Born in London in 1874, a scion of a family long prominent in the British Empire. The son of the 1st Baron Revelstoke (a director of the Bank of England and a senior partner at Baring Bros.), he was educated at Eton and at Cambridge, and joined the diplomatic service in 1898. In 1904 he became a journalist and reported the Russo–Japanese War in Manchuria; later he was a correspondent in Russia and Constantinople. He is credited with having discovered Chekhov's work in Moscow and helping to introduce it to the West. Baring is remembered as a versatile, prolific and highly successful writer, who produced articles, plays, biographies, criticism, poetry, translations, stories and novels. He is regarded as a representative of the social culture that flourished in England before World War I and his work is highly regarded to this day for the acute intimate portraits of the time.

● MAURICE

Baring

The Coat Without Seam

HOUSE OF
STRATUS

This edition published in 2001 by House of Stratus, an imprint of Stratus Books Ltd., Lisandra House, Fore St., Looe, Cornwall, PL13 1AD, U.K.
www.houseofstratus.com

Typeset by House of Stratus.

A catalogue record for this book is available from the British Library and the Library of Congress.

ISBN 0-7551-0091-3

"…pray for me while I am on live that God send me good deliverance."

Sir Thomas Malory

à
Monsieur le Chanoine
Mugnier, en respectueuse
affection.

CHAPTER I

"When I grow up," said Christopher, to his sister Mabel, "I mean to be an explorer and to write a huge book of travel like Marco Polo."

They were sitting on the banks of an island of the river Seine. They had rowed there in a boat, unsupervised, for it was the month of August when their Governess, Mademoiselle Altmann, took her holiday.

Christopher Trevenen was nine years old, and his sister Mabel was ten. They were the children of Benjamin Trevenen, the scholar and publicist, who was taking his holiday with his wife in the town of Vernay, in the north of France. They took a house there, which belonged to an English lady, every year for the months of August and September. Vernay was a sleepy town on the banks of the Seine. It boasted of no mineral springs, and its only hotels were primitive and unstarred in Baedeker, but it possessed one inn which was marked in the confidential manual of the Greedy, where it was said that you got the best *Entrecôte à la minute* in France. Vernay was rarely visited by tourists and there was no Casino, no theatre and no English colony: that is why the Trevenens, or rather why Mrs Trevenen, chose it. The house they lived in was outside the town, a white house with grey panels, polished floors and cool rooms that smelt of lavender. There was a lawn in front of the house and a flower garden behind it.

Benjamin Trevenen was a northern Irishman by birth. He had been educated in England: at Winchester and at Oxford. He came from a line of Irish gentry; he was a younger son. At the death of his only brother he inherited a house and an estate in County Antrim, which he sold owing to agricultural troubles. He did well at school, and at Oxford in History, and when he went down, he became a Fellow of St Olaph's College. A few years later, while he was spending his summer holiday abroad, he made the acquaintance of a certain Général de Sarthenay, and his wife, who were taking the waters at Haréville with their two grown-up daughters. Benjamin Trevenen fell in love with the second of the two daughters, Geneviève.

The General judged all men by one simple standard: whether they were *bien* or not *bien*. Benjamin Trevenen was, according to his standard, *bien*: and, indeed, there was something reassuring about Benjamin, for Trevenen had about him, besides the refinement of a scholar, a racial distinction which was manifest not only in his hands, his head and his hair, but in his manners, which were the natural good manners of an earlier age. His vocabulary, too, had the ease and polish of the eighteenth century without a touch of pedantry, although by temperament he was shy and even prim.

There were, of course, material and religious questions to be settled. On the material side all was well. Geneviève had a *dot*. Benjamin was well off and had no relations and obligations. So far he had done well. He had written articles for the serious reviews, not only on historical subjects but on foreign politics and his name was well-known.

The General was a Catholic, but although personally pious, anti-clerical. His wife was a Huguenot, tolerant, moderate and sensible in all things; a *republicaine bleue*, unlike her husband, who was a Bonapartist.

As for Geneviève herself, she was so far a fervid Catholic. She had been brought up at a convent where she had been moulded by a remarkable nun, Soeur Marie Agnès, who had left the world of gaiety for ever, when she was a girl, to nurse the wounded in the Crimean War. Geneviève was short and fair, with pale grey eyes, clear cut features, and strong practical hands. She was fond of reading, she had a passion for history, and she and Benjamin met on common ground. She also shared his liking for botany and long walks. The marriage took place in France, a few months later. And the following year Benjamin Trevenen became a Catholic. He had been brought up without religious guidance, but, although he had lived in northern Ireland, a part of the population where he had lived were Catholics, and his leanings had been towards the Catholic rather than towards the Protestant ideals of the Irish. He had been inclined from his childhood to take the side of the minority and the opposition. Benjamin on his marriage gave up his Fellowship, partly because he did not want to live at Oxford as a married man, and partly because he was offered the post of Foreign Editor on a large London daily newspaper, an undertaking which attracted him still more, as he was interested in foreign politics. He and his wife settled in London, at Chiswick, and they spent their holidays in France with Geneviève's parents as long as these were alive; after their death they took the house at Vernay. Christopher was a shy boy, with the light hair and the keen grey eyes of his mother, the absent-mindedness and lurking obstinacy of his father.

Mabel was unlike her father and her mother. Her eyes were blue and her hair rebellious; she was dark; she was talkative, high-spirited and gay. The studies of the two children were directed by their Governess, Mademoiselle Altmann, an Alsatian, who was chosen because she knew German, as well as French. They were supervised and supplemented by their mother. Christopher, his mother said, must learn German, as it would be necessary for him *one* day. She was never more precise than this, but the children knew that she meant the day of the *revanche*, for their mother often hinted that the time would come when Europe would have to fight the Prussians. Their father, too, was sometimes heard to say that Germany was the danger: indeed he was one of the first to write on the subject in the newspapers. Mademoiselle Altmann was supposed to have a French heart, and to be dreaming of the day of emancipation. But the children reflected that if her heart was French, her mind and her manners were German. She liked Mabel, who was quick and industrious, but she had no patience with Christopher, who was dreamy, obstinate and inattentive. He affected to dislike the German language. The children were neither of them afraid of her, but they lived in different worlds between which there seemed to be no bridge. Mabel was Irish to the core. She was expansive, agreeable and careless. She was adventurous and fond of fun. She was unpunctual, always losing everything, and innately untidy. This distressed her mother, who was scrupulously attentive to detail, practical, always busy and who always had time for everything.

Mrs Trevenen went to Mass every morning at eight; she managed the household; supervised the cooking; kept the accounts; said her rosary every day; and yet she had time to read the modern French and English books and reviews that came out and to study Italian and Gaelic. She had written and published a life of Saint Francis of Assisi, which was well reviewed in the newspapers, as well as a guide to the churches in northern France.

The children saw little of their father, for in London he worked at night, and was not to be disturbed in the morning. During the holidays he was busy writing a book. When they did see him he was more shy of them than they were of him. He treated them courteously and made conversation with them, as if they were grown-up strangers.

With Mademoiselle Altmann they lived at least on the same plane, although they both of them disliked her. She was strict and enforced discipline – a dry, pointed, unimaginative woman, with a slightly red nose and glossy hair, who intended to do her duty, and succeeded whatever the cost. She was there to teach the children, and she taught them. They laughed at her behind her back; they teased her indirectly and subtly, but they obeyed her.

Their religious education was thorough. Mabel was to go to a convent later. At this epoch the children did not make their first Communion until they were at least twelve years old. Mabel enjoyed going to church and was naturally devout, but religious instruction fell from Christopher like water from a duck's back, and left him impervious. He resented having to abstain on Fridays, saying the rosary bored him to a pitch of pain, and he disliked feeling different from other people. Above all things he was afraid of being thought French, and he took pains before strangers to pretend that he could neither understand nor speak the language.

Mrs Trevenen spoke English, and you would not have taken her for a French woman. This was probably because she had had an English nurse as a child.

Christopher and Mabel were thrown back on themselves, but, whereas Mabel was gregarious and willing to make friends with other children, with the children they met at Monsieur Blanc's classes of French literature, and at a Gymnasium which they attended once a week, Christopher kept to himself and took pains to appear less amiable than he was. He felt that his father thought him stupid, and that in his mother's eyes he was inefficient, because he was unable to respond to his father. She was always scolding him for his distractions and forgetfulness. He was not without gifts. He had a natural facility for languages. He had no difficulty in learning Latin; and German or French came to him easily, although he affected to dislike the one and to ignore the other. But he did not deceive his masters, and Monsieur Blanc said that if he tried he could be the best boy in his class, were it not for his incurable absent-mindedness. His mother sighed when came in report after report to this effect, and when Mademoiselle Altmann said the same thing, but she hoped that when he went to school he would do better. He was not particularly fond of reading; that is to say the story books and the fairy tales that enchanted his sister left him cold. He thought them silly. But he had a passion for history, books of travel, and out of the way scraps of knowledge, a passion which his father might have fostered and shared with him had he understood how to set about it. He had a quick retentive memory and he was fond of epic poems, such as Southey's "Thalaba," certain parts of "Paradise Lost," and some passages from Chateaubriand which his mother read aloud and which he only half understood. Mrs Trevenen read aloud the French classics to her children, and every now and then they had to recite a fable of La Fontaine in the drawing room – a performance which they both of them detested.

The society of Mabel, although she teased him and although they frequently quarrelled and sometimes even fought, sufficed for Christopher. He was devoted to his sister. They were both quick tempered.

He would often tell her his dreams and ambitions for the future, and they were just now in the middle of one of those exchanges of mutual confidence that Mabel enjoyed.

"I shall discover countries," he went on, "that have never been heard of."

"Oh yes!" said Mabel, "like the '*Voyage au centre de la terre.*'"

"Oh, that's all rubbish!"

"Mamma says that a great many of those things may come true some day."

"But I mean *real* travel. I shall go to Mecca and the Forbidden City, to Eldorado – like Ponce de Leon."

"You will have to learn Arabic first."

"I mean to learn Arabic. I know I can if I choose."

Mabel laughed.

"You're ashamed of knowing French."

"French is a girl's language."

"Papa says that French is based on Latin and that Latin is the first of all languages. But I know I shall never get further than *mensa*."

"That's because you're a girl."

"You just said French was a girl's language."

"You said Latin."

"But papa says French *is* Latin."

"He never said that: French is French and Latin is Latin."

"But he did say it; what will you bet? I don't care anyway. When I grow up I am going to be a prima donna and sing at the Opera and have the horses taken out of my carriage and be dragged by cheering crowds through the streets of Warsaw."

"Then you'll have to practise scales better than you do now. Mademoiselle says you scamp your scales."

"Oh, the piano! I hate the piano. I like songs," and here she began to sing her favourite song of the moment – these favourites changed almost weekly:

"But Oh! that my heart had wings,
I'd fly like the blue bird far,
Away and away to the end of the day,
Where the cool and the palm trees are."

"Mademoiselle says that song is *nauséabond*."

"She doesn't understand any music except German music."

Mabel had a pretty voice and a good ear, but she was incapable of receiving sustained musical instruction.

"Perhaps," she said, rather wistfully, "I might come with you on your travels and we would be troubadours."

Christopher laughed.

"They only existed in the Middle Ages."

"Well, gypsies exist, and I would like to be a gypsy. The Queen of the Gypsies."

"Queen Mab! I thought you wanted to be a prima donna?"

7

"I could be both. Gypsies often do sing."

"They squawk."

"Won't you take me with you on your travels?" she asked, plaintively.

"I'll see about it," he said, condescendingly.

"At any rate I could do the cooking."

Christopher laughed.

"Mamma says you haven't the head to be a cook. She says that cooking, like everything else, wants brains."

"I can make toffee," said Mabel.

The conversation dropped.

It was a hot afternoon.

"Let's bathe," said Mabel.

"We haven't got bathing clothes or towels," said Christopher.

"What does that matter?"

"I don't mind, only mamma said you weren't to because of your chest."

"My chest is all right."

Mabel disappeared behind a tree and presently she was in the water.

Christopher, who was longing to bathe himself, soon followed suit.

They stayed in a long time, longer than they realised. It had become more and more sultry, and the sky was overcast when they came out.

"We had better get home quick. We shall be late for tea," said Christopher, after they had dressed.

They got into the boat and began to row home.

"We had better say nothing about the bathing," said Mabel, after they had been rowing for some time.

Christopher looked at Mabel and laughed.

"You should see your hair," he said, "you couldn't keep the bathing a secret with hair like that. You look like a mermaid."

"I believe it's going to rain."

They might have thought of this before, as during the last half hour there had been every sign of an approaching thunderstorm.

And now a few heavy drops began to fall.

"It's too late to go back," said Mabel. "I don't mind. I like thunderstorms."

"Never mind," said Christopher, "we shall soon be home. You had better have my coat, I can scull better without it."

He threw her his coat.

At that moment there was a flash of lightning in the distance, a peal of thunder and then, almost immediately, it poured with rain.

They were not far from home, but far enough to get soaked to the skin. When they reached the boat-house, they would still have half an hour's walk before they got home. They waited in the boat-house till the shower was over and then they walked home.

Mabel was shivering.

"At any rate, they won't notice we've bathed," she said.

Their mother met them at the door.

"Come upstairs," she said to Mabel. "You must get to bed at once and have a hot *tizane*."

She bundled the children into the house.

"How could you let your sister get so wet!" she said to Christopher. "You know her chest is delicate."

"We were caught by the rain on the river," said Christopher.

Mrs Trevenen made a gesture of despair.

"You will end by killing your sister," she said.

Nothing was said about the bathing. They were both so wet from the rain that it was not noticed.

CHAPTER II

Mabel caught a chill. She had had chills before and her chest was delicate. Two or three days later, the word pneumonia was pronounced and anxiety spread through the house. The local doctor was sensible and efficient, but he called for outside assistance, and a physician came from Rouen, but threw no new light on the situation. Mrs Trevenen nursed her child with the help of the children's nurse, who had been her nurse. Mr Trevenen said nothing, but blinked and murmured optimistic nothings which it was obvious he did not believe.

Days passed and the crisis came; it was successfully tided over, and the household breathed more freely. Throughout Mabel's illness Mr Trevenen had continued his regular work. He was writing, in the holidays only, a history of the Merovingian Kings.

On the first of September, a date which Christopher was to remember for the rest of his life, Mabel was said to be out of danger. In the afternoon, Christopher went out for a walk by himself. His mother was resting, and his father was writing at a small table in the garden. Christopher strolled into the town. He wanted to buy some barley sugar and he passed the church. His mother had told him to go to the church and put up a candle to Our Lady as a thanksgiving for Mabel's recovery. He strolled into the church, which was large, fine in period, with some tawdry modern alterations. There was a beautiful stained glass window. Christopher went to get a candle, but could not find one. He dared not leave the commission undone, so he rang the sacristy bell, expecting the old woman who looked after the church to come out. But instead of the old woman the Curé himself appeared. Christopher knew him well. He generally came to dinner on Sundays. The Curé, who was fond of children, had always been kind to him, and, much to his disgust, had paid him the honour of asking him to assist at the *quête*. That is to say, he had to walk hand in hand with a little French girl who went round with the plate for the collection. Christopher had made every excuse to avoid doing this, but when, after having purposely forgotten to tell his parents of the Curé's invitation, the Curé had told them himself, he was obliged to do so, and he had suffered acutely. The Curé, who was an old man with grey hair who took snuff, greeted him kindly, asked after his sister, and when Christopher told him the news and what he had come for, the Curé said that of course he must thank *La Sainte Vierge*; he himself had said Mass for Mabel that morning.

The Curé fetched him a candle, and they went together to the Altar of Our Lady, and put it up.

"We will say a prayer together," the Curé said, and they knelt down at the altar rails.

When they had finished, the Curé asked Christopher whether he would like to see the *trésor* of the church. He then took him into the sacristy and showed him some beautiful vestments, and a chalice that dated from the time of St Louis.

"And now," said the Curé, when they had seen everything, "I will take you to my house and give you a *Baba* before you go home."

As they passed through the church again, they passed a chapel where, over the altar, there hung a faded piece of reddish brown fabric in a frame behind a glass.

Christopher asked what it was.

11

"That," said the Curé, "is a relic. It is a Holy Coat, and for many years it was thought by many to be the Coat without Seam, for which the soldiers drew lots after Our Blessed Lord was crucified; and indeed many made pilgrimages here to see it. But the story was always doubtful, and the people of Treves claim that they have the Holy Coat in their Cathedral, and that it was presented to them by the Empress Helena in the fourth century, and it seems probable that our relic, although certainly of the greatest antiquity – it was brought here by Charlemagne – is not that Coat. Some people have called our relic the *Cappa pueri Jesu*, the Garment of the Child Jesus. During the revolution the Curé – it was in another church then – cut it up in four pieces and hid them because he feared the Coat might be destroyed. In 1795, some of the pieces were brought back."

Christopher had always been interested in the story of the Coat without Seam, and he asked the Curé how it had been found.

The Curé said, "I will tell you about that presently."

They walked into the presbytery, a little house with a garden where pears hung heavily on a sunburnt wall, and flowers blazed: nasturtiums, sunflowers, snapdragons and lavender. They sat down at a table in the garden, and an old woman called Amélie brought the Curé a bottle of blackcurrant wine and some cakes flavoured with rum. Christopher enjoyed his little feast and, while he was eating his cake, the Curé told him the story of St Helena, and the finding of the Cross. When he had finished, Christopher was silent for a while, and then asked the Curé what had happened to the Coat between the time of the Crucifixion and the finding of the Cross.

"We do not know," said the Curé. "These things are a mystery and we are not meant to know everything; otherwise, what would be the use of Faith? 'Blessed are those who have not seen and yet have believed,' Our Lord said. There are so many things we do not know. Indeed, so few things that the wisest of us, the holiest as well as the greatest, savants do know, that we must be content with the crumbs of knowledge that fall to us."

"Are all the stories of relics true?"

He had been taunted once in London by an English boy who had told him that the manufacture of false relics was a profitable trade, and a sign of the rottenness of his Church.

The Curé guessed what was in his mind.

"Many people, my child," he said, "especially those who have not the privilege of belonging to our Holy Church, do not understand the difference between what we call an article of Faith and a pious opinion. If the faithful believe a certain relic to be genuine it is a pious opinion, but, short of evidence which has been declared to be certain by holy and inspired authority, it is not necessarily an article of Faith. People often attack the authenticity of relics, but they are inclined to forget that tradition is sometimes in itself valuable evidence. It is a pious opinion to venerate the relic we possess, but you are not obliged to believe that it is really a garment that belonged to Our Lord if you do not wish to. We do not know. Its history is too obscure. All we know is that it has been here for over a thousand years. But there can be no harm in reverencing any object which has been held to be holy by generations of the faithful."

"But is the Holy Coat without Seam at Treves?"

"It may well be," said the Curé. "Its history is said to go still further back than ours."

"But I can't understand," said Christopher, "how it can have lasted so long before Saint Helena found it without being lost."

"The fate of all objects, not only holy relics, is extraordinary," said the Curé, "and sometimes nothing short of miraculous. Think of the iron crown of Charlemagne and the many objects that have reached us not only since the days of the Greeks and the Romans but since the days of the Egyptians and the Assyrians. Everything is more durable than the dust out of which man himself is made. That his body is perishable is of no importance, because the soul is imperishable, and on the Last Day he will be given a new and imperishable body."

"But a piece of stuff," objected Christopher.

"We have pieces of stuff that are over two thousand years old and which clothed the ancient Egyptians."

"I wonder what happened to it directly afterwards," Christopher said, after a while.

"When I was a child," said the Curé, "not older than you, I read in a story book, a book of the lives and legends of saints, a story that will answer your question. Shall I tell it to you?"

"Oh, yes, please do, M. le Curé."

"Well," said the Curé, "the story was something like this:

"When the soldiers drew lots for the Seamless Coat of Our Lord, the soldier who had won the Coat was pleased, and as soon as the soldiers were released from their duty, he took it home to his wife. The soldier's name was Marcus, and his wife was a Jewess. He gave the Coat to her and made her promise that she would never give it away, and she asked if it would not be better to sell it, because they were poor. But Marcus was frightened at the idea; because they knew, they who had been on Mount Golgotha, that something extraordinary had happened.

"Now Marcus and his wife, whose name was Miriam, had a child, a little boy, who was only a year old and they loved him very much.

"The next day, while Marcus was away on duty, the child fell sick, and Miriam did not know what to do. She tried to find a physician, but it was the Sabbath Day, our Saturday, and the Jews would not come and tend her child on the Sabbath Day.

"She was at her wits' end. At last she thought of a certain wise man, who lived hard by in the poorer part of the city, and who had the reputation of being able to cure the sick. But

people were afraid of him because they said that he trafficked with the Evil One. But at last she went to him and told him that her child was sick, and that nobody would help her because it was the Sabbath Day. The Wise Man laughed at this, and said that he did not mind working on the Sabbath Day. He followed her to her home and examined the child who seemed to be worse. He said he could cure the child, but that he must be paid first, and Miriam told him that she had no money. Her husband was only a common Roman soldier and had only his pay to live on.

"The Wise Man said he did not ask for money. She asked him what he wanted, and he said the Coat without Seam, which her husband had won when he and the other soldiers had cast lots for it with dice on Golgotha.

" 'I cannot give you that,' she said, 'not while my husband is away, because I promised him never to part with it. But I am sure he will give it you when he comes back, if you cure our child. Only be quick, because the child is very ill.'

"But the Wise Man said she must give it him at once.

"Then Miriam wept and implored him to wait until her husband should come home; he could not be long because his watch ended at the ninth hour.

"But the Wise Man refused to do anything unless she gave him the Coat, and he went away and left her.

"Miriam fetched the Coat when he was gone and looked at it, and then she covered her son with it to keep him warm, and she tried to sing him to sleep. And the child seemed to grow better from that moment.

"Presently the Wise Man came back again and said he must have the Coat. If she did not give it him the child would die.

"Again she begged him to wait till her husband came home.

"And he offered her money. But Miriam refused to sell him the Coat, and she said she believed her son was getting

15

better.

" 'If you can cure him yourself, you do not need me,' the Wise Man said, and he went away and left her.

"Presently Marcus came home and Miriam told him what had happened, and how she had refused a large sum of money. At first, he was angry, saying it was true he had told her not to sell the Coat, but when the child's life was at stake she should have done it.

" 'But our son is better,' said Miriam. 'He grew better as soon as the Coat touched him.'

"And Marcus looked at the child and said, 'No, he is not better. He is dying.'

"Then the Wise Man came back, and he brought with him another Roman soldier of higher rank, a sergeant. And he told the sergeant that Marcus and his wife owed him the Coat in payment for what he had done for their child, and that they refused to give it him.

"And Miriam denied the story, and told the truth.

"The sergeant asked the Wise Man why he needed the Coat, and the Wise Man said that he wished to destroy it because the Nazarene was a false Prophet; and Miriam said that this was not true. The Wise Man needed it for his magic.

"When the sergeant heard this, he coveted the Coat, and he ordered Marcus to give him the Coat, saying he would give it to those in authority.

"And while they were talking, Miriam screamed, 'It is too late. My child is dead.' And the sergeant commanded Marcus to give him the Coat, and Marcus refused. And then the sergeant threatened him with severe punishment for disobedience, and summoned soldiers to arrest him, and he ordered Miriam, to give him the Coat; but Miriam said she would die first, and she screamed for help.

"At that moment, a Centurion walked in, and asked what the tumult meant, and why Marcus was bound. And the sergeant said that he had wished to destroy the Coat, as it

*belonged to the Man who had called Himself the King of the
Jews. And Marcus told the Centurion the whole story.*

*"Then the Centurion ordered the soldiers to unbind Marcus
and told everyone to leave the house, and the Centurion asked
Marcus why he had not given up the Coat; and Marcus said
that it was his by right.*

*"And Miriam said, 'What does it all avail now? My son is
dead, and nothing can bring him back to me.'*

"And the Centurion said, 'Is the child dead?'

*"And they looked at the child and found that he was
breathing, and the child got well; and Marcus and Miriam
became Christians from that day."*

The Curé paused.

"That is the story such as I read it in an old illuminated book
that had many legends and pictures, as far as I can remember
it."

"And is it true?" asked Christopher.

"It may well be true," said the Curé, "but there are many
such legends, and some of them may well be only the dreams
of the pious, but if that is so, they are beautiful dreams, and
there is no harm in our believing them. But now it is time for
you to go home, and you shall take something with you."

And the Curé fetched a pear from his wall and gave it to
Christopher, and he gave him too a medal to wear round his
neck – a medal of St Christopher.

"And I have something else for you, too," he said and he gave
Christopher a wooden flute, called a *mirliton* in French. "This
used to belong to a nephew of mine, whom I was very fond of,
and who died many years ago. But toys should not lie unused,
and that is why I will give it to you."

Christopher thanked him very much. He was delighted
especially with the flute. It would do well for his games with
Mabel.

When he got home, his father met him downstairs. His

mother was upstairs with Mabel.

She was not so well. Christopher was told to take a book and be quiet. He dared not play on the wooden flute.

He had his supper early and went to bed.

The next day, Mabel was no better. She had had a relapse, and the doctor from Rouen came again, and then M. le Curé, and she received the last Sacraments. Christopher was allowed to see her for a moment, and she smiled at him, but she did not speak. She looked very white. The next morning, they told him Mabel was dead.

Christopher did not cry. He said nothing. He could not realise what had happened. It was as if the whole world he had lived in had crumbled to pieces. His father and his mother thought he did not care, and they were surprised and grieved and shocked. His father, Christopher noticed, looked different, not exactly older, but as if his face was scarred. Christopher was allowed to see Mabel once more after she was dead. She was lying on her bed, covered with flowers. Round the bed, there were tall candles as in church, and at the foot of the bed two nuns dressed in black were praying.

Mabel looked as if asleep, more beautiful than she had ever looked: happy and contented. But Christopher was frightened at the sight, nor did he feel inclined either to cry or to say a single prayer as he was told to do.

His Mabel was not there. She had gone away for ever, and to some place he could not reach, far beyond any thought.

His mother was quiet and calm and went about her business as usual. They all had black clothes, and he was taken to Rouen, and a black suit was bought for him. Mabel was buried at Vernay in the churchyard which was a quiet place, overgrown with long grass, sweet-briar and wild flowers. Christopher was taken to the Requiem and held a candle in his hand. He did not seem to realise what was happening, and his parents could not understand him. The Curé would have understood if Christopher had spoken to him, but he did not dare, and there was no time as it was settled that they were to go back to England at once.

While the boxes were being packed, Christopher remembered the *mirliton*, the wooden flute, which M. le Curé had given him and which he had forgotten during these last days. He took it to the garden and began playing on it. His mother at once rushed out into the garden and said, "Don't make that noise, Christopher. You are disturbing your father. He is busy."

And when she came back into the house, she said to the nurse, "*Vraiment, cet enfant n'a pas de coeur.*"

"At that age," the nurse said, "children forget easily."

"Perhaps it is better so," said Mrs Trevenen, and she sighed.

Christopher was in the passage while they were talking; the door was open, and he overheard what they said, and he felt something bitter rising up in him – a hatred of the whole race of grown-ups, especially his father and mother.

His father was as usual busy writing.

"He goes on writing," thought Christopher, "and nobody scolds him, and what did he know of Mabel? What would they do if they knew that I had *killed* Mabel?"

For Christopher was convinced that it was the bathing in the river that killed his sister, and this thought pursued him like a dreadful demon, and gnawed at his heart; but nothing in the world would have made him reveal his secret burden, nothing except perhaps sympathy and that alas! was not forthcoming.

CHAPTER III

When Christopher was ten years old the question of his going to school arose. It had frequently arisen before, but as it was a point on which his parents disagreed, Mrs Trevenen had always shelved it. Now it could be shelved no longer. Benjamin wished to send his son to a public school. Mrs Trevenen had no objection to his going to a Jesuit college. The Jesuits she said were the only people who kept boys out of mischief and taught them anything. Her father when the question was discussed disagreed with his daughter on this point violently. He admitted the Jesuits were admirable for small children and possibly kept boys out of mischief, but he denied the scholastic advantages of their education. They produced, he said, the average cavalry officer but nothing better, and as Christopher – who was only seven years old at the time of these discussions – showed no signs of military vocation, it was absurd to send him to a Jesuit school. He was in favour of an English public school.

"He will lose his Faith," said his mother.

"He will lose it twice as quickly under the care of the Jesuits," said the General.

Mrs Trevenen suggested other Catholic schools she had heard of: the Oratory: Cardinal Newman: what could one have better?

Then Benjamin spoke up. He had as an Irishman a particular

pride and prejudice. He cherished a dislike of a certain type of Irish squireen which he imagined to be the fruits of Catholic schools in England. He knew nothing about the Oratory, but he sided with his father-in-law, and Mrs Trevenen wisely changed the subject. Now the question was raised again and had to be settled. Mrs Trevenen again pleaded for the Oratory. Benjamin, who on most subjects temporised and compromised, revealed an invincible obstinacy.

"Well," said Mrs Trevenen, "he had better not go to school at all. After all boys learn nothing at school except bad habits, and I am determined that our son shall be taught something."

The idea of Christopher not going to school did not shock Benjamin and he was delighted at the compromise.

"He can go to classes," he said, "and perhaps he would learn more at home, but it depends on what he is to be."

"He has a gift for languages, he must go into the Diplomatic Service," said Mrs Trevenen.

Christopher had been asked once rather shyly by his father what he would like to be, and he had said an explorer.

His father had said that this was not a profession, it was an accident.

The question was settled.

Christopher went for three years to a Dame School in London. After that a tutor came to the house three times a week to teach him Latin and Greek. His mother taught him French herself, his German remained dormant. Mademoiselle Altmann had left soon after Mabel died.

Christopher did not accept the arrangement without a protest. He wanted to go to school. He begged to be allowed to go to Winchester, his father's school. He was told that Winchester did not take Catholics. He then asked to be sent to Eton. He was told it was too expensive.

He played a trump card: Westminster where boys lived at home: but the trump card was of no avail. His mother was not against school because she wanted him at home; far from it.

He saw the struggle was hopeless and this strengthened his feeling of bitterness against the race of grown-ups. He detested his Dame School and did his best to learn as little as possible there, which was not difficult. But his mother became aware of this, and it was then that the tutor was introduced.

The tutor was a lecturer at one of the London colleges. His name was Jackson; he had the gift of making the classics uninteresting; his one idea was to spot questions that examiners might set in examination papers and words that would be useful for prose.

He would say for instance, "*Sine ullo dilectu.* Translate it, 'Hobson's choice.' Useful phrase for prose."

Mr Jackson revelled in a neat epigram and tried to make Christopher appreciate Tacitus before he was sound on the four concords.

In the holidays his parents went abroad. They no longer stayed at Vernay although his mother made a pilgrimage thither every year.

Sometimes they stayed with some French cousins in Brittany. When her elder sister died Mrs Trevenen inherited her father's house near Angers. After that, they went there yearly.

When Christopher was fourteen it was settled that he should go into the Diplomatic Service. He still wanted to be a traveller but he knew it was no good saying so.

He was to go to a German family when he was seventeen for a year, and then to Cambridge or Oxford for at least a year. After that for a term to Mr Spark, the crammer.

He grew up quickly and when he was twelve made his first Communion. He was a big boy for his age. This event, which he had been told by his mother would be the greatest event of his life, left him to his own disappointment religiously unmoved, not that he was harassed with doubts. He accepted what he was taught as a matter of course, but, although he was impressed and agitated by the importance of the occasion, he felt no spark of the religious fervour which he had expected to feel.

His religious instructors were satisfied with him because he had a clear mind and a retentive memory. He knew the catechism thoroughly. When he went to Confession the day before his first Communion, he startled the priest, a sensible Oratorian, by telling him that he had murdered his sister and that he had never dared confess it. When the priest heard Christopher's story he did his best to reassure him and convince him that there was no guilt in the matter.

But Christopher was not convinced. He thought the priest was trying to be kind to him, and he was too much upset by the importance of the occasion to take in the clear explanations.

His father gave him a missal and his mother gave him a Rosary. He wore a tail coat for the first time, but he went through the ceremony as one in a dream and only remembered being frightened lest he should trip up on the stone floor.

When he was seventeen his father had an attack of bronchitis in the autumn, and was ordered to spend the winter abroad. This made his regular work impossible, but his newspaper arranged that he should write on foreign politics from Rome. Benjamin Trevenen was well-known and accustomed to contribute to the serious reviews under the pseudonym of *Scrutator*. Christopher spent the winter with his parents at a *pension*, and he learnt Italian with care. It was necessary for him to learn a third language for his examination.

He went with his mother and father when they were received in audience by the Pope, and his father showed him the Roman antiquities and the churches in detail.

Rome had little effect upon him. He did not care for archaeology. Churches, picture galleries and ruins bored him.

He made no friends. He was overgrown, for his age, shy and silent, but firm and strong, fond of walking, and his chief hobby was the solving of the chess problems in the *Illustrated London News*.

He still read books of travel and at his own request he had

lessons in Arabic from an Italian. He continued his Latin and Greek with a priest.

His parents went back to London in the spring and spent some time later in France, and, early in the following year, Christopher was sent to Germany, to a family at Dresden.

There he made the acquaintance of someone who might have been a life-long friend, a certain Godfrey Mellor who had just left school and who was working for the Civil Service.

Godfrey Mellor was quiet, observant and musical. He took Christopher to concerts and to the Opera. But Christopher did not like classical music and distressed Mellor by saying that Wagner was the only composer worth listening to, but that even he was too long-winded. They had one taste in common and that was the game of chess.

For the first time in his life, since the death of his sister, Christopher felt that he had made a friend. Someone with whom he could exchange thoughts and to whom he could say what he thought.

They discussed every subject under the sun: especially religion. Christopher's religious faith vanished at this time like a puff of smoke. He asked Mellor one day what he thought about religion, the Christian religion, and Mellor said in a slow gentle manner, "I think people believe all those things because they want to."

"I agree. I was brought up as a Catholic, you know."

"A Catholic?" said Mellor, "all that must be still more difficult to believe… I can't understand how any one can believe what Catholics have to believe."

"My father and mother do," said Christopher, "but then they are old-fashioned."

"Do you discuss it with them?" asked Mellor.

"No, never, because they wouldn't understand, and I don't want to shock or to hurt them. It's not their fault that they are old-fashioned, besides I think one must always respect Mythology. The intelligent Romans paid honour to the Gods and the Augurs and all that although they knew it was nonsense."

Christopher had read a great deal and wandered in the by-paths of literature. Mellor read little but he was better informed than Christopher because he took in *The Times* and read it every day.

Christopher was overripe in some ways and callow in others; he had read Jean Paul, Kant, Mommsen, Gregorovius, Strauss, Renan and Schopenhauer, whose works affected him greatly.

Mellor knew of their works by hearsay and was mildly interested by what Christopher told him of them. Christopher's friendship with Mellor might have made a lasting difference to his life. Unfortunately, just before he left Dresden the following February they quarrelled. It was over a game of chess.

They were fairly well matched, but Christopher was the better player. He bet Mellor twenty marks he would give him two pawns and beat him ten games running. He won nine games. Two days before Christopher left Dresden they were playing the tenth game. They were sitting in a *Bierhalle* and each of them had a glass of beer beside him.

The game was fairly even, but Mellor was if anything slightly in the more advantageous position, when he made a false move, but as he did so he said in a low voice, "*j'adoube.*"

There was a good deal of noise going on in the restaurant and a band was playing. Christopher was lost in thought and did not hear him. Mellor was thinking the position out; he saw his mistake and took the move back.

"You can't have that move back," said Christopher.

"But I said '*j'adoube.*' "

"I didn't hear you. Even then you have no right to move the piece."

"I did say it. I didn't know you mightn't move it."

"Very well."

They played on and Mellor won the game. Christopher paid

him his twenty marks but, as he did so, he said, "You wouldn't have won if I hadn't let you have that move back."

"It wasn't a question of 'letting,' it was my right," said Mellor. "I said *'j'adoube.'* "

"You had no right to move the piece: only to touch it: but it's a pity you didn't say it more distinctly," Christopher said satirically.

"You don't believe me?" Mellor inquired quietly. "I am not in the habit of cheating at chess."

"You mean I am?"

"No, I only mean what I said."

"I was listening with all my might and I didn't hear you say anything."

This was true. Christopher thought he was listening but in reality he was in an abstraction. He had no idea how absent-minded he could be.

"But as I tell you now, I said it, you ought to believe me."

"I don't believe you," Christopher said savagely. He knew now that Mellor was speaking the truth.

"The truth of the matter is, you cannot bear being beaten," said Mellor, quietly.

This was true. Christopher had never been beaten by Mellor before.

Christopher saw red and threw his glass of beer in Mellor's face, who wiped it with a handkerchief, called for the waiter and said, "*bezahlen bitte.*"

He paid for the beer, Christopher paid for his share and they went out.

They met in the evening at supper and Christopher was silent. He knew he had been in the wrong and that he would only have to say a word and Mellor would smile – and all would be well, but he could not bring himself to say that word, and Mellor was too shy a man to take the initiative, so Christopher left the next day without saying goodbye to Mellor and their friendship came to an end.

His father was promised a nomination for Christopher for the examination for the Diplomatic Service, and it was settled that he was to go up to Oxford in the autumn and for his examination as soon as there was one after he had been a year at the University.

His father and mother spent that winter in Rome.

Christopher joined them in February. It was thought that he had been long enough in Germany for the present and that it would be a good thing for him to perfect himself in Italian.

He stayed there till the middle of April, when his father caught a chill and fell ill once more. It was bronchitis again. This time it developed into double pneumonia, and Benjamin Trevenen died after a three weeks' illness. He was buried in Rome.

When Trevenen died there were many articles published about him and the brilliance and usefulness of his work. His fame as a political publicist was European, but this did not mitigate the fact that he had left his affairs in a deplorable state. Mrs Trevenen found herself left with nothing but her slender marriage settlement and her father's house in France. There was, of course, no more question of Christopher going into the Diplomatic Service.

It cannot be said that he was greatly grieved by his father's death. His father had always been kind to him but they had never ceased to be shy of one another. Ever since the death of his sister, Christopher felt incapable of any strong emotion.

Mrs Trevenen consulted her friends in London, among others the Foreign Secretary, who was a friend of her husband, and Mr Spark, the crammer. They advised her to let Christopher try for a Student Interpretership in the Levant. To do this he had to pass an open competitive examination (in French and Latin, with Greek, Italian and German as optional subjects). If he passed it he would have to go up to one of the Universities chosen by the Secretary of State and study Oriental languages (Turkish, Arabic, Mussulman Law) there for two years. During that time he would receive a salary of £200 a year.

He would have to pass further examinations at the University, and, if he passed these, on leaving the University he would be appointed an assistant and assigned to a Mission or a Consulate in the Levant, with a salary of three hundred a year, and a further examination had to be passed before he could make any further advancement. Christopher accepted this situation. There was an examination in May, which he was too late for. There was to be another one in September. He would go up for that. Mr Spark said he thought Christopher could get through the examination if he spent a term with him. His French and German were exceptionally good and so was his Italian. His Latin was up to the average.

The difficulty was the expense.

It was settled that Christopher should attend the lectures at Spark's during the summer term, and his mother with the help of Mr Spark arranged that at the end of July he should take a tutorship with an Austrian family; there was a Countess Linsky who wished her son to have a companion who would talk English to him. Christopher would have plenty of spare time to himself to work and would hear German spoken. He would go up for his examination in September and if he passed go to St Crispin's College, Cambridge, which was the University chosen by the Secretary of State for student interpreters for the Levant. Mrs Trevenen at once set about to make the best of the situation. She sold the French property which had belonged to her father, and as soon as Christopher had finished with Spark she sold her London house. She took an apartment in Paris, and obtained from the newspaper which her husband had worked for a post as a political correspondent. She published a book which her husband had left finished all but a chapter, and which she finished herself with the help of his notes. It was on England's Foreign Policy. She did not publish his work on the Merovingian Kings which was twice as long, although only seven chapters had been finished.

Trevenen's book made a stir and had a comparatively large sale. Mrs Trevenen was able to pay her husband's debts and even to give Christopher a small allowance.

At Spark's he worked hard and made no new friends. There he found Godfrey Mellor who was cramming for the Civil Service, before going up to Oxford. They did not do more than nod to one another.

CHAPTER IV

Countess Linsky was a widow. She lived with her daughter and her son in the castle of Birkenberg, which was halfway between Vienna and Prague.

It was a white-washed building with pointed turrets situated on the top of the hill. It was uneven, and the rooms were rambling like a rabbit-warren. In the valley there was a village with red pointed roofs on which the storks nested, and hard by there was a small pellucid river, a water mill, and smiling green meadows.

Countess Linsky was an old lady with shrewd eyes and an infectious laugh. Her son Karl, who was sixteen years old, was delicate. He had short, rather curly hair, and a gentle, wistful expression like that of a spaniel. His sister, Alex, was seventeen, and just out. She was short, with light brown hair, clear, dark blue, laughing eyes, and a quiet smile that seemed to search the whole room like a sunbeam.

There was another aunt in the house; an aunt by marriage. They called her "Aunt Berthe." A Countess Felsen. She was a Frenchwoman, tall and rather large, with soft grey eyes and tawny hair like a soft muff that had white streaks in it. Her daughter was with her. Her name was Elsa.

Elsa was the same age as Alex. She was fresh and pretty, with a snub nose and pale blue eyes, and fair hair. She was not a beauty, but she reminded you of a white rose.

Christopher liked Countess Felsen at once. She was gentle and reflective, and purred like a good-natured cat. She was a widow and had a married son.

There was an English nurse in the house called Hanna. But she was too old to do much. She sat sewing all day in the deserted schoolroom. She was devoted to the children.

Countess Linsky and her cousin approved of Christopher's looks. He was grown up now and no longer overgrown. His features were good and had a certain dignity about them. "He has got a good head and fine eyes," they said. But there was something sullen in his expression and he was silent. If he smiled he was disarming, but it was difficult to make him smile.

Karl was a gentle creature. He was lazy, fond of nature and sport, uncultivated, that is to say, he never read a book, except a German translation of Mark Twain, and spoke with a slow, lazy drawl, but every now and then he would twinkle and bubble with fun, and in the evenings he would play the piano by ear with an exquisite sense of rhythm.

He was friendly and affable to Christopher. Every day they were supposed to do an hour's English reading. But as neither Karl nor Christopher could fix their attention on what they were supposed to read – Shakespeare and Walter Scott – the lesson generally ended by Karl showing Christopher his stamp collection or in rambling conversation. They had no topics in common except stamps, which amused Christopher, as anything did connected with travel. But Karl was the sort of person who could talk to anyone, and it was impossible, however little one said oneself, to feel embarrassed with him.

After Christopher had been a week at Birkenberg, his mother asked Karl how he liked him.

"I like him very much," he said, "*ein ganz guter Kerl, sehr zahm*, very tame for an Englishman."

"I don't know whether he is so tame," said his mother.

Christopher was happy. He liked being abroad where people

took him for granted, where he did not have to pretend that he was not half French and a Catholic.

He had plenty of time to himself which he spent working for his examination, in the library, and he went for long walks in the woods with Karl.

He did not see much of Alex at first for she was busy with her cousin.

One night, after dinner, they were sitting in the long, low, drawing room; the girls were busy painting, Karl was playing the pianoforte, and Christopher was talking to Countess Linsky and Countess Felsen. They were talking of a question of conscience. Christopher, who had been silent, suddenly said:

"I don't think I have got a conscience."

Countess Linsky laughed, and Countess Felsen looked at him with a puzzled expression.

She asked him what he meant.

He became a little confused.

"If one does things by accident, one is told they don't matter."

"Of course they don't," said Countess Linsky, "there is all the difference in the world. My dear friend, you don't mean to say that it is the same thing to push someone out of the window and to throw him out on purpose."

"I believe it might be the same thing to me."

Countess Linsky laughed.

"Then we must be careful never to go near a window with you."

"The tame *Engländer* will never throw anyone out of the window," said Karl, looking up from his playing.

"I don't believe I've got a conscience, all the same," said Christopher.

Countess Linsky laughed again.

"That only means you have never done anything very bad and your conscience is so good that you don't notice it."

They talked of other things.

The next day Countess Felsen took Christopher out for a walk.

He found he could talk to her more easily than to anyone he had ever met. He felt he did not mind what he said to her. She seemed to understand everything and to be interested in everything, and he felt that he had known her all his life.

All at once she said to him:

"What you said about not having a conscience interested me, but I didn't quite understand what you meant."

"I meant," said Christopher, "that it is just as bad to do things by accident as on purpose, and that if I did something bad on purpose I shouldn't mind more than if I had done it by accident. I mean I think remorse is a sin – a disease."

"But remorse is not conscience," said Countess Felsen. "Conscience tells you what is right and wrong. Remorse is what you suffer from doing what you know to have been wrong."

"All the things I have done which seemed to me most wrong I have done by accident," said Christopher, "and those are the things I have minded. When I have done something wrong on purpose I have never minded at all because I meant to do it."

Countess Felsen smiled with understanding.

"I know what you mean," she said, "I used to feel like that sometimes when I was your age, but you know one deceives oneself, and one changes."

"Do people change?" asked Christopher. "I am reading a German translation of a book by Turgenev, and he says that man is the same from the cradle to the grave."

"Possibly," she said, "but children have a conscience, you were probably aware of your conscience as a child."

"I don't think I was," said Christopher, "at least it was all second-hand – all done for me. I was told some things were wrong and some things were right, and I often did the things I was told not to do and nobody minded, and when I did something which I thought was right I was punished. So I ended by never saying."

"You probably had nothing serious to hide. Children make mountains out of such mole-hills."

"I did. I had some things to hide."

"Things which seem very silly now."

"Not altogether. I had one serious thing."

"Really serious?"

"Really serious."

"We all have our serious things at every age," she said, "and then we look back and see they were not so serious after all."

"But this was serious."

Countess Felsen lit a cigarette.

"You see I had a sister, Mabel. I was fond of her."

"Younger than you?"

"No, a year older – she was – she was the only person I have ever been friends with. We understood each other."

"I know, I had a brother – he died."

"She was delicate, and I was told never to let her bathe, and I let her bathe."

"That happens to all children. That is not serious."

"Yes, but we got wet afterwards, in a thunderstorm – and she caught cold – and she died."

"And you thought it was your fault?"

"It was my fault. I knew I had killed her – but I didn't tell anyone."

"Didn't you go to Confession?"

"Yes, but I never confessed that – not till my first Communion."

"And then?"

"I told the priest, and he said that there was no guilt, and that I had been foolish not to confess it before."

"Of course. He was quite right."

"But why? After all, I did kill my sister. I let her bathe."

Countess Felsen laughed.

"You are not much older now than you were then. You didn't mean to kill her."

"That's just it. If I had killed her on purpose I shouldn't have minded so much. I should have meant to do it. It was because it was an accident that it was so awful."

"That means, not that you hadn't got a conscience but that you had too much conscience. You tormented yourself with scruples. Don't you see that you can't know what you would have felt if you had killed her on purpose, because you never would have wanted to kill her?"

"I used to be angry with her, and I sometimes felt that I could have killed her – gladly."

"Every child in the world has felt like that sometimes, and always will, and when they do something wild or rash or violent in such moments, they mind afterwards."

"Not more than I minded as it was. I couldn't have minded more."

"You loved your sister very much?"

"Very much."

"More than your father and your mother?"

"I never knew my father properly, and my mother has never liked me."

"Don't say that. You don't know – you can't tell – you have no idea how greatly mothers sometimes love their children without showing it. Sometimes they can't show it, however much they long to."

"But I do know. My mother has always done her best not to let me see it, but I couldn't help seeing that she loved my sister and that she didn't love me. You see I wasn't jealous. And my mother wasn't unkind. She took pains to be kinder to me – only that was just the difference. I couldn't help seeing it. My mother was *fair*. Too fair to me. Unfairer to Mabel."

Countess Felsen sighed. She understood the situation.

"I think," she said, "that you got things into a tangle and that you haven't quite unwound that tangle yet. It will unwind itself later on. When one is young one doesn't see things in their true proportion. But nothing I can say will be of any use to you. One can't help people, especially young people, by giving them advice. But I am sure that, so far from having no conscience, you have too much, otherwise you would have no religion."

"That's just it," said Christopher, "I have got no religion. Please do not say I told you this. Please do not tell Countess Linsky or Karl that I said this. And please do not think me a hypocrite because I go to Mass. That is all I do. I go to Mass on Sundays, but I do none of the other things. I never go to Confession even at Easter. But I think the Catholic is the only religion, if one must have a religion, and I do not want to disturb and shock other people. It would kill my mother if she knew I was saying all this. Not because she is fond of me, but because she would think it such an awful thing, such a disgrace, like having bad manners."

"But, my dear Christopher, that is nonsense. She would only mind because she is fond of you. Your mother is a clever woman, a woman of intellect and character. I knew her when she was a girl, and I knew her father. You must know that religion with her is not a convention."

"I don't say it is. I know it is real for *her*, but – "

"But what?"

He was going to say – "she is old-fashioned," but he thought it would be rude, so he said:

"She is different."

"When I was young I lost all Faith, too," said Countess Felsen, "but it comes back sometimes, and then one looks back at the time when one was without it as a part of one's education. To find the right path one has to try wrong paths first."

"But how does one know it is the right path?"

"One knows it in the same way one knows whether one is outside or inside a house. You are warm inside and cold outside. Inside there is a fire."

"But if you don't feel cold outside?"

"Till you find the fire you do not know how cold you were."

"I don't see that one is any the worse off, if one doesn't

know."

"You can't understand that till you feel the fire. You had Faith as a child?"

"I accepted everything I was told as a child because I didn't understand what it meant."

"And about the future life – when we are dead?"

"I would like to go out like a candle."

"But it's not a question of what we like. Supposing we don't."

"Oh, of course one can't prove it, but all the probability lies – "

"Some people – and not only religious people – some great minds think, and have always thought, that life after death is more probable than the contrary."

"Yes, but if one doesn't feel it, there is nothing to be done. I don't feel it. I am made like that."

"But what you don't see is that nearly everyone feels like you do at some time or other in their lives, but they change."

"You think I will change?"

"I am sure you will. Our natures may not change, but our opinions are always changing. Everyone we meet makes a difference to us."

"I can't imagine myself thinking differently."

"Do you like poetry?" she asked.

"No, I don't understand it. I like some German poems because they are simple. I like prose. Travel, facts, adventures. True things. And I like things put simply. All English poetry, ancient and modern, seems to me so complicated."

"Then you would have liked to be a traveller?"

"Oh yes, I should like to go to Africa and India and Thibet and Arabia."

"But you will go to the East."

"Yes, as a clerk in an office," he said, bitterly.

"Who knows what that may not lead to? Your mother wrote to Countess Linsky and said you had the makings of an Oriental

37

scholar."

"The most I can rise to is to be a Consul General or chief dragoman somewhere."

"One never knows what one may not rise to. When people write novels they make their characters fulfil their purpose. Every character is in the story for some particular object. Why shouldn't it be the same with the universe?"

"I daresay it is, but I am sure I have been cast for a very minor part."

"Perhaps Napoleon said the same thing when he was a penniless *lieutenant d'artillerie*?"

"But he had ambition, and I have no ambition except – "

"Except what?"

"Except for things I cannot possibly achieve – explorations."

"Explorations!"

"I should like to make a discovery, to discover a lost temple or a lost relic – like Saint Helena! I would like to go to Mecca or the forbidden city to find some unknown flower or some wonderful jewel, or an undiscovered race. I know this is silly. I am talking as if Rider Haggard's stories were true. You are laughing at me."

"I am not laughing at you. It isn't silly, because such things do happen. Think of Schliemann. And another thing is – we most of us get what we pray for. Our prayers are answered."

"I don't pray. I can't."

"Every one of your hopes and dreams is an unconscious prayer. Nothing is lost in the universe."

"Do you mean to say you think I shall ever discover a lost temple, or something like that?"

"I think it might happen when you least expect it. Keep an open mind. Do not think that doors are shut in front of you. Remember everything is possible. In the meantime you must pass your examination. It is always best to think of the thing that is immediately in front of one, and to do that as well as one can."

"You are right. I must pass my examination for my mother's sake. She has done a lot for me."

"Yes, that is just it. There is always someone else one has to think of, thank Heaven. There's your mother. One is never isolated in this world. One's life is bound up with those of other people. In some ways it makes things more difficult, but in other ways it makes everything easier."

At that moment they met Karl, dressed in green, with a feather in his felt cap. He was carrying a gun. He yodelled to them, and they walked home together.

CHAPTER V

Christopher had been attracted by Alex at the first glance. He had never met anyone so easy in his life. She reminded him of Mabel. But his admiration made him doubly shy with her, and he avoided her. She, too, was busy with her cousin, so for the first weeks of his stay at Birkenberg he hardly exchanged a word with her except at meals. He watched her with admiration, and sometimes when they all played games together in the evening she would gently tease him. He got on better with her cousin if by getting on one means conversation, but he was not attracted by her.

A Serbian professor arrived at the house, a certain Doctor Jacobi, who lived in Paris, and was a friend of Countess Felsen.

He was talkative and dogmatic, a short man, with piercing eyes and a black beard.

One evening after dinner they were talking of ghosts, and somehow or other the ghost in *Hamlet* was mentioned.

"Hamlet," said the doctor, "was mad. His form of madness is well known to us nerve doctors. He was suffering from auto-hallucination, and Shakespeare understood that very well."

"But," said Christopher, "other people saw the ghost."

"They were infected with his hallucination. Nothing is more catching."

"But they saw it first," said Christopher.

"Then he caught it from them."

"I am sure Shakespeare meant the ghost to be a ghost," said Christopher.

"Of course he did," said Countess Felsen.

"No, no, no, it was a study of a particular hallucination," said the doctor. "Shakespeare was ahead of his time. He had of course to express himself in a way his public would understand."

"Jacobi doesn't believe in ghosts," said Countess Felsen.

"That is just as well," said Karl, "he won't see our ghost."

"Is there a ghost here?" asked Christopher.

"No," said Countess Linsky, "that is all nonsense."

"Alex and I have both seen it twice," said Karl.

"Don't, Karl, don't talk such nonsense, you know I don't like it," said his mother.

Jacobi, Countess Linsky, Karl and Countess Felsen, and her daughter settled down at the card table, and began a rubber of whist.

Alex, Karl and Christopher went out on to the terrace.

It was a perfect August evening. The fields were half reaped. Over the dark rim of the fir-clad hills there was a silvery halo which heralded the approach of moonrise.

"Have you really seen a ghost?" asked Christopher.

"Yes, I saw one on this terrace, but it was naughty of Karl to talk about it, because it was the night before Uncle Paul, my father's brother, died, and Mamma doesn't like us to talk about it."

"Where did you see it?"

"We saw it here on this terrace, didn't we, Karl? It was just like *Hamlet*. The lamps were lit in the drawing room, as they are tonight, and one saw the light through the window. Papa and Mamma and the others were playing cards. Uncle Paul was abroad in Paris. It was a hot night in August, just like tonight, and Karl and I went on to the terrace. We were just going to bed, and we had gone out to look at the moon. And I said to Karl, 'there is someone coming along the terrace,' and he said, 'that is Joseph (the butler),' and then we saw a man who looked like a monk, and then he disappeared. If I had been alone I should have thought I had seen nothing, but Karl saw it, too. Later we heard that Uncle Paul died just at that moment. We didn't know he was ill."

"Did you ever see it again?"

"No, we didn't, but I believe other people did. Hanna saw it once, but she won't talk about it. It always means something sad."

The full moon began to rise above the hill, large and rosy. Alex looked at it thoughtfully.

"It was naughty of you, Karl, to talk of the ghost. You know Mamma doesn't like it."

Karl laughed.

"I couldn't help it. Jacobi is so stupid about everything."

"Stupid!" said Alex. "He is a great *savant*, a great doctor!"

"He is stupid, all the same. He'll think we are mad now, like Hamlet. Have you ever seen a ghost, Mr Trevenen?"

"No, and I don't believe in them."

"Then you are as bad as the doctor. You think Hamlet was mad."

"I don't understand *Hamlet*. I should enjoy it if only it wasn't written in blank verse. But then we always had to learn long pieces from it by heart."

"I always imagine it happening here on this terrace," said Alex. "We saw it acted once, in Vienna. It was lovely. Do you like plays?"

"Yes. I haven't seen many. I liked the plays in Dresden."

"Oh, the Opera! It must be lovely there. Have you ever heard the *Fledermaus*?"

"No, never. I'm not musical. I don't like difficult music."

"But that's not difficult. Karl, go and play a tune from the *Fledermaus*."

Karl went in and began to play.

"He does play well," said Christopher.

"You don't play?"

"Not at all. I haven't any talents."

"Mamma says you are a *savant* and know all languages."

"My father was a scholar, he knew a lot. That's why I know nothing. I believe children of parents who know a lot never learn anything."

"But you have travelled a great deal?"

"I have only been to France and Rome and Dresden."

"Oh, Rome! Did you like Rome?"

"I liked the Campagna. I liked Dresden better. At Rome there is too much to see – and it's all dead."

"Did you go to the top of Saint Peter's?"

"Yes, I did, and down in the catacombs. How well Karl plays. I like that kind of music."

"So do I. That's a *walzer* – Strauss. Only it makes me sad. I don't know why gay music makes me sadder than sad music. Can you dance?"

"We used to go to dancing classes, I and my sister, when we were small. I have never danced since."

"Do you remember your sister?" Alex asked, gently.

"Oh yes. I was only nine when she died."

"But that was a long time ago."

"I shall always remember her."

"Was she like you?"

"No, she was pretty, she was like – " He was going to say "like you," but he checked himself and said instead: "She had blue eyes and she was fond of fun."

"Was she younger than you?"

"No, a year older."

"What was she called?"

"She was called Mabel, but I used to call her Mab, after Queen Mab. Because she had funny ideas. She thought she was going to be a prima donna or a Gypsy Queen."

"You must miss her. I know how I would miss Karl. Brothers and sisters are unlike anything else. Grown-up people are not the same, are they?"

Christopher looked at Alex and saw that her eyes were filled with tears. He thought he had never seen a more beautiful face. Her smile was like sunshine, but her sadness was more beautiful, a searchlight of pity in a still harbour.

He said nothing and they were silent for a moment. They listened to the noises of the night in the valley. Some lights were twinkling. Karl had stopped playing, but presently he began again and played a tune that sounded like spring.

Aus mei - nen Thränen sprie - ssen viel blü - hen - de Blu-men her - vor

"What is that tune?" Christopher asked.

"It's called 'Aus meinen Thränen spriessen.' The words are by Heine. Do you like Heine?"

"I never have liked any poetry yet, I have never understood it, but – "

Christopher was not sure whether he would not like Heine now. He had only read German verse as an exercise; he had never thought such sentiments could have any relation to real life, but now – everything had become different.

He listened to the song. When Karl had finished he said:

"Do tell me what the words are. I have forgotten them."

Alex repeated the words.

Aus meinen Thränen spriessen
Viel blühende Blumen hervor,
Und meine Seufzer werden
Ein Nachtigallenchor.

Und wenn du mich lieb hast, Kindchen,
Schenk' ich dir die Blumen all,

Und vor deinem Fenster soll klingen
Das Lied der Nachtigall.

"Yes, I like that. I think that is beautiful. It's simple. Anyone could understand it."

Alex laughed.

"How silly you are. You can't pretend not to understand poetry!"

"I understand that sort of poem," he said, "at least I do now – now that I have heard the tune; but I don't understand most poetry. I understand what the words mean, but I don't see the point of saying in a complicated way what could be said simply."

"What sort of poetry do you mean?"

"Oh, the speeches in Shakespeare and all that sort of thing."

"I like Shakespeare," said Alex, "he is wonderful. *Romeo and Juliet*. And his songs! Oh! his songs." She began softly to repeat in her soft, careful, foreign English:

"Fear no more the heat o' the sun,
Nor the furious winter's rages;
Thou thy worldly task hast done,
Home art gone, and ta'en thy wages:
Golden lads and girls all must,
As chimney-sweepers, come to dust."

She repeated the whole poem.

"Don't you like that?"

Christopher thought of Mabel, of Vernay; he felt inclined to cry; when he had felt inclined to cry before there had been a bleakness and desolation about his grief.

Now he was feeling sad, and the sadness, instead of being dark and bitter, was irradiated with moonshine. He was enjoying it. It was as if he had been touched by an enchanter's

45

wand.

"I didn't know that," he said, "you see I have only read Shakespeare as a duty."

"Shakespeare understood everything. Especially young people. I always think someone must have been unkind to him. He talks so painfully of ingratitude, but although he is sad and tragic he is never bitter, he is sweet. He is like Beethoven. Out of his great sadness there comes a fountain of joy."

"I can't understand Beethoven."

"Have you ever heard his symphonies?"

"Never, only quartettes, and things like that."

"Oh, but you must."

Christopher felt he could understand even Beethoven if he were with Alex. "But you are musical, you see, and I'm not."

"You are, but you don't know it. You must be musical if you like Karl's playing."

"But that is easy, simple."

"So are Beethoven's great things. I always think that all the great things, the greatest things, are simple. It is the second-best things that are so complicated."

"When I was at Dresden, I had a friend who was musical, and he used to take me to concerts. I couldn't understand any of the music, but he loved it."

"Chamber music, I suppose?"

"Yes, chamber music; I thought it awful. And then we used to go to the Opera. I annoyed him because the only music I liked was Wagner."

"Oh, Wagner! I adore Wagner! Didn't your friend like him?"

"Yes, he did; but not so much as the other composers."

"I understand. Musicians are often like that. That's why it is a comfort not to know too much, and to be able to like anything. I know nothing about music, but I just enjoy anything. It's the same with books. Tell me about your friend. Was he a professional musician? Did he compose?"

"Oh no! But he had a friend there who did, a man called

Solway, who used to play beautifully, I believe, but I couldn't bear his playing. The only playing I have ever liked is your brother's. I could listen to that for hours."

"He *is* musical, but he doesn't know how musical he is; he can play anything he has heard, but he can't read a note of music."

"And can you play?"

"Not like that. I play with notes, very painfully."

She laughed. "You must have heard me practising in the morning. Scales."

"Yes, I have heard it sometimes."

"Did your sister play?"

"No, but she sang; she had a pretty voice, and she was fond of music. She liked everything, just as you do. She used to sing Irish songs and French songs. She sang a song I used to like very much called '*La Pimpolaise.*'"

"Karl can play that. Karl," she called through the window, "play the '*Pimpolaise.*' It's a Breton song," she said. "Your mother is French, isn't she?"

"Yes," Christopher said, without any warmth of response.

"That's so nice. I love French songs – but I like German poetry better. We had to learn such a lot of Racine and Corneille."

"So did we."

"And we hated it."

"So did we."

"The *songe d'Athalie.*"

"Yes, and *Fables.*"

"That was worst of all."

"I had to say one on Sundays after luncheon."

"Did you have a governess?"

"Yes, she was a German, she was supposed to be Alsatian, but she was really German. We hated her. She was strict, but we used to laugh at her."

"And we had a French governess called Mademoiselle

47

Josselin. Karl and I used to tease her dreadfully because she didn't understand German, and she never could learn a word. I'm thankful it's all over, last year it wasn't."

"Did you come out this year?"

"Last winter we went to Vienna. It was great fun, you must come in the winter. I love Vienna, but I want to go to England so much. I have never been there, but I feel I know what it is like. And London."

"I hate London," said Christopher, "it's awful."

But he felt it would not be at all awful if Alex were there. He saw himself showing her all sorts of things.

Karl came out and said:

"Mamma says you are to come in, Alex. She says you will catch cold."

They went indoors.

Christopher asked Karl to play something else, and he played a valse called "*Sei nicht böse.*"

Christopher sat and listened, looking at Alex, who took up her needlework.

They made Karl play for the rest of the evening. It was late when they went to bed. Christopher went to bed, but not to sleep. His brain was on fire. The tunes he had heard – one of them at least – kept ringing in his head, and the vision of Alex's eyes was before him.

He had never seen anyone like her in his life. Could it be, he suddenly asked himself, that he was in love? He tried to sleep and failed; he lit a candle and read a little, but he could not pay attention to his book, nor take in what he was reading. He blew out the candle, and in the dark he saw the terrace, the lights in the valley, the rising moon, Alex in her white frock, her eyes, her blue eyes, filled with tears when she talked of Mabel.

"Tomorrow I must read Heine," he said to himself, "it's not so silly as I thought it was."

CHAPTER VI

The next morning when Christopher woke up he felt before he was quite awake that some wonderful thing had happened or that some treat was in store for him. He had not felt like that since the first days of the holidays at Vernay, when he used to wake up and gradually realise that Mademoiselle Altmann had gone for her holidays.

That morning as he worked with Karl, he was absent-minded. They were reading "Quentin Durward."

"Do you like Heine?" he asked Karl.

"I like the songs that are set to music and the tunes, but I think the words are so childish. I like Schiller's ballads much better. Heine is always crying. It is so silly."

Christopher asked Alex to lend him a volume of Heine, and that afternoon he went for a walk in the woods by himself, and took the book with him. The others had gone to pay a visit to a neighbour.

He sat in the woods, smoking and reading the lyrics.

"Karl," he thought, "isn't old enough of course, to understand this. But I understand it." He felt old. "This is the only readable poetry that has ever been written. Why can't other people write simply?" He thought of the Greeks and the Latins. "The Greeks were simple, but I don't expect they felt things in this way. The Latins? Virgil is tiresome. Horace is like La Fontaine's fables.

Dull. Catullus?" He had read Catullus, bits of it – for work, not for pleasure. "Perhaps he is better. I must try." But all thoughts of books vanished – books were dead, and Alex was alive.

The world was empty without her. When would he see her again? At teatime. They had tea in the schoolroom with Hanna.

Would she be back for tea? Would he be able to talk to her again after dinner? On the terrace, perhaps? She never played whist. She didn't know how to. Her cousin played. Her cousin was thought pretty, but what was she in comparison with Alex? Karl admired her. Was Karl in love with her? No, he was too young. What was the use of his being in love with Alex? He could never marry her. Her mother would never let her marry a penniless interpreter. He was not even an interpreter yet. Austrians were proud. He was only a tutor. They looked down upon him. They were kind to him, but they probably looked upon him as belonging to an inferior race. It didn't matter. He didn't count. There was a gulf between them, and yet things like that happened. Was it more extraordinary than his mother marrying his father? But they had had enough money to marry on. After all, his father's family was a good one, so was his mother's; he was as good as they were. Why should they look down upon him? What right had they to despise him? It was only money. Money, money, money; that was all that mattered in the world. And he would never have any money. If he ever should have any it would be for his mother. It was she who was giving to him so far. He must pass his examination. He didn't want to be an interpreter. It was the last thing he wanted. It would be like the ordeal of Tantalus, to be near all the things that interested him most – the East: Persia, Arabia – and yet not to be able to taste it. To be a clerk, a book-keeper, a Vice-Consul. How would he endure it? How did anyone endure anything? Money was all that mattered. There were rich people and they did what they liked, and the people without money slaved.

Could he make money? Could he become rich? Why not? People did become rich. If he were rich they would be glad to let him marry Alex. Yes, but would she marry him? No, there was no chance of that. She could never love him. Perhaps she loved someone already. Perhaps she was engaged to be married.

How foolish he was. He was just like Perrette in the fable, counting her chickens before they were hatched. Perrette. How he wished that Alex was a farmer's girl, like Perrette.

But if by any miracle she were to – no, these things didn't happen. He didn't believe she hated him. Her face rose before him. The tears in her eyes when they talked of Mabel. Why think of the future? These things were settled. Kismet. But supposing they were settled in his favour? Then nothing, no mortal agency could prevent his marrying Alex. He thought of his conversation with Countess Felsen. She believed in *prayer*. But then all people of her generation believed in prayer: his mother, his father. He remembered his father saying his rosary in the evening at Vernay, with his grey eyes looking straight into space. Did he believe all that, or was it only because he was an Irishman? But he had been born a Protestant. All Irishmen were the same, Catholics or Protestants, they all believed in something of the kind, and it was only a chance which camp they belonged to. Whichever the camp, they were just as violent.

But his father was not violent, he was mild. Yes, but obstinate. His mother? Yes, but she was French. She had inherited prejudices and customs. "I am nothing," he said to himself, "I am half one thing and half another. I shall fall between two stools. I am not an Englishman and I talk English. I am not an Irishman. I am not a Frenchman. And I have enough of the three elements not to be at home anywhere. My father ought never to have married my mother. And yet if I married Alex? If Alex wanted to marry me I would not let that stand in my way. It wouldn't matter so much as I too am foreign."

He got up and walked on through the woods.

It was a beautiful still afternoon. The world was lapped in warmth and sunshine. He had left the wood. Slight noises came from the fields and villages. Distant crowings. The harvest was nearly done. He passed a little girl, leading a flock of geese with a switch.

He looked at his watch. He must be back in time for tea, he thought, or he would miss Alex.

He got back in time for tea. Alex and Karl and Elsa were already there, bubbling with laughter, teasing Hanna, who scolded them as if they were children. They had had such a funny afternoon.

That night after dinner they didn't play whist, but a round game, with counters, called *Le Nain Jaune*, all of them except Karl, who sat reading Mark Twain. Christopher asked him to play a tune.

He played some student and folk songs. Christopher asked him to play some of the tunes set to Heine's words, but he said he only knew one.

"Play that one," said Christopher.

"I've forgotten it," he said, "I will play something better." And he played "*Ach! Du lieber Augustin*" over and over again.

"Let's dance," said Alex.

The game was at an end.

"If you dance you must dance in the dining room," said Countess Linsky. "Leave the door open and you will hear the music."

"But if Karl dances there will be no one to play," said Alex.

"I will play for you," said Countess Felsen, and she sat down and played a valse.

They pushed the chairs and table out of the way in the big high dining room, and Karl began at once to dance with Elsa.

"You must dance with me," said Alex to Christopher.

"But I don't think I can."

"I will teach you."

They began to whirl round. Christopher felt awkward; he knew he was out of time, but Alex danced so well that he got through better than he had expected. He felt as if in heaven as he held her in his arms.

The dance came to an end.

"Now," said Alex, "I will show you what you do wrong."

She took hold of his hands and taught him the steps of the *trois temps*.

They asked for another tune and they danced again. They whirled round and round till they were out of breath. Then they sat down.

"Let's go out on to the terrace for a moment," said Christopher. "It's so hot."

They went out on to the terrace and looked into the night. There were no clouds. It was a still and starry night.

The moon had risen some time ago.

"I enjoyed the book you lent me," said Christopher.

"I thought you would. They are so lovely."

"He must have been unhappy."

"Yes, poor man. He was dreadfully ill...and then he was a Jew."

"And despised by everyone, I suppose."

"I don't know. He lived abroad, in Paris. But he was famous in his lifetime."

"Would you have despised him?"

"I would never despise anyone who wrote beautiful things like that. But I think he was bitter and mischievous, and if he was hated it was partly his own fault."

"If people are unhappy and lonely that makes them bitter and mischievous, I suppose."

"Yes, but you know I think great men, very great men, are never bitter – men like Goethe and Shakespeare."

"I don't think I understand them. They are on the top of a mountain, but I think I could understand people like Heine better."

"What did you do all the afternoon?"

"I went into the woods and I read a great many of those poems, almost all of them."

"I knew you would like Heine after our talk last night," said Alex, and she smiled. Again Christopher felt as if in Heaven.

"She doesn't hate me, she doesn't despise me," he said to himself.

They were called back by the others and they danced again, and then Countess Felsen said she could play no more. It was time to go to bed.

Two days later they went for a picnic.

Countess Linsky and Countess Felsen went in one carriage and took the provisions. The four others went in another carriage. They went into the woods.

There they made a fire and baked potatoes in the ashes and fried some fish which Karl caught in a stream. The young people went for a walk. The carriage was to meet them further on. For a time they walked together, then Karl and Elsa went on ahead, leaving Christopher and Alex behind. Alex told him about her life and made him tell her about his. They talked of Mabel and France and Rome, and his parents and his mother.

"She must be a wonderful woman," said Alex.

"She is," said Christopher. "There is nothing she can't do. I feel so ashamed of being so unlike her and of being able to do so little for her."

"But you will some day, I am sure. I think you will be a great man some day. Famous. As famous as Heine."

Christopher laughed.

"I shall never write poetry," he said, "I couldn't string two lines together. I wish I had been born a composer."

Alex laughed.

"I thought you hated music!"

"So I do in a way, but if I were a composer I feel I could express more things in music than one can in words."

"Yes, that is true."

"But I shall be nothing like that…nothing. I shall never create anything."

"You may be a great *savant* or a great statesman, or rule one of those Eastern places. My mother thinks so. She was telling the people where we went the other day about you, and said you were remarkable. She said your father was remarkable, too. Very famous. *Welt-berühmt.*"

"My father, but he was different. I am not in the least like him."

"Perhaps you are like your mother."

"No, I am like neither of them…a sort of ugly duckling."

"But the ugly duckling changed into a swan. He *was* a swan all the time."

"Those things only happen in fairy tales. But I feel all this is like a fairy tale."

"All what?"

"My living here and knowing you, and walking with you in this wood. But soon it will come to an end and it will be like a dream."

"I shan't forget," said Alex

"Nor shall I. I shall never forget."

They walked in silence. The sun was setting and shining through the large stems of the trees, which shone red. It was cool in the great still wood.

"Let's sit down for a moment," said Christopher.

They sat down in the moss under the tree.

Christopher lit a cigarette.

"Give me one, please," Alex said. "I love smoking, but I am not allowed to except on great occasions."

Christopher asked Alex about her future plans.

They would go to Vienna in the winter; after Christmas.

"We always spend Christmas here, and a lot of relations come; the house is full. It is great fun. We have a Christmas tree, and act a play and paint the scenery ourselves. It is getting late," said Alex, suddenly. "We must pick up the others or we shall be scolded."

They got up.

"Wait a moment," said Christopher. "I want to tell you something."

Alex looked at him and smiled radiantly.

"What is it?" she asked. "Is it a secret?"

"Yes," he whispered. "It is a great secret. I love you."

She blushed and her smile did not vanish. It became more radiant still.

"I will tell you a secret, too," she said. "I loved you from the first moment I saw you."

They were in each other's arms, and the setting sun and the silent woods sealed the sacrament of their kiss.

Then they heard someone calling.

"Quick, they are coming," said Alex, and they hurried on to meet the others.

CHAPTER VII

It was September. Christopher would have to go back to England in a fortnight. His examination was at the end of the month. After the day of the picnic in the woods the world had been changed for him. He trod on air and put away all thoughts of the future. He managed to see Alex as often as he could, but he seldom had an opportunity of seeing her alone for long. Thanks to all sorts of small stratagems they used to meet in the garden or the library, where he worked by himself. Countess Linsky did not know what was happening. She saw that Christopher was in good spirits. She liked him and was glad that he was enjoying himself. One day Countess Felsen said to her: "I believe that young Englishman has rather a tender spot for Alex." Countess Linsky had laughed as if such a thing were beyond the region of possibility.

"He is so young," she said, "boys of that age always have a spark of sentiment. I have nothing against it."

"But what about Alex?" Countess Felsen asked.

"Oh, Alex is a strange girl, she is quite fancy-free. All that will come later."

"I wonder," said Countess Felsen.

In the meantime Christopher was brooding over all sorts of plans.

If he passed his examination; if he could only somehow or

other make some money… How? By writing? One didn't make much that way…he could pass further examinations, couldn't he? Then get transferred into the Diplomatic Service, and then would there be no insuperable objection to his marrying Alex? Perhaps his marriage could bring this about. Perhaps his mother could manage it. He believed she could do almost anything. He had talked of this to Alex, and had told her he supposed her family would think their marriage out of the question.

But Alex had said: "Why? Everything is possible if one is once determined to do it."

Christopher was so happy in the present that he accepted what she said. He talked no more of the future, but only of the present. But at night he would brood on the possibilities.

Could they run away? But that wouldn't be fair on Alex. What would they live on? No, his mother must arrange things, she and Alex's mother. After all, Countess Linsky respected his mother and he was sure they would get on if they were to meet; but for the greater part of the time Christopher put all thoughts of the future away from him and lived only in the present. He was catching glimpses of Heaven.

One morning, shortly before the day when he was to leave, he was sitting in the library working at Latin. He was reading Latin, which was one of the obligatory subjects for his examination. He was reading Catullus, and to his astonishment he found the writings of that poet full of passion.

"This is better than Heine," he said to himself, as he read the lyrics written to Lesbia.

Presently Alex came into the room.

"Mamma and Aunt Berthe have gone to the village," she said, "and Karl and Elsa are in the garden."

"Is Karl in love with Elsa?" asked Christopher, who now took an interest in the love affairs of other people.

"No," said Alex, "he is too young; but he will never be in love with Elsa, nor Elsa with him. Elsa loves someone else. He is away, but he is Karl's great friend, and they talk of nothing else. I have come to tell you that today I am going to tell Mamma that we are engaged to be married."

"Do you think you had better do that?" said Christopher. He was alarmed for the moment.

"It must be done some time. I am sure she will be pleased. She said you had a great future before you. I heard her say so."

"Very well, I expect you are right," and Christopher for a moment floated on an ocean of pleasant illusion. How wonderful it would be if she said: "Go and be happy, my children," but at the same time a presage of approaching disaster seemed to overshadow him. "You are sure we had not better wait?"

"Wait for what?"

"Very well, you know best."

"You see you are going away."

"I know, next Wednesday."

"I know, I have marked every day in my diary."

"You will write to me?"

"Every day."

"And when you walk on the terrace after dinner you will think of me?"

"I will go out on to the terrace every evening at nine. And if there is a moon I will say, 'Herr Mond, please greet my heart's love,' and if there is no Herr Mond, I will say, 'little stars, please be kind enough to do my commission for me,' and if there are no stars I will ask the sky, and if it is raining I will ask the lamp. But I will pray every evening to Saint Christopher because he is your saint, isn't he?"

"Yes," said Christopher, doubtfully.

"You believe in St Christopher, of course. He is such a good saint, almost as good as St Anthony."

"You think the saints do look after us?"

"Yes, I am quite sure. St Anthony does important things for one. I mean not only finding the things one has lost, although he does that, too. There is another Christopher – Christopher Seredy. He was not exactly a saint, but he died a martyr's death in Hungary. Have you ever heard of him?"

"Never."

"I will show you his story."

Alex went to one of the bookshelves and fetched a large flat volume bound in old calf. She opened it on the large table.

It contained a story written in manuscript in a large clear modern German script. It had illuminated pictures.

"I did this," she said. "I copied out the story from an old illuminated book. The original isn't here. It is locked up somewhere because it is precious. I copied it out, not all of it, because it was too long. I copied it because I liked the story and it was too difficult to read in the old manuscript. So I translated it and copied it out and made these pictures. My father helped me, and I did the pictures for him one Christmas as a surprise."

Christopher looked at the pictures with admiration.

"But they are beautifully done," he said.

"They are only copies and very childish. I will read you the story.

"It was the 28th of August, the day of St Augustine of Hippo, the eve of the day on which the martyrdom of St John the Baptist is commemorated, and the King and all his army were assembled at Mohacs. The King had summoned a Council that evening, for the Hungarians were in two minds whether to give battle against Solyman and the Turks on the morrow, or whether to retreat and to join hands with the armies that were marching from Slavonia and from Transylvania.

"And Francis Perényi, the Bishop of Grosswardein, was summoned to that Council, and Caspar Seredy, who was the keeper of the Treasure House and the guardian of the Holy Vessels, the relics and the crown of St Stephen. But of treasure

60

there was not a gold coin left, and even some of the holy Vessels had been melted down to pay the soldiery. Now Christopher, the son of Caspar Seredy, the keeper of the Treasure House, had lately been taken prisoner by the Turks. They had caught him spying, so they said, but this he had denied. And Caspar went to Solyman and begged of him the life of his son.

"And Solyman said: 'I will give him you in return for a Turkish hostage,' knowing well that there were no Turkish hostages in the hands of the Hungarians.

"And Caspar spoke of ransom (but where would he have found the wherewithal to pay the ransom?), and Solyman frowned on him and said the Turks were soldiers and not merchants. They would have gold and plunder enough in due time. As for prisoners and spies, they would be put to death either before or after the battle.

"And Caspar came away, sorrowing.

"And he returned to his home and to his wife, Elizabeth, and wept."

"Look," Alex said, "this is a picture of his wife, Elizabeth."

"But he said that all was not yet lost, for he had met with a French soldier of fortune, who was fighting for Solyman (it was King Francis, being fearful and envious, who had urged Solyman to fight the Hungarians), and the Frenchman had said that peradventure he might aid Christopher to escape.

"And at nightfall the Frenchman came to Caspar's house and said that Christopher was free; and in the neighbourhood, hard by, but guarded, and that he would deliver him to his father, at a price.

"And Caspar asked after the price, for gold and silver had he none.

"And the Frenchman said that he needed neither silver nor gold. It was a relic he needed; a Holy Coat which had been

given by Elizabeth, the daughter of Andreas to Louis, Landgraf of Thuringia, as a marriage gift.

"Now this Holy Coat was that Coat without Seam, for which the soldiers had cast lots after the Crucifixion of our Most Blessed Lord. Saint Helena had found it in Jerusalem, being warned of its whereabouts in a dream."

Christopher started when he heard this. He felt something pressing on his brain. Something he had forgotten. Then all at once he saw before him the church at Vernay. It was a still hot September afternoon. The town seemed asleep. The white houses blinked in the sun. He saw the dark cool empty church, smelling of incense. The dark East window, with its rich brown, faded yellow, and gorgeous blue jewels of glass; the Lady Chapel where he had put up a tall candle in thanks for Mabel's recovery; the side altar over which a faded piece of red stuff hung in a gilt frame; the Curé taking snuff in his blazing garden; the nasturtiums, the snapdragon, the lavender, the sunflowers; the heavy pears on the sunburnt wall. He could once more taste the blackcurrant wine, and the rum in the baba, the juicy pear. He could hear the reedy note of the little *mirliton*, which the Curé gave him, and he remembered in every detail the story of the Coat which the Curé had told him of.

Alex went on reading:

"And Caspar said to the Frenchman: 'The Holy Coat belongs to Hungary. It shall go before us into battle, like a banner, high above our Host, and you bid me sell it to the Infidel, and thereby sell our Blessed Lord a second time.'

"But the Frenchman said he would not deliver the Coat into the hands of the Infidel. He needed it for himself, for his ancestors had fought in the Crusades, and he would take it home and hang it in the Chapel where his ancestors lay buried, in the Chapel of his Castle in Poitou.

"And Caspar blamed him for serving the Infidel, but the

Frenchman said the Hungarians were the more baneful foe of his country.

"'Give me the Coat,' he said, 'and I will restore your son to you.'

"And Caspar said to himself: 'Get thee behind me, Satan.' And Caspar was summoned to the Council, and the Frenchman took leave of him and of his wife, and Caspar went out to the Council.

"But Elizabeth bade the Frenchman stay, saying she would send a last word to her son, and when Caspar had left them she said to the Frenchman:

"'If I give you the sacred Coat will you swear my son shall never hear of this?'

"And the Frenchman swore upon the Rood her son should not know, and he likewise swore that the hand of the Infidel should not touch the Holy Coat, but that he would take it home to his own country, to the Chapel in his Castle in Poitou.

"And Elizabeth gave the Frenchman the Holy Coat.

"And the Frenchman went his way.

"And presently Caspar returned from the Council and with him was Francis Perényi, Bishop of Grosswardein, and they said that the King and Paul Tömöri, the Commander-in-Chief, would give battle on the morrow, and they would have under the standards but twenty-five thousand men against the three hundred thousand men of Solyman, and his three hundred cannon.

"And Elizabeth said to them: 'In whom do they put their trust?'

"And Caspar answered: 'In the Coat without Seam which shall go before us into battle, like a banner, high above the Host.'

"And presently Christopher, Caspar's son, entered the house, saying he had escaped from the Turks. And they told him the King would give battle on the morrow, and Francis, the Bishop of Grosswardein, said: 'Tomorrow there will be

twenty-thousand Hungarian martyrs on the field of Mohacs, and it would be well that they should be canonised at once.'

"And Caspar said: 'The King has said that if the Coat without Seam shall go before us into battle we shall yet prevail over the infidel.'

"And Christopher said: 'Shall the Coat without Seam be taken into battle?'

"And Francis, the Bishop, said: 'Yes, but against my will and in spite of my counsel.'

"And Christopher said: 'Where is the Coat without Seam?'

"And Caspar said: 'It is here in this house, in safe keeping with what is left of the Holy Vessels.'

"And Christopher said: 'Show me the Coat.'

"And Caspar said: 'We shall all of us see the Coat betimes on the morrow.'

"And Christopher said: 'Nay, I must see it now, it is thanks to the Holy Coat that I am free, for I thought of this Coat in my prayers.'

"And Caspar opened the cupboard where the Holy Coat was kept. And the Coat was not there. And Elizabeth confessed that which she had done.

"Then when Christopher had heard all she had to tell and how she had given the Holy Coat in exchange for his life, he said:

"'I must go back forthwith and deliver myself into the hands of the Turks.'

"And his father said him not nay, and his mother asked pardon of him.

"And Christopher went back and was slain, but whether after or before the battle it is not recorded. And what befell the Holy Coat is not known save that it fell not into the hands of Solyman, and some say that the Frenchman took it home to his Chapel in his Castle in Poitou, where it hangs to this day. And on the morrow the battle was fought, and twenty thousand Hungarians perished on the field of Mohacs, as

Francis the Bishop of Grosswardein had foretold.
  "May God have mercy upon their souls."

"That is the story," said Alex, "and here you see is a picture of the battle."

"And what happened to the Coat without Seam? Was it taken back to France?" asked Christopher.

"I don't know. There is a church at Treves which claims to have it, and there is a church in France which claims to have it as well. But it is certainly not in Hungary."

Christopher told Alex the story which the Curé at Vernay had told him.

"It is strange," he said, "that this story should have cropped up in my life again. The first time it was just before something sad. I hope it doesn't mean that something sad is going to happen to me now."

"I think it will be the contrary," said Alex, "I think that something wonderful is going to happen to us."

A bell rang.

"That means," she said "we must get ready for luncheon."

CHAPTER VIII

After luncheon that day it poured with rain. Christopher sat in the library with Karl, who was busy carving something rather elaborate with a fret-saw.

Just after luncheon Alex managed to whisper to Christopher that she was going to tell her mother, and she followed her into her sitting room. She stayed there about an hour. Christopher was pretending to read a book. Every now and then Karl said something to him, but his voice had that tone of aloof abstraction, not asking for an answer, peculiar to people who are engaged in some engrossing manual occupation. It was about half-past three when Alex broke into the room, half opened the door, and made a sign to Christopher. He obeyed her signal.

"What has happened? Is it all right?" he asked.

She looked white; her eyes were bright but dry.

"No," she said, "not at all now…but it may become all right… she wants to see you now…at once… You must be careful… she was so surprised, it was a shock to her."

Christopher followed Alex to her mother's sitting room. As she left him she said, "Be careful," then she ran up the small spiral staircase that led to her room.

Christopher found Countess Linsky standing up in front of the fireplace. It was a small room, built in one of the turrets of the house. Over the chimney piece there was a large crayon portrait of Count Linsky in a Hussar uniform. There were water-colour portraits of Alex and Karl as children, and a large oil painting of the carnival at Rome, some water-colours of Naples and Sicily, temples, ruins and mountains, and a picture of the Madonna and Child copied from Andrea del Sarto. There was a large writing table full of knick-knacks and some arm chairs covered with a faded cretonne. There was a little table too, with a glass top, full of snuff boxes, watches and medals.

"Come in, my dear boy, and sit down. I have asked you to come because I want to talk to you at once," Countess Linsky said, pointing to one of the arm chairs, and sitting down on the other. Christopher sat down.

"Alex has been here, and she has told me everything. It was a surprise to me. I am to blame for that. I ought to have known better. I understand what has happened. It is only too natural. I am going to be frank with you and talk to you as if you were my own son. There can be no question of marriage. You are both far too young, and you would have nothing to live on. Alex will have very little, and you have yet your career to make. I am sure you will do well, but you must know that at present it would be absurd for you to think of marriage with anybody."

"Oh yes," said Christopher, "I understand that, but if later I should be in a position to marry, would you let me marry Alex? Would you let us wait?"

"Do you think that would be fair on Alex?"

"I would not wish to bind her in any way…but may we not be engaged, she could always break it off if she wanted to…if there was someone else she liked better…if she changed her mind?"

"That would be binding her, binding her in the most, in the most – I cannot think of the word, in the most thorough way."

"I don't see why."

"You must take my word for it. It would not be fair on her. It would prevent her ever thinking of anyone else if she felt she was bound in loyalty to you."

"But supposing she wanted to be bound in loyalty to me?"

"Alex is not old enough to know…she is a child, and you will forgive me for saying so, you are not old enough yet to know your own mind."

"I shan't change my mind."

"That is what we all think when we are your age."

"That is what people always tell young people, but over and over again they have been proved to be wrong. My mother married when she was young. She never regretted it."

Countess Linsky sighed, wondering whether this were true, and thinking that even if it were true, the ultimate result was hardly a signal example of a successful marriage.

"Even if you are right," she said, "that is neither here nor there. You would not have a penny between you to live on. If my husband was alive he would not hear of it."

"I love Alex, and she loves me," Christopher said.

"I know, my dear boy, don't think that I don't understand, but unfortunately love isn't enough in this world."

"I don't care how long I wait."

"Is it fair on Alex to ask her to wait indefinitely?"

"If I pass my examination, there are other examinations I could pass, and one gets so much more a year – I might get into the Diplomatic Service."

"An expensive profession."

Christopher felt he had no arguments in his armoury. "There are always ways of making money," he said lamely. "I could go to America."

"I think it would be foolish for you to throw away the chance which is open to you now for what? What would you do in America?"

"My father had friends there."

"My poor child, all that is vague, and life in America like everywhere else is a struggle for existence."

"I know plenty of Englishmen who have made money in

America."

"Do you think you have any talent for business?"

"No, I don't, but I might be a journalist."

"A journalist!"

"My father was a journalist," he said defiantly.

"Your father was a scholar, and a publicist, who wrote in the reviews and newspapers on important subjects. That was different. He had a distinguished career at the University before he began to write."

"Why couldn't I do the same?"

"Certainly you could, but so far you have not done what your father did in his youth."

"I haven't had time."

"That is why I say you must at all costs pass your examination."

"I agree about that, but if I do, and if I get on well, and if in three years' time I *should* be in a position to marry, would you let Alex marry me?"

"If you were in a position to marry in three years' time I don't say I would refuse, it depends upon what sort of position you were in, but I can have no binding engagement. It is not fair on Alex. You must see that. You must consider that for the present it is all over, and you must not write to her."

"Not write?"

"You must see that it would not be fair on her. If you are fond of her you must understand that."

"If she wanted to she could always break it off at a minute's notice."

"No, no, no, I can't have it, however unreasonable and however cruel this may seem to you now, you must believe me when I tell you that I know I am right."

"I suppose so," said Christopher, "but if circumstances were to change, if in two or three years' time I could marry, and Alex still wanted to marry me, you would not prevent it?"

"Certainly not, if I were satisfied that you were in a position to support Alex decently."

"That is enough for me," he said and he got up.

"Believe me, I am really sorry for you, and don't think I am being cruel on purpose."

"Nobody is ever cruel on purpose," Christopher said bitterly, and he went up to his room. There he found a note from Alex.

"I am to go to my cousins at Felsenstein tomorrow," she wrote. "It is perhaps better. Don't be disheartened – I shall never change, whatever happens. I am praying to St Anthony and to St Christopher, and I am sure all will come right in the end. I shall not come down to dinner tonight. I couldn't bear it. I shall say I have got a headache, but I will be in the kitchen garden early tomorrow morning, at nine. I go away at half past ten, by the eleven train. I love you."

Christopher sat by the open window of his room. It looked out on to the terrace. The weather had cleared up. There was every promise of a beautiful evening. He sat and pondered. "What was there to be done? What could be done?"

"It is no good my praying to St Anthony," he said to himself. His mother he thought might possibly do something. He was to go to Paris as soon as the examination was over, until he went up to Cambridge if he passed. If he passed! If he didn't pass? What would happen then? Nothing could be done until he passed his examination. He must pass.

Presently he heard voices. Countess Linsky was walking on the terrace. She was talking to Countess Felsen.

"I told you something of the sort was happening," said Countess Felsen.

"Who could have thought of such a thing? And they seriously expect me to consent to their being married! Imagine if Fritz were alive and I had said to him 'Alex wants to marry the English tutor'!" She laughed.

That was enough for Christopher. He got up and left the room and went out of the house into the village. He stayed out for a short time. He was in a fury of passion. Then he came back, and began writing a letter to Countess Linsky, a passionate letter telling her she was a snob and mercenary and only cared for position, titles and money. As soon as he had finished it he tore it up. He went down to dinner. The priest from the village was dining there, and this made things easier. After dinner there was a rubber of whist, and Christopher went for a stroll with Karl in the garden. Karl said nothing about the situation, and Christopher imagined that Alex had not told him about it.

Christopher had felt it necessary during the whole evening to exercise self-control. So far he had succeeded.

But when he came in, and the priest and Karl had said good-night and gone, and Countess Linsky said to him in a friendly way, "Good-night, Christopher," the rage that was bubbling in him burst out.

"I wonder you say good-night to me," he said. "I am nothing but a tutor. But I wish to tell you that I will be a tutor in your house no longer. I will leave tomorrow. You can make the necessary reduction from my monthly salary. Wages, perhaps I ought to say. I will not stay a moment longer in your house."

"My dear Christopher, what is the matter?"

"When you were walking on the terrace this afternoon, I couldn't help overhearing the beginning of your conversation with Countess Felsen. Don't think I was eavesdropping. I left the room at once, but what I heard was enough to prove to me how you regard me. And I want to tell you that you have no right to despise me. My father came from one of the oldest families in Ireland, a family as old or older than yours, and my mother, you know too, is of good family although you probably despise her because her father was the son of one of Napoleon's Generals, and hadn't got twenty-six quarterings. Thank Heaven! But the only difference between us is money, and money is all you care for; if I was a millionaire, or some half-witted Prince or Duke or Count with acres of land and no brains, you would be delighted for me to marry Alex, as it is I am only a tutor. But, I want you to know that I despise you as much as you despise me. I think you are a pack of snobs!"

He walked out of the room and banged the door.

Countess Felsen went after him and made him follow her into the library.

"I insist on your listening to me for a moment," she said. "I understand what you must be feeling, but you must not be so hot-headed and unreasonable. It is ridiculous of you to talk to my cousin like that, besides being very rude."

"Oh! I know I have never shown her proper respect!"

"Don't be so silly, Christopher, you know in your heart you are talking nonsense. You know quite well that she does not despise you."

"But I heard her say that to you on the terrace."

"You must realise that it is a thing we might all have said, she was looking at the absurd side of it. It would strike any old person as absurd that two children, and you are only children, should talk of marriage, and you, before you have even begun your career, when you haven't even *got* a career yet! You know my cousin is fond of you. You know we are all fond of you. Try and look at the matter from her point of view, for a moment. Try to imagine yourself having a daughter and someone coming to you and asking to marry her."

"A tutor?"

"Leave the word 'tutor' out. You know that has nothing to do with it. You know what my cousin feels about your parents. Christopher, believe me. Listen to sense."

"I only want to go," he said.

"You can go when you like...but first go and say good-night to my cousin and say you are sorry."

"Yes, I suppose I have done an unheard of thing. It's an unheard of thing for someone to speak... "

Countess Felsen interrupted him –

"Whoever one is, and wherever one is, one is always in the wrong if one is rude. My cousin is an old lady and you are a young man and an Englishman."

"I'm not an Englishman; I'm nothing."

"You are half French and that's all the more reason why you should be civil."

"I am nothing but a mongrel."

"Don't be foolish, Christopher. Go and say good-night."

He was silent.

"Do, to please me."

"I will to please you. You have always been kind to me, and I don't believe you do despise me."

Christopher went back to the drawing room and found Countess Linsky sitting at the card table doing a patience.

"I have come to apologise for being rude," he said in a trembling voice. "I am very sorry… " his voice broke.

"My dear boy, that is all right. We will forget all about it. I know, I understand what you are feeling."

She held out her hand.

Christopher kissed it and then rushed out of the room. He was shaking with sobs.

The next morning he said good-bye to Alex in the garden and told her what had happened. They had a brief parting as Alex had to catch a train, but they swore eternal love and fidelity to each other.

"Mamma says we are not to write," she said.

"I will write, but I will not send the letters. I will write to you in a copy book and perhaps later I will be able to send it to you."

"And I will write to you every day in my prayers. Write to me in yours."

"I will try, but I am bad at praying."

"But you must pray for my sake."

"Then I will."

"Every day?"

"Yes, every day."

Alex gave him a bunch of lavender and pansies that she had picked.

"And I want you to keep my Heine."

"I will keep it always."

"Good-bye, my dearest, dearest heart, *Herzallerliebster*."

There were final kisses and tears and she rushed away. Fate made things easier for Christopher, because by that morning's post he got a letter from Spark urging him to come home at once for final instructions before the examination. He left the next day. Both the Countesses wished him an affectionate farewell, and Karl came to see him off at the station.

He said nothing but he was so gentle and sympathetic that Christopher felt he must know everything.

The examination was a week earlier than had been anticipated. Christopher went to Spark for a final brush up, then he went in for the examination. Directly it was over he went to Paris to see his mother.

While he was there he received notice from the Civil Service Commissioners that he had passed.

CHAPTER IX

When Christopher saw his mother, he told her what happened to him at Birkenberg, but she knew about it already because Countess Linsky had written to her. She told him she agreed with Countess Linsky. It was out of the question for him to think of marrying at present. It was absurd to think that Countess Linsky should entertain the idea of such a thing for a moment.

"But later," said Christopher, "supposing I were better off?"

"The girl," said his mother, "will be married by that time. She will marry someone of her own race."

"But it isn't as if there were the usual difficulties. I am a Catholic."

"You belong to different worlds," his mother said.

"But, after all, one might have said that about you and Papa."

"When we married, we had enough to marry on, and you have nothing."

Christopher saw that it was idle to discuss the matter.

He went up to Cambridge at the end of the month to St Crispin's, and was given rooms in college.

St Crispin's was a small college.

The Master was a don of the old-fashioned school. He was an Irishman by birth, and seemed more like a squire than a don.

He was dark with pronounced features, a rubicund complexion, and long white scholarly hands. He stooped and was short-sighted. He was fond of riding, Italian opera, and old claret, and he kept a tame tortoise, called Hannibal. He played the flute and was a passionate gardener. He was social and entertained largely.

St Crispin's, which was a small college, was frequented mostly by undergraduates who were fond of riding and untroubled by any scholastic ambitions, but it also contained a set which modelled themselves on the more serious lights of contemporary literature and conducted a journal called the *Cambridge Forum*, and also a small nucleus of scholars who kept to themselves.

The Master received Christopher genially. He had known his father. He asked him to dinner, where he met several other dons. The talk ranged from politics to Alpine climbing, from Alpine climbing to French towns, with a plentiful admixture of archaeology, from French towns to Italy, thence via opera to Handel, and from music to the extinction of the ballet (the Master related his father's reminiscences of Taglione), and thence over the Golden Bridge of Mrs Crummles to Dickens. Dickens led to Thackeray, and Thackeray to Stevenson. Then the port and the claret were passed round on silver wheeled decanters, and the conversation settled down to wine.

Christopher sat between two dons: one was a Fellow of Salisbury who had a classic head and a clear-cut utterance, and took a dispassionate interest in psychical research, and the other the well-known Master of Ipswich, a comfortable man of the world, an expert in French vintages and Parisian restaurants as well as the leading authority on the Ice Age.

After dinner, the Master, accompanied by the Fellow of Salisbury, played some airs on the flute. Christopher hardly spoke during the whole evening.

He was invited to breakfast by undergraduates, and asked to join various clubs and societies.

The leader of the literary set, the editor of the *Cambridge Forum*, asked him to tea to meet some friends but found him wanting, as he had not read Dostoyevsky. At that time, this was an exotic taste. The riding men left him alone; and so did the scholars.

But Christopher had work to do of his own.

He had to study Turkish, Arabic, and Mussulman law. These were obligatory subjects. But optional subjects were necessary to him as well if he wished to get on, and of these he chose Russian and modern Greek. These subjects of study brought Christopher into contact with two men who exercised a considerable influence over his life.

The first was Professor Sackbut who taught him Arabic and Turkish. His face was remarkable. It looked as if it had been modelled in wax. His long black hair reminded one of pictures of an Eastern Saint, and his steady grey eyes were luminous without being bright. He was small and thin, and it seemed as if his body were being consumed by the inward flame of his knowledge and his ideas. There was no subject that he did not seem to have mastered. Besides all his Oriental studies (he was translating Hafiz and the Persian poets) he had written a book about Marcello and an illuminating monograph on Hogarth. He was familiar with the modern literature of most European countries and read Tolstoi and Ibsen in the original.

Sackbut at once perceived that Christopher had a vocation for Oriental studies but he was not an encouraging teacher. He seldom made comments and when he did they had a sharp edge.

He despised most modern scholarship and he was a formidable critic. But it was impossible to be with him for any space of time without being stimulated, for there was no subject on which he had not some original view and some first-hand knowledge.

Christopher attended his lectures and went to him for private instruction. Every week he had to read him an essay.

Sackbut's methods of instruction were unorthodox. The first thing he did with Christopher was to make him write an essay on Rome.

A few days later he asked Christopher to dinner in his rooms at Anselm's. There were no other guests.

During dinner Sackbut talked of Germany. He disliked the Germans except for their music. Christopher confessed to not being musical. "But," he said, "I like Wagner."

"All unmusical people do," said Sackbut, "you don't have to be musical to respond to a railway accident."

There was a silence. Christopher felt small.

Sackbut asked Christopher if he had seen Shakespeare acted in Germany.

"They act him well in spite of the incredible silliness of their Shakespearean criticism."

A little later he said, "Germany is the danger. Your father saw this. They will oust us in the Near East…you will have to look after that," he smiled grimly. "And Bismarck says that the grave of the British Empire will be South Africa."

Christopher asked Sackbut whether he thought the German Emperor was a great man.

"Certainly not," he answered, "he is energetic and he can stir up ideas but he will never create. He has none of his mother's knowledge. She is a great woman. Besides which he is too impulsive."

"I admire him for getting rid of Bismarck," said Christopher.

"It was fine from the histrionic point of view, but it is a calamity for Germany. Bismarck, the Sultan, and the Pope were the only three great Powers in Europe."

"What about Lord Salisbury?"

"The greatest statesman in English history since the 18th century, as your father said. He has a policy. He has and has always had profound insight and foresight. But he preaches to deaf ears and he is shackled by our parliamentary system. The

Sultan and Bismarck till this boy upset the apple-cart could do what they liked."

"You don't admire German literature?" asked Christopher.

"German literature is a by-product. The Germans found their highest expression in their music. Music is their art."

"But Schopenhauer, surely he is great?"

"Schopenhauer is a poor rehash of Oriental philosophy as you will see in time. He is one of the few Germans who can write prose. He is witty; that is why you like him. But you must give up all that second-hand stuff now, and go to the fountain-heads."

After dinner, Christopher had to read his paper aloud.

Sackbut sat smoking and made no comment.

When he had finished he said: "You have been taught nothing and what is worse you have been crammed, which is the negation of education. That is not your fault. But you have picked up a few things, probably from your father and your mother. It would have been strange if you had not. You have inherited, I think, some sparks of your father's insight. Of course you have none of his knowledge. However, things might be worse. You would I think have fared worse at a public school. You are a Catholic?"

"Yes," said Christopher with hesitation.

"You have read St Thomas and Bossuet?"

"I'm afraid not."

"Only Newman, I suppose?"

"I'm afraid I have never read Newman."

"That's a pity; he would have improved your style, which at present is atrocious. You have caught a dreadful jargon from leading articles and worse still from German books. But there are gleams in your essay."

He then pointed out error after error and fault after fault, without looking at the MS. He seemed to have memorised Christopher's unfortunate effort.

"You must begin at the beginning. For your English read Swift and Sterne, and for your French, Sainte-Beuve and

Renan, but principally Sainte-Beuve, as Renan is a little sticky; leave German alone."

With his Russian teacher, Professor Yakovlev, Christopher's experiences were different.

Andrei Semenovitch Yakovlev was a large man; bearded and dark with friendly twinkling brown eyes. He was untidy. His waistcoat was always undone at the top and his tie out of its place. His long shabby black coat was covered with grease stains. Yakovlev asked Christopher to his rooms after dinner and brewed him glasses of delicious tea with the help of a samovar.

Yakovlev asked him no hard questions.

"I will teach you Russian in six months. No, in five months. You have facility, and know other languages, which is the important thing. Russian is only another form of Greek. The important thing in languages is the framework. Once you have that, and you have it, you have only to fill in the details. You will soon be reading Pushkin and Turgenev with me. And Soloviev. They call him the Russian Newman. You are a Catholic?"

"Yes," said Christopher, "I was brought up as one, but I am not one now, I mean I don't believe in it."

"That does not matter, you will learn in time. You have never studied theology, I suppose. But I will teach it you, in Russian."

"But you are, I suppose, Orthodox?"

"Yes, I am Orthodox, what you call Greek Church – the son of an Old Believer. But the doctrine, the dogma, the belief is the same for me, and for you, with one or two details different. The theology is the same. That is to say I believe in all the Catholic doctrine you were probably taught as a child."

"All of it?"

"Of course, all of it! If one believes part of it one cannot help believing all of it. If you believe in a thumb you believe in a body."

"I have no Faith."

"No, I suppose not. But you will have Faith when you are older."

Yakovlev talked to Christopher indulgently as to a very backward child. "Young men lose their Faith. If they have been brought up with Faith and they are not losing it afterwards they will hardly be knowing, I suppose, what it means. That is why God takes it away from them and gives it back."

"I cannot see how one can reconcile Faith with modern knowledge."

"One cannot. But then modern knowledge, and ancient knowledge too, is only a temporary thing. It changes like the fashion. I myself can remember many changes. I may live to see many more changes. The scientific dogmas of a period are only working hypotheses. What is scientific dogma in one age, is laughed at by the next age. We believe that the earth goes round the sun, but the scientists before us, and they were being just as clever as our scientists, believed that the sun was going round the earth, and even now for practical purposes sailors have to pretend to believe the same thing."

"Do you think that men will ever believe the sun goes round the earth again?"

"Not according to our rules. It is like a game of cards in which you win if you take all the tricks, but the game may change for another in which you win if you take no tricks at all. Our whole system may change for another one. It matters very little if the sun goes round the earth or the earth goes round the sun; not more than whether you must take tricks or lose them. What matters is to see things in their true proportion, and to realise that dogmatic materialists are not being above religion, but they are being below it."

"Yes, but if you haven't got religious Faith, you haven't got it."

"Of course not, but you must pray for it. You cannot get what you do not want and ask for."

"I'm not sure I do want it. At any rate I cannot pray."

"Then ask some very good nun to pray for you."

"Have you always believed?"

"Oh, when I was your age I went through the usual superstitions. I believed in Hegel, etc. But I always respected the Holy Images. I have a very old one here. I will show it to you."

Yakovlev fetched an Ikon from the next room.

"This came from Kazan. It worked many miracles. And some day I will be taking it back again."

"Did it work miracles for you?"

"Only once."

Christopher laughed.

"Why do you laugh?"

"I was laughing because I was wondering what Professor Sackbut would think of that."

"He would not laugh. He knows the East too well. He at least believes in gods. He is a very clever man. He knows enough to know that he knows nothing. He only lacks one thing."

"What is that?"

"Courage. Courage can only come from love, and from unselfishness. You see scholarship has frightened him. It has given him a shock and he has never recovered. Scholarship makes cowards of us all. Happily I am no scholar."

"Professor Sackbut says you are one of the greatest authorities in Europe."

"That, my friend, is not saying much. Have another glass of tea."

After a month at Cambridge, Christopher's impression of his principal mentors was that whereas Sackbut was as bitter as alum, Yakovlev was, apart from his technical knowledge, a child; just as a great painter or musician can be blind on other subjects.

CHAPTER X

Christopher made his first Cambridge friend through Professor Sackbut. This was an undergraduate called Suckling who was studying Oriental languages and was destined for the Indian Civil Service. Suckling was the son of a clergyman, and his mother was a brilliantly clever woman. Suckling had inherited her quickness, he was keen, energetic and ambitious, and acutely alive to the absurd side of things.

He was impatient of dullness and boredom, and Christopher interested him. But he was more gregarious than Christopher, and belonged to a club, a dramatic, and to several debating societies. He was at King's. He tried to enlarge Christopher's circle of acquaintances, but Christopher refused to mix with a larger world or to belong to debating societies. He said he was too busy.

Suckling was athletic and fond of rowing, and at the same time cultivated, but he did not belong to any literary set. He read widely for his pleasure, and his memory was astonishing.

One night Suckling asked Christopher to dinner; he was anxious for him to meet two of his greatest friends: Lawless of Trinity, and Spence of Trinity Hall.

He told Christopher he wished him to make a good impression on Lawless who he said had real character, and was well worth knowing.

Spence was the step-son of a well-known barrister who had married an American widow whom he had met in San Francisco. He was sixteen years old when his mother married again. He had been to school in America, but he followed his mother to London, and after a year at a crammer's went up to Cambridge.

Lawless was a Winchester man.

The dinner was at Suckling's rooms at King's.

Bruce Lawless was good-looking, fair with amiable blue eyes, and had been told by Suckling to be nice to Christopher; and he tried to do his best.

When Christopher came into the room, the two others were talking rowing shop. Lawless stopped and said," How do you do?" and then asked Christopher several civil questions, but he could obtain no response.

Presently Spence arrived. He was tall and broad, with a funny pug face and sad grey eyes.

"Boys," he said, "I'm late."

He was introduced to Christopher.

"You're the guy who's learning Sanskrit. I've forgotten mine."

Lawless asked him some question about the river. Spence was a rowing man.

"Don't," he said, "rowing shop makes me tired. I want to talk about Omar Khayyam. I like him. He grabbed the cash and let the credit go."

When they sat down to dinner, Spence drowned the table with talk and all would have gone well if Lawless hadn't had the misfortune to say when an acquaintance was mentioned as a candidate for a society that he and Suckling belonged to –

"Oh, no, we can't have him. He coached my younger brother in the vac' and he never washed."

Christopher took this as an indictment on all people who coached, and on himself in particular.

"I was a tutor to a boy in Austria before I came up," he said defiantly.

Lawless turned scarlet and confused and said that he had not meant anything against coaches.

And Spence laughed and said to Christopher, "You mustn't mind Bruce. He's all right, but his brain's addled from too much rowing."

But Christopher did mind him. He took a violent dislike to him, which was to last all his life.

After dinner, Spence sat down at the piano and played and whistled. He played by ear.

Then he said, "We will now beat it to my rooms. I have arranged a poker game."

Christopher excused himself, but Spence insisted on his going with them.

They went to Spence's rooms in Trinity Street, and Spence made some shandygaff.

"This," he said, "is a soft drink."

Christopher drank a glass of it and felt better. Then he had some more. Two or three other undergraduates strolled into the room and a game of poker was started. Christopher said he would rather not play.

Spence did not insist, but said, "It's a pity because you have a real poker face."

Christopher sat in a chair while the others played and they seemed to be a long way off.

The reason of this was that the shandygaff was made of audit-ale and champagne. Then they got bored with playing and Spence fetched a banjo and whistled and sang. They all joined in. Then Spence preached a sermon like one of the dons. The evening party developed into a bear fight. A good deal of furniture and glass was broken. At midnight they went home. Christopher could not remember how. The next morning, Christopher had a headache. He had liked Spence as much as he had disliked Lawless.

"But what does it matter?" he said to himself. "I shall never see either of them again."

There he was wrong.

He told Suckling that it was no good his trying to make him like Lawless.

"You see," he said, "we belong to different worlds."

"Nonsense," said Suckling, "Lawless's father's a great traveller and has written fearfully interesting books about Spain."

"I don't care what his father is. I can see in Lawless's face that he looks down on people like me."

"That's nonsense, too. He is the most charming fellow, and very modest, he will probably get his Blue and besides that he is not a fool. He may get a First. I believe he will be a great man some day."

"Oh yes, it's easy enough for him. He will go into Parliament. He has got money and position to start with."

"His father isn't at all well-off."

"Perhaps not, but isn't his uncle Lord Wisbeach?"

"Yes."

"And won't he inherit the title, the estate, half a dozen estates?"

"He's none the worse for that. It's not his fault."

"I daresay not, but it's silly to talk of his not being rich."

"What does it matter if he is, if he is a good chap."

"I see nothing in him. I think he's conceited, narrow-minded and insolent."

"That's simply silly. He's the least conceited man in the world. I think he has got beautiful manners."

"What you call beautiful manners, I call condescension."

When Suckling talked to Lawless about Christopher, he said, "Queer chap; rather difficult, isn't he?"

"Very," Suckling said, "but worth while."

"Well, perhaps I shall succeed better another time. I expect it was my fault."

About a week later, one evening when Christopher was

working in his rooms, who should stroll in but Spence.

"May I come in?" he said. "I'm tired and I want to talk."

Christopher was immensely surprised to see Spence, but not displeased, and he fetched him some whisky.

Spence drank it neat, and some water afterwards.

"That's what I like," he said, "a chaser. It's funny I can't ever get used to English ways, although I've lived in this country ever since I left school. I guess you're not used to them either. You've been around too much. Besides which, you're only half English. Don't get mad. I'm not English at all. That's why I can say what I like to you. They tell me your father was Irish, and your mother was French, and you're a Roman Catholic, all that's almost the same as being an American. My grandmother was English and my father was half Irish, so what is there to choose between us? I like this place. But the boys get on my nerves sometimes, and the dons make me tired all the time. They are terribly slow. A New York bell-hop would make rings round the quickest of them."

Spence then poured out the whole story of his life: his childhood in the West, with extraordinary tales of his father's good nature, talents and violence; and the ups and downs in his circumstances which ranged from great wealth to extreme poverty. His father had been a gifted lawyer, too fond of drink. Then his mother's second marriage and his introduction to English life. He was now naturalised. He liked his stepfather. England and London had seemed terrible to him at first; but he had been to an excellent crammer's who lived near Cambridge, and in company with five or six boys who, having spent five years at Eton and other public schools, had not learnt enough to pass either Smalls or the Little-go, he got into Cambridge.

"And now I'm here. I like this place well enough, but sometimes I just pine for the sight of a nigger. Some people are born to be kind of exiles, wherever they go, and you are one of them."

"I'm not an exile, because I've got no real home," said

Christopher.

"You'll have a home all right when you marry. They say one's home is where one loves."

"I shall never marry," said Christopher, getting red.

"It's as bad as that, is it? I knew the minute I saw you what was the trouble. I expect you fell for a girl in Austria, when you were out there on that coaching game. We went to Vienna one holiday, and I could have fallen for all of them. When I have been here for two years I'm going to a German University for a time if my step-dad lets me. I'm supposed to be working for the Bar. You are going in for the Orient."

"I am a Student Interpreter," said Christopher, "and if I get through my course, I shall be attached to a Mission as an Assistant. When my father died, he left no money and I've got nothing of my own. My mother has to work at journalism as it is."

"Now, see here, in England you make no end of a fuss about that sort of thing. In the States, they think nothing of it. A man thinks nothing of changing his profession once every six months. He thinks nothing of being ruined at one moment and rich another and making good. You are so stodgy here and so stiff. For the love of Mike try to be a little more elastic in your ideas, or you will never get anywhere."

"It's all very well for you to talk. Your stepfather is a successful man."

"Yes, and why? Because he's made good. Why shouldn't you make good, too? My father started at the bottom of the ladder and worked his way up. And my stepfather most certainly did. I don't know if I shall ever get called to the Bar, but if I don't I shan't just hang round; I shall do something else. One gets what one wants in this world."

"Do you think so? I wonder."

"I believe one does in the long run. Of course I don't say you'll marry the first girl you fall for."

Christopher was silent and got red again.

"I guess you'd better forget all about her," Spence said. "Austrian *Comtessen* don't marry Student Interpreters."

"I don't think it is in very good taste for you to talk to me about my private affairs," said Christopher savagely.

"To Hell. Good taste be damned! That's where you English are so darned silly. You're always making rules for yourselves. You know perfectly well you're just crazy to talk of nothing else."

"Very well," said Christopher, "if you want to know. While I was in Austria, being tutor to an Austrian boy, 1 fell in love with his sister and we got engaged to be married. And her mother…"

"Oh, I know what her mother said. 'Good-bye and no flowers by request.'"

"Yes, that was it."

"And you are saying to yourself that you'll be eternally faithful, make good and marry her when you have made good."

"That's about it."

"But Sonny, it will be too late. She will have married someone else by that time."

"Of her own world?"

"Yes, of her own world, which is no better than yours, but it's there. She'll probably marry a cousin once removed with forty quarterings and a doll's house outfit on the top of a hill."

"But supposing she doesn't want to?"

"She won't want to now, but she won't see you maybe for three years; you've got to be up here two years I reckon before you start on your business; well she is sure to be lonesome after a while. One can't live on memories, however pleasant."

"Some people have waited."

"You make me tired."

"My father married a Frenchwoman, when he was a young man."

"Did they have to wait?"

"No, they had enough to marry on and married."

"Well that is a different proposition. If you take my advice you will write the girl a fine letter, and say you understand everything, and you do not want to bind her in any way."

"I can't do that, it wouldn't be true."

"It will come better from you than from her."

"Don't you think that sort of thing ever comes right?"

"Not outside fairy story stuff."

"Well, I shall wait whatever happens. She can do what she likes. But I won't be the one to give up hope first."

"That's because men are more selfish than women."

"You think it's selfish?"

"Sure, what else is it anyhow?"

"I don't ask her to do anything. I make no claim. I only claim the right to be faithful for myself: to keep my promise."

"Be as faithful as you like, but don't let her think she has to be."

"You may think me silly, mad, selfish, or anything you like, but I swear to you, that I shall not look at a girl, till I hear from her that it is all over. All our business, I mean."

"Well that won't harm you any. You will have all the more leisure for your Sanskrit and Omar. And now I am going to beat it. So-long, and forgive me for being so fresh as to butt into what I knew was damned private."

Christopher laughed.

"I didn't mind," he said.

"You bet you didn't," said Spence laughing, and he went away whistling.

CHAPTER XI

According to the Foreign Office regulations, Christopher was obliged to reside at the University not less than nine months of the year. As the Christmas vacation was short it was not worth while his attempting to visit his mother, so he stayed at Cambridge, but managed to get away for Christmas. He went to stay with Suckling's parents in Essex. The Lent term and the Easter term went by. Christopher made no new friends, but considerable progress in his Oriental and Slav studies. He could read Russian easily, and Professor Sackbut was satisfied with his Arabic. He spent his Easter holidays at Cambridge and part of the long vacation. In August he went to see his mother in France. She was living in a small apartment at Versailles. She wrote a weekly article on French politics and literature for the *Daily Messenger*, and a monthly article in the *Carlton Review*. The subject of Alex was not mentioned between them. Christopher had not heard from her, nor had he written to her, but Countess Felsen had sent him a card on New Year's day. His mother had made herself a circle of agreeable friends. She received on Sunday afternoons, and at her flat, Christopher met some distinguished Frenchwomen and Frenchmen.

He had not forgotten Alex. She lived in the background of his mind, "in some close corner of the brain." There he both enjoyed and missed her, and so far he had kept the rash promise he had made to Spence that until he received his dismissal from Alex, he would not look at another girl.

It was one Saturday evening, by the late post, that Christopher received a letter written on foreign paper with a foreign stamp and post-mark.

Without the help of these, merely by the handwriting, Christopher knew who the letter was from.

The Concierge's wife had given it him just before dinner. He had not time to open it.

He had dinner alone with his mother and directly afterwards he went out. It was a hot August evening. He strolled towards the town with the letter in his pocket.

He was not going to open it till he was isolated from importunity.

When he had reached a small café he used often to frequent, he ordered some coffee and sat down.

It was not until the waiter brought him the coffee that he took the letter from his pocket.

He turned it over and over in his hand: it was thin.

The sight of the paper, and of the handwriting: a large sloping handwriting, in violet ink, summoned before him a series of pictures of Birkenberg.

He saw the white castle, the green valley, the clear river, the sleepy village, the green woods, the red stems of the tall trees, the goose girl, the high dining room, the long, low drawing room, with its wood fire, Karl in his green suit, Countess Linsky sitting at her patience, Alex on the terrace, Alex in the garden, Alex at the dining table, Alex in the schoolroom at tea, Alex in the woods that afternoon in the slanting sunlight.

He opened the letter: as he did so, it would have been impossible to say whether it was joy or fear that he was feeling.

It was a mixture of both.

He read the letter. It was very short.

"My dear Christopher,

"I am engaged to be married to Hermann Zekes who is a kind of cousin of mine. We are to be married at the end of the month. My mother sends you her love.

"Yours very sincerely,

"Alex."

Christopher lit a cigarette and said to himself, "Well, of course, it had to happen. What do I care?"

But that feeble bluff was no use. He cared in a way he had never dreamt of. He had never thought he could care like that.

He asked for a postcard and he wrote on it:

"Dear Countess Alex,

"Just received letter. Please accept heartiest congratulations and my best wishes for your future happiness. Please remember me respectfully to your mother.

"Yours sincerely,

"Christopher Trevenen."

Then he began to wonder.

He wondered whether she was happy: whether she was in love: whether this had been a sudden rapturous love affair which swept her off her feet, brought her a new life, and blotted out the past or whether it was a marriage of convenience arranged by the respective parents, and whether in reality she detested this cousin.

How he would like to know. But which would be best or rather worst?

All he should wish for was her happiness.

But who knew which of the two paths would lead to happiness?

Well, that was all over. A chapter definitely finished.

"Tomorrow to fresh woods," he said to himself. "That seems to be the end of every sorrow, of every mishap. One turns the page and begins another chapter. Fresh woods! Fresh woods!"

The next day was Sunday. He went into Paris and strolled about the Boulevards. He looked at the theatrical announcements pasted up on the kiosks. Most of the theatres were shut. Only the Théâtre Français and the Opera went on faithfully through the hot deserted season. What was going on at the Français? *Cabotins* by Pailleron. He would like to see that. He had an early meal at a Duval and then he clambered up to the cheaper seats in one of the upper galleries.

Sitting next to him there was a girl dressed in black. She had black hair and dark dancing eyes and a powdered face but she was neat. During the entr'acte they talked to each other.

Yes, she liked the play, but she preferred the classical repertory. That is why she always came to the Français on Sunday night. Last Sunday it had been *Cinna*. She had enjoyed that. She did not care for modern plays. They were so undistinguished. She came here every Sunday evening when she could manage it, with her cousin, her cousin wasn't here tonight. She should have met her at the *guichet*. She must have been detained. She shared an apartment with her cousin, who was older than she was.

"Do you go a great deal to the play?" asked Christopher.

"No, only on Sundays. I am busy during the week. I cannot go out at night during the week. They would not let me."

"They" was at present not further defined.

After the play was over, Christopher asked his new friend to come and have something at a café. He had to catch the twelve-thirty train back to Versailles, and she had to catch so she said, the bus.

But there was just time for something.

Christopher's friend, her name was Annette Le Grand, chose a *syrop de groseille*, and he ordered a bock.

"I suppose really you would like champagne," Christopher said with a laugh, when they brought the *syrop*. "Unfortunately I can't afford it."

"Oh champagne!" she said with an expression of disgust. "I hate champagne."

Before they parted Annette and Christopher agreed to meet the following week. She could not meet him before.

"But why must we wait for the evening?" said Christopher. "Let us meet in the morning and spend the day in the country."

Annette agreed. She would like to spend the day somewhere in the country, and come back in time for the play.

The following Sunday was a beautiful day. They met in Paris early at the Gare St Lazare. Annette said she wanted to see the pictures in the Louvre, so they spent a little time there, and then, after they had breakfasted at a Duval, they took the train for St Cloud. There they strolled about in the stately glades and sat near the ruins. The sunlight slanted through the tall trees, and Christopher thought of the afternoon in the Austrian woods; but these were "fresh woods." He would put away all thought of the past. And indeed now it seemed easy, for Annette's company was to him like the sunshine of a new spring. They talked, they laughed, they sat in the shade, and when Christopher whispered to her that he loved her, she showed no surprise, and made no resistance to his embraces. She merely smiled on him, and seemed to be filled with joy.

When they got back to Paris, and had dined at a Duval and Christopher said, "Why should we go to that hot stuffy theatre?" Annette asked what the play was.

It was *L'Aventurière*.

No, she did not care for that.

After a moment's reflection Annette said: "I can take you *tonight* to my cousin's apartment until it is time for you to catch your train, because *tonight* she will be out."

They went some distance in an omnibus and then they

walked some way towards Montmartre; they stopped at a house, and Christopher followed Annette up what seemed to him to be an interminable flight of stairs, into a dark little apartment, which seemed to have no windows. Annette lit a lamp. The small sitting room was tidy and neat. There were flowers in the vases on the chimney piece, a few books in a small bookcase and a cheap reproduction of Millet's *Angelus* on the wall and a photograph of a young man in dragoon's uniform in a leather frame on the table.

Christopher looked at it. "That is my cousin's brother," she said, "he is doing his military service."

Annette fetched a dog's-eared yellow paper-bound book of verse. She showed Christopher her favourite poems, which were by Musset. Annette hoped to go on the stage, some day. (At present she had told him she was employed in a big shop.) That was why she went to the Théâtre Français. It was to get hints for diction. Christopher asked her to read out a poem to him. She began to read. He looked over her shoulder.

> "Un soir, nous étions seuls, j'étais assis près d'elle
> Elle penchait la tête, et sur son clavecin
> Laissait, tout en rêvant, flotter sa blanche main."

Christopher took her hand and pressed it.

> "Ce n'était qu'un murmure: on eût dit des coups d'aile
> D'un zéphyr éloigné glissant sur des roseaux,
> Et craignant en passant d'éveiller les oiseaux."

Annette read the lines in a conventional manner, imitated from the most approved models, but Christopher thought he had never listened to sweeter utterance.

> "Les tièdes voluptés des nuits mélancoliques
> Sortaient autour de nous du calice des fleurs."

Like Paolo and Francesca they got no further with their reading that day.

Towards eleven o'clock they heard steps on the staircase.

"You must hide," said Annette. "It's my cousin. She must not find you here. She is serious."

"Hide! Where?" said Christopher. "In the next room?"

"No, here under the table."

"What is the use? If it's your cousin, she is bound to know I am here."

"No, no," said Annette. "I will arrange matters and I will get you out when I have put her to bed."

She made Christopher get under the table, and she turned out the lamp and went to the door.

Presently, she came back and said: "It was nothing. It is not she. It is only the *voisin*. But you must go at once."

They arranged to meet on the following Sunday.

"Couldn't we meet before during the week?" asked Christopher. "Couldn't I meet you at your shop?"

"Oh no, *chéri*, that would be quite impossible."

"But why not?"

"Because I am busy and because it wouldn't do."

"But why not in the evening after you have done your work?"

"Because of my cousin."

"She wouldn't know."

"Oh, but she would. Now you must go. *Bon soir, mon amour.*"

She gave him a last kiss and looked at him sadly.

"*Tu sais, tu es gentil.*"

The following Sunday Annette and Christopher met again in the morning and went to Passy. They spent the afternoon on the Seine and landed on an island.

Christopher was blissfully happy.

When they came back in the evening and had dinner,

Christopher said, "Now let us go to your apartment."

Annette said it was impossible, that evening. Her cousin was there, and she wasn't well. It was out of the question.

Annette said she would like to go to the Français, but Christopher after looking at the poster and seeing *Le Monde ou l'on s'ennuie* would not hear of it.

"I know what we will do," he said, "we will go to the Folies Bergères."

Annette expressed reluctance to go there.

"It is so hot and noisy there," she said. "Especially at this time of the year."

"Yes," said Christopher, "but where else can we go?"

Other places were suggested by Christopher and rejected by Annette. Finally she consented to go to the Folies Bergères. "For a little while, but I must get back early, tonight," she said.

They went there, and looked on at the entertainment for a little while. Then Annette said she was thirsty and must have something to drink.

Christopher took her out to the bar, and they sat down at a small table.

While they were there who should Christopher catch sight of in the crowd but Spence.

He smiled when he caught Christopher's eye and made as if to go out, but Christopher beckoned to him, explaining to Annette that Spence was his greatest friend and that he wanted to introduce him to her.

Spence pushed his way through the crowd towards them.

Till he got up to their table he had not been able to distinguish Annette's features. He had only seen that Christopher was in female society and noticed no more than a hat.

Christopher introduced him and as Spence looked at Annette, it was all he could do to suppress a start.

But as Christopher turned to speak to the waiter to give an order, Annette looked at Spence and put her finger on her lips. Christopher did not observe this. Spence explained that he was passing through Paris on his way to Switzerland. He was with his mother and his stepfather, but they were dining out with some serious friends. He had already been two or three days in Paris and was leaving the next day. They were staying at the Continental.

They sat talking for some time and presently Annette said she must go home.

Christopher said he would drive her home but she refused. She would rather go by the bus. There was one handy. She made arrangements for the following Sunday with Christopher, and she said good-night to both of them. Spence took Christopher to supper at a small restaurant that he knew of in the Boulevard.

"Well," said Spence to Christopher while they were having supper, "I suppose you kept your promise?"

"Yes, I did."

"It was called off?"

"Yes, you were right. She is engaged to be married to a cousin."

"How long are you staying here?" asked Spence.

"Not long, only a fortnight longer."

"You like it?"

"Yes, I'm happy now, *now*, because I have found out at last what real love, real disinterested love can mean."

"Yes, yes," said Spence, thoughtfully.

When Sunday came Christopher was punctual at the station – where Annette had promised to meet him. But she was not there.

He went to her apartment; he was not sure it was the right house, and rang the bell there, but there was no answer. He wrote to her that evening, telegraphed, sent a *petit bleu*, but received no answer.

He called twice more at the apartment.

The first time nobody answered the bell. The second time the door was opened by a deaf old woman. She knew nothing of any Mademoiselle Le Grand, and Christopher could get nothing out of her.

There had been a mademoiselle living there, but Christopher could not understand whether the old woman was alluding to Annette or to her cousin or to neither. Whoever had lived there, had gone and left no address.

Christopher neither saw nor heard of Annette again. The following Sunday he waited half an hour at their usual meeting place at the Gare St Lazare, and in the evening he went to the cheap places in the Théâtre Français where a classical play was being performed; but there was no sign of Annette.

On the Monday he was obliged to go back to Cambridge.

CHAPTER XII

Christopher's second year at Cambridge did not greatly differ from his first. He made no new friends. He worked hard and gave satisfaction to Sackbut and Yakovlev. He stayed most of the time at Cambridge, but just before Easter his mother fell ill, and he went over at once to Versailles. He was in time to see her before she died. She recognised him and pressed his hand, but she was too ill to speak. She died the day after he arrived. She left him her savings which did not amount to much. He went back after the funeral, as soon as he had got through what business there was to be done, for his last term at Cambridge. Once more he seemed to have closed a fresh chapter. Annette had left an empty place in his heart which was not filled. He never alluded to her when talking to Spence, nor did Spence allude to her either. In the long vacation, he spent a little time with Spence, whose parents had taken a house in Normandy.

In September, he went up for his final examination and passed it. He was appointed to Constantinople as an assistant. He proceeded thither at the beginning of October in the lowest spirits, like a boy going to a private school for the first time; but there was one bright spot on the horizon. Spence had given up all thoughts of the Bar and had been appointed Honorary Attaché to the Embassy at Constantinople. He meant to spend a year there and after that to go into business in London.

Christopher arrived at Constantinople on a cold drizzling autumnal day. The city seemed to him wet, shabby, muddy, dirty and bedraggled. A very slut of a city, and he never experienced a more poignant impression of melancholy than when he drove up the hill to Pera for the first time: through the untidy streets, on the cobbles and the dirt, and saw the pariah dogs and heard the nasal wail of the muezzin from the distant minarets. But this melancholy impression did not last, for two days later the sun came out and Stambul shone like a soap-bubble with all the colours of the rainbow.

Spence was already there, and had taken a house. His fellow secretaries lived at the Embassy, but there was not room for him. Spence too preferred living by himself, and one of the reasons he had taken this house was to be able to put up Christopher who, after some argument, consented to live with him, provided he was allowed to pay something towards the rent.

Christopher lived the same kind of life at Constantinople as at Cambridge. He worked at the Dragomanate which was in the Embassy. He made friends with nobody on the Embassy or Consular Staffs. He had luncheon once at the Embassy, and sometimes had tea with the Consul and the Head Dragoman; he was a member of the small Club.

Spence led a life of his own also. He had no great friend on the Embassy Staff, but he had several friends among the foreign missions.

He had not been long at Constantinople before he fell in love with the daughter of the American Minister.

Christopher made friends with the Servian Minister, whose name was Turçin, a man of wide culture. His wife was remarkable. She was said to be an Armenian by birth. She was dark, with a beautiful white skin and large liquid eyes. She spoke all languages and seemed familiar with the literature of every country. She was an accomplished musician.

Just at this time, the Armenian question was beginning to

102

become acute. While Christopher was still at Cambridge Lord Salisbury was at the Foreign Office, much to the delight of Sackbut. Every now and then, Christopher received from Sackbut short and pithy letters in his scholarly handwriting about the political situation.

"The Turk," he wrote, "will get the best of you, for the powers will never agree, and the Germans will ultimately profit by the situation."

There was a massacre of Armenians at Trebizond, shortly after Christopher's arrival; afterwards massacre followed massacre in other places until the beginning of the New Year.

At first, Christopher was inclined, under the influence of Sackbut, to be cynically pro-Turk, but this influence was counteracted and finally undermined by that of Madame Turçin, by whom he was attracted. Whether she was an Armenian or not, she was a Catholic and violently pro-Armenian, and she soon made Christopher see eye to eye with her.

His letters to Sackbut became changed in tone and impassioned, so that one day Sackbut wrote to him as follows:

"I think you are losing your intellectual balance. You must see that as long as there are Turks and Armenians in the same country the Armenians will squeeze the Turks because they are cleverer, and the Turks' sole method of keeping even with them will be to massacre them occasionally. As for stopping the massacres, as for getting the Turks to reform, you can only do that by coercion , and that will not be done unless the Powers are unanimous. Which is impossible."

Christopher wrote back saying among other things:

"I daresay you are right. I daresay it is impossible to get

the Powers to agree, but I don't see that this absolves us.
I think it is criminal for us not to go on trying to stop
these appalling massacres. I daresay you think I am
sentimental. But it is not that: it is merely an elementary
sense of justice: elementary Christian morality. As for
the Armenians squeezing the Turks, I admit they are
clever and may get the best of them in bargains, but it
seems to me absurd to talk of the Turks having anything
to f e a r from the Armenians. I admit they d o fear
them, but I maintain that it is fear born of ignorance,
prejudice, superstition and tradition. It is one of those
intangible fears that are based on nothing. Like the fear
some people have of Freemasons, others of Jesuits,
others of Jews. It is this unformed and baseless fear
which is at the root of most persecutions."

Sackbut wrote back saying he did not consider such fears to be always baseless or intangible. He himself regarded the Jews as a real danger to the world.

"*I think,*" he wrote, "*the Russians are right not to give them liberties; if they do, they will find themselves at the mercy of the Jews.*"

Nothing was done by the Powers. In the summer there were more massacres, and in August came the famous raid on the Ottoman Bank, and the wholesale slaughter in the streets of Constantinople.

Christopher was an eye witness and the sight entered into his soul. It was a part of his duties to help with reports and he did his best to make it excruciatingly clear that the massacres had been organised and carried out according to plan.

In England people wrote to the newspapers; sermons were preached; indignant speeches were made; meetings were held indoors and out of doors; poets wrote sonnets, and cartoonists dipped their pens in vitriol; but nothing was done.

Christopher was possessed by the subject, and he would

probably have quarrelled with Sackbut had they met face to face. As it was, Sackbut understanding his frame of mind was cautious, and confined himself to saying that the Liberals found it easy to be virtuous at the expense of others.

Christopher's remarks in his reports were toned down. But he could not believe that nothing would be done.

He found in Spence a sympathetic listener. Spence shared his views and his indignation, as far as he was capable of sharing anything at a time when he was in love. He was pressing his suit, and apparently with success.

One evening in October, the year after Christopher had arrived at Constantinople, Madame Turçin asked him to dinner.

Besides his host, a short fair dapper little man, and his hostess there was a middle-aged man who was introduced to him as Stephen Alishan. Before he arrived, Madame Turçin told Christopher that he was an Armenian refugee from Trebizond. He was a Gregorian Armenian. The Greek Christians had been protected by the Russians, the Catholics by the French. The Gregorians and the Protestants had no one to protect them.

His wife and his children had been massacred in a church. All his property had been looted and destroyed. He had escaped by accident.

After dinner he told the story dispassionately as if it had happened to someone else. But there were sorrow and fire in his deep-set eyes and lines of suffering on his face that one felt nothing in the world could ever efface. He dwelt little on his own losses which he seemed to accept with sublime resignation, but in detail on the sufferings and the heroism of those who had preferred death and torture to apostasy. There had been many such among the Gregorian and Protestant pastors.

He spoke with indifference of the loss of his goods. He had been, so the Turçins had told Christopher, one of the richest men in the Near East and had possessed an unrivalled collection of missals and church ornaments.

"I have only one thing left," he said to Madame Turçin, "and I have brought it to you because my wife would like you to have it. She was so fond of you."

"But you must keep it yourself," said Madame Turçin.

"No," said Ahishan, "I am sure it is her will that you should have it. You have befriended me and I wish you to have it. It is a record of the Fourth Crusade: stories of the Crusaders written in Greek and illuminated. There is nothing remarkable about it, but the pictures are interesting. And there is one story which is striking. I will read it you. It is quite short."

Alishan sat down at the table near the lamp and read aloud the Greek story in English which he spoke beautifully.

"It was in the month of April, in the year of Grace 1203, in the Abbey of the Castle of Boemond, not far from the city of Constantinople that a Greek maiden named Sofia was about to take the veil.

"Now Sofia had a brother named Constantine who loved her dearly, and when the day appointed for the ceremony was at hand and Sofia had made ready and had put on her bridal apparel, he besought the Lady Abbess and his sister to wait for a year, but his sister said to him: 'My Lord is awaiting me, My Lord and thine.'

"When the Lord Bishop had come and all had been made ready and they were about to enter the church, news came to them of ill-omen. The Normans and the Franks, drunken with wine, were about to enter the Abbey, and with them was one Ulrich of Tone, an evil man.

"Now in that Abbey there was a holy relic: That very Coat without Seam which had been stripped from Our most Blessed Lord on Good Friday and for which soldiers had cast lots on Golgotha. For it had been brought thither from the Holy Land, and many pilgrims visited the Abbey to pay honour to the Coat."

Christopher started when he heard this and he saw the room at Birkenberg and Alex bent over the book she had illuminated.

"And when the Abbess was told of the approach of the Franks she said: 'We must save the Coat without Seam.'

"And the Abbess concealed the Holy Coat in one of the pillars of the church which opened by virtue of a hidden device. And Ulrich and his men entered the church.

"And Ulrich demanded the Coat without Seam, for he swore that a forefather of his ancestor had captured this Coat from the Turks when Lord Raymond stormed Jerusalem and the Coat had been stolen from his forefather by guile.

"He would fain hang the Coat in the church of his city. But the Abbess said him nay. And when Ulrich beheld Sofia in her bridal attire he asked who was this bride, and they told him she was Sofia, the sister of Constantine, and about to take the veil.

"And Ulrich said that unless they gave unto him the Holy Coat there would be no ceremony that day.

"And the Abbess said him nay. For the Coat she said belonged to God alone. And Ulrich swore that unless they gave him the Holy Coat he would take Sofia to be his bride.

"And Constantine adjured the Abbess to give Ulrich the Holy Coat lest his sister should suffer shame.

"But Sofia said they must strike no such wicked bargain for her sake.

"Then Ulrich laid hands on Sofia, but Constantine cried out that if Ulrich would swear to him not to molest his sister he would reveal to him the secret place where the Holy Coat was hidden.

"And Ulrich swore upon his sword.

"And, despite the prayers of Sofia, Constantine touched the secret pillar and its door was opened and the Holy Coat was manifest.

"Then said Ulrich: 'I shall take the Holy Coat and the Bride

as well.'

"*And Constantine fell upon him with his sword and they fought, and Ulrich prevailed and Constantine was slain.*

"*And Ulrich said: 'Now shall I be wedded to this bride in this church and the Holy Coat shall be my wedding garment.'*

"*And Ulrich took the Holy Coat in his hands, but no sooner did his hands touch the Holy stuff, than he fell upon his knees and repented him of his sin.*

"*And he said to the Abbess: 'Tell me what I must do to atone for my sin and I will do it.'*

"*And the Abbess bade him take the Holy Coat home to his city and hang it in the church, that people might come from far and wide to honour the Holy relic.*

"*And for himself he must enter the religious life in his city and serve God until the hour of his death.*

"*And Ulrich went his way and took with him the Holy Coat to his city in the Germanies, where it hangs in the church until this day.*

"*And on the day the Franks and the Greeks fought in the city of Constantinople, the castle, the Abbey of Boemond and many other dwellings were destroyed by fire and the dwellers therein were put to the sword.*"

"Is it known what happened to the Coat afterwards?" asked Christopher.

"Some say it is at Treves, and there is a church in France which claims to have it," said Alishan.

Christopher left early that evening saying that he had work to finish before going to bed.

CHAPTER XIII

When Christopher reached home his mind was in a ferment. This story had again cropped up. So far this had always betokened an approaching crisis in his life. How strange these coincidences were! There seemed to be no crisis now. It was curious that he did not realise it, but he was, at that moment, in the heart of a crisis. He sat reading a book in a chair, but his mind paid no attention to the meaning of the words. Presently Spence came in looking happy. He had been dining with Norton, the American Minister.

"It's fixed," he said. "Clara has said yes. Parents' consent asked for and given. We are to be married before Christmas."

"Well, I do congratulate you," said Christopher, "it's splendid."

Spence told him the details of the evening and of his talks with Mr and Mrs Newton, but Christopher found it difficult to listen.

"What is the matter with you?" said Spence at last. He had been at first so much absorbed in his own feelings that it was some time before he was aware of Christopher's abstraction.

"I was dining with the Turçins tonight and I heard an awful story. There was a man there called Alishan, an Armenian refugee from Trebizond, a charming man, cultivated and quiet. He has lost everything. His wife and children were killed while they were in church; his house was burnt, isn't it terrible? And he's only one among thousands, and we sit still and do nothing, just because we are all so damned jealous of one another. And we call ourselves Christians! What a farce it is, isn't it?"

"I guess we can't move without the others."

"Yes, but what I feel is, if we, or say, we and the Americans, gave the lead, the other Powers would have to follow our lead for very shame."

"They won't; directly we do something the Russians or the Germans or the French do the opposite. The Turk can always fix the deal so as to hold four aces."

"Oh, I think it's sickening, to think one can do nothing."

"And we certainly cannot."

"I'm not so sure"; an idea suddenly came into Christopher's head. "Do you know what I mean to do?"

"What?"

"I mean to write to the *Daily Messenger* an analysis of what the policy of the Government has been during the last year, and an account of what has happened – the result. Just to show up that it has been like a game of jealous children which has not done any one of them any good, and has ended in the massacre of thousands of innocent men and women. Massacre and torture, and the destruction of some of the best, of the only fruitful elements in the country."

"But if you do that, you will be fired."

"If I do that I shall be fired," Christopher repeated, and at that moment he realised the crisis which faced him. "And supposing I am fired?"

"What will you do?"

"It doesn't matter what happens to me. As long as my mother was alive it mattered, but now it doesn't matter. I shall find something to do."

"And all your work will have been for nothing, and your future will be thrown away."

"What is my future here? Consul-General or chief dragoman

at the best."

"Well, that's fine, and a living, anyhow. I guess you've got to live."

"I can find some job as a translator. If not, they might take me at Cook's office."

"You can't do that sort of work, you don't know how."

"I might get something at Cambridge. I could coach people in Eastern languages."

"Maybe. But I wouldn't have you do anything in a hurry, not while you're worked up. Think it over."

Christopher did think over it.

He thought of nothing else. He slept little that night, and he brooded over burning phrases that leapt into his mind. The next day he said nothing about it to Spence: but he began to write a draft of his letter in his spare moments. At any rate he would write a letter and see how it turned out. He would settle whether to send it later on.

It took him about a week to finish, as the official work was heavy.

Towards the end of October he finished the draft of his letter. He was pleased with it. It made bitter reading. At the time he received intimation that his work was considered satisfactory, and that he would be appointed Acting Vice-Consul at Van at the end of the month. Now the moment of crisis had come. He must settle what to do. He laid the situation before Spence, late one evening.

"Well, let's hear what you've written, anyway," said Spence.

Christopher read out his letter; it was two columns long. It made good reading. It was forcibly written. It was clear that the writer knew what he was talking about, that he was sincere, burning with indignation which was all the more effective from being expressed with restraint.

"That's some letter," said Spence. "It's darned good, but you will be fired all the same if you hand it to the Press."

"I shan't wait to be fired," said Christopher.

"What's the hurry? Why not wait and see if you can't find another job first?"

"Well, I've got to settle now at once because of this new appointment. If I accept this Vice-Consulate, I can't send the letter."

"Well, I quite understand what you feel," said Spence. "I know how mad and sore you are about this business, and it's enough to make anyone mad and sore, but I figure it out this way; there is no use in us small fry butting in. It can't help any. I believe it may do more harm than good."

"I don't see how it can do any harm. Somebody writing from the spot with first-hand knowledge always commands attention. Otherwise people are inclined to say: 'Oh, all that is bound to be exaggerated, and we needn't believe half of it.' "

"Sure, they do say that, and we know all too well that there's mighty little exaggeration going around. Rather the reverse. But how will it help?"

"It may not help, but if I feel I must do it."

"Of course, if you must, you must. But all the same, one has to go on living, however many Armenians are beaten up."

"I remember you once telling me that Americans never minded scrapping one profession and taking up another."

"Sure. But then you see you ain't no American, Chris. There's not enough pep to you."

"I feel sure I could find some work."

"Before you hand them that letter, why not write Sackbut and see how he feels about it?"

"Sackbut. He will help me. He won't like this letter, but if I chuck the Service he will help me to find some work in Cambridge, I'm sure, coaching or something."

"Yes, but why not send him the letter first?"

"What's the use? I know what he would say. I know what he thinks. He is at the bottom of his heart entirely pro-Turk. He doesn't care a button about the Armenians."

"Sure. Not two hoots."

"He would think it insane of me."

"I'm not so sure I don't either."

"Not after all you have seen?"

"I think you're right to feel mad. But I think there is yourself to think of, and it's not as if you were making the sacrifice for anyone else."

"But if one isn't true to one's ideas, I don't see how one can go on living."

"That's right, but supposing you could be useful here later on, and I guess you will be, ain't it rather a pity to throw away the chance?"

"As things are now I never could be useful."

"But things change even in Turkey."

"Well, I shall have to settle it by tomorrow."

"Then, think it over once more, tonight."

Christopher spent one more sleepless night brooding over the problem.

By the morning he had come to the conclusion that he had better not send the letter to the Press. After all, who was he to arrogate to himself the position of arbiter of international policy? He only saw one corner of things; but Lord Salisbury had the whole map of Europe in his mind and the whole future of British policy to think of. Besides, what good could it do? All might have been well, if he hadn't been invited that day to luncheon by Mr Norton, the American Minister. Spence wished him to go.

Christopher went. He found Mr Norton a polished lawyer with humorous eyes, silvered hair and a quiet manner; his wife tall, handsome and perfectly dressed, with a steady, even keel of conversation. Then there was Clare, the daughter, only just out, radiant with youth, and happiness streaming from her laughing, grey eyes.

There was also a guest, Hubert Strang, MP, an English

Liberal who had come out to glance at the Eastern question.

Hubert Strang had been many years in Parliament. He took a tempered interest in foreign countries. His upbringing had been Nonconformist, but his education Westminster and Cambridge. He was a supporter of Liberal Italy, and no mean Dante scholar. He was prodigal of forensic rhetoric and sometimes of indignation, but cautious when votes were in question.

He was small and sallow, and there was something about him that reminded you sometimes of a jockey and sometimes of a priest.

He had a smooth, silvery, clear-cut and slightly husky utterance, and quiet eyes from which every now and then there darted a lurking sting.

Christopher knew him well by name, and he had spoken at some public meetings on the Armenian question, so he took it for granted he was sound on that subject.

When the topic was mentioned, as it was bound to be mentioned sooner or later (and it was mentioned sooner), Strang said:

"I am convinced since I have been here that nothing which we have heard and nothing which has been said about these dastardly outrages has been exaggerated. A strong feeling has been aroused in the country. At a meeting I had the other day at Shelborough" (he was alluding to a coming by-election) "the audience were much moved by what I told them." He paused and tears came into his voice. "I spared them nothing, and I told them that the conscience of the nation had been touched" (his voice had a "dying fall").

"I had a great reception, especially when I mentioned that ruler whose name reverberates, as Dante put it, throughout the corridors of Hell –

E per l'inferno il nome tuo si spande."

He mouthed his quotation succulently and snapped his lips.

"And dark as the picture was which I painted to them, it was mild in comparison with the lurid truth that I have learnt since my arrival at Constantinople."

"But I think that now we may safely say that there is less fear of any recurrence of these appalling crimes."

"There are very few people left to kill," said Christopher.

"Quite. Quite. It is terrible," Strang sighed, "and I feel we are all to blame, our party as much as the present Government. We should never have allowed matters to reach this pitch."

He outlined some of the things that ought to have been done. Mr Norton pointed out a few of the difficulties that might have stood in the way of the policy he outlined.

"Of course, of course," said Strang, "one knows the difficulties, and it is easy to be wise after the event. But I fear the Turks no longer fear us, and feel that they can do as they please."

"Were you in favour of coercion, Mr Strang?" asked Norton.

"Coercion might have been possible had the Powers agreed; of course now it is out of the question. I met Welby last night, who has been sent out as a special correspondent by the *Daily Messenger*. He has visited all the worst districts, and he kindly showed me the article he intended to send. It was accurate, I believe quite accurate, and vividly written. But I told him that he would only harm the cause he was anxious to defend by publishing his plea in its present form. Whatever may have been right in the past, it is too late now. He agreed with me and said he would recast the article. It would entirely misfire in the constituencies if they thought we were being led towards war with Russia. I advised him to concentrate on reform and the urgency of relief."

"Then you think that at present the massacres ought not to be written about?" said Christopher.

"Not at present, and not in that way. Mr G will do what is necessary, and the public will follow him. We do not want a

Press campaign because it would be sure to bring about a reaction, and do us untold harm."

"Do you mean the Liberal Party, Mr Strang?" asked Norton.

"We are all Liberals on this subject, without any distinction of Party," said Strang, suavely. "Nobody in England wants the country to be faced with the risk of a war with Russia, and nobody wants fresh massacres to occur. But there would be a danger of both if a spirit of Jingoism were to be aroused. I told our Ambassador frankly what I thought of the situation, and he agreed with me that indiscriminate Press hysterics were undesirable – highly undesirable."

"But I do not see Welby as a man who would write at random," said Norton. "He talks Turkish and Armenian, and I believe he thinks in Arabic."

"Quite. An admirable publicist, like my young friend's lamented and illustrious father," he bowed to Christopher, "but unlike your father, whom I knew well, he is no politician."

"My father," said Christopher, "thought the Germans were the danger in the Near East and everywhere else."

"If that is true, it is a reason why we must not alienate Russia," said Strang.

"I understand then, Mr Strang," said Norton, "that you are of the opinion that the Powers can do nothing."

"I am in favour of reforms being pressed on the Turks, but I think there is a right way and a wrong way of doing this."

"As far as I can see," said Norton, "the only way the Turk understands is to bump him off the side-walk; if you don't do that to him he will do it to you."

"I saw a poor woman yesterday," said Mrs Norton, "whose whole family had been burnt to death. She only escaped by a miracle."

"Terrible," said Strang, "and what makes it more terrible still is that all this perhaps need not have occurred. I may be prejudiced, but I am sure if Mr G had been five years younger, and in office, it would not have occurred."

"I can't say I believe your Liberal Government found the Turk any easier to handle than your present Ministers do," said Norton.

"The Turk," said Strang, with an air of finality, "is unspeakable, eternally sick and eternally convalescent."

Having disposed of the subject he turned to Mrs Norton and asked her if she'd ever been to Brusa.

When Christopher went home he despatched his letter to the *Daily Messenger*.

CHAPTER XIV

The *Daily Messenger* published Christopher's letter, and Christopher sent in his resignation and informed the Ambassador.

When the Ambassador received Christopher's letter he sent for the Chief Dragoman and asked him what it was about. The Chief Dragoman was a man of ability and judgment and was interested in Christopher, although he did not know him well. He was at a loss to understand what had happened.

"He was doing well," he said. "He is a fine Arabic and Turkish scholar, and his father and his mother were remarkable people: I think it is a case of *cherchez la femme*. I think he is in love with Madame Turçin."

"That explains everything," said the Ambassador. "Well, there is nothing to be done. He tells me he has written to the Press."

"Yes, it is in the *Daily Messenger* that came today. It is a violently anti-Turkish and anti-Governmental diatribe. He told me he had done it and I begged him to stop it by wire. But, it was then already too late. He has deliberately burnt his boats."

"Then we can do nothing for the boy. I shall read the letter with interest. It is always interesting to learn from the young."

"It is well written," the Chief Dragoman said.

"What will he do?" asked the Ambassador. "Has he got anything to live on?"

"Nothing that I know of, but he says he will teach. He is able enough and he knows enough to find a job, but of course it is rank folly."

Christopher took leave of the Turçins and his acquaintances. Madame Turçin and Spence were the only two he minded leaving. And he felt both these partings.

He dined with the Turçins the night before he left and Madame Turçin said to him: "This is the worst of our horrible career. As soon as one makes friends one has to go somewhere else and one may never see them again. I think you have done well to get out of it, but I am sorry, for I thought we were going to be friends."

"Oh, but I wasn't a diplomat and never should have been one, I was a failure."

"Who knows, we may meet again soon," said Turçin, cheerfully. He had a neat optimistic mind. "We may be appointed to London some day."

When Christopher said good-bye, Madame Turçin looked at him sadly and said: "Good-bye, I think what you did was noble and I beg you never to regret it however foolish it may seem to you afterwards."

Spence saw him off at the station the next morning. There were not many passengers for the Orient Express: a French diplomat and his wife on leave and a King's messenger.

Spence was silent and thoughtful.

"It's a shame you can't stop and be my best man," he said.

"We shall meet in England," said Christopher, "you'll be coming over in the spring."

"Yes, if all goes well."

"I've no doubt about that."

"Well, you see it's like this," said Spence, "everything looks so good, so darned good, that it has me scared, scared of some sudden raw deal."

"Don't think of such things."

The officials began to fuss. A brown-coated attendant told Christopher it was time to start.

"So long," he said.

"Till the spring, Chris," said Spence, and waved at him as the train steamed slowly from the station.

Christopher leant out of the window and saw Spence's large figure move slowly away.

It was the last time he was ever to see him.

And although he felt no such presentiment, he was aware of a strange tightening in the muscles of his throat.

As soon as he reached England, Christopher went straight to Cambridge.

He went to see Sackbut not without fear.

Sackbut who was profoundly vexed at what had happened received him calmly.

"You have thrown away a career for an idea," he said, "that is better than exchanging it for a mess of pottage. Even if the idea be a false one, which you know I think it is. Your letter made a sensation. But it is a sensation that will only last a few days, and you will have all the wrong people on your side. You will be in the sad but common position of a Liberal who disbelieves in Liberals."

Christopher sadly acknowledged that this was true already. "I needn't have anything to do with them," he said.

"The trouble is the other side won't have anything to do with you. But we must see what we can find for you to do."

Sackbut found Christopher some pupils whom he could coach in Turkish and he took a small lodging in the town.

He went to see Yakovlev.

Yakovlev listened to his whole story gravely and said:

"It is a pity; I say it is a pity not because I do not admire people who sacrifice something for an idea, but because I am not sure whether your nature can bear the consequences. Your ideas spring from rage and are spurred by reaction and so may easily turn to sourness instead of to balm. And the essence of sacrifice is balm. But I fear you will not attain it. You will always be too angry. If you had some religion all would be different."

"I have seen too much of practical Christianity," said Christopher bitterly.

"You mean you have seen too much of human nature which is radically bad. Too much of unchristian Christians. That does not affect the question."

"I am afraid it does for me," said Christopher.

"Well, we must hope," said Yakovlev with a smile. "I wish you had shown me that letter before you had published it."

"But, surely you agree…?" interrupted Christopher.

"It takes a very big man to be angry," said Yakovlev. "You must attain to great calm and self-control before you can scourge the money changers away from the temple and upset their tables."

Christopher stayed on at Cambridge. He was very poor but he still had something of his last year's salary left. He was able to make some money by writing in the reviews. They accepted his articles on the East. Sackbut found him some pupils.

In the spring he got a letter from Spence saying that Clare Norton had caught typhoid fever.

Six weeks later he heard again that she had died.

Spence laconically stated the fact and Christopher wrote to him as briefly to say he was sorry. They understood one another. Spence was probably the only man who completely understood Christopher, unlike as they were.

Christopher was not surprised to hear when war between Greece and Turkey broke out that Spence had enlisted on the Greek side.

One morning in May, when he was coaching a pupil, a telegram came for him. He put it by till his pupil left him and forgot it for a time. He remembered it just as he was going out.

It was from Mr Norton and it told him that Spence had been killed.

Christopher had not experienced so sharp a sense of loss since the death of Mabel. He had suffered from the parting with Alex, but not in the same way. There was something so final about death.

He spent the whole of the vacation at Cambridge, except for a few weeks with Spence's parents, who again had taken a house in France for the summer.

It was towards the end of the Michaelmas term that he received a note one morning from Yakovlev asking him to call when he could. He went that same evening.

"I think," said Yakovlev, "I have found something for you. There is a man called Sir Joseph Claydon. He is a Member of Parliament. Very rich. Cotton. He retired from business to go into Parliament. He has married a long time ago a Russian, the daughter of one of the Moscow merchants. Anna Feodorovna Losova. I have known her very well in the time. He is looking for an undergraduate or someone who has finished with the University and who wants work. To be a kind of secretary. He has bought a house called Westleigh which has a large library and he wants someone to look after it. Also as I said he is an MP. He is a Liberal and interested in Eastern questions and fond of Russia. He cannot bear the Turks and is angry with the Government. He read your letter; the letter that made the fuss, and he was pleased with it. Now his wife writes to me and asks if I know anybody who would do and she asks me what you are doing, and whether I know you, and whether you would do for the work, and like to do it. Would you like to do it?"

"I don't think so," said Christopher, "I don't want to be the slave of a *nouveau riche*. I can make enough to scrape on somehow."

"Sir Joseph Claydon is a character," said Yakovlev. "He speaks Russian and reads Juvenal for his amusement. His wife is nice and cultivated and knows interesting people. I think you would like them and you would have plenty of time to yourself. At any rate let me write and tell them you are here and you can see him, and if you do not like the thought of him you need not go. It is a pity to miss such a chance."

"Very well," said Christopher.

A week later Christopher went up to London to interview Sir Joseph Claydon in his house in St James's Place.

He was shown in to Sir Joseph at once.

Sir Joseph was between fifty and sixty: large, square, and rubicund, with short, reddish whiskers.

He went abruptly to the point. His voice which was low and suave was not what one expected from his rather rough exterior.

"I want a secretary," he said, "but not for my accounts and business letters. I have a typist who does that. But I want a man who knows something. Who can look up things for me and help me with my speeches. A scholar and not a damned fool. I want someone who can look after the library. There is a fine library at Westleigh. I read; I like old books but I don't know much about them and I haven't time, and there is Heaven knows what in this library," he groaned, as if it were a burden. "I read that letter of yours in the *Messenger*.

"You were perfectly right, only of course a young man has no business to say such things. If he does he gets sacked, but of course you had to resign. I like you for saying them. Now I would give you £300 a year, you will live with the family and you could have a month's holiday every year if you want it. I should expect you to live at Westleigh and in London during the session, if I wanted you. I am told you know foreign languages, Eastern tongues and God knows what, and that you can look after books. Yakovlev says you know a lot. I think you would do for me. You needn't answer me now. And I haven't made up my mind myself. I shall let you know definitely in a week. What college were you at?"

"Crispin's."

"Good, I know the Master. Good fellow. I knew your father. I liked him although we differed on politics. You are a Roman Catholic?"

"Yes, but… "

"You needn't go into that. I don't care if you are a Mahommedan."

Then he got up suddenly and said, "Well, good-morning. You will hear from me and you can give me your answer when you hear."

For a week Christopher heard nothing.

He was just beginning to think the incident was closed when he got a letter from Sir Joseph saying that if he wished to accept the post of librarian and secretary he could enter upon his duties at once as soon as the Cambridge term was over.

Christopher went to consult Sackbut.

Sackbut did not know Sir Joseph Claydon but he knew all about Westleigh. It had belonged to the Glastonbury family and Sir Joseph had bought it as it stood from a distant relation of the late Lord Glastonbury who had died childless.

"Of course you will accept?" he said.

"I think not," said Christopher, "I have seen Sir Joseph and I didn't dislike him, but I don't think I should please him. I think it would be a mistake. I should probably be sacked again."

"I think you are foolish," said Sackbut. "I don't know Claydon, but I know about him. He is a Liberal but he is not a humbug. The Master of Crispin's told me about this offer last night. Claydon wrote to him about you and he recommended you strongly. He knows Claydon well and he is a sound man. Headstrong, but fair and kind. He knows something too: reads the classics and Russian. As for the library at Westleigh, I have seen it, and it is an education in itself. You will have time to go on with your own studies. Time to write articles if you want to, and not so many as you have written so far, and better ones. Of course you've had to do it up till now for the money. Now that won't be necessary, which is an excellent thing. You were already beginning to deteriorate in your writing. If I were you I would go quietly on with my Eastern studies and then some day write a really serious book on some Oriental subject: Persia if you like. You can keep in touch with the serious Press, so that if you want to write in the future they will take what you write. We shall have the Eastern question with us for many a long day. You can't learn enough about it. The great thing is to go on with the ground-work. So far you have only crammed, and scraped the surface. And then there is Claydon's wife. Yakovlev knows her and says she is a delightful woman. And you will meet interesting people. People worth knowing."

"But the worst of it is," said Christopher, "Sir Joseph is an ardent Liberal and probably thinks I am one too, because of my letter, and when he finds out that I'm not…that I hate the whole pack of politicians, Liberals and Conservatives and the Liberals worst of the two, what will happen then?"

"Nothing will happen. Claydon is a man of sense. He doesn't want people to agree with him. All you have to do is to help him to say what he wants to say. His opinions will be no business of yours and he will not trouble about your opinions, he will only trouble about your facts."

"Very well, I suppose I had better have a try."

So Christopher accepted the offer and went to Westleigh just before Christmas.

CHAPTER XV

Westleigh, which was not far from London, was a square red brick Queen Anne house, and stood in a park at the end of a long avenue of stately trees. Sir Joseph had left the house as he found it, except for putting in electric light, hot-water pipes and a few bathrooms. He did not worry much about furniture and artistic things, but he liked a good picture and was proud of his possessions. He liked things to be good and he had an instinctive horror of trash. The rooms were high and panelled, furnished with the flotsam and jetsam of various periods – 1700, Georgian, early and mid-Victorian. The library was long and low and had not been touched. It contained a fine Vandyck over the chimney-piece, otherwise it was full of books and books of the rarest and most beautiful description. There were Aldines, Elzevirs, Shakespeare folios and quartos, Restoration comedies, French illustrated books of the eighteenth century, besides missals and illuminated MSS. There was also a fine collection of engravings and coloured prints, books of travel, and some Oriental books which were of great interest to Christopher. There was enough food here to occupy his mind for the rest of his life.

He was welcomed by Lady Claydon. She was the daughter of a rich Moscow merchant. She was large, dark, calm and sensible, cultivated and intelligent. They had one daughter who was sixteen years old and at school, but who had come home for her holidays. She was called Anne and took after her mother.

Christopher was taken into what was called the breakfast room, a square room with white panels and cupboards full of old English china.

There was a large table with an opulent tea and a samovar. Lady Claydon gave him a warm welcome. "We shall be able to talk Russian," she said. "Andrei Semonovitch says you speak it so well and you learnt it so quickly. My husband can speak it if he chooses but he pretends he cannot."

She told him that she too had admired him for writing the letter he had written, and she blamed the Russian Government for their inactivity.

"Our politicians," she said, "think that they have only to do nothing about Turkey, and one day Constantinople will fall like a ripe plum into their lap." She sighed. "I feel they will be disillusioned some day. I should like Russia to have Constantinople and to see St Sophia a Christian church once more, and I think it would be best for the world, but, but... "

Sir Joseph came in later and drank four or five cups of tea. He was excited about an article on Crete in one of the evening papers. "I shall have to speak on the subject," he said, "after Christmas, to my constituents. You will have to help me with my speech. They do write such damned nonsense." His constituency was in one of the towns in the north of England.

Christopher at first found the life easy and agreeable. Sir Joseph gave him little to do. He enjoyed the library, and discovered fresh treasures every day. He took Sackbut's advice and went on in his spare time with his Oriental studies. All went well for the first two weeks.

At the New Year some guests arrived. There was pheasant shooting, and the guests were of three categories – sporting, political and artistic, for Lady Claydon was in touch with the artistic and literary world. Politics were represented by two

Members of Parliament and their wives, sport by the same Members and a Colonel Stockton, a neighbour, and the arts by Sir Francis Macbride, the composer, and his wife and daughter.

The Members of Parliament, who were both Liberals, were civil to Christopher with a friendly patronage which irritated him acutely. He longed to explain to them that he detested Liberalism and disbelieved in Liberals more than he did in Conservatives, and that he had done what he had done instinctively and not in obedience to any political creed, but fortunately he held his tongue. He disliked both the Members of Parliament: Vincent Langley, the smooth, portly brewer who exuded wealth, as did his tall, languid wife, who wore long sweeping rich stuffs and was slightly condescending; and Whitelaw, a dark active Scot, quick-witted and canny. He found relief in the society of the Macbrides, that is to say, with Lady Macbride who was handsome and half Italian, and their daughter Esther, who was at present studying music at the Royal College of Music with a view to being a professional pianist.

She was now only fifteen, not grown up, with her hair in a plait, but she looked grown up and showed promise of beauty. She was well set up. She held herself well. She had the carriage of an Italian peasant and great clear eyes. She was a friend of Anne Claydon. Christopher sat next to Esther Macbride at dinner, the first night of her arrival, and he confessed to her at once that he was unmusical. She laughed and said she liked him all the better for that because she found it impossible to talk about music.

"Even with professionals?" he asked.

"That is different, but then that is like talking shop and I cannot bear the ordinary conversation about music."

"Why is it," asked Christopher, "that one cannot bear to talk about anything one really knows something about, even if it is only a little?"

"I think it is because people are always striking wrong notes, and wrong notes matter when one has an ear for anything."

"Are Austrians musical?" asked Christopher.

"Yes, more musical than anybody."

"I stayed in Austria for a little while and I knew an Austrian whose playing I used to enjoy. When do you start your career?"

"As soon as I have finished with the College of Music, I shall go to Germany, to Leipzig, to study there for two years or more, and then when they think I am ready, I will try and play at concerts if they think I am good enough. But I daresay I shan't be good enough."

"Do you want to be good enough?"

"Of course."

Esther's attention was then monopolised by her neighbour, and Christopher had to talk to Mrs Whitelaw, who was handsome, athletic, and an authority on sports, games and most other questions. She talked indulgently of Sir Joseph's shooting.

"I don't call pheasant shooting sport at all," she said, "but it's good for Jock, as he gets away so little now."

"They say the pheasants here are difficult to shoot," said Christopher. Mrs Whitelaw smiled indulgently and changed the subject.

"I hear Sir Joseph has an indoor tennis court," she said.

"Yes," said Christopher, "do you play tennis?"

"I do when I can get a real game," she said, "but I cannot endure pat-ball."

She didn't ask him whether he played and Christopher felt he was being treated as an inferior.

"I'm fond of tennis," he said.

"I don't let my boys play tennis," she said, "I think it spoils their keenness for cricket and football."

After dinner the men sat for a long time.

Sir Joseph was fond of Burgundy and proud of his cellar.

The conversation turned on the Dreyfus case. The news had just come that Major Esterhazy, who had been tried by Court Martial sitting with closed doors, had been acquitted.

"It is the most monstrous thing," said Langley.

"The whole staff of the French army," said Whitelaw, sipping his port, "are as corrupt as they can be, rotten to the core, every man Jack of them."

"I don't agree with you," said Colonel Stockton who had lived in France, "I don't say the man may not be innocent, but I think people talk nonsense about Courts Martial. It's the fairest form of justice that exists."

Langley and Whitelaw laughed.

"Well," said Sir Joseph, "I'm not an anti-Semite but there is no doubt that the man was a Jew. And as to Courts Martial, you remember what Dr Johnson said about a Court Martial – that he didn't believe any of its members had spent half an hour in balancing probabilities."

"That's just what makes them so much fairer," said Stockton. "They go by common sense instead of by lawyers' quibbles."

"I believe," said Sir Joseph, "that their decisions are often right although their procedure is wrong."

"What do you think of it, Trevenen?" said Whitelaw to Christopher.

"I think Dreyfus is guilty," said Christopher. "The French staff who have seen the evidence must know more about it than we who haven't. At any rate, it is no business of ours."

"You didn't think the Armenian massacres were no business of ours, young man," said Whitelaw, "and I respect you for it."

"I think it is our business to defend Christians when they are persecuted," said Christopher.

"But not Jews, eh?" said Whitelaw.

"Not to interfere," Christopher went on, "with officers of another state who are trying an officer for treason."

"But my dear fellow," said Langley, "we know that the evidence was forged."

"I don't think we know anything."

"We know enough to know there is something radically wrong. Why did they try Esterhazy *in camera*?"

"For reasons of State; we should have done the same," said Christopher.

"The French are an extraordinary people," Langley went on, "I was arguing with a Frenchman the other day who is convinced that Dreyfus is guilty and when I said the opposite, he said, 'Ah! but you haven't seen the man.'"

"I think that's a very sensible remark," said Christopher.

"Well, thank Heaven, it is not a principle of British justice," said Langley.

"I don't think British justice is any fairer than any other," said Christopher hotly, "any fairer than Chinese justice, for instance."

"You mean you don't believe there is such a thing as justice as administered by the law?"

"Yes," said Christopher, "I think it would be just as fair in the long run to toss up whether a man is guilty or innocent as to try him by our system, and would save a lot of time."

Langley laughed good-humouredly.

"I mean it seriously," said Christopher.

"Well, if they teach boys at Cambridge that sort of paradox, I shall send my boy to Oxford," Langley said sharply.

Christopher was silent and turned red.

That was the first and last time that he ever joined in discussion publicly with any of Sir Joseph's guests.

"I am amazed at what you say," Langley continued. "Every time I read a Judge's summing up, I am lost in admiration at the fairness and level-headedness of our Judges. A Dreyfus case in England would be impossible."

He then embarked upon anecdote.

When they left the dining room they found Lady Claydon sitting in what was called the gallery at a tea table in front of the samovar. A rubber of whist in another room was arranged for Sir Joseph. Lady Claydon asked Esther whether she would care to play them something. She consented at once, looking at Christopher and smiling as she did so. She sat down at the grand pianoforte, and Christopher was amazed. The music was not intelligible to him, although she was not playing anything difficult. But he felt that Esther had genius. Her personality astonished him and it astonished him in one so young. He was amazed at the uprightness of her carriage, the sweep and mastery of her hands, her absence of self-consciousness and the expression in her eyes. She was rapt in what she was doing. She seemed to sink her personality in the music; to efface herself and to present you humbly with the composer's message. Christopher thought she looked like a priestess performing a holy sacrificial rite.

She played two pieces and then her father, a small mild man with wide tawny hair and dreamy eyes, said: "That is enough, Esther. You played the Schumann well. You must practise the Chopin."

After that they settled down to a round game.

CHAPTER XVI

The guests stayed for the inside of a week. There was a shoot every day. The only guests whom Christopher spoke to were Esther and her parents; but he did not have much talk with them. They told him he must be sure to come and see them in London. They lived in Kensington.

In February Parliament met and the Claydons went to London. Christopher went with them. He began to settle down to his new work. Sir Joseph went to the House of Commons every night during the week. Sundays he spent at Westleigh, as a rule with the family, but sometimes he would invite a friend or two. He never had large weekend parties. Anne went back to school.

In London Christopher might have made friends with some interesting people, for several artists and men of letters came to the house: Walter Bell, the painter, Hodgkinson, the essayist, and Sir Humphrey Law, the scientist; but whenever Christopher was introduced to anyone of interest, he not only made no effort, but he shut up like an oyster. When they asked him to their houses, he always found some excuse for not going. He made no new friends except the Macbrides, and he did not see them often. Esther went to Germany after Easter, and was not to come back until Christmas.

Sometimes the Claydons would give a dinner party, and they

asked Christopher several times, but he always had a reason for not being able to come. This annoyed Sir Joseph, who said to him one day:

"I have got Rowley dining here next week," (Rowley was a prominent lawyer and a Conservative) "and I very much want you to be there as it will be a help to me for you to hear him talk."

Christopher at once put on his business manner and said that of course he would be there.

When the dinner came off, Rowley, who was an anti-sentimentalist and held the same views on Liberals as Christopher, was civil to him, and all would have gone well had not China been discussed. Christopher said something in favour of Chinese civilisation and Rowley, who was generally fond of paradox, took the orthodox occidental view, and caught him out in argument, whereupon he withdrew into his shell. So Sir Joseph's experiment failed.

When Christopher was not working for Sir Joseph, he worked for himself. He went to the British Museum. He hunted among the second-hand book shops. He rarely went to a play, never to a concert, but sometimes to the music-halls. Since the affair with Annette he had had no new sentimental adventures, although it is probable that he would have fallen in love with Madame Turçin had he stayed longer at Constantinople. But his first two love affairs had left him bitter. Too bitter to be cynical, although he once said to his friend Suckling, whom he saw from time to time, that sentiment in love affairs was a mistake and that the most honest women he knew were those who were to be met at the promenade of the Empire.

At Easter, the Claydons went to Westleigh, and a few guests were invited. At Westleigh, Christopher led a life of his own. When there were guests he never appeared except at meals. He never joined in the general conversation. If he was asked to join in something, an expedition, a game, he made the excuse that he had work to do and retired to the library. He did whatever he had to do for Sir Joseph conscientiously, and he looked after the library, not only with care but with love. He managed to do work for himself, but Sir Joseph kept him busy. As Sackbut had prophesied, the library proved to be an education in itself.

Sir Joseph was satisfied with him, highly satisfied with his work, but puzzled and irritated by his behaviour. And yet there was nothing he could complain of. Christopher was hard-working, willing, conscientious, intelligent and civil. But never did he open out for a moment, never was the barrier of his reserve for a moment broken down. Sir Joseph was large-minded and tolerant.

"He's a rum fellow," he said to his wife after Christopher had been there some time, "and he's all right; he does what one asks him to do, and he does it well. He's got a memory, and he's a damned good chess player; but I wish he wouldn't be so damned...so damned stand-offish."

"Poor boy," said Lady Claydon, "he is shy and proud, and he does not want to interfere."

"But can't the fellow see I should like him to interfere?"

"It is difficult for him."

When they were alone, Sir Joseph would sometimes read something from the classics with Christopher after dinner, or a Russian book with his wife and Christopher. At such moments, Christopher would talk and comment and take interest, but as soon as the reading was over, he would relapse into his reserve. Sometimes they would play chess.

If Sir Joseph asked him for an opinion he always gave it; and on business, that is to say, political matters, he would express himself with freedom and point, but he drew a sharp distinction between his private life and the work which he was paid for doing; as long as it was a question of business, he would be talkative and expansive; directly it was a question of everyday matters, he was civil but unresponsive.

He seemed to be happy as long as there were no guests in

the house; when there were, especially if they were politicians, he withdrew into his shell.

He liked Sir Joseph, but was inclined to misjudge him, and he liked Lady Claydon; but she was right in saying that he was proud; he was suffering from being a dependant. He had been too bruised already to take the situation lightly. He was longing to go away, to do something else, but he had no particular ambition now, and he saw no opening available to him. He had no plans for the future; he saw for the present no avenue of escape. Since he had been with Sir Joseph he had twice written an article in a review, which had won Sackbut's grudging approval. That year and the next went by quickly it seemed to Christopher. The Claydons spent it in London and at Westleigh. In the summer of the second year they went abroad, and Christopher took a month's holiday. He went with his old Cambridge friend to Russia. They went by sea to St Petersburg and thence to Moscow and the country, and stayed with a family called Daskov, at Susieki, their estate. Yakovlev had given them a letter of introduction to the Daskovs. They stayed there a week and Christopher enjoyed himself. Madame Daskov in writing to Yakovlev afterwards said:

"Quant à vos Anglais l'un ne dit rien et l'autre dit trop. Jean qui pleure et Jean qui rit. Nous avons préféré Jean qui pleure.

"Il est bien, et bon, a good sort. *L'autre est gentil, très intelligent mais moins bien.*

"Jean qui pleure comprend tout sauf la musique. Er ist gar nicht musikalisch, gar nicht. L'autre est musicien et joue mal, c'est à dire trop bien. Jean qui pleure a le caractère difficile, ce qui serait égal ici, mais je pense qu'en Angleterre il doit se faire facilement des enemis. Il paraît que la femme du Monsieur chez qu'il travaille est la fille du vieux Losov. Jean qui pleure a une tête intéressante. Tête de frondeur. On voit bien qu'il a du sang français ou est-ce le sang irlandais? Ses

yeux sont étranges. Des yeux d'illuminé. Camille Desmoulins.
Le reste de sa personne tranquille. Un scholar."

The Claydons spent the whole of the following autumn at
Westleigh, and at Christmas the Macbrides arrived with
Esther.

The South African war had broken out. Sir Joseph was a
Pro-Boer and so was Christopher; this made for harmony.

Esther had grown into a beautiful girl. Her hair was done up.
She was tall, and there was something noble about her. She
was radiant too with the happiness that comes from work:
work satisfactorily accomplished. Christopher felt shy when he
saw her, as if she were a new person whom he had never seen
before. There were other guests in the house; Solway, a
musician, Yakovlev, Stockton, and the Langleys. Esther played
the pianoforte by herself in the day time.

Christopher, when he saw her, felt that he was meeting a
stranger. It was not that he found it difficult to talk to her, nor
that he could not get on with her. He could get on with her all
too well. He felt he was on the brink of making friends, and he
did not want to. He was determined never to have an intimate
relation with any other woman in his life. So he deliberately
shielded himself behind an iron mask of reserve.

He avoided her society and kept to himself as much as
possible. This was easy until Yakovlev arrived.

Yakovlev had not been many hours in the house before he
understood the situation.

One afternoon, the day after Yakovlev's arrival, he took
Christopher for a walk through a leafless wood. It was a bright
day in January, frosty and dry, and Yakovlev had it out with
him.

"I think," he said, "you are behaving foolishly. These people,
Claydon, and especially Anna Feodorovna, are fond of you, and
instead of making things easy for them you make everything
difficult. You are always hiding, always getting into the

background."

"They are very kind to me, and I don't think, no, I know, Anna Feodorovna does not look down upon me, but Sir Joseph's friends do. They look upon me as a paid servant, which I am. I am nothing better than a paid servant."

"If you would only not think about yourself so much and a little more about other people! We are all of us servants, paid or unpaid. I am a paid servant. Sir Joseph, he is a paid servant, although he receives no salary, but he is a servant of the State all the same."

"I think Members of Parliament are the parasites, not the servants of the State."

"You talk like our young *intelligentsia*, and you have no right to talk like that. You have seen already too much to talk like that. You know perfectly well that the Macbrides, who are artists, do not look down upon you."

"No, but the Langleys do."

"Then why bother about them?"

"Well, I will try and do better. But the truth is, I cannot stand this life, and I see no way of escaping from it."

"Nonsense," said Yakovlev, "this life suits you very well."

Yakovlev's words had an effect on Christopher. That night he sat next to Esther at dinner, and he was more forthcoming.

After dinner, he found himself next to Solway, and asked him what he thought of Esther's talent.

"She is wonderful," he said, "an artist of the greatest promise. She has taught me things about Beethoven which I had not guessed."

"Will she become a great professional performer, a great celebrity?"

"She ought to. She is the finest pianist I have heard since Yanota, and there is no nonsense about her playing. It is the real thing. Of course she may… " he stopped.

"She may what?"

"She may marry, and give it all up."

"That would be a great pity."

"It would be a disaster."

"But I suppose she might marry and *not* give it up."

"Yes, of course, if she married the right person."

"I am not at all musical, but I thought, when I heard her play two years ago, there was something remarkable about her playing."

"She has improved out of all knowledge since she went to Germany, and they have not overworked her."

"I haven't heard her play this time. She played one evening, but I was busy."

"I will ask her to play tonight."

Esther played after dinner. Her parents, Solway, Lady Claydon, Anne and Christopher listened.

There was the usual rubber in the other room.

Sir Joseph was learning bridge.

As Esther played in the long, dim, dignified empty gallery with its white panelling, its silver sconces, and portraits by Lawrence, and landscapes by Bonnington, Christopher was spellbound. He did not heed the music, but he was captivated by her presence and her personality: the way her head was set upon her shoulders; the fire in her eyes, the nobility of her brow, and the wonderful shape and play of her hands.

She played some Bach, then some Schumann, and then, at Solway's request, a Sonata by Beethoven.

Solway asked for Op. III.

"I can't play that before you," she said to him.

"But I want to hear you play it," said Solway.

"We shall have to hear what you can do with it some day," said her father.

Her mother sat looking like a sibyl, dark, handsome and inscrutable. She said nothing.

Christopher put in a word, "Please play it," he said. "I have always hated Beethoven until now."

"Very well," said Esther, "and now you will hate it still

more."

She played the Sonata.

When she had finished, Solway said: "I knew she could do it."

"Yes," said Macbride, "she played it well, but she will play it better than that some day."

"What did you think of that?" Yakovlev said to Christopher.

"I can understand that that is beautiful, although I don't understand it all."

"I find," said Yakovlev, "that for a man who is not musical you like music very much."

After that, Solway and Esther played a symphony arranged as a duet.

Christopher enjoyed that still more.

When it was over, Lady Macbride said, "There is nothing like the dear old C Minor, but the *Andante* makes me always say to myself, '*Also gehen wir spazieren.*'"

Esther was asked for another solo.

She laughed and said:

"It's a great shame on Mr Trevenen who hates music, but I will try and play him something that will please him."

She sat down and played a Viennese *Walzer*: *Wein, Weib und Gesang.*

She played it with an intoxicating sense of rhythm; so much so that Anne got up and said, "I must dance."

Yakovlev said, "All right, I will dance with you," and they moved the chairs out of the way and whirled round the room.

Yakovlev, in spite of his heavy frame, danced in perfect time, and with gusto.

Christopher was longing to dance.

Never had he been so keenly sensible of the power of sound: he saw once more the dining room at Birkenberg, and Alex's face rose before him; Countess Linsky, the terrace, the moonlight, and Countess Felsen and Karl, and the castle and all that happy past.

Yakovlev and Anne at last stopped exhausted, at least Anne said she could dance no more, and Yakovlev said to Esther, "You have a sense of rhythm that would make the dead rise from their graves. I have never heard anyone play dance music better."

Then most of them went to bed, but Christopher sat up talking with Yakovlev.

"That girl is an artist, a great artist, and she will always be a great artist," Yakovlev said, as he lit a cigarette and sipped his tea. "But whether she will make a professional career is another matter."

"What is to prevent her?"

"Life, my dear friend, life is stronger than art. She will most certainly fall in love. It is impossible for someone who plays like that, with so much temperament, with such a sense of rhythm, not to fall in love."

"But haven't all great artists fallen in love? I should have thought it was not only good for their art, but indispensable."

"Yes, it is good for their art, but she seems to me like a person who will not be able to do two things at once."

"She will have every opportunity – her father is well known, and he will look after her. She seems to me sensible, and I think that all that matters is that she should not marry the wrong person."

"You mean she ought to marry a musician?"

"Not necessarily, a musician; no, I think it would be far better for her to marry someone who is not a musician, not a professional at any rate, but someone who would understand the artistic life. If she married a country squire or a complete Philistine her career would be ruined. She is beautiful, isn't she? and so simple."

"Yes, she reminds me of the girls in my country."

"Yes, that is true, she reminds me of the Daskovs' girl."

"Alexandra Petrovna?"

"Yes, only Esther Macbride is more beautiful. If only she

marries the right person! There is one thing to be thankful for at any rate, she won't be forced into some absurd *mariage de convenance.*"

"She may choose that kind of marriage."

"I don't think so, that kind of marriage is always chosen by the parents."

"No," said Yakovlev, "not always."

CHAPTER XVII

When the Claydons went to London after Christmas, Christopher became a frequent visitor at the Macbrides' house in Kensington. Esther was to have gone back to Germany at once, as soon as the holidays were over. But she had a bad attack of influenza, and the doctors said she must have a rest before she went back to work. Christopher went to the Macbrides' on Sunday afternoons when they were at home and stayed there for supper. The house was small; papered with Morris wall papers and furnished with old English furniture, but it was generally full of people, chiefly the young. There Christopher met Solway, who was at that time just beginning to appear in public as a pianist, Walter Bell the painter, and his old friend Godfrey Mellor who was now a clerk in a Government office. They greeted each other amiably but they never became friends again. Suckling had passed into the Civil Service and had gone to India.

On Sunday afternoons the Macbrides' house used to be full. After supper there would be music, and Christopher, although he had not become more musical, enjoyed listening to Esther's playing. He would press her to play, and he was always greatly disappointed if Solway or someone else sat down at the pianoforte.

His reserve towards her had melted. She had made it melt.

143

She chaffed him, teased him, gave him tunes to guess and made him play five-finger exercises.

There were often other students in the house; young people who were learning music or who were at the Slade School. Lady Macbride presided over the proceedings, handsome, imposing and absent-minded. She had a certain Italian languor which she had inherited and a touch of German sentiment. She had been brought up in Germany. A pre-Raphaelite atmosphere still hung about her, and she looked like a Rossetti picture. Macbride had a dreamy appearance and a jovial manner. He enjoyed making salads himself, sometimes cooking an omelette, playing drawing-room games, and doing conjuring tricks which he did badly. He was fond of puns.

After Easter, Esther went back to Germany, but Christopher continued to go to the Macbrides' house on Sundays. He came to be regarded as a member of the family.

This new intimacy made a difference to his life. He became less reserved with the Claydons and he no longer evaded their invitations when they asked him to one of their dinner parties, although he was never a talkative guest when there were strangers present.

In August the Claydons went to Paris to see the Exhibition. The Macbrides had a small house on the south coast of England, called Merrydown, and they invited Christopher to spend his holiday there.

Esther had come back for her long holiday.

Christopher arrived laden with books but they spent most of the time boating and bathing. In the evening, there was music. Macbride was composing a trio and he played his composition as it progressed. Besides Christopher, Solway was staying in the house and a Miss Shipley, an old lady who was a friend of Lady Macbride. She was original, musical and cultivated, voluble and loudly enthusiastic.

The time passed by quickly and at last the time came for Christopher to go back to Westleigh. It was a hot Sunday in

September. They had spent all day sitting on the beach. They had had dinner, and the windows of the little drawing room were open on to the small garden. Beyond the garden there was an orchard and not half a mile away the beach and the sea. Macbride had been correcting the exercises in counterpoint of a pupil which had been sent to him.

He was laughing to himself as he corrected them.

"Come here, Ronnie," he said to Solway, "and look at these fifths."

They both had a good laugh over the extravagant fifths of the pupil, and then Macbride suggested a game of draughts, which they sat down to. Lady Macbride was bending over an embroidery frame, and Miss Shipley was playing a patience. Christopher and Esther were stripping lavender on to a newspaper.

"A little music I think," said Miss Shipley, "yes, a little Schumann on this moonlight night. A little Schumann if you please, dear Esther." She raised her voice. "It would be such a treat. Such a *great treat.*"

"I think it's really too hot to play and it will disturb the draughts players."

"They won't listen unless you play a wrong note and that is not likely. Just a song."

"Very well," said Esther, and she sat down and played Schumann's *Lotosblume*, and after that another song.

"There, it's too hot to play any more," said Esther when she had finished the second song.

"Thank you, my dear," said Miss Shipley, "I always think that Schumann transports one into a solid world of cypresses and fountains."

It was quite still and there was a slight murmur from the sea. Moths were flying about the lamp.

Esther went out into the garden and Christopher followed her.

They walked through the garden into the orchard in

silence.

"What was that you were playing just now?" Christopher asked her presently.

"The first song is called *Die Lotosblume* and the second one *Aus Meinen Thränen Spriessen*. The words of both of them are by Heine. Are you fond of Heine?"

"I used to be."

Christopher remembered that the second song was the song that Karl had played at Birkenberg the night he had first talked to Alex on the terrace. How long ago it seemed now! He had forgotten the tune, and he was surprised to find that the recollection of it, and of the circumstances which had attended that playing, affected him no more than the memory of a dream.

"I sometimes wonder," he said, "whether everything that happens to one is no more than what we see in dreams, when once it is over."

"I forget my dreams," said Esther, "instantly, and the things that happen to me in real life seem to me real, long after they are over."

"So they do to me, or at least they used to, but some things are like dreams. When I was small we used to live a great deal in France, and that to me is like a dream now, and I had a sister whom I was very fond of, and she died when I was small, only nine years old, and that to me is like a dream, but for a long time afterwards it was terribly real."

"Nobody I have been very fond of has died yet," said Esther, "I don't know how I should bear it."

"I think one gets used to everything. When I first went to the Claydons as Sir Joseph's secretary I thought I couldn't bear it, and never should be able to. I never disliked them. They were always kind to me. But now I like being there."

"You don't mind going back?"

"Going away is always horrible especially when one has been enjoying oneself, and I have been enjoying myself so much here. How quickly it has gone!"

"In a flash. You must come next year."

"But you will come back before the summer?"

"Oh yes, at Christmas, and then I may stay for good, or I may stay another year in Germany. It depends on what they say, and on what father thinks."

"And then your professional career will begin."

"I don't think I shall ever have a professional career."

"I thought you lived for nothing else."

"I do, but somehow or other I don't think it will happen. I think it will be only a dream. Have your dreams come true?"

"No, none of them. I used to dream when I was a small boy that I would be an explorer and discover new countries, and then later on I had all sorts of other silly dreams, but they none of them came true."

"I think dreams – that kind of dream, is often only the shadow of the real dream that comes later and does come true."

"But you don't think music is your real dream?"

"Somehow not. I don't believe I am good enough. I am good enough in a way, I think; but not good enough for it to mean my whole life; and it must either be that or nothing."

"But you want it to be that?"

"Oh yes, but what is the use of wanting?"

"I think one gets what one wants."

He remembered having said or heard this before but he could not remember where, nor when.

"I wonder," and Christopher remembered that when he had said or heard this before the other person had said "I wonder." He felt a curious click in his brain. "I think it may be true," she said, "but the question is *when*?"

"When do you go back to Germany?" asked Christopher.

"In a fortnight. We shall miss you here very much. Father will miss you," she laughed. "You know it is so funny he won't believe you are not musical, he says you always like the best things."

"Isn't that simply because I like the things you play?"

"No, I don't think so. He thinks you choose the best things."

"Perhaps I choose the things you like best."

"Perhaps. It is an odd thing I always know when you like something, and when you don't. I know it better than I do when I am playing to people who are supposed to be more musical than you are."

"When you are playing can you feel what people are thinking?"

"Oh yes, and it is almost impossible to play to someone who doesn't like it. It makes an enormous difference – all the difference."

"And yet you don't mind playing before me, although you know I understand it so little."

"You don't understand the grammar of music, but you understand the thought and the feeling, and it is that which matters. You have a sense of rhythm."

"I don't understand other people's playing. I don't understand Solway's, and he plays well, doesn't he?"

"Oh yes, better than I shall ever play, but I think you have to be musical to understand his playing."

"I used to be friends with someone who comes to your house sometimes, and who is a great friend of Solway's – Godfrey Mellor. We quarrelled, at least I quarrelled with him. He used to try and educate me, and he said Solway's playing was wonderful, but he couldn't get me to understand it. But I could listen to your playing for ever."

"Could you?"

"Yes, for ever. I seem to understand it. It seems to me like a message in a foreign language which I don't know, which I can't speak, but which I understand, without knowing it. A message from another world."

"Music is a message from another world."

"Only your music – only when you play, to me. I believe I do know in a kind of way what is good and bad. At least I believe this: when one has been used to the best in anything – just used to it without knowing anything about it – the second best is intolerable. And you see with you I have been used to the best. I shall miss it dreadfully."

"Nobody plays at Westleigh?"

"No, thank Heaven."

"But Lady Claydon is musical?"

"Yes, but he hates it, and Anne can't play anything but scales."

"Anne is such a nice girl. I love her. I think it is partly because she is half foreign; that always makes a difference."

"I'm half foreign."

"I know, and that is why I think I never found you difficult."

"I never found you difficult, at least not when we first met. I did when you came back to Westleigh at Christmas two years later. I felt as if you were a stranger at first."

Esther laughed.

"That was your fault. You tried to be difficult. You treated me suddenly like a stranger, as if you had never seen me before."

"Yes, it was my fault. I was absurd. I was shy."

" You don't feel like that now?"

"Oh no! not now," he laughed.

"And you won't be like that again, even if I stay away a long time? When we meet again you won't suddenly treat me like a stranger? I feel you might."

"Oh! not if you stay away for years. But you won't stay away very long this time, will you?"

"I hope not. It depends."

"Will you write to me sometimes?"

"Every day if you like."

They had walked while they had been talking through the orchard and they were now standing on the edge of the beach. Before them there was a rampart of shingle and then a stretch of wet sand. The sea and the sands were silvery from a large golden moon. The waves made a soft sleepy noise.

"Every day?"

"Yes, every day."

"Do you mean that?"

"Yes, I do mean it," said Esther.

"Then you mean you will miss me?"

"Yes," she said, "I shall miss you."

There was a tremor in her voice. What did it mean?

"Would you like not to miss me? I mean not to have to miss me? Could you like me like that?"

"Yes, I think I could."

"I mean enough to marry me, for you to belong to me for ever?"

"Yes, I think so."

Esther whispered the words so softly Christopher scarcely heard them. He took her gently into his arms and kissed her again and again, and the moon and the sea and the shining sand and the dark orchard behind them, seemed to bear witness to their troth.

They stood in each other's arms for what was to them an eternity.

Then they heard someone calling.

"They are calling us," whispered Esther. It was impossible for them to move; impossible to go; for Time had stood still for them and the noise of the sea, the light on the waves and the sands, the dark orchard trees, the stillness and the warmth were a part of a lasting miracle and Christopher tasted one of those magical moments that come to mortals but once in a lifetime.

They heard footsteps. The spell was broken and the enchanted walls that enclosed them vanished.

Solway came up to them.

"I have been sent to fetch you home," he said, "they were beginning to get anxious. We thought you must be rehearsing the third act of a Grand Opera," and he hummed an air from

Faust.

"So we were," said Esther laughing.

Solway noticed nothing and went on humming. "Gounod is very good, all the same," he said to himself. Then he turned to Esther – "Your father beat me three times running. Do you know it is very late? Your father wanted to try over that third movement before we went to bed, but it's too late now."

They walked back in silence.

"At last, children! You are late!" said Lady Macbride as they went into the house. "But it was my fault. We have been arguing about Kruger as usual, and your father and Ronald were playing so busily and we all argued so loudly that we never noticed how late it was getting."

"I am thankful you are back," said Miss Shipley, "we should have come to blows. They have been calling me names."

"I do hope you haven't caught cold," said Lady Macbride.

"No mother darling, it is very hot outside."

"Yes, it's a lovely night, but the moths are so tiresome and I thought I saw a bat at one moment. What a beautiful night!"

Der Mond ist aufgegangen
Und überstrallt die Well'n;
Ich halte mein Liebchen umfangen,
Und unsre Herzen schwell'n.

"Do you remember quoting that to me, darling," she said to her husband, "that evening on Lake Como when we were engaged?"

"Yes," said Macbride, "I remember being bitten by mosquitoes and that you caught cold, and I recommended some *Como*mile tea. I do hope Esther won't catch cold again just before going to Germany."

They went upstairs.

Esther went to her mother's room and told her that she was engaged to be married.

"*Ach! Du lieber Gott!*" said Lady Macbride who always spoke German on sentimental occasions, although she had no drop of German blood in her veins. "Engaged! engaged! but who is he? who is the *Brautigam*?" ...as if there had been a thousand possibilities.

"Christopher, of course, darling."

"Ah well!" she gave a sigh of relief, "I thought it was the Leipzig professor. But, my dear, Christopher is not at all musical in spite of what your father says. Your father will insist that he is musical because he turns over when he is told to. But what will you do with an unmusical husband?"

"Mother darling, what does music matter?"

"Well," sighed Lady Macbride, "it was to be your bread and butter, but in a way you are right. It does not matter as much as all that: well, I am glad. I like Christopher, but we must tell your father. I don't know what he will say."

"But father adores Christopher."

"Yes; but your father is sometimes obstinate. You had better go to bed and let me tell him by myself." She kissed Esther over and over again, and then she cried, and they both cried, and then she took Esther to bed. After all this was done, Lady Macbride broke the news to her husband.

He said nothing at first.

Then he said: "I like Trevenen. I think he is an intelligent man, but I will not have Esther's career interfered with. There shall not be any question of marriage until she has made her *début*. I will not have her career ruined; I will not have it interfered with in any way, for a moment."

"No, of course not, darling."

"And there can be no question of marriage for two years."

"Well, we mustn't make things too difficult for them."

"Esther is too young, and she must finish her studies first, and then we will see, but I have nothing against Trevenen, nothing. I know no one whom I would like better as a son-in-law. He is the only man I have ever met who can turn over properly, and yet he says he is not musical! He never makes a mistake. But what will they live on?"

"What did we live on when we married, darling?"

"Love, dearest, love and hope."

"Well, they have plenty of love I am sure; we must supply the hope."

CHAPTER XVIII

The news of his daughter's engagement had astonished Sir Francis. Esther's marriage was a possibility he had not yet thought of. He had regarded her as a professional musician and as nothing else. There were objections. There was in his mind the question of Esther's career. There was her youth. She was not yet eighteen. There was the question of means. Christopher's means. There was the religious question. The Macbrides were Protestants.

The last question was the more easily solved. Macbride had no objection to his daughter marrying a Catholic. He himself held no dogmatic views; and he knew that Christopher was not a bigot. Esther, he said, was too young to marry. He had only been twenty-five and his wife nineteen when they married, but when his wife reminded him of this, he said the case was different. He had had a future before him as a musician (he was being wise after the event) but what was Christopher's future? Would he be a private secretary for the rest of his life? Supposing Sir Joseph Claydon were to die? What would Christopher do? He had barred the door himself to all Government employment. He had no prosperous relations, and no prospects. After much argument and discussion it was settled that there was to be no formal engagement and that nothing was to interfere with the completion of Esther's studies and the interests of her career.

She was to go back to Germany; they hoped she would appear publicly in January, if the professors were satisfied.

If in two years' time Christopher had found some opening he would have nothing against the marriage if Esther still wanted to marry him. But she was not to consider herself bound in any way. She was to be free.

All this was explained to Christopher, who accepted the situation.

He asked whether he might write to Esther. This was allowed. But he was not to expect daily letters from her. It would interfere with her work. She could write to him when she had time.

"But I may always send him postcards?" said Esther.

"Postcards?" said her father. "Well, *picture* postcards, they do not take up much time."

Esther and Christopher bade each other good-bye, and Esther promised she would write every day, even if it were only a picture postcard.

Macbride said good-bye to Christopher in the most friendly manner, but his last words were:

"You must remember there is to be no formal engagement; and if, in the course of the next year or sooner, if at any moment Esther wishes to change her mind, she is not to feel in the slightest way bound. There must be no question of anyone saying she has *behaved badly*."

Christopher said he understood.

"She shall be as free as air," he said.

"You see, my dear boy," Macbride said, "you must understand my being selfish about Esther. It is not of myself I am thinking but of her. I consider that she has a career before her, and I will not let anything interfere with that. I will fight for her, for her career, like a tiger, and we are just approaching the critical moment for her. Her start is imminent, and I cannot have anything interfering with that: her whole career is at stake."

"But I wouldn't interfere with her career for a moment," said Christopher. "I want to help her with her career as much as I possibly can."

They all went to see Christopher off at the station.

Lady Macbride wept, and Miss Shipley said:

"There is nothing so heart-rending as a railway station, except perhaps old dance music found in a drawer."

When Christopher arrived at Westleigh, he told Sir Joseph what had happened.

Sir Joseph listened to the whole story, and then said:

"Macbride has behaved with sense. His daughter is too young to think of marrying at present. She is not yet eighteen. Let her finish her studies and start her career, and in the meantime we will look round and see if we can't find something for you."

Christopher, in spite of the sadness of parting with Esther, was happy. He was in another world.

He wrote to Sackbut and to Yakovlev and told them what had happened.

Sackbut answered, "Don't let this interfere with your studies either. If you make a name for yourself as an orientalist, well and good; we will get you a place at the British Museum, and you will be able to marry. You must work, work, work."

Yakovlev wrote in another strain:

"Your news," he said, "has been no surprise to me. I thought that something might happen when I met Miss Macbride at Christmas. I congratulate you both, but I agree with what her father says. I think that she is too young to marry. I am not against young marriages in general, but she has not developed yet, and there is much, oh! so much, to develop. In a year's time she may not want to marry at all, or she may – you won't be angry at my saying this – want to marry someone else. She is much younger than you are in a sense. She has not *bitten* anything yet in life. There is all the difference in this world between seventeen and eighteen for a woman. But I hope for your sake that all will be well."

Lady Claydon was sympathetic, and so was Anne. She was now coming out: and was ready for her first season.

She had grown up into a handsome girl.

Esther kept her promise about the postcards, and sometimes she wrote long letters. She was working hard, and they were satisfied with her. Her studies would be finished by Christmas, and she would appear in January. She would not come home for Christmas as she did not want to make a break in her work. The Macbrides settled to go to Leipzig for her first appearance. Christopher was to go with them. All through the autumn Esther wrote to Christopher regularly. He received something – either a postcard or a note every day, and at least once a week a letter. She was, she said, working hard. In one of her letters she said: "*I have met an old Cambridge friend of yours, called Lawless. He is the brother of one of my fellow pupils. He is in the Army and is just back from South Africa where he was wounded. He is working at German because he wants to pass into the Staff College. He is going to learn Russian, too. He is musical, and it is a comfort to find someone who can talk English and not merely speak it.*"

When Christopher read this he was jealous. He told himself it was absurd, but he could not help it.

In her next letter, Esther did not mention Lawless, but a few days later, she wrote: "*We all went to the Opera last night,* FIDELIO – " then there followed a string of German names, "*and Mr Lawless – it was great fun. We all had supper together afterwards.*"

Christopher remembered the dinner at Suckling's when he had met Lawless for the first time, and how he had taken a dislike to him. They had met several times later, but had never exchanged more than a few words.

A week later, Esther mentioned him again. Christopher made no comment on these mentions. As Christmas drew nearer her letters became shorter. She was working hard for her first appearance and she said she felt almost too nervous to write. She said nothing more about Lawless. Just before Christmas when Christopher was preparing to start for Germany he caught measles and was three weeks in bed. When he was convalescent he had an attack of bronchial pneumonia. It was no longer possible for him to think of going to Germany. Esther's first appearance came off at the end of January and was a success. She was well received, and even the Press, which was not inclined to favour a woman, and an Englishwoman, and was anti-English owing to the Boer War, grudgingly admitted that her performance was creditable. Christopher, who had been sent to Brighton to get well, received telegrams from Macbride and from Esther telling him of her success. He was back at his work by the time Parliament opened. Esther's parents came back to London directly after the concert. Sir Francis had to be at the College of Music. Esther stayed on to play in another concert in Vienna some weeks later. She was to come back to England at Easter for good. There was the possibility of her giving a recital in London in the summer. Sir Joseph Claydon asked the Macbrides to stay with them for Easter.

A few days after the Claydons and Christopher had arrived at Westleigh, and the night before the Macbrides were expected, Christopher was sitting alone in the library. Sir Joseph was reading a report in his study and Lady Claydon and Anne were busy cutting out some clothes which they were making for a bazaar.

Christopher was browsing idly among the books when he chanced to fall on a small MS volume bound in calf, which he had never noticed before. It was called "The Memoirs of Sister Mary Agatha." The book, dated 1830, was retrospective. It went back to the days of Dr Johnson.

It was written in a clear flowing bold handwriting. Christopher began to read it.

The authoress declared at the beginning of her narrative that she intended to tell the story of her life in order that others might possibly derive profit and edification from the record of the vicissitudes and trials she had suffered and the peace she had ultimately found.

She was the daughter, she wrote, of an Irish squire, "tall and well-shaped," and she had run away from her home to go upon the stage.

There followed the record of early struggles, failures and want: of her first successes; her early marriage to an actor; and how at last she achieved a position on the stage, and become a favourite of the public. She was not, she was careful to explain, a great actress, nor famous, but she had sprightliness and wit and had charmed the public in Comedy.

Christopher skimmed through the book rapidly, reading a passage here and there. Her first appearance and her first success interested him as it made him think of Esther. He skipped the record of various vicissitudes in stage-land, and out of it, and then his eye was suddenly arrested by a chapter entitled "The Coat without Seam."

"I was at that time (the chapter began) *a lover of gaiety and seldom missed an opportunity of satisfying my love of pleasure and vanity. Harry and I at this time were both of us playing in the same comedy. My husband had a good part, and had taken the fancy of the town. I had a small part. We had lodgings in St Martin's Lane.* All for Love *was to be revived at Drury Lane and Harry was in eager expectation of being cast for the part of Antony.*

"Both Harry and I had arrived at the critical moment of our stage career. Harry seemed in a fair way to achieve substantial success, had it not been for his unfortunate occasional propensity to the bottle and the gaming table. In both of which vices he was wont to indulge too freely when fortunes and funds were low; but he had not at that time become either a drunkard or a gamester.

"*It was at this most critical moment in our careers that I met Sir Horace Beaufort. He first caught sight of me as I was standing at my window and he was driving by in his coach. He came to Drury Lane Play-House that night and sent me a missive bidding me to the Assembly. I was loth to go and asked Harry to take me home. But Harry that night had promised, so he said, to sup with some old school-fellows who had been present at the performance. I went to the Assembly and Sir Horace was there, the cynosure of all eyes with his velvet coat cut in the French fashion and embroidered with gold, and his waistcoat of cloth of silver.*

"*He advanced to me with a low bow and begged the honour of dancing with me, an honour which I immediately granted with a low curtsey. I danced with him all night.*

"*On the following afternoon he waited upon me, and made his addresses with the utmost vehemence, but I repulsed him and referred him to Harry. He laughed at me and said I was a fool to waste my youth and my beauty on a drunkard and a profligate. Sir Horace expended a wealth of eloquence and passion and appealed to my vanity and my greed. He protested that he could not live another hour without me, and he offered me a house in London, a house at Richmond; jewels, brocades, lace, finery, and an equipage. I told him that I had no desire to become a lady of the town and that I loved my husband in spite of his faults. He vowed that I should become not a lady of the town, but the lady of the town; that I was born to be a Queen, and that he would furnish the kingdom. I protested that my kingdom was on the boards and that when the lights were snuffed and the applause was silent I must go back to my humble lodging, and study. Otherwise, I should lose my crown and forfeit my kingdom. I cut short the interview, but he entreated me not to let him despair, and as he took leave of me, I bade him farewell with a laugh and a smile. I was in two minds; for dancing with him at the Assembly I had enjoyed the highest pleasure I had as yet experienced.*

"The next morning I received from him an impassioned letter, in which he called me 'most divine and adorable creature,' and poured out the desire of his heart. For a week I would not see him, although he came nightly to the playhouse, and every day I received an impassioned letter. During these days Harry was moody and sullen, chiefly, I thought, because his fate was in the balance and he was afraid of an adverse turn of affairs.

"At last I received a letter from Sir Horace in which he protested that if I would not listen to his suit he had determined to take his life, and although I knew full well that such protestations are the small change of the profligate and the smarts, I knew that there was something about me which had taken possession of his being and which for the moment held him as the hook holds a fish. I was informed on credible authority, that he had no eyes for any of the reigning beauties. I wrote to him and said that I would be the next morning in the sale room in King's Street, for I was anxious to purchase a certain piece of French brocade, which was to be sold by auction and which I had set my heart upon. I intended to wear it in the next comedy.

"I went to the sale room early, and I found Sir Horace awaiting me with impatience. The effects for sale were the property of a French nobleman who had been ruined in the Variations, and consisted of pictures, finery, silks, stuffs, snuff-boxes and knick-knacks.

"Sir Horace pressed his suit more vehemently than ever before. He repeated that he would die if I would not consent to become his mistress, and he attempted to dazzle me with the brilliant prospects he offered; and indeed the pallor of his countenance and his dejected looks and distracted behaviour all lent colour to the sincerity and the vehemence of his feelings.

"The dealers and bidders began to arrive and I vowed to

give him his final answer before the sale was ended. I was still in two minds; on the one hand there was the prospect of wealth, ease, luxury, finery; and love, ardent and sincere, even if it proved to be fleeting; on the other hand there was Harry, full of failings, it is true, not over-faithful, prone to drink and to gaming, but affectionate, and after all my first love, and the sharer of my early struggles and trials, and whom, in spite of all, I loved, and to whom I owed duty. There were also the precepts of my religion which I had not altogether forgotten, although I practised them so seldom and so ill.

"I should, I knew, be committing a mortal sin, but so headstrong, and so frivolous was I at this time, that such considerations weighed but lightly upon me. I thought too of Sir Horace, and I could not deny that I returned his passion.

"Our conversation was interrupted by the sudden entry of Harry, who appeared on the scene just as the auction was beginning, in a state of joyful agitation. He told me that he had great news, and that he had been cast for the part of Antony in the revival of All for Love. *I congratulated him and inquired who was to play the part of Cleopatra. He was abashed and murmured the name of Mrs Bradshaw, but I laughed at him, knowing she was too old. Then he mentioned Mrs Green, who was at that time at the height of her fame, and as he did so the demon of jealousy and envy entered into my soul. I expressed my displeasure and vowed that this woman was bent on my discomfiture. And when Harry admitted that it was true he was to play Antony to her Cleopatra, I exclaimed that I had always known of his treachery and her wiles, and that she had filched my part and stolen my husband; that he loved her with a guilty passion. I paid no attention to his protestations, which were now silenced, as the auction had begun and Harry had left the*

auction room. All this while Sir Horace remained on the other side of the room examining the pictures, and feigning indifference.   Harry   knew   nothing   of   our   closer acquaintanceship.

"The first lots offered for sale were relics of the French Royal Family: a copy book that had belonged to the late Dauphin, which was knocked down to a French Abbé who was there, bent and shabby and covered with snuff. Other lots followed, and among them the piece of silver brocade on which I had set my heart. This was bid for and bought for the price of twenty guineas by Sir Horace. He looked at me as it was knocked down to him, and smiled.

"Then a garment was put up for auction. It was faded and reddish brown in colour, and so old and so frail that it looked as if it might crumble away. The auctioneer said it was of peculiar interest. It was the property of the same French nobleman, and was said to have been brought from the Holy Land to Germany and from Germany to France. It had been in the family of the late owner since the year 1526, and had escaped destruction by the merest chance, when the mansion of the late owner had been destroyed during the excesses of the Jacobins. It had always been venerated as a relic of the greatest antiquity, and there was a legend, the auctioneer smiled as he said this, which some of the pious believed, that this piece of stuff was the identical Coat without Seam which was taken from Our Saviour by the Roman soldiers after the Crucifixion, and for which they had cast lots.

" 'Even if we cannot quite credit this tale,' the auctioneer said with a smile, 'there is no doubt of its extreme antiquity.'

"The bidding began and the Abbé bid five pounds; another bidder at once made it guineas, and the bidding went up by degrees to two hundred pounds. At that moment the Abbé withdrew disappointed from the contest, but he remained in

the auction room. When the bidder said two hundred pounds and the Abbé *was silent, another bidder entered the fray, and nodded, and the bidding between these two went up step by step to the great sum of three thousand pounds. At this sum the bidding ceased. At the very moment when the auctioneer said, 'Three thousand pounds, any more bids, any more bids, please?' I had resolved in my heart that I would leave Harry and become the mistress of Sir Horace. He was standing opposite me near the auctioneer on the other side of the green baize table. I looked at Sir Horace and I nodded. And the auctioneer took my nod for a bid and said, 'Three thousand guineas, any more bids?' There were no more bids, and the piece of stuff was knocked down to me.*

"When the auction was over, I went up to Sir Horace and told him that I had bought the piece of red fabric for the price of three thousand guineas and that I had not a penny to pay for it. He said he would pay it gladly, and asked me what I purposed doing with it. I said I needed it as a present, as he would see, and I walked up to the Abbé, and with a low curtsey I presented him with the Coat, and the Abbé knelt down and kissed my hand, and thanked me for it with tears.

"Then Sir Horace said to me: 'So tonight?'

"And I said, 'No, Sir, not tonight, and never.' But he protested, 'You nodded me your consent, and the auctioneer thought you were bidding. I understood your glance.'

"I told him this was true. I had indeed meant to nod my consent, and the auctioneer had indeed thought I was bidding. I had no intention of buying the Coat. I had meant to leave my husband and become his mistress.

" 'Well, what then?' asked Sir Horace.

" 'Instead of which,' I retorted, 'I purchased a piece of stuff, and changed my mind. Farewell, Sir, and for ever.'

"I never saw Sir Horace again and... "

At that moment Sir Joseph entered the library.

"I forgot to tell you, Christopher," he said, "that there are some young folk coming tomorrow, friends of Anne's. A girl called Jane Ellis, and two young men: Stockton's boy and a friend of his, who is in the same regiment, called Lawless."

CHAPTER XIX

The next day the Macbrides and Anne's young friends arrived by the same train. Christopher was troubled and gloomy before their arrival. The news of the arrival of Lawless displeased him, although he admitted to himself that his displeasure was unreasonable; Lawless was, so Lady Claydon had told him, a friend of Anne's; young Stockton was thought to be fond of Jane Ellis, who was Anne's best friend. But there was the coincidence of once more coming across that story.

Christopher said to himself that he knew this was only a coincidence, but every time that coincidence had happened before, it had meant trouble. This was the fourth time. What could it portend? He wondered whether the old Curé at Vernay was alive, and what he would think of it.

"I must find out, and if he is still alive I will translate the story into French and send it him as a Christmas present," he said to himself. The guests arrived late, in time for dinner.

Christopher did not think that Esther was greatly altered. She was a little more formed, and still more beautiful, he thought; more grave, more serious, and there was something a little foreign about her. At dinner Esther sat between Christopher and Lawless. On Christopher's other side was Lady Macbride. She was full of Leipzig and the concerts and Esther's success.

"Oh! it was so beautiful," she said; "we missed you so much.

It was better than anything we had expected, and they gave her flowers and laurel wreaths with ribbons. Professor Krause, her teacher, you know, was delighted, and he has hardly ever been known to praise; and to think of you lying at home with measles, it was horrible! Francis was so unhappy about it. He said you would have enjoyed the music."

It was not until the middle of dinner that Christopher was able to talk to Esther. He had thousands of things he wanted to say to her. When the opportunity did come, he said:

"How did you come back, by Flushing or the Hook of Holland?"

"The Hook."

"It is more comfortable, isn't it?"

"They say so, but I like the other way better."

"Did you have a smooth crossing?"

"No, it was awful. I think it always is awful. And poor father was fearfully ill. He lost his portfolio, too, and all his scores. I don't know what we should have done without Mr Lawless."

"Did he come with you?"

"Yes. He wasn't there – not at Leipzig, I mean, for the concert. He came out to fetch his sister, who was coming home too."

There was a pause. Then Esther said:

"Are you really quite well now?"

"Yes, quite well."

There was another pause.

After a time Christopher said:

"I wish I could have been there."

"Yes, it was a shame, but you didn't miss much. I played badly at the first concert. The second was better. What have you been doing all this time?"

"I thought I had kept you well informed of my doings."

"You never said much about what you were doing."

"You never asked."

"I have had so little time to write lately. I had to write in such a hurry I never had time to think what I was writing, but I wrote to you very often."

"Not so often, lately."

"That was because of the concerts, and then father and mother being there."

There was a pause.

Christopher wanted to ask her whether she was glad to see him.

"You see it was terrible," she said; and she told him of what her life had been like lately: the second concert, the rehearsals, the panic beforehand, the relief afterwards.

"But I mustn't talk of all that; nothing is so boring as travellers' tales."

"Travellers' tales?"

"And music shop. Doesn't Anne look pretty now she is out? She is becoming a beauty."

Lady Macbride then asked him a question, and the conversation became general.

And then Esther talked to Lawless.

While Christopher talked to Lady Macbride, he caught every now and then fragments of what Esther and Lawless were saying. They laughed a great deal. They were sharing reminiscences.

"Do you remember that evening?" "Do you remember that day?" "Do you remember what Fräulein X — said, and what the Professor did, and that night at the *Wienergarten*?... The opera... "

"Yes, wasn't she wonderful!... What a performance... I like the third Act best of all – *Fritzi... Erich... Lottchen... Fräulein Salbe*...that *cor anglais* passage... *Kuvernal*"...names... fragments of intimacy, of a new intimacy kept on coming up... fragments of experiences, pleasures, mishaps, and jokes shared...jokes he could not understand and allusions that escaped him.

There was no pause in their conversation.

Later on, Esther turned to him again, leaving Lawless to talk to Lady Claydon.

"How is your book getting on?" she asked.

"What book?"

"I thought you were writing a book on some sort of Turkish things."

"My Persian translations?"

"I meant Persian."

"I haven't begun it. I was ill and that interrupted everything, and then I was busy in London."

There was another pause and Christopher felt it was impossible to open the door which would lead at once to the old intimacy.

"You won't go back again to Germany now?" he said at last.

"Oh no; I am here for good."

Lady Claydon made a sign, and the men were left to themselves. Lawless was asked to move up between Sir Joseph and Christopher.

"We haven't met since Cambridge," Lawless said to Christopher.

"It seems a long time ago now."

Christopher felt his old shyness and dislike for Lawless rising in him, but he said to himself that he must not show it, it was ridiculous.

"Yes, it is a long time."

"And since then you have done a lot. You passed all sorts of exams?"

"Yes, and then I got the sack from the Public Service."

"Oh!" said Lawless, uncomfortably. He was vaguely aware of Christopher's history. He turned red and said: "I thought you had written something that everyone praised tremendously."

"It was for that I got the sack."

Lawless felt he had made things worse.

"What a jolly house this is!" he said.

Then Sir Joseph interrupted their conversation by urging them to have some more Burgundy.

After dinner, the older people played bridge and the younger people played poker, but Christopher refused to play. He said he liked looking on.

Esther was asked to play the pianoforte, but she said she was too tired.

The next morning the young people went out riding, except Christopher, who was working, and Esther, who was going to practise.

Christopher settled down to his work for Sir Joseph. He wrote and answered letters for him daily, and indeed Sir Joseph gave him his letters, hardly indicating what he wanted said, and he was invariably satisfied with the way in which Christopher dealt with them. When he had got through his work he thought he might at last have a chance of talking to Esther alone. He went to the gallery, expecting to hear the noise of arpeggios. When he got there he found Lady Macbride by herself.

Christopher asked where Esther was.

"They have come back from riding," said Lady Macbride, "and they have taken Esther up to the tennis court."

Christopher walked up to the tennis court. When he got there he found Stockton playing Anne and Miss Ellis, and Esther and Lawless sitting in the gallery. Esther did not play.

"Come and watch them," Esther said to him.

"I can't stay," said Christopher, "I've got some letters to finish for Sir Joseph."

He went back to the house. He was possessed by jealousy. All his vague fears and doubts had become definite. He had been blind. He ought to have seen that Esther was now different the moment he had set eyes on her. It was clear that she no longer loved him, and that she loved Lawless. Well, she would be able to marry him without difficulty. He had prospects.

At luncheon he avoided sitting next to Esther. After luncheon it rained, and it was settled that they should play tennis in the court: Lawless, Stockton, Miss Ellis and Anne made a four.

Esther said she would look on, but after luncheon she asked

Christopher whether he was not coming up to the tennis court.

Christopher said icily that he was sorry, he had too much to do.

"Oh! do come," she said. "You have been working all the morning, and I haven't had a word with you yet."

"No, you have been better employed."

"It's not kind of you to say that," Esther said, with tears in her eyes.

"Do you want me to come?"

"Yes, of course I do."

"Very well," his heart melted, "I will."

When they started, Esther and Christopher lagged a little behind the others.

"Why are you so beastly to me?" Christopher said.

"I'm not," she said, "it is you who are being unkind. Look, Christopher, you must be reasonable. Before we came here, before mother accepted the invitation, father had a long talk with me and said that if I came here it was on the understanding that there was no definite engagement between us, and we were not to behave like an engaged couple. Otherwise he would not come. Then he repeated what he has said before a thousand times, that when I am properly started, if you can come to him with some definite prospects, so that we could have enough to live on between us, he would have nothing against our being married. But he won't hear of anything happening for two years; and till then, he said, we must behave to each other like ordinary friends. If we can't do that, he said, then we must not see each other at all, or write, so I do entreat you to be sensible, or you will spoil everything."

"I understand that, but you have been treating me as less, well, than an ordinary friend, and others as more than ordinary friends."

"What others?"

"Lawless."

"What nonsense!" she said, turning crimson.

"It's no use deceiving me, Esther, you are changed. I felt it directly, last night at dinner. You have forgotten. You are different. You are tired of me. Bored with me."

"Oh! don't talk like that, please."

"Of course, I know, I'm nothing at all."

"Oh don't, don't, please, please."

"But it's true; you're different when you are with him. Everyone notices it."

"How can you be so silly?"

"Well, you can't deny that he's in love with you. Madly in love. There's no doubt about that."

"How can you say such things?" She turned crimson again.

"He can't look at anyone else…and then the way he looks at you. His face lights up when you come into the room. He scrambles over the furniture to talk to you."

"But you don't understand; it's all different."

"I know it's all different. That's just what I'm saying."

"I didn't mean that. I meant that I, that we… "

"Oh! what's the use of going on like that, Esther? You know that it's all over. I know, of course, I can't compete with him. I'm nothing but a dependant. He's well off. He's good-looking."

"Oh, Christopher don't, please, please."

She began to sob.

They had reached the tennis court.

When they went into the little dressing room downstairs where the shoes were kept, Esther said:

"Leave me alone for a moment. I will come up presently."

She was still crying.

"I'll wait," Christopher said.

"No," she said, and she beckoned him away.

He went up to the gallery by himself and looked on at the game for about ten minutes in silence.

He was joined by Lady Claydon and the Macbrides and Esther. She had regained her composure, and was talking naturally, even gaily.

Christopher stayed a little while and then went home. He went to the library, but he could not work. He walked round and round the room, smoking cigarettes.

Had he been a fool? Was it all nonsense? Then various pictures and incidents rose in his mind. Esther's expression when she was talking to Lawless at breakfast that morning; their jokes at dinner; the way he looked at her...all they did not say. But perhaps he was to blame; perhaps it was his fault. He must try to be more self-controlled. He was behaving foolishly. If he was not careful he would himself create the situation he most feared.

He would try and do better.

They met again at tea. Lawless was in the highest spirits, so was Miss Jane Ellis. She was a radiant, fair creature, with fair, laughing, insolent eyes, half American. She chaffed Christopher.

"What have you been doing?" she said, "mooning away in that stuffy old library. Sir Joseph told us you had nothing to do. Why didn't you come and play with us? We had some grand fun. Anne and I beat the two men in one set. Tomorrow we must make Esther play."

Christopher was not next to Esther at dinner that night, but between Anne and Lady Claydon. Esther sat between Sir Joseph and Lawless, and Christopher watched them carefully.

Esther talked to Sir Joseph, nearly all through dinner, and Lawless talked attentively to his neighbour, Anne. But towards the end of dinner, Sir Joseph turned to Lady Macbride, and then Esther and Lawless seemed to open a sluice of conversation, which lasted till the end of dinner. Esther was talking to him with ease, and his laugh kept on ringing through the room, and his blue eyes were full of a blinding gaiety.

"I wonder why I can't laugh like that?" thought Christopher.

After dinner there were charades. Christopher refused to act. He said he preferred to be in the audience. They did not press him.

Lawless turned out to be a good actor. Esther and he played the part of two Germans. Macbride was convulsed with laughter; so were Sir Joseph and Lady Claydon. "Lawless is playing for Esther," thought Christopher.

Jane acted well too.

When it was all over and they were going to bed Esther said good-night to him and smiled sadly, as much as to say: "I haven't hurt you, have I? At any rate it's all right now." Then she went upstairs with her mother. The men had gone into the smoking-room. Christopher had no wish to join them. He took a book and went upstairs. He passed Anne and Jane Ellis who were gossiping on the staircase.

"It's a pity you didn't act, Mr Trevenen," said Anne. "I am quite sure you can act."

"Oh!" said Jane, with a laugh, "he's sore because Bruce Lawless has grabbed his girl."

Unconsciously she had hit the bull's eye.

Christopher went to his room, but not to bed. He sat up writing Esther a letter. He wrote till far into the night, and poured out the bitterness of his soul on paper. It was past two when he finished the letter. It was a bitter letter and a wild letter. A letter of unbridled recrimination, savage accusation, and blind anger. The letter of someone who has been caught like an animal in a trap, and, mad with pain, bites savagely and at random. He recorded in detail every incident of the last two days, and scheduled a whole list of unintended and baseless grievances. He noted and misconstrued what she had said and what she had left unsaid. He harped on every little harmless thing he had heard her say to Lawless, and found a fantastic meaning and intention in everything she had done and left undone. He went back on her letters and the lack of them. He racked up incidents she had referred to, and others of which he had been kept in ignorance. He accused Esther of fickleness, heartlessness, and self-centredness. He accused her of being intoxicated by the ambitious egotism of the professional artist, and at the same time of being worldly and snobbish, and ruthlessly vain. His accusations contradicted one another. Finally, he went back upon the past and all the happy hours they had spent at Merrydown. She had, of course, forgotten all that. He told her how everyone had noticed the changed situation, and that Jane Ellis had made him a public butt on account of it. "It is all over," he ended, "nothing can ever be as it was before. You had better cut me out of your life and forget that you have ever known me."

Then he went to bed, but not to sleep. Do what he would, Jane Ellis's words kept ringing in his head. "He's sore because Bruce Lawless has grabbed his girl." It wasn't true. It couldn't be true. Lawless might want to, but Esther loved him, and him only.

The next morning, when he came down to early breakfast, he found a letter from Yakovlev, from Cambridge, telling him that Sackbut was seriously ill. He had had an operation which was successful, but the doctors feared for his heart. He was weak but conscious, and had asked for Christopher several times. "I think," wrote Yakovlev, "that he would like to see you, only if you do come, come at once, or else it will be too late."

When Christopher went to Sir Joseph after breakfast, after they had gone through his correspondence, and Sir Joseph had given him a few brief instructions, Christopher told him about Sackbut, and said he would like to go to Cambridge.

"Of course, you must go," said Joseph, "I shan't be wanting you. You can go and stay there as long as you like. I shan't want you till after the holidays, not till we go back to London, on Monday week, but come back whenever you like. You had better go this morning and get down to Cambridge this afternoon. You had better go by the eleven o'clock train. You will just have time. Can you manage that?"

Christopher said he could manage that easily. It wouldn't take him a moment to pack.

Sir Joseph rang the bell and ordered the electric brougham to take Christopher to the station.

Christopher went up to pack. His letter to Esther was in his pocket. But now he was going away he felt he could not leave it behind him. He would see her, and tell her he was going.

When he had finished packing and rung for the servant, he went downstairs and met Lady Macbride in the sitting room. He asked where Esther was.

"She is practising in the gallery," said Lady Macbride. "Don't disturb her please."

"I'm going away to Cambridge, a friend of mine is ill. Do you think I could say good-bye?"

"Oh! I'm so sorry! By all means go and say good-bye, but don't keep her long."

Christopher went towards the gallery. He heard the sound of a few chords being played, but the music stopped before he reached the door.

He opened the door noiselessly. Esther was sitting at the pianoforte; but she was not playing, and she was not facing the music-desk, but someone with whom she was engaged in conversation. It was Lawless, who was sitting on a chair next to the pianoforte, bending towards her. They were absorbed in talk, and they did not notice him open the door. Christopher shut the door and went. They must have heard this, because she at once began to play a feverish run.

The electric brougham was at the door.

Christopher left his letter for Esther on the table.

CHAPTER XX

When Christopher arrived at Cambridge he went straight to Yakovlev's rooms who said he would put him up. Sackbut, he said, was better. Yakovlev at once noticed that something had happened to Christopher and he thought that the news of Sackbut's illness was not enough to account for it, but he asked him no questions and Christopher made him no confidences. The next morning (which was Good Friday) he went to see Sackbut. He found him in bed looking wasted and waxen, propped up on pillows, as if the veil of flesh between life and death had worn thin. The nurse said he must not stay long.

Sackbut looked at him and smiled and pointed to a large pile of typewritten MS which was on a chair near the bed.

"That is," he said, "my Persian book, all that is written of it; the notes and the rough plan."

"Oh! it's not finished?" said Christopher.

"No, but I'm finished. I want you to finish it, you are the only person who can finish it. It has taken me all my life to begin it. It won't interest more than a dozen people – not as many – but that does not matter."

He paused. This speech had tired him. And then he said: "I want you to try."

"I couldn't do it," said Christopher.

"These things are only sand-castles," said Sackbut, "but it is our duty to build them if we can, otherwise we have no right to encumber the beach. Remember that life is a compromise, and we must live, and let live, and the only way people like you can *let* live, is to work. I want you to write that book. To finish it. I can't talk any more. Good-bye. This, as they say, is my last request."

He pressed Christopher's hand.

The next day Sackbut was not well enough to see anyone. Christopher received no news from Westleigh. Sackbut got weaker and was unable to see anyone again. He had no relations alive, and his Cambridge friends were away. He drifted slowly and gently to death and died on Easter Tuesday, peacefully, from heart failure.

Christopher stayed at Cambridge until the funeral, which was on the following Saturday, and attended by representatives of various learned bodies. Sackbut left everything he had to Christopher. It was not much; but Christopher reflected bitterly that with what he was earning at present he would have had enough money, with what she had, to marry Esther. He made up his mind to leave Sir Joseph at once, and he wrote to him telling him so, saying that he had been left enough money to be able to live independently, and that he wished to devote himself to journalism: he would like to go away as soon as it was convenient. He stayed at Cambridge till the following Monday and then joined the Claydons in London. On the day he arrived in London, before he saw Sir Joseph, he went to see the editor of the *Daily Messenger* whom he knew and who had hitherto taken his articles, and asked him to take him on his staff in any capacity. The *Messenger* badly needed a correspondent for St Petersburg at that moment; someone who knew French and, if possible, Russian. Christopher was the very man. The editor could not give him an immediate answer. He would have, he said, to consult the owner, but he held out hopes. Christopher found no letter from Esther and did not expect one. He dined alone with the Claydons, and neither Sir Joseph nor Lady

Claydon seemed to be aware that anything had happened between him and Esther. If they were aware of it, they did not show it. They talked of the Macbrides, who had gone back to London on Easter Tuesday.

When Christopher was left alone with Sir Joseph, after dinner, Sir Joseph went straight to the point.

"I'm delighted to hear you've been left some money," he said, "but why should you go? Won't this windfall facilitate your marriage? Mind you, I could keep you on as a secretary; you wouldn't have to live here, unless you liked, but I should be delighted for you and your wife to live at Westleigh in the summer as much as you liked, and in London you could just come to me in the day time."

"It would have facilitated things," said Christopher, "and it is kind of you to make me such a generous offer, but there is now no question of my being married."

"Oh!" said Sir Joseph, "of course you know your own business, but I shouldn't do anything in a hurry. As far as I am concerned you can go when you like. I shan't want you to wait till I get someone else, because I shan't get anyone else unless I find someone later who could be as good as or better than you for my purpose, which is not likely. I mean I shall just let Miss Taylor deal with the correspondence and let the library take care of itself. As for what you used to do for me I can't get anyone to do that, unless I find a duplicate of yourself, which, as I said, is damned improbable. Of course I am sorry to lose you. And not only selfishly sorry; however, as I say, I shouldn't be in a hurry. You haven't been offered a definite job yet by that newspaper?"

"No, not definitely."

"Well at any rate, you had better stay till that is settled, and when they offer you something definite you can go."

"That is very kind of you," said Christopher.

A few days later he had an interview with the owner of the *Daily Messenger*, who offered him the post of Correspondent at St Petersburg at a reasonable salary. He accepted it. He was to go out as soon as he could.

Christopher at once told Sir Joseph.

After asking him a few practical questions, he said:

"You know what I think. I should like you to stay and I think you would be wiser to stay, but I repeat that I suppose you know your own business best and now that you are going you had better go as soon as you can. I know it's no good pressing you to stay."

"I'm afraid not," said Christopher, "I know I must seem ungrateful and I am sorry."

"Ungrateful! Fiddlesticks, a man must manage his life his own way. I was only thinking of your future. I shall be sorry to lose you, I shall miss you and so shall we all."

Christopher settled to leave London for good the following week.

When he said good-bye to Lady Claydon she asked him whether he was sure he was not making a mistake. Christopher was uncertain whether she was alluding in a covert way to Esther, and he said, "No, I'm not making a mistake."

"We will all miss you very much and you must let us know what happens to you."

"I will."

Lady Claydon gave him letters of introduction to friends and relations of hers. So did Yakovlev. She and Anne saw him off at the station.

"Remember if things go wrong, you can always come back to us," Lady Claydon said to him, "I don't think you will find anyone else in the library."

"Sir Joseph will probably find someone who is more capable than I am," he said.

"Don't forget," said Anne, "to send us a postcard every now and then."

"I won't."

They waved at him as the train left, and Lady Claydon made

the sign of the Cross.

There was deep snow on the ground when Christopher arrived in St Petersburg. He went to the Hôtel de France and he lived there for the first three weeks, and then he moved into the apartment of a Russian lady who took in lodgers and English pupils, and to whom he was recommended by one of the other correspondents. Her name was Elena Dimitrevna Klauer. She lived on the top floor of a large house in a street between the Nevsky Prospect and the Nikolaev station. Christopher settled down there to a life of comfortable discomfort. Elena Dimitrevna was middle-aged, short, and small, the widow of a minor official who had got into trouble for his political opinions. He was half German; she was entirely Russian, but had been brought up in Paris and Germany, and had at one time been a fine musician. She was cultivated and had worked all her life quietly and cautiously for the Liberal cause. She was a Liberal and a dogmatic free-thinker. Her ideals, which were in reality revolutionary, and her anti-religious principles, which were on paper nihilistic, were tempered by common sense. She was an admirable teacher and a good housekeeper. She bustled about the house and did her work with precision and energy. She had grey hair and soft grey eyes and she was always dressed in black. She was fond of English people but found them, as a rule, politically invincibly ignorant.

Her niece Olga was a musician and cared nothing for politics. She was gay and full of life. She hoped to be a professional pianist.

To the outward eye nothing could have seemed more uncomfortable. Christopher had no sitting room and his bedroom was warmed by a lukewarm stove. There were two small living rooms in Elena Dimitrevna's flat; a sitting room proper which contained a grand pianoforte, a palm tree, and a photograph of a man playing a violin duet with a pianoforte player, to a group of listeners on a sofa, called "Beethoven," and a dining room where the samovar was nearly always on the

American-cloth-clad table and where everyone sat and smoked. There were double windows and layers of cotton wool between the panes. The house was always full of people.

Elena Dimitrevna and her niece both gave lessons in Russian to pupils. At present she had one, an Englishman, who was working for the Staff College. Christopher saw little of him because he spent most of the day working.

The household consisted of the niece Olga, a young girl with bright brown eyes and tousled hair, and two girl students: one of them, Sofie, who was dark and languid and studying for the stage, and the other, Kitty, who was alert and red-haired and working to be a professional violinist. There was a schoolboy, Misha, who played the flute. There was a constant noise of music in the house: violin, pianoforte and flute, and scales and trills went on from morning to night. Elena Dimitrevna seemed to be unaware of it.

Christopher used to get up late and drink coffee in the dining room about half-past nine. Then he would do any writing he had to do and stroll towards half-past twelve and go to the Hôtel de France, where he met other correspondents, read the newspapers, and garnered the news of the day.

If there was a dearth of news, or news which needed elucidation or discussion, he would go round to the Ministry of the Interior where he knew one of the officials, or sometimes to the British Embassy. He would go back to the Hôtel de France and have luncheon either with one of the other correspondents, or with a Russian, or sometimes he would go to some other restaurant. Then he would concoct a telegram if there was anything worth sending. After that he would stroll about the streets, pay visits, or shop, and then go home. Supper was at nine. The big meal of the day at Elena Dimitrevna's house was at two o'clock in the afternoon, or later, but Christopher always took that meal in the town. He would do his writing after dinner, if he was writing an article. Then, later, he would go to the dining room where he would be sure to find some of the inmates of the household, and probably some of Elena Dimitrevna's friends. They would drink tea and smoke cigarettes and sit talking late into the night. Sometimes he would go to a Play or to the Opera. He found the work easy and interesting. He wrote a weekly letter and telegraphed any news that seemed to him of importance. He had no wish to make any intimate friends, and he made no use of the letters that Lady Claydon had given to him. Her friends lived in Moscow, but Christopher might easily have gone there. Yakovlev had given him some letters of introduction as well: one of them to a professor of Eastern languages, and the other to a well-known doctor. Christopher went to see these and through them he made the acquaintance of other members of the *Intelligentsia*.

He made friends with one of the secretaries at the British Embassy, a certain Harold Lawrence, and what brought them together, oddly enough, was music. Lawrence was musical, and went to all the concerts, and Christopher sometimes went with him. This was not due to any new musical understanding on his part but simply to the thought of Esther.

The winter went by. Christopher did his work well, and his editor was pleased with him. So were the Russian officials, since he took as Conservative a line as was compatible with the policy of the newspaper. This was not difficult as the *Messenger* was for the moment anti-Jingo, and consequently pro-Russian.

It was one morning in June that the next event of importance happened to him. He was sitting in the hotel downstairs, awaiting the arrival of Lawrence whom he had asked to luncheon and reading his own newspaper, the *Messenger*, when his eye caught the name of Miss Esther Macbride. It was a short article about a pianoforte recital which had been given at the Regent Hall.

It was headed: "Miss Esther Macbride." The article began with a paragraph classing pianists in various categories; those who made you uneasy by their temperamental uncertainty, those in whose hands you felt secure, and those who startled you, and revealed something new. Miss Macbride, according to this critic, in spite of her youth, belonged to the last category.

"Complete serenity ruled her performance of the variations in F minor of Haydn." He caught the words: "faultless phrasing," "well-graded tone." And then "Beethoven's Sonata Opus III."

Was this, he wondered, the sonata which she had played at Westleigh, the sonata her father had said she would play better some day? Christopher wondered whether he had thought she had improved; whether that "some day" had arrived. The critic said that Miss Macbride possessed the classical sense in perfection, and the warmth of temperament that went with it.

But it was in the Chopin Sonata – "the stock piece of beginners" – that had followed, that the critic said that Esther had revealed herself and astounded her audience. Here she had shown something more than distinction. She had proved more than equal to the occasion. The phrases in the right hand in the first movement "had cut like a knife," and this was all the more remarkable in the performance of a beginner of Miss Macbride's sex and youth. The critic ended by saying that she had well deserved the ovation she had received, and that she had proved herself to be "a worthy offspring of her illustrious father."

Remorse came over Christopher as he read this article. He felt that he had been to blame for everything, that he had misjudged Esther and made a hash of the situation. "Perhaps it's not too late to put everything right," he thought, "I will send her a telegram."

Just as he was about to write out a telegram he was interrupted by the arrival of Lawrence.

No sooner had they sat down to luncheon than Christopher felt he must talk about Esther. He asked Lawrence whether he had noticed the account of her concert in the *Messenger*.

"Oh! yes," he said, "and I wished I had been there to hear her. She ought of course, to be good. The daughter of such a father. He is the best composer we have had since Purcell, and I believe she *is* good."

"You have never heard her play?"

"No, I have never heard her play myself. But I was talking the other day to Bielov, the composer. He heard her play at Leipzig and said she had genius. He said it was not only a question of promise, although of course there was any amount of promise, but of accomplishment. He said that what she did now was remarkable and he had never heard an English person, man or woman, play as well. He said she ought to have a great career if she goes on with it."

"Why shouldn't she go on with it?"

"When women artists marry, sometimes it's all up with their career."

"But she isn't married," Christopher said.

"No, but she's engaged."

"Engaged?" Christopher felt the room swimming round him. He did not ask to whom. He felt he knew.

"Yes," Lawrence went on, "engaged to a very nice fellow. It was in yesterday's *Morning Post*. Bruce Lawless. He's in the army."

"Oh! really," said Christopher, with a show of indifference, "then I suppose that may mean an end of her career."

"Not necessarily. They will be well off some day, if not now. He is Lord Wisbeach's heir and will inherit something. Lots of married artists have made successful careers."

"You have never met her?" asked Christopher.

"No, I have never met her. I have met her father and I know Bruce Lawless."

"Is he musical?"

"Yes, musical enough," Lawrence laughed, "it would be a pity if he was too musical."

"I suppose it would."

They talked of other things and Christopher spoke and answered mechanically. When luncheon was over he had no notion what they had discussed.

But Lawrence had talked the whole time and had apparently not noticed Christopher's distraction. A suspicion began to take root in his heart; that there had been a plot on the part of the Claydons.

Christopher went for a walk by himself along the quay.

He absolved Lady Claydon from any complicity in it, "Because," he said to himself, "at least she is not a snob." But had not Sir Joseph at Anne's suggestion asked Lawless to Westleigh?

He had sometimes suspected that Anne looked down upon him. He was sure that she had thought that he was not worthy of Esther. He recalled to mind small details, incidents, and sayings, which seemed to confirm this view.

Sir Joseph had no doubt thought it absurd for him to marry Esther...and yet he had seemed to encourage it...and Sir Joseph was a straightforward man...eminently straightforward. And yet...he had not pressed him to remain. He had accepted his decision at once. He had not argued with him. Supposing his sudden decision had made everything easy for the Claydons? Or was he perhaps being unjust?

The Claydons must have known that Lawless was in love with Esther? They must have known it before they asked Lawless to Westleigh.

Perhaps Sir Joseph knew nothing of the situation before, but once Lawless was at Westleigh he must have known; he and Lady Claydon must have known after he had left for Cambridge; and then, when he said he was going for good, he supposed that it seemed to Sir Joseph the easiest way out of the situation. But, if that were true, how double-faced it was of Sir Joseph to talk to him as he had done...and Sir Joseph was an honourable man. Did people behave like that? Did people seem to be one thing and really prove to be another?

Or did the most honourable people lose all sense of honour and feeling directly money was at stake? Did they put money affairs in one compartment, and everything else in another?

Treachery! treachery!…that was the factor he had never faced. That was – no doubt – what had made Shakespeare so bitter… treachery was there like a snake at the roots of life, and he had never noticed it.

What did it all matter now? What did the cause matter? The result was there, unchangeable, irrevocable, and permanent.

The longer he brooded on the subject, the more firmly convinced he became that Esther's marriage had been engineered by the Claydons, and when, some weeks later, he read an account of Esther's wedding at St Mary's, High Street, Kensington, and that Mr and Mrs Lawless had gone to spend their honeymoon at Sir Joseph's country seat, Westleigh, in Eastfordshire, his resentment against the Claydons was firmly set. He made up his mind never to have anything to do with the Claydons again. The thought of this scheme which he credited the Claydons with, ate into his mind and corroded it like a canker. Just as the thought that he had murdered Mabel had blighted his boyhood, so did the thought that the Claydons had betrayed him blight his manhood. The first disillusionments he had suffered in his life; the abrupt end of the Alex episode, the brief episode with Annette, were as nothing compared with this. They had wounded him. This soured him. It brought his last fort of illusion, dream, and hope to the ground.

He had nothing to set in its place.

CHAPTER XXI

Yakovlev had written to the Daskovs about Christopher, but they were not at St Petersburg that winter. In the summer they went to their country estate, Susieki, and they asked Christopher to stay with them, but he declined the invitation.

In the following winter, at St Petersburg, they asked him to their house, to an evening party. He went; there was music and a *Liedersängerin*, who sang some German songs, and a group of charming, cultivated people. The Daskovs asked him to come any Sunday evening he pleased, but Christopher contented himself with leaving cards, and never went back. Madame Daskov, who was energetic, persistent, but busy, gave him up as a hopeless case.

"He isn't musical," she said, "and my house bores him."

But she remained willing to make friends with him at any moment, had he made a sign.

He stayed a year at St Petersburg without coming home. He contracted no sentimental ties; and he used to argue that the Russians were a people who understood how to keep sentiment out of love affairs. Some of them smiled when he said this. After he had first settled down to his work, he determined, as he could get through with it easily and satisfactorily and still have time for himself, to devote his spare time to his Eastern studies. He had not given up the idea of producing something himself, and he still dreamt of editing and completing Sackbut's book. Sackbut had worked all his life on a book which was to be an exhaustive study of Persian poetry, but as he had told Christopher, when he was dying, he had got no further than what he had called his notes. Sackbut's notes, although exiguous in content, were richer in subject-matter, and more packed with thought than the completed work of other men, and with these notes there was a translation of Hafiz's *Odes*, nearly finished. Sackbut had left behind him the outline and groundwork of just such a book as Christopher had always dreamt of writing himself, and he felt that he would be able to fill in the outline, and write an introduction giving an account of Sackbut's life and personality. But he kept on putting off doing this, and at the end of his first year, he found that besides what he had done for his newspaper, he had frittered his time away, drinking tea and smoking cigarettes with stray acquaintances. He found life in St Petersburg not only easy, but comfortable, and he enjoyed his independence. He scanned the musical news in his newspaper daily, to see if there was any mention of Esther's name, but he never found it, except once, among the births, where in due time after her marriage, he saw that she had given birth to a son, in Halkin Street. She had moved west, he noted. "She has given up her career," he said to himself, and this made him more bitter than ever.

His second year in Russia went by much as the first, except that he went to England for a short time in the spring, to see Brierley, the editor. He did not go near the Claydons.

Lady Claydon sent him a card at Christmas, and at Easter. He acknowledged these with thanks, but never added a word of news, or a friendly question.

In the summer time, Elena Dimitrevna and her household moved to the suburb of Tsarskoe Selo, and Christopher followed them there and went to St Petersburg every day. At Tsarskoe, they led the same kind of life as in St Petersburg, except that the samovar was stationed in a verandah instead of in the dining room.

It was in the summer of the second year he spent in Russia that Christopher received a letter from Lady Claydon telling him that her daughter Anne was engaged to be married to Bertram Wallace, a rising politician, and one of the hopes of the Liberal Party. She asked him to the wedding.

He wrote back as follows:

"Dear Lady Claydon,

"I am delighted to hear your good news, and I hope that your daughter will be happy. It is very kind of you to ask me to the wedding, but I fear it will be impossible for me to get away. I am very glad you are satisfied with what I have been writing.

"Yours sincerely,
"Christopher Trevenen."

When he had written so far, he felt impelled to add a postscript:

"The real reason," (he began his postscript) *"why I do not come is not because I cannot get away – I can get away quite easily – but because it is altogether too painful for me to see your daughter or any member of your family.*

"Surely you must understand this, by now.

"Of course I know and understand fully that I received nothing but kindness from you, and of course having known a few Russians before I came here and having got to know a great many others since I have been living here, I understand even better than I did before how rare it is for a Russian to be a snob.

"At the same time you must realise that I always felt from the first that Sir Joseph looked down on me. I was

useful to him and he was kind to me, but he was kind as he would have been to any paid dependant. He regarded me as belonging to another sphere.

"This was all the more galling to me, and to my mind frankly ridiculous, considering our respective lineage, but there is no barrier in the world greater than that of wealth and the rank that is the result of money. Sir Joseph despised me from the first, because I was poor. He was careful not to show this overtly, but I was none the less conscious of it, as any person who is in the least bit sensitive could not fail to be.

"Do you remember that evening when we were sitting after dinner in the gallery and you were reading the newspaper and said: 'Kate is going to be married'? And I wondered who Kate might be; and Sir Joseph said: 'Who is the young man?' and you said, 'Oh, it's not a very young man. It's Mr Ainslee.' And Sir Joseph said, 'Oh, the Schoolmaster.'

"Ainslee was a schoolmaster, and there was nothing odd in Sir Joseph mentioning it, but it was the tone with which he said it.

"And do you remember when Lawless arrived how everything was arranged so that he and Esther might be thrown together? Do you remember how you kept it dark till the last moment that he was coming at all? Sir Joseph and you had not mentioned him; the night before they arrived I was reading in the library, Sir Joseph came in and said he had forgotten to tell me that some young people were arriving the next day, friends of Anne, and he mentioned all the others first, and Lawless' name last, casually, and you both of you gave me to understand that Lawless was attracted by Anne. It turned out she hardly knew him. She couldn't have known him long, as he came back from South Africa late in the autumn and then went to Germany. And, just

before he arrived, he had been to Leipzig, nominally to fetch his sister, but really to see Esther. Not a word was said about that. Not a word was said about his having been in Germany before, and you must have known all about it. Even Esther told me that. Looking back on things now, I remember how you and Lady Macbride used to exchange meaning glances when you looked at me, and Lawless and Esther, especially that night they acted in the charade.

"Of course I know perfectly well, as Octave Feuillet says in one of his books, that neither the truest maternal love, nor 'l'esprit le plus délicat,' nor 'la pié té la plus haute ,' can teach mothers the difference between a beau mariage and a bon mariage. I understand that you were all of you in duty bound to ensure Esther making a beau mariage, and not, as you would have thought had she married me, a very bad marriage, but what I cannot forgive Sir Joseph for, and you must have known what he was doing – is that he allowed me to think he was in favour of my marrying Esther.

"Instead of telling me that he knew it to be out of the question, he let me think it would be arranged some day. He said, 'We will see what we can find for you,' and he said that Esther and I could live at Westleigh. And all the time he was helping the Macbrides to find a way out of the situation.

"When I came back from Cambridge, and told him Sackbut had left me some money, he said, 'Won't that facilitate your marriage?' Those were his words, when he must have known at that moment that his scheme had been successful, and that Lawless and Esther were practically engaged!

"That is what I cannot forgive, what I shall never be able to forgive, because although men of business may call it common sense, and men of the world may call it

necessity, and life, it is in my opinion treachery, and nothing can alter the fact.

"Sir Joseph would never have dreamed of behaving to anyone like Lawless in this way, and it was not because he had a treacherous nature – I know better than anyone all about his honesty and straightforwardness, in most matters, – but it was because in this matter, the matter of marriage, he looked upon me as something which did not count, a negligible quantity. I belonged to a different category, the category of people who don't count, and whom people don't marry. I am sure you did not think of this scheme, and that you would not have minded Esther marrying me, but you were nevertheless a party to it. You helped Lawless and you did not help me. You too had to give in to the beau mariage. And as for Anne, she openly showed that she thought I was not good enough for Esther, and she did all that was humanly possible during those days to encourage Lawless, and to throw him and Esther together. And then the hypocrisy of all that fuss about her career! What has happened to her career now? I suppose her career is to entertain soldiers' wives at tea parties at Aldershot, and to produce future cannon fodder?

"It is for this reason I have not written and not been to England to see you, nor seen you when I was in England, and I fear that it is a reason which cannot help being permanent.

"You will forgive me for writing as frankly as I have done, and I feel certain that you will at least understand what I have been feeling, and what I have gone through. I may have been wrong in writing as I have done, but I felt I could not keep silent any longer.

"Yours sincerely,

"Christopher Trevenen."

193

When he had finished the letter, he felt compelled to add yet another postscript:

"I am not surprised at Sir Joseph acting as he did, nor do I blame him. He is a business man, and business men cannot help looking at matters from a business point of view, but what really hurt me is that you, with your intuition and unworldliness, should have taken the same line and become willingly or unwillingly an accomplice in this dastardly plot."

He sent this letter off, and received an answer at once from Lady Claydon, telling him that she thought his letter so foolish, wrong-headed and absurd, that she could not even discuss it with him.

This confirmed Christopher in thinking that he had been right. Lady Claydon could not discuss the matter with him because she had no case, and she was obliged to be loyal to Sir Joseph.

Christopher had in the meanwhile settled down to his life at St Petersburg. He felt as if he had never lived anywhere else, and that the past was a dream. He was comfortable, if he was not happy. He had no great friends, but a number of easy acquaintances, English, foreign and Russian. He might have gone on living indefinitely in the cosy atmosphere of Elena Dimitrevna's flat, with the small group of people who regularly frequented it, and the girl students and his journalist friends, had it not been for public events. He had made no friends in St Petersburg society. The Daskovs had left Russia for good, and settled at Nice, and he had been true to his purpose not to form any new intimacies. His work for his newspaper had continued to find favour with his editor, the public, and experts like Yakovlev and Lady Claydon, until relations between Russia and Japan became strained. Even then all went well for a time, as his newspaper was on the whole anti-Japanese, but when the war between Russia and Japan broke out, his editor warned him that he must be careful, as England was the ally of Japan. This did not deter Christopher from speaking his mind. He wrote that if Japan won the war the Pacific would become a Japanese lake, and that it was to England's interest that Japan should be beaten. This point of view, strongly expressed, and frequently reiterated by Christopher, proved, contrary to the editor's cautious hesitation, not unpalatable to the readers of the *Messenger*, and all went well till internal troubles started in Russia, in October 1905.

About these events and the troubles that followed, Christopher continued to take a reactionary line, and this ruffled the readers of the *Messenger*. They were most of them good Liberals, and had only been pro-Russian in the Russo-Japanese war question because the Government were pro-Japanese.

Christopher was told to modify his tone. He obeyed on the surface, but by means of carefully selected omission and well-timed emphasis, he managed, subtly, to do the opposite. His public and his editor did not at first notice it, and might never have noticed it, had it not been for the swelling tide of public events. But the Russians noticed it; and his fellow-correspondents noticed it. Lady Claydon noticed it, and suddenly wrote to him towards the end of October. She wrote as if nothing had happened. She said that she had admired his articles until the outbreak of the internal troubles, immensely, but that now he was going too far, and she thought he was being wrong-headed, and it was a great pity.

"I know the Liberals here" (she wrote), *and they won't put up with it. My husband is already annoyed. I met Brierley"* (the editor of the *Messenger*) *"the other day, and he says he regards you as the best correspondent they have had for years, but it would be impossible to keep you in Russia, if you go on writing as you have*

done. He says he has asked you to modify your tone, and hopes you have done so. I beg you also to do so, it would be a pity to lose such a valuable post, just as events are becoming so interesting. I am coming out to Russia myself for a few days, as there is some property in which I have a share that must be sold. Every landowner will have to give up at least half of his property to the peasants, and I am going to sell my share. So I hope to see you. It is not really necessary for me to come, but they want to discuss it with me and I want to see my father."

Yakovlev also wrote to him that he was going too far. All this had the effect of making him more cautious for a while. Lawrence was annoyed at the line Christopher was taking, and asked him to dinner one night, not so much with the purpose of discussing the question, as in the hope that Christopher might hear and be influenced by other views, expressed by intelligent people. Christopher went. The dinner was at Lawrence's small flat, which was on the ground floor of the Quay close to the Embassy. He had asked a Professor Mihailov to meet him, who was a friend of Yakovlev, and one of the most enlightened of the Liberal leaders; a large, fat, comfortable man with a beard and thoughtful eyes. He had also asked a man called Mousourov, who was a landed proprietor and had been to the war, with the Red Cross. He had known him before, but did not know what were his political views. Christopher found the guests assembled. Mousourov was a tall, middle-aged man with sandy-coloured hair and pale grey eyes, and wore a *pince-nez*. There were also a Pole called Vezlitsky, who was to stand for the Duma, and a correspondent of one of the Conservative newspapers, called Jameson. The latest piece of news was that the Government had officially declared that the granting of Polish constitutional liberties was postponed. The topic came up directly they had drunk their vodka, and sat down to the dinner table, and Vezlitsky, who was a tall, eloquent man with a rich vocabulary, began to inveigh against the Government.

"They forget," he said, "these officials forget that they are Asiatics and we are Europeans, and they forget that we once occupied Moscow."

"Yes," said Mihailov, "you occupied it and left it, and we occupied it and stayed there… "

In two minutes, Mihailov, who was supposed to be the most enlightened and broad-minded of all the Liberal leaders, was engaged in a bitter controversy with Vezlitsky, and was expressing the most violent views. This was the last thing that Lawrence had either intended or expected.

What made it worse was that Mousourov not only agreed with Mihailov but went much further: "I am opposed to any form of Duma," he said, "you cannot draw up a Constitution for Russia, any more than you can for China. The desire for liberal reforms based on western examples is a fictitious agitation of the *intelligentsia*, a fad: it can only end in disaster."

"I agree," Christopher said, "with all my mind. Of course the whole agitation has been got up by the Jews. It's international, and not national."

"Whenever I hear the word 'Jew,' 'free-mason,' or 'Jesuit' in a political discussion," said Mihailov, "I withdraw my attention."

"So do I," said Lawrence.

Christopher had forgotten this had once been his view.

"You can make all the reforms you like, but you can't change the character of the people," said Mousourov.

"You mean, every country has the government it deserves," said Jameson.

"Yes," said Mousourov, "we can eat all sorts of mushrooms, and other countries are poisoned by them; and I don't think our Government is worse than any other, Eastern or Western."

"That is what I say," said Christopher.

"If I thought that," said Mihailov, "I should become a

naturalised Turk."

"There have only been two forms of Government in Russia," said Mousourov, "Autocracy and Chaos. The old formula, Autocracy tempered by Assassination. And at present we have no autocrat, and so there is chaos."

"What about Witte?" asked Jameson.

"Witte is not an autocrat: he is a man of business, and therefore a temporiser. If he were an autocrat, there would have been no question of the Duma, or anything else."

"What I say," said Cliristopher, "and I have said it over and over again in the Press, and I mean to say it again, is, that it is no business of ours. We are always being virtuous at other people's expense."

"That's not what you thought about the Armenians," said Lawrence.

"I think one has the right to defend the Christian races," said Christopher. "But I hate the pro-Armenians in England as much as I hated the pro-Boers."

"Are you a Christian?" said Mousourov.

"No," said Christopher, "I am a Catholic by birth, but I don't practise."

"I understand. I think I understand," said Mousourov. "One more question. Were you a pro-Boer yourself?"

"Yes."

"Ah, I understand exactly. You are, my friend, a real reactionary – reactionary in the sense that you *react*. React against the prevalent Liberal or Conservative opinion, as may be. I am sorry for you. You will all your life be against vivisection and against the anti-vivisectionists. *Triste sort!* That is to say, an impossible situation. You will be ground like a mill stone between warring contradictions and opposites. You will never be at home in any camp."

"I hate camps and catchwords," said Christopher.

Mihailov and Mousourov, having been brought together by the common political opponent, were now talking on friendly terms.

"But perhaps," said Mousourov to Christopher "you will marry, and then your wife will change all that."

"I don't think so."

"You don't believe in marriage?"

"Marriage is all right for the wealthy."

"Marriage," said Mousourov, "is difficult for any kind of Christian, and very difficult for a Catholic, who is the complete Christian, but all right for a Turk. I agree with the Turks. A harem and a bow-string, and there would be no problems and no problem plays, thank Heavens, and no Alexandre Dumas *fils*, and no Ibsen, and no sad case of Anna Karenina throwing herself under the train, to get out of the hopeless tangle."

"And there would be no Romeo and Juliet, and no Tristan and Iseult," said Christopher.

"No, exactly," said Mousourov, "and what a good thing! You think of Romeo and Juliet only, that is the selfishness of youth. You do not think of King Mark, nor of Mercutio and Tybalt and Paris and the others who were killed that Romeo and Juliet might exchange soft nothings over the garden wall."

"Their death reconciled the two families and healed the quarrel," said Christopher.

"Well, you fall between two stools there, too. You are a romantic, *and* a realist. *Je vous félicite, mais je vous plains!*"

The dinner lasted long, and the discussion after dinner went on far into the night, and whatever subject was mentioned always came back in the end to politics in general, and to Count Witte in particular. When Christopher left, and said good-bye, Mousourov said to him:

"Good-night. If everyone was like you, the world would be impossible, but it is a good thing that some people should be like you. I repeat, *je vous félicite, mais je vous plains.* You have fallen from Heaven between two stools."

CHAPTER XXII

Lady Claydon arrived at St Petersburg, a few days after this dinner. She stayed at the Hôtel d'Europe, and sent word to Christopher that she was there. He went to see her, and Christopher felt suddenly that the hatchet had been buried for ever. "I am going to Moscow," she said, "and you must come with me."

Christopher had only twice been to Moscow for a short time, and was quite glad to go there again. They travelled together. Christopher went to the hotel, and Lady Claydon went to her father's house, which was now occupied by her eldest brother: Alexander Fedorovitch Losov. Her father lived in the country. The next day they travelled to her father's house a four hours' journey from Moscow in the government of O— . They started at midnight, and arrived at four o'clock in the morning. There was a day train. "But," said Lady Claydon, "the servants like one to arrive in the night. They enjoy the bustle."

There was a bustle when they arrived. A samovar was brought, and they were met at the door by Lady Claydon's father, Feodor Losov, a tall bearded man who wore high boots and a long black cloth coat. The house was large, roomy and comfortable, two storeyed and built of wood. It was furnished in modern fashion, and there were many pictures by French impressionist painters: Monet and others.

These had been collected, Lady Claydon said, by her brother. Her father endured rather than liked them.

There was a large mechanical orchestrophone in the house. Feodor Losov greeted Christopher warmly, and after they had had tea, they went to bed.

The next day Feodor Losov showed him the grounds. There was a park, a garden, a kitchen-garden, a frozen pond, and some barns. The estate was the joint property of Feodor and his family; his son's and his daughter's consent was necessary before any part of the whole could be sold. Everything was mantled in snow. Losov spoke despondently of the political situation. It was, he said, the fault of the Liberals and of the vacillating policy of the Government. It was also, he said, partly the fault of the English who had subsidised the Japanese and were no doubt subsidising the revolutionaries in Russia. He said this good-humouredly to Christopher, explaining that his daughter was an Englishwoman now. "She is a *Miladi*."

"The English are very sly," he said, "very cunning, and they don't know it. Ah! Queen Victoria! She was a great woman! Very cunning. Very wise. Well, the long and short of it is I wish to sell two-thirds of the land, to the peasants and Sasha" (that was his son) "is willing to sell his share: he cares nothing except for new fashioned pictures and all that decadent stuff, and you must settle," he said to his daughter, "what you want to do with your share. There is a farm."

"I want to sell the whole of my share," said Lady Claydon, "it is of no use to me."

"You can sell it, but you will get nothing for it."

"It's better than having it taken, and the house burnt into the bargain. Have you had many disorders here?"

"No, not here. Everything has been quiet, but in the next estate, the Semonovs', everything was destroyed. The peasants got drunk. It was the steward's fault. He was a fool. A German."

Lady Claydon interviewed the steward with her father, and

she also interviewed a deputation of three peasants. Christopher was present at this interview. The sale was agreed upon, and the peasants' terms disputed and accepted, and when the conversation was over, one of the peasants said to her, "Tell me, Anna Feodorovna, when will the *levelling* be?"

"What *levelling*?" she asked.

"When we shall all be equal and there will be no rich and no poor – no *Masters*?"

"That will happen," she said, "when 'the lobsters sing'[1] or when the Kingdom of Heaven comes; but even there the angels are not equal; for there are angels and archangels, and one star differs from another in glory, as it says in the Scriptures; they are not *equal*."

"That is true," said the peasant. "After the 17th of October the Governor came to the town and made a speech and told us that the Gasudar in his graciousness had given us liberty, but he said it was liberty to behave well and not behave badly, and the Elder said to him 'that, your Excellency, is just as it was before.'"

He chuckled.

"And yet times are different. *Those* times have gone by. We have got some more land, and some day we shall have it all, for it stands to reason that the land is God's gift and must belong to those who till it."

"And a nice mess you will make of it," said Feodor Losov, "when it all does belong to you."

The peasants sniggered, sighed, and went away.

"They are as obstinate as mules," said Losov, "and if you try to do something for them, they think you are trying to cheat them."

The food at Losov's house was rich and copious. In the afternoon they drove for a time in a sledge through snowbound fields and frozen woods, and through the village. They dined early and sat up late, and Losov turned on the orchestrophone.

1   *Kogda rak svisnet*

Lady Claydon had to get back to England. It was not necessary for her to stay for the conclusion of the business which could all be done by procuration. The next day Lady Claydon and Christopher took their leave and went back to Moscow, by day this time. Losov came to see them off at the station, and he cried as he said good-bye, and blessed his daughter. When they were in the train and the journey had lasted about an hour, Lady Claydon said to him:

"I want to tell you, Christopher, that when I got that letter you wrote me, that angry letter, I was startled at first and hurt, but after a time I understood. You were of course wrong; when Bruce Lawless arrived in our house we had no more idea he would marry Esther than the man in the moon, and I don't think, poor girl, she had any notion of it herself."

"But why did you ask him?" said Christopher.

"We asked him because he was a friend of Colonel Stockton's son. They had both been together in South Africa, and Stockton's son was invalided home, and Lawless was wounded and they came home together. If you hadn't gone away, it would never have happened."

"Yes, it would, she was in love with him. I saw it. I shouldn't have wanted her to marry me if she was in love with someone else. I can forgive you. I'm sure you didn't mean to do anything against me, but I shall never forgive him. He has ruined her career."

"Her career, my poor friend! She would never have had a career! She was not strong enough. She nearly died when her baby was born, and the doctor said it was *impossible* for her to become a professional pianist. And besides, I doubt if she had enough talent. Her talent was that of thousands of young girls, all very well in a drawing room."

"No, that is where you are wrong. I am not musical, but I could see that she had genius. I am sure if she had never met Lawless, she would have been a great, a very great artist. I have a musical friend in St Petersburg who agrees with me, and

Bielov the composer heard her at Leipsig, and he agreed too."

"But then, if she had married you, it would have been the same."

"We should not have been married so soon. She would have had time to get settled in her career. She was too young to marry."

"If she was too young to marry, she was too young to lead the life of a professional pianist."

"I don't agree at all. She was leading it as it was."

"She was studying – that is different. How could she have travelled all over the world playing and practising? It would have killed her."

"She needn't have travelled. She could have stayed in England."

"But if artists don't travel, they don't become known, and they don't get engagements."

"Well, I am certain she has genius. I suppose she never plays now?"

"Never in public."

"Is she happy?"

"I think she is. There were two children, but the second one died."

"Poor thing!"

"He is doing well."

"Has he inherited anything?"

"No, his uncle is still alive."

"Well, at any rate, she will not have to work for her living."

"Don't be so bitter."

"I am not bitter, about her, but I am bitter about him. He took her away from me deliberately. He always hated and despised me, and he will never be able to appreciate her."

"Think what you like about him, but I do not want you to think badly of my husband. I never showed him your letter. He would not have understood. How you, who know him, could think him capable of such a thing!"

"Money spoils the best natures, and business men put money matters in a separate compartment."

"But, my poor child, he was fond of you and ready to do anything for you. He wanted you both to live with us."

"Till Lawless came."

"We never gave him a thought until we heard of the engagement. It was a complete surprise to him."

"Very well, we won't talk about it again."

"But you don't think badly of my husband?"

"I know *you* didn't mean to do anything against me."

"Christopher, you will make me angry. I want you to believe me when I promise you that *he* had nothing against your marrying Esther – on the contrary – and that he knew nothing about the Lawless affair till it happened. Do you believe me?"

"I believe you to be perfectly sincere."

"Yes, but I want you to believe that he was, and is perfectly sincere."

"Sincere? Yes. Don't let's talk about it any more, please."

They did not refer to it again. In spite of all that Lady Claydon had said, Christopher still obstinately clung to his view about Sir Joseph's conduct in the matter, but he said to himself he could not help it. It was not his fault.

Lady Claydon went straight back to London from Moscow on the following day.

Christopher was going back to St Petersburg when a strike broke out in Moscow. He had to stay on, because the trains were not running. The lift stopped working at his hotel, and the electric light was turned off. The next day the shops were shut. Two days later, a band of revolutionists, mostly students and schoolboys, seized a school, refused to surrender and threw a bomb at an officer and killed him. Finally they surrendered after killing an officer and five men and causing seventeen casualties. There were barricades in the town, and artillery fire and a fight round one of the big works, and all the time life went on more or less as usual. Cossacks and dragoons scoured the streets every now and then, and the populace looked on with curiosity. There were no trains running till after Christmas day. Christopher sent a telegram to his newspaper. After Christmas the whole thing petered out. Troops arrived to restore order. There were few casualties on either side of the combatants, and as usually happens in such affairs, nine-tenths of the people who were killed were onlookers among the public. This was often due to their incurable curiosity. Some houses were destroyed, and the printing houses of one of the newspapers.

The inhabitants complained bitterly. Some blamed the soldiers and others the revolutionaries, but there was no enthusiasm. Christopher went back to St Petersburg and wrote an account of what had happened to his newspaper throwing the blame entirely on the revolutionaries who he said were childish and had been led by school children. There was some truth in this, but it annoyed his newspaper, as some of the other newspapers published lurid accounts of fighting and atrocities.

Christopher wrote again to say all these stories were exaggerated and some of them pure invention.

Brierley, the editor, wrote to him and said he could *narrate* what he liked, but he need not relate things in so partial a manner. They were as a matter of fact delighted to get his news, and it had been fortunate for his newspaper that he had happened to be at Moscow.

In April the elections took place, and in May, the first Duma assembled. Christopher wrote a picturesque account of the opening, but as soon as proceedings began which led to a deadlock between the Government and the majority of the electors, Christopher took the side of the Government and said that the Liberals were silly, and the revolutionaries childish. When the Duma was dissolved in July, Christopher applauded the move. This was more than the readers of his newspaper could stand. They complained in no uncertain tone, and the owner of the newspaper, a Liberal who had been made a peer by Gladstone, and who had followed him after the Home Rule Bill, said that something must be done. He was determined not to lose Christopher, but he realised that his attitude on Russian affairs was doing his newspaper harm. So he suggested that Christopher should exchange places with their correspondent at Rome. Christopher did not care if he stayed in Russia or if he went away. He cared not a button for the political situation in Russia. It was true what Mousourov had said to him, he was a real reactionary, and a natural supporter of all "lost causes and impossible loyalties," but never the loyalty or the cause which you expected. He accepted the offer without hesitation. He felt it was time he was going. He had quarrelled with nearly all his friends about the political situation. Elena Dimitrevna still tolerated him because she said that all Englishmen, whether Liberals or Tories, were all of them conservatives, because they were all of them egotists and could not help it. But most of the Russians he had met at her house or through Yakovlev would no longer speak to him.

He accepted at once, partly for this reason and partly because he was obliged to, for he would not have enough to live on, if he cut himself adrift from his newspaper.

The idea of going to Rome attracted him. He thought he would be able to resume research work on his own account and to set about editing Sackbut's literary remains. He had not begun to do so at St Petersburg. The days had gone by so swiftly and so easily that he had had far too much time to himself to have any real time for himself: that is to say for work.

He was to go to England at the beginning of August. A few days before he left he was walking on the quays. It was a hot August day and the Neva looked serenely blue, and the spire of St Peter and St Paul's glinted in the sunshine. He was walking absently, thinking of what the next move in his life would be like when somebody called him.

It was Madame Turçin who was taking her dog out for a walk. He had not seen her nor heard of her except for an occasional postcard since he had been at Constantinople.

"Fancy our meeting here!" she said. "I knew you were here, as we read your articles in the *Messenger*. We have been appointed here to the Legation and we have just arrived. We must see a lot of each other."

"I am just going away alas!" said Christopher, "I have been appointed to Rome."

"To Rome? We have just come from there. We were there two years – just after Paris. That is unlucky. But that always happens in life. You will like Rome I am sure. We were miserable at leaving. We had so many friends there. My husband will be so displeased. He admires what you have been writing. I do not agree with your articles but I admire them. He agrees. Do come and see us before you go. We live in a flat in the Konniushenny Pereulok. Come tonight and have dinner with us. I cannot stay now as I have a visit to pay in one of these houses."

Christopher went to dinner with the Turçins. They talked of old times at Constantinople, and Madame Turçin told him about Rome.

"There are many nice people," she said, "and all sorts of little worlds which are like separate spheres, but they all revolve in the same system and they all touch each other at points. I will give you some letters of introduction. There are some nice Russian diplomats. The English you will know in any case. I need not bother about the diplomats; you will get to them, those you want to know, by yourself. I will give you letters to people you would not find out by yourself. There is a German philosopher who lives a retired life, and then there is a Madame D'Alberg whom I think you would like. We knew her in Paris."

"Who is she?" asked Christopher.

"She is the widow of D'Alberg the writer. You – a student of Eastern things – must know all about him."

"Oh, Auguste D'Alberg, the *savant*?"

"Yes. He died you know three years ago, and Madame D'Alberg lived on for a little while in Paris and then she found she could bear it no longer, and so she migrated to Rome. She was Irish or Scotch by birth, I am not sure which. A charming woman. They had such a nice *salon* in Paris and knew all the interesting people. Now she lives a more retired life, but people are discovering her. She is a person who cannot remain really secluded for long. She is too clever and too attractive."

Christopher stayed there till late, and before he left Madame Turçin gave him some letters for Madame D'Alberg and others.

When the moment came for him to leave, he was overcome with melancholy. Elena Dimitrevna was living at her *datcha* at Tsarskoe, but she came up to see him off. So did her niece Olga, and so did Kitty and Sofie and Misha. Olga was now a professional pianist. Sofie had tried the stage but had only been moderately successful in the provinces, and was about to go again on tour. Kitty was still studying the violin. Lawrence came to see him off as well, but none of his Russian friends, with the exception of Mousourov, whom he had met several times since he had made his acquaintance. They all met at the station, and Elena Dimitrevna was lamenting.

"It is such a pity," she said, "such a great pity, when we at last get as a correspondent someone who knows Russia and speaks Russian that he should be impregnated by these old-fashioned, conservative, reactionary *Black-gang* ideas. Oh! Christopher Beniaminovitch! Why did you write like that? It was perversity I am sure. For I believe in spite of whatever you say, that you are really a Liberal at heart, even if you are the only English Liberal that exists. You were noble about Armenia."

"The truth is," said Mousourov, "that you know too much about Russia and newspapers can't stand the truth. They do not want the truth. They want a fairy tale, small blame to them. The truth is tedious, and besides that, it is dangerous. The truth is like dynamite, and when the newspapers get hold of a story that is really true they do not dare to publish it."

"Oh! the truth," said Christopher, "that is what they cannot stand, and I only gave them small doses."

"Well," said Mousourov, "in Rome you will have the treat of being a Catholic and anti-papal, and anti-papal and not pro-Governmental. That ought to suit you down to the ground. But I prophesy that Rome will get the better of you. Rome is not a place for *frondeurs*."

"Well you must write to us; Heaven knows if we shall all be alive, if the Government goes committing such follies! Just fancy!" said Elena Dimitrevna.

"You will enjoy the Vatican library," said Lawrence.

"Oh yes," said Kitty and Sofie in chorus, "and the Forum and the Colosseum by moonlight."

"I am sorry, dreadfully sorry; don't forget us and send us a postcard sometimes," said Elena Dimitrevna. "There is the third bell, it is time for you to go – good-bye," and as the train moved slowly from the station she made a surreptitious sign of the Cross and wiped her eyes.

"The old Eve still persists in spite of her 'free' thought," said Mousourov in a whisper to Lawrence. "*Grattez le Jacobin…*"

CHAPTER XXIII

Christopher arrived in London in August, and at once went to see Brierley, the editor, an intelligent and active man.

"Well, this has been a sad business," said Brierley. "You are the best correspondent we have had, and you throw the whole thing away just as things are becoming interesting and the revolution is beginning."

"The revolution is over," said Christopher, "the Liberals have waved the European banner of ideals and it is too heavy for their feeble Slav hands. The revolutionaries are powerless and the Government is incompetent, so for the moment it is stalemate."

"But surely something will happen?"

"I suppose so – something may happen any minute; only everything in Russia takes ten times as long to happen as it does anywhere else – or longer. I had quite enough of it. I am sick to death of both sides. A plague on both their houses!"

"If you had thought more of your paper, and less of these party squabbles, we should still be getting news from you. However, you are going to Rome, for Heaven's sake don't fall foul of all parties there. You had better have some leave and get there at the beginning of next month."

Christopher left the office and walked down the Strand. There he met a large man, whom he did not at first recognise.

"Hullo, Chris!" the man called out. It was Suckling – Suckling, whom he had not seen since Cambridge. He had grown fat. His face was lined, and had the mark of the tropics on it.

"This is splendid," said Suckling. "I am home on leave. I am going down to my father's this afternoon. You must come with me. My wife is there, too; she will be delighted to see you."

Christopher went with Suckling to the country. The Claydons were abroad, and this relieved Christopher from having to make up his mind whether he would go and see Sir Joseph. He stayed two weeks with Suckling, who, he found, had achieved success and with it disillusion. His wife was pretty and delicate. He then went to Cambridge, and stayed a few days with Yakovlev. He found Yakovlev just the same, more sorry than angry about the events in Russia, and prognosticating a gloomy future. They sat up discussing the situation there, late into the night.

"The trouble about our country," said Yakovlev, "is the dead level of mediocrity. The lack of great men. And directly a great man emerges he does too much and ruins the country like Peter the Great, and it takes a century for it to recover."

Yakovlev said to him the night before he left:

"I am sorry you have left Russia. I do not say your ideas were altogether wrong, but you annoyed your readers on purpose. You were mischievous. Sheer *polissonnerie*. You only told half the truth, and you know it."

"Yes," said Christopher, "but the half that never *is* told. The other people are allowed to write what they like, and half of what they write is not true at all."

"You could have said all you wanted to say without annoying anybody, with a little care, but you're bitten by *le plaisir aristocratique de déplaire*. However, now that you are going to Rome I don't think there will be any rock in the way against which you can be shipwrecked except the rock of St Peter, and I suppose, whatever you think, you know better than to tilt against that."

"I shall say what I think," said Christopher. "I have no love for the Vatican. I think they are behindhand there, obstinate, narrow-minded, proud, backward, and, above all things, stupid."

"Behindhand, possibly, and slow; but remember they have behind them a policy which is two thousand years old, and they can afford to wait – and you won't have much to do with the Vatican. But if you do, remember that *qui mange du Pape en meurt*, and you are not stronger than Napoleon and Bismarck."

"Oh! I shall leave all that alone," said Christopher. "I don't feel strongly about Italian politics, and they will let me say what I like about Italian things. As for the Vatican, it is the Aunt Sally of the English Press. But I mean to get on with my own work and to edit what Sackbut left behind him."

"That is an excellent idea," said Yakovlev. "He would have been annoyed at your leaving Russia, just now, when it is so interesting, and things are happening every day."

"I had had enough of it," said Christopher, "and the nonsense people talk about it, both here, and there, makes me sick."

"Turgenev," said Yakovlev, "says that man is either a Hamlet or a Don Quixote. You are a Don Quixote, only you have none of the Spaniard's kindness and humility. If you are a Don Quixote you should be chivalrous."

"Don Quixote, fortunately for him, was mad."

"He was very sane too."

"You mean that I am neither mad nor sane?"

"Neither mad, nor sane *enough*."

"I will try and improve," said Christopher, and he laughed.

"For a person who is steeped in oriental literature, it is surprising how little of the oriental serenity you have assimilated."

"I suppose it is my Irish blood."

"Yes, but I should have thought that would have been tempered by your mother's common sense."

"That is because I am neither one thing nor the other; an exile everywhere."

"We are all of us exiles," said Yakovlev, "one must carry one's country with one. The Kingdom of Heaven is within."

"Yes, for those who have found it."

They were silent.

Christopher looked at Yakovlev, and envied the Faith that shone like a quiet dream in his large eyes. After all, if it were only a dream, what a comforting dream!

The next day Christopher went to London, and the day after he started for Rome.

He found the town hot and empty. He stayed at first at a small hotel, and then moved into a *pension* called the Helvetia, which was managed by two ladies: an impoverished Italian widow, and an Irish spinster, a Miss O'Connor who belonged to the Gedetic Society and believed that the earth was flat. The *pension* was small and comfortable, and not far from the Piazza di Spagna. There was a heterogeneous collection of inmates: the Italian lady's son and two nieces, a young American student who was studying archaeology, a retired English Consul and his wife, two young Englishmen who were learning Italian and working for the Foreign Office, an Italian sculptor, a German lady and her daughter, two American girls, and a Polish widow. The people to whom the Turçins had given Christopher letters of introduction were all of them away, so was the British Ambassador. Christopher called on the First Secretary and made the acquaintance of some of the staff, also of his fellow-journalists. Life seemed quiet after Russia; dull and stagnant. Christopher wandered about the town, and visited the spots he had seen as a boy, and looked up some old acquaintances. It was not until the end of October that he met Madame D'Alberg. She had been away at a watering place. He had left cards on her and his letter of introduction, and then he had forgotten about her.

One day he received a card from her saying she was

delighted to hear from her old friend Mina Turçin, and that she hoped Christopher would look in some evening after dinner. As she did not name any definite date Christopher did not like to go by himself and he thought no more about it.

Then, one night about a month later he was asked to come, after dinner, by a Russian called Pavlov, to whom Madame Turçin had also given him a letter.

Pavlov was the last scion of an old family – he was a widower and his children were dead. He had once been rich, and he was now poor. At one time, he had owned a large estate in the south of Russia, and a magnificent collection of Italian pictures. All that had gone. He now lived in a small apartment in the Via San Niccolo da Tolentino. His ivory-coloured face and sunken grey eyes had a mournful dignity, and his bare shabby clothes had an eighteenth century air about them. There was an atmosphere of the past about him but his ideas and opinions on art and literature were advanced. His historical scholarship was remarkable, and he composed religious music and played the organ in his spare time. In his flat he still possessed the last relic of his happier days, a small hand-blown organ, with four stops and a mellow tone. In politics he was a Conservative, and he was fervently orthodox. He had read Christopher's articles, and agreed with every word of them. He never asked people to meals; he was too poor, and there was no room. He hardly ate anything himself. But people went to see him after dinner and he had friends in many worlds.

The first time Christopher went to see him he found four or five people in the room.

There were the Russian Minister to the Vatican and his wife, a cosmopolitan Italian called Scalchi, who spoke English like an Englishman; a Russian lady, Countess Mühlendorff; a philosopher, Konitz, who was half Polish and had written a book about Wagner; a German professor called Wildenspruch; and sitting talking to him was a lady. Pavlov introduced him to everyone – among others to the lady, but he did not catch her name. The conversation was general and ranged over all sorts of topics. Pavlov talked of the Russian situation, and congratulated Christopher on the line he had taken, saying it was so rare that anybody had the courage to tell the truth about Russia in the newspapers.

"The revolutionary troubles," he said, "will soon fizzle out now that we at last have a strong man at the head of the Government; for Stolypin is a strong man; a strong man and an honest man."

The lady in black seemed to be listening attentively, but Christopher thought that she was really far away. She was sipping lemonade and talking to Scalchi. Christopher was sitting next to them and made a third in their conversation, although he hardly said anything. Scalchi was talking about an actress whom he had seen at Vienna.

"I believe she is wonderful," said the lady.

Christopher said something about the Art Theatre at Moscow.

"Oh! I believe they are quite wonderful," said Scalchi. The lady said nothing.

Christopher asked her if she cared for plays.

"I haven't been to the theatre for a long time," she said, smiling.

Christopher looked at her, and noticed she was dressed in black, with a black lace shawl over her shoulders, and thought to himself, "She is in mourning, and I have said the wrong thing." They went on talking: at least Scalchi, who seemed to know her well, talked, and she listened. Christopher observed her. She was pale, remote and still, with the stillness of deep waters; no longer young, but not yet middle-aged. She had not lost her youthfulness of line and figure. She had ripples of dark hair, and her face in repose was sad. Christopher thought he had seldom seen a sadder face. It was a young face, and the sadness in it seemed inappropriate and ill-allotted, an unfair, unmerited load. But then there were her eyes...her eyes...with their long lashes; what colour were they? Brown or blue? or black? When she smiled an elfin gleam lit up her face, which gave one the idea that at some time or other her spirits had been, and perhaps even now were at moments wild. There was twilight in her eyes, but it gave hints every now and then of some radiant dawn. They were like some curious precious stone, that is dark in the daytime, and has strange golden lights at night.

Presently she got up and said good-night, and Christopher noted that she moved with a deft grace, which had the effect of a musical phrase; something completely satisfying and right, which was the result probably of perfect proportion, and made one forget to ask whether she was tall or short, and she was not tall. As she was going, Pavlov said to her:

"Mr Trevenen is a friend of the Turçins."

"Oh, yes," she said, to Christopher, "Mina Turçin wrote to me about you and I asked you to come and see me some evening," she smiled, "but you never came. Do look in some time. I am nearly always in in the afternoon, or after dinner."

Christopher had of course guessed that she was Madame D'Alberg. Had he not done so, Pavlov would have enlightened him.

"You should see Madame D'Alberg," he said, after she had gone. "She is exceptional…only it is not easy: in spite of what she says, she is hardly ever at home, and she never goes out *dans le monde*. Poor woman, she is sad! He was a great loss, and she was devoted to him. She is difficult to know, but it is worth while."

About a week later Christopher went to leave cards on Madame D'Alberg. He thought he would leave cards before he ventured to go there in the evening.

She lived on the second floor of a large *palazzo* in the old part of the town. You walked up two long flights of steps to it. He asked if she were at home, meaning to leave cards, and was shown in before he knew where he was. Madame D'Alberg was sitting in a dark high room crowded with furniture arranged anyhow, with photographs of French and English people and of English pre-Raphaelite pictures.

To reach her sitting room you went through a room which was lined from floor to ceiling with books. She was not alone; there were the German professor, Wildenspruch, whom he had met, an archaeologist, Scalchi, and a middle-aged Italian. They were engaged in an intimate conversation, and Christopher felt they had changed the subject directly he arrived. He made a few commonplace remarks, and they talked of one thing and another; he went away as soon as he thought it was decent, feeling uncomfortable at having come at all. As he was going away, Madame D'Alberg said to him, "You must come one evening. Come next Thursday, you will find a few people."

Christopher would have accepted her invitation; unfortunately before Thursday came, an incident occurred which modified his mode of life. Madame Turçin had given him a letter of introduction to an Italian lady, a certain Madame Torelli, who received every Tuesday evening, and at whose house you met artists, men of letters, and musicians. Christopher went there one Tuesday, and there he again met the Russian lady whom he had met at Pavlov's: Countess Mühlendorff; she was old, clever, soured and spiteful. He found her in one room – there were many rooms and they were all of them crowded – talking to Pavlov. They were sitting against the wall. He said, "How do you do?" and spoke to them for a moment, and then an American, Mrs Castleton-Wyse, whom he knew, emerged from the crowd and spoke to him; and he left them, but he was still in earshot. As he was exchanging small talk with the American lady who was asking him how he liked Rome, and telling him that Rome was the home of every thoughtful person's soul, he could distinctly hear every word that Pavlov and Countess Mühlendorff were saying. Up till now they had been talking French, and they were now talking Russian. Pavlov knew that Christopher spoke Russian, but he thought he was out of earshot, and, like many foreigners when they know that Englishmen speak their language, never wholly realised that they understand what you are saying – a kind of ostrich theory.

"Who is that Englishman?" Countess Mühlendorff was saying. "He was at your house the other night."

"He is the correspondent of an English newspaper: the *Daily Messenger*."

"Oh, a reporter!"

"He writes very well about Russia. Yakovlev gave him a letter to me, and says he is a capable man."

"My dear friend," said Countess Mühlendorff, "take my advice and have nothing to do with reporters. You cannot trust them. I have been caught twice. I once made friends with a Mr Edwards, who was very clever really, very intelligent, *très brillant*, and one day in the course of conversation I let something slip, and something I ought not to have said, but I forgot and thought and talked as I would to you, and it came out in his newspaper! It did not much matter, but it taught me a lesson; at least, it should have, but I did not learn it. Some time later I made the acquaintance of a Mr Lowell – he wrote serious articles in reviews, and in the newspapers too. I thought him remarkable and that he was a man one could trust. One day I told him something which I thought he ought to know, but I told him in the strictest confidence. He sent the news at once to his newspaper, and of course they made use of it. That taught me a lesson, and I have never had anything to do with a reporter since then. They cannot behave as gentlemen, and I don't blame them, because their first loyalty is to their newspaper."

"But Yakovlev says that this Englishman is a gentleman. He knew his father."

"As if that mattered! It is of no consequence what he was or what he was born, once he is a journalist he is a journalist, and they are all alike."

At that moment Pavlov said, "Take care, he might hear you and he understands."

"He couldn't have heard," said Countess Mühlendorff, "and if he did, it would be a good lesson for him. I shouldn't mind saying all that to his face."

Christopher left the house shortly afterwards, and he made up his mind that this was the last time he would go out in Roman society. It was the last time they would have the chance of meeting a reporter, as far as he was concerned. He did not go to Madame D'Alberg's, on Thursday, and he determined that he would never go near her house again. Nor would he go and see Pavlov. The stray remarks of Countess Mühlendorff which he had overheard modified his mode of life in Rome. He gave up attempting to know any Italians unless they were officials or people whom he could see on business, and he associated entirely with journalists, Bohemians or men of business. He was asked to the British Embassy, but he refused the invitation, and he only went there on business.

One day, just before Christmas, he met one of the American secretaries, called Wilding. He had been a friend of Spence. He had not been in Rome long, and was only just married. Christopher had met him at Spence's father's house in London. He was alert, fair-haired and amiable.

"Well, it's fine to see you. You're the first friend I've met, and if one keeps one's eyes open here, one sees quite a lot of people one doesn't know."

"I'm married now and my wife will be just crazy to know you when she knows you were a friend of Spence's. You must come and dine with us, come next Wednesday. We have two Austrians coming, a young couple, newcomers like us, and old Mrs Castleton-Wyse."

"I'm afraid I can't."

"Got a date?"

"No, it's not that – I never dine out."

"But why?"

"Because people here don't like meeting 'reporters.'"

"Gosh! That doesn't go with us… You can't say that to me. Why, some of my best friends, some of our best friends, are newspaper men, and you know as well as I do that we don't hold with any of that Lord Chesterfield stuff. No, sir."

"But the Austrians wouldn't like it."

"I say they would. They are the cutest little couple in the world, and she's a peach."

"What are they called?"

"Search me! I've forgotten, it's a name that sounds either like soda water being poured into a drink, or a sneeze, or a bark. But you'll come?"

"All right. I'll come."

CHAPTER XXIV

Christopher went to dinner with the Wildings. There were only six people. His host, his hostess, who was young and unspoilt and came from Chicago, and Mrs Castleton-Wyse, who was one of the Roman social institutions. Christopher had hardly got into the room when Count and Countess Zekes were announced and Christopher found himself face to face with Alex.

"Let me present you to Countess Zekes," said his hostess to him.

"Mr Trevenen and I are old friends," she said. "We met years ago at my mother's house in Austria."

Christopher sat between Alex and his hostess at dinner.

He had not seen Alex for thirteen years.

Would he have known her? Yes, anywhere.

She had developed into an exquisite woman. There was the same radiance she had always had: but now there was a sovran elegance about her. She was thinner, she seemed taller. Her shoulders were dazzling. She was the essence of distinction, so distinguished that one felt that it almost prevented her being as beautiful as she might have been.

What was exactly the same about her was her blue eyes, and her smile.

"I had no idea you were in Rome," she said to him, "we have only just arrived. Before this we were in Berlin. Are you at the

Embassy?"

"Oh! no, I am a journalist. Foreign correspondent to the *Messenger*, or perhaps I ought to say, a reporter."

She laughed.

"You write in the newspapers, just fancy. I must read what you write. I never do read the newspapers, but Hermann does. He has to. He has probably read your articles."

"Where have you been all these years?" he asked.

"Hermann was in the army two years after we married, then after he got into the diplomatic service we were sent to Paris, then to Madrid, then to Sofia, and then to Copenhagen." The sound of her voice brought back the past to him. He saw the woods at Birkenberg and the library where she had shown him a book she had illuminated. The terrace and the garden where he had last met her. He looked at Zekes, a tall, broad-shouldered dark man, with black eye-brows and rather a sullen mouth and wondered whether she was happy.

"Do you like diplomacy?" he asked.

"It has its good points," she said, "and it has its nasty things like everything else. And you – what have you been doing?"

"I passed my examination as a student interpreter and I was sent to Constantinople and then I wrote an angry letter about the Armenian massacres and I had to leave the service, and I became a journalist. I was in Russia at St Petersburg for four years, and then my newspaper didn't like what I wrote, so they sent me here."

"I suppose you were too revolutionary."

"No, too Conservative. I write for a Liberal newspaper."

"That is like you," she laughed.

Her laugh was the same. He remembered the night they danced in the dining room.

"Karl is married," she said, "and mamma died three years ago."

"And your aunt?"

"Aunt Berthe? She is still alive. And do you know the first

person I met here was Jacobi. Do you remember him?"

"Oh, yes. He said Hamlet was a medical case."

There was a pause in the conversation.

"Fancy you two knowing each other," said Mrs Wilding. "Now that's what I call a real stroke of good luck. And you met at Vienna?"

"I was a tutor in Countess Zekes' family," said Christopher.

"Now fancy that. Countess Zekes," she addressed Alex across Christopher, "Mr Trevenen, my husband tells me, is one of the most brilliant correspondents the British Press has ever had, and we are really lucky to have him here, and I hope, Mr Trevenen, that you will stay here as long as we do. Mr Trevenen was the friend of one of my husband's oldest school chums. He was killed, poor boy, in the Grecian war. Such a shame. He was such a bright boy."

After dinner, the men went into Wilding's little den to smoke their cigars. The flat consisted, besides this, of two sitting rooms, and a dining room. Zekes began to talk about Russia. Christopher observed him. He was good-looking, but there was a hint of possible future grossness and his eyebrows were curiously arched upwards towards the temples. He had a loud laugh.

"The Emperor of Russia was perfectly right to dissolve the Duma," said Zekes.

Although Christopher agreed with the sentiment, he was faintly irritated.

"All that business of comparing what is happening in Russia with the French revolution, as so many reporters do, is such nonsense."

"What do you say to that, Christopher?" said Mr Wilding. "Mr Trevenen writes the foreign news in the *Messenger*."

"All revolutions work out on the same formula," said Christopher. "And so far the likeness has been startling. The Emperor of Russia is in exactly the same position as Louis the Sixteenth."

"Oh! But the Russians and the French are so different," said Zekes. "The Russians will never make a revolution. They are weak, they give in. But now it is over."

"It is not over," said Christopher. "That is how revolutions always begin."

"*Tout cela finira en queue de poisson.* The moment they feel the strong hand they give in. All they need is *une main de fer.* You English have understood that in dealing with the Irish."

"The Irish have never given in," said Christopher. "And never will. They have smashed the machinery of the House of Commons in order to compel the English to face the Irish question, and they rule English politics now and they will go on doing so till they get the right to manage their own affairs. Dr Johnson said that there was no instance even in the ten persecutions of such severity as the minority in Ireland have exercised over the majority. And it has been useless; the Irish are undefeated, and unconquerable."

Christopher's eyes were flashing and his face was white.

Zekes, feeling that he had inadvertently lit a powder magazine and being a slow, sleepy, good-natured man, thought he had better change the subject.

"Then," he said, "you think the Emperor was wrong to dissolve the Duma?"

"Not at all," said Christopher. "They were wrong ever to convene a Duma."

Zekes was puzzled, and laughed good-humouredly.

"*Mon cher Monsieur,*" he said. "The Emperor was obliged to do something of the kind. He was right to give them a Chamber where people can *talk*, but what they need is a reasonable chamber elected on a sensible system with a good strong man at the head of the Ministry, who will put through the necessary reforms, and they have got the man now."

"You can't reform Russia," said Christopher, "not on western lines."

"Then you are a Panslavist?" said Zekes, good-humouredly.

"In Russian politics, of course."

"If you knew the Slavs as well as I do you wouldn't talk like that. Russia has always been governed by Germans. Every steward on every estate is a German."

"The estates don't count; and how can you expect Prussians to understand Russia?"

"Germans are not all Prussians," said Zekes, who was becoming annoyed.

"The Prussians are the rulers; as for the others, they are a herd of drudges under direction."

Zekes ignored the remark and turned to Wilding.

"I see," he said, "your Ambassador is giving a ball."

Christopher felt hatred rising in him against Zekes, and he was on the verge of saying something violent, when Mrs Wilding came into the room and said:

"We are going to have a little bridge. Do you play bridge, Mr Trevenen?"

Christopher said he did not.

Countess Zekes did not play, and she and Christopher went into the next room.

"It is so strange to see you again," said Alex.

Christopher said nothing, and lit a cigarette.

"What were you discussing in the smoking room for so long?"

"We were talking politics and I, as usual, was rude. I was rude to your husband."

Alex laughed.

"Hermann won't mind," she said. "He is so used to people getting angry when they talk politics."

"He wouldn't mind it from others...no, I am wrong. He *would* mind it from others. He would challenge them to a duel, if they said the kind of thing I said to him. He doesn't mind it from me. He thinks I don't count, and rightly."

"What nonsense."

"It isn't nonsense. I know exactly what he thinks of me."

"Hermann is fond of Englishmen."

"Yes, of people who have ten thousand a year and hunt in Leicestershire."

"All that is nonsense, we will talk of something else. I want to ask you something very much, may I?"

"Of course."

"You will not mind?"

"No, of course not."

"It is this. Did you forgive me?"

"Yes," said Christopher, "I did. Not at first. Not for a long time, although I never blamed you. I blamed the whole universe. But of course I knew it was impossible. We were very young."

"Very young. And very foolish."

"And were you happy? Are you happy?" asked Christopher.

"Oh yes," she said. "I have two children, a boy and a girl. There was another, the eldest, but he died when he was three – a boy, that was a great sadness. But the others are a great joy to me. And you?"

"Oh, I have made a mess of my life and I suppose I always shall. I was engaged to be married six years ago, and it came to nothing through my fault."

"Could you have married?"

"Yes, as things turned out, but I made a mess of it."

"And she?"

"She married someone else. And lived happily ever afterwards."

At that moment the door opened and someone came into the room.

Mrs Wilding, who had been told of her arrival, came to meet her. "Well, I declare," she said, "this is really kind of you, Carrie. Countess Zekes, this is one of my dearest friends, Carrie Clyde. Carrie, this is Countess Zekes of the Austrian Embassy, and Mr Trevenen of the *Messenger*, their brilliant correspondent. Come and see Joe. We are playing bridge, but now that you are here, we will have a little music. We have just finished the rubber."

Miss Clyde, who was fair and handsome, went into the next room, and presently they all came back. Another secretary from the American Embassy arrived and they talked together for a while and lemonade and tea were served. Then Miss Clyde was asked to sing.

"You have brought your music, haven't you?" said Mrs Wilding.

"Well, I have brought it," she said. "But isn't everyone just dying to talk?"

"Now you know perfectly well, Carrie, that we just love music. Count Zekes is very musical and so is Countess Zekes and I am sure Mr Trevenen is too."

After a little more pressing, Miss Clyde fetched her music and sat down at the pianoforte. She sang some songs by Brahms, and an Italian song. She had a fine voice and had been well taught.

"Do you sing any Schumann?" Countess Zekes asked.

"Yes, I will, if you like, certainly. What would you like?"

"Oh, the *Dichterliebe*," said Countess Zekes.

Miss Clyde sang the *Dichterliebe*, and when she got to the second song, "*Aus meinen Thränen spriessen*," Alex looked at Christopher. When she had finished, and everyone was applauding, Alex said to Christopher: "That was the song Karl used to play." He remembered that night on the terrace and he also remembered the night at Merrydown when somebody had played it. But all this he was surprised to find, meant nothing to him. Nothing at all. Alex was to him like a perfect stranger, and even what was more the thought of Esther meant nothing to him. All that was over. He was surprised to find that this was so.

When the party broke up and he was saying good-bye, Countess Zekes said to him:

"You will come and see us, won't you?"

"I'm afraid I never go out," said Christopher.

"But you must come and see us. We have a *jour* on Mondays, but don't come then. Come any other time, and telephone first."

"I'm afraid I never go out," said Christopher. "I think," he said, looking at Zekes, "that it is a mistake for gentlemen to ask reporters to their houses." And he left the room.

Christopher walked down the Via Settembre, past the station where the fountains were flashing in the moonlight. He wondered why the meeting with Alex had not opened the wound that Esther had inflicted on him. It had not. He said to himself, "I no longer care. All that is as if it had not happened. I feel nothing. That side of me is dead. I wonder whether I shall ever feel anything of that kind again? Ever really mind anything again? *Really* mind? No, of course not; but I suppose on the whole it is better not to."

Three days later, Alex wrote him a charming letter and begged him not to be silly but to come and see her. She asked him to luncheon. He wrote back, saying that he had seriously meant it when he said he did not go out.

"I went to the Wildings," he wrote, *"because he was an old friend of an old friend of mine, but I never do go out. I find it impossible. You mustn't think me rude. I cannot do it. I appreciate your kindness, but we live in different worlds. I have tried the experiment of going into other worlds than my own and it has always failed, as it is bound to do."*

He changed his mode of life. It was necessary for him to see a certain number of people on account of his work, but he resolutely refused to go out in society. He would not go to the Wildings' house, nor even to see Pavlov. He settled down in his *pension* and resumed his Eastern studies.

He began to work upon Sackbut's papers. He found this work absorbingly interesting. At the same time it filled him with despair. Sackbut knew too much. He began to make closer friends with the inmates of the *pension*. The two Englishmen there were aloof and shy. One of them had smooth hair and well-tied ties tied in a bow and that aristocratic carelessness which irritated Christopher like a red rag. The other was curly-haired, observant, mischievous, and fond of books. Christopher did not like him either.

Then there were the Italians, who were friendly, especially the sculptor Ansoni, who looked like a decayed nobleman. The German lady and her niece kept to themselves; the Polish lady sometimes read Russian with him. She was sentimental and insinuating, and he had long political discussions with her. She was an ardent Liberal and did not believe that a Liberal could ever do wrong. There was also Whitehead, the American student of archaeology; he was super-refined and had no roots in any continent.

CHAPTER XXV

Christopher's life went on quietly in this groove until after Christmas. One afternoon at the beginning of February, he went to the Museo Nazionale, and he was about to buy his ticket of admittance when he found himself face to face with Madame D'Alberg.

"Such a stupid thing has happened to me," she said. "I want to go into the Museum and I have paid my cab and I find that I have no money left. Can you lend me some *lire*?"

Christopher said that of course he would.

"Are you going in too?"

"Yes."

"Then let us look at the things together, unless you are one of those people who must be alone in a Museum or in a picture gallery."

"Not at all," said Christopher.

They went upstairs and looked at one thing and another. Madame D'Alberg showed Christopher the things she admired most, and pointed out what her husband used to admire and quoted what he had said about this and that.

After they had been there some time, she said:

"This is great fun. Great fun for me at least. I so seldom go to a Museum by myself."

"Would you like me to go away?"

She laughed.

"That is not what I meant. What I meant was that I so often have to show Museums to people who are staying in Rome or else go to them with people I don't want to go with – this is a holiday."

"I suppose you see a great many people?"

"Not many, but always the same people. Rome is a place where people have settled habits and make nests, and several people have made a nest in my house." She laughed. "Old men chiefly," she went on. "I have a fatal attraction for the old. When we lived in Paris and my husband was alive, a certain number of people used to come and see him every day and discuss serious things. They got used to seeing him, and when I migrated here some of them followed me."

"I suppose you knew a great many people in Paris?"

"Yes, any amount of people, my husband did at least, till the Dreyfus case upset everything."

"Which side were you on?"

"It was a dreadful tangle. I was for Dreyfus, but not altogether for the *Dreyfusards*. My husband was against Dreyfus – but not entirely for the *anti-Dreyfusards*. He was a strong revisionist."

"I understand that. I have been like that, in that situation all my life. I mean I have been for the Dreyfuses but against the *Dreyfusards*. In that case I was not even for Dreyfus. I mean, I think he was guilty."

"I am sure he was innocent, but he was made a – what is it called? not a stumbling block, and not an Aunt Sally?"

"A stalking horse?"

"Yes, that is it. It changed our life, because there were friends who used to come and see us every day of their lives, who could no longer come because they could no longer speak to each other."

They walked on and looked at something else. They came to the head of the dying Persian.

"I think," said Madame D'Alberg, "that that is one of the most beautiful things in the world."

"Yes," said Christopher, "it expresses something indomitable. A man who has got to die and doesn't mind. I prefer that to the Christian morality people, who die meekly. I like people to die defiantly."

"Perhaps they didn't know any better."

"You mean it was because they were barbarians. I don't agree. Take the orientals. They are not barbarians, and take any oriental however well-educated, or however ill-educated, not one of them will mind death. They know too much about that sort of thing. They know death doesn't matter."

"But you don't think that?"

"Yes, I do."

"You don't seem to me at all like an oriental. I don't think you have any of the oriental indifference. Your father was Irish, wasn't he?"

"Yes, but he was very serene."

"And your mother?"

"My mother was French. She was a Mademoiselle de Sarthenay."

"How stupid of me! We knew her, at least my husband used to know her quite well. She came to live in Paris for a time and then didn't she go to Versailles?"

"Yes, she did."

"And I used to read your father's articles, and now I must read yours."

"Oh, mine are not worth reading."

"Do you go on with your oriental studies? Mina Turçin said you were an oriental scholar."

"Yes, I have begun lately. I was a friend of a scholar called Sackbut. He left me an unfinished book to edit."

"We knew him too. He used to come and see us in Paris. I hope you will edit the book. My husband admired him more than anyone."

"I shall try; but journalism fritters away one's time. I did nothing all the time I was in Russia, but I have more time here."

"Yes, and you have the Vatican library."

They walked on and looked at other things. They talked about the Turçins, Constantinople, Russia, Pavlov, Rome, France, Italians, friends. The time went quickly. Christopher found himself talking to Madame D'Alberg as if he had always known her.

At last she looked at her watch and said: "I must go now. Do you know it's very late? We have been here hours. You must come and see me. Come some evening – next Monday."

Christopher explained that he never went out.

"If you mind people," Madame D'Alberg said, "you must come when there is no one there. There never are many people in my house. Only Wildenspruch and Altamura, and sometimes Pavlov."

"You will think me very odd, but I don't want to get into that set."

"It isn't a set."

"Perhaps not, but they all know each other so well and I don't know them."

"One must make a beginning. However, I understand you. I felt just like that when I married. I felt I should never make friends with anyone in Paris; not real friends. Well, you must come some day when there is no one."

"Very well," said Christopher, and he fetched Madame D'Alberg a cab.

When the following Monday came, Christopher felt an inclination to visit Madame D'Alberg, but he resisted it.

"There's sure to be a crowd of people," he said to himself. When dinner was over at the *pension* he settled not to go and went into the *pension* sitting room. It was a large high room. The signora's son was playing the mandoline and one of the signora's nieces was accompanying him. He was playing the opening song of the *Cavalleria Rusticana*. The German lady and her daughter were sitting by the table bolt upright, knitting. The Polish lady was discussing politics with Ansoni, and the Signora and Miss O'Connor were discussing domestic matters. The others had all gone out. Christopher sat down on the sofa, but became restless. He thought he might go after all, later. Then he suddenly said that he had to go out, and he took a cab and drove to Madame D'Alberg's house. There was no one there when he arrived.

"This is nice," Madame D'Alberg said. "Sit down and smoke and we will have a good talk."

They began talking. Madame D'Alberg asked him about the *pension* and made him describe the inmates one by one. She seemed to know what they were like before he described them.

"There is a signora's son," he said, "who is in business and plays the mandoline."

"Yes," she said. "The *Cavalleria*."

"And laughs at the nieces."

"Yes," she said, "because they go to picture galleries. Does he say *'preferisco un buon piatto di maccheroni?'*"

"He does," said Christopher, "and the Englishmen, at least one of them, teases one of the nieces too. One of the nieces is artistic and the other is philanthropic. Then they have tremendous discussions with Miss O'Connor about the earth being flat, and Ansoni, the sculptor, agrees, and Whitehead, an American, very seriously proves why it is impossible, although he says the usual proofs are absurd."

"And what do the Germans say?" asked Madame D'Alberg.

"Oh, they say nothing."

They talked on and on and he was enjoying his talk when Scalchi was announced, and he was almost immediately followed by a Russian lady who was handsome, middle-aged and full of herself, and began to tell everyone in detail the plans she had made for organising a fête and a bazaar at which artistic objects in wood, wool and stuff would be made by Russian peasants, and sold. Scalchi began to chatter, a Frenchman was announced, and Christopher got up and said good-bye.

"You must come again soon," said Madame D'Alberg.

Christopher said he would, but he thought to himself: "Not I. It is no use. It is impossible to see her by herself. The house is obviously always full of people. I was a fool to go." But how he had enjoyed his conversation with Madame D'Alberg as long as it had lasted, and how soon it had been interrupted! "What a pity it is that one cannot see her without that chattering crowd. Of course they go there every day. I shall never see her again."

About a week later he went to the Protestant Cemetery. It was a soft February afternoon. There were milky clouds in the pale blue sky.

He ran into Madame D'Alberg at the gate.

"I am so glad to see you," she said. "I'm afraid you were bored the other night, but it isn't always so bad. You must come again. I'll telephone to you next time when I know it's safe." She laughed.

They walked up the hill.

"Do you often come here?" asked Christopher.

"Yes, often. My father was buried here. I come to look after the grave. Here it is, not far from Shelley's. This was his favourite spot in Rome."

They paused opposite the grave. There was a marble tablet, with a laurel wreath, carved in marble, and an inscription just giving the name: "Walter de Luce" and the dates of his birth and death.

"We lived at Florence," said Madame D'Alberg, "but my father one winter had a wild desire to come to Rome. I think he knew he was going to die and he wanted to die here. So we came here for the winter and he caught cold and died."

"That is exactly what happened to my father," said Christopher. "He is buried in Rome too, but in the Catholic cemetery."

"I wish I had been born a Catholic," said Madame D'Alberg. "As it was I was brought up like Perdita on the sea coast of Bohemia."

"Your father was a genius, wasn't he?"

"No, not a genius. He had talent; too many talents, and too much of each. He was half Scotch and half Irish, and the two elements fought against each other. When he was young the Scotch side won, and he painted portraits, and one or two beautiful landscapes. You have probably seen some of them. Then he married my mother. She was English, she had a beautiful voice and she was studying for the opera, but she gave up the idea when she married."

"That always happens, doesn't it?"

"No, not always; most singers are married. But when one artist marries another, I suppose it is rare for both of them to go on, although that happens sometimes. My mother worshipped my father and believed in him. They went to Italy directly they were married, and lived in Florence, where I was born. My father was making quite a lot of money by his pictures. At least he could have made a lot, but he was always thinking of something else: music, musical instruments, chemistry, carving, even astrology. Our household was extraordinary. The untidiest villa in the world. The most fantastic life. Luckily we had an angel called Giovanni, to look after it. After a time my father gave up painting because he thought he had discovered the secret of making stained glass. The way they used to make it in the Middle Ages – he put all his money in experiments, and lost it. He only made one window. Then my mother died. My father was ill and dreadfully poor, but full of another scheme, a complicated musical instrument which he thought he could invent. But we had no money. We sold everything and he had some good pictures by other people, and this brought in a little. Then he insisted on going to Rome and we struggled there in the winter. That is where I met Auguste D'Alberg. We got engaged almost at once. Father died directly after that – we were married in Rome quietly and then after a little journey we went to Paris and there I lived for the rest of my life, till I migrated here after my husband died. That is all my story."

Madame D'Alberg arranged some flowers she had brought with her on the grave.

"Did your mother ever regret having given up the stage?"

"Oh, never."

"And would she have been a great singer?"

"I think she would have been a great success. To begin with, she was beautiful. She had large black eyes, and a fine presence. And her voice was magnificent. It would have filled the Colosseum, but the funny thing was, she wasn't in the least musical. She could sing in tune. She couldn't sing out of tune, but that was like a bird. But she had no idea of the difference between good and bad music. She used to make my father despair by the things she preferred singing. He was the soul of music and used to play any instrument."

"And you?"

"I know nothing about music and have no talents of any kind, but I suppose I know what is bad. I inherited that from my father. He used to compose songs too, but he never would write them down and everything in the house used to be lost."

"Was your mother practical?"

"Oh, no, not at all. She had everything that goes with the artistic temperament, except good taste in music. I believe she would have been a great operatic singer, a great actress, I mean, because when you heard her sing something good, when my father used to make her sing something good, she used to sing as if she understood it."

"I expect she did unconsciously."

"Oh no! She frankly preferred songs, like 'The Lost Chord,' and 'The Better Land' and the worst Hymns Ancient and Modern, to anything else."

"But she never felt a wish to go on the stage afterwards?"

"No, she never gave it a thought. She was happy except when my brother died. I had one brother. He died when he was little, six. He was older than I and I can only just remember him. He caught cold and I thought it was my fault."

"Oh, did you?"

"Yes, it's a thing that often happens to children and it makes them miserable for years."

"It does."

"My father and my mother had a happy life in spite of everything. They enjoyed the sunshine. They enjoyed seeing people. He enjoyed his experiments."

"Did he give up painting altogether?"

"Practically, although he painted something every now and then if they wanted money. I think he would have been a really good painter if he had gone straight on, when he started."

"Marriage spoilt both their artistic careers."

"Yes, but they were happier like that. And after all, what do careers matter?"

"You think they don't matter?"

"I think it's the quality of life that matters. For instance I think it is more important for you to edit Sackbut's book, or try to, than to be a successful journalist. But I have stayed here far too long, boring you with my life's history. You must come and see me again in the evening."

"I will come," said Christopher, but he was determined not to go to her house again. "Because," he said to himself, "it is useless."

They walked down to the gate of the cemetery and Christopher saw her into her cab.

CHAPTER XXVI

It was only a few days after this meeting that Christopher was asked by telephone from Madame D'Alberg to come and have luncheon with her the next day, to meet an old friend. He went and to his astonishment he found Madame Turçin. She had been ordered south, as she had suffered from bronchitis in Paris, and she was on her way to Naples. She was staying for the inside of the week at Rome, at an hotel. She had left her husband in Paris, and she was in deep mourning, as her mother had just died. There was no one else at the luncheon. Christopher was glad to see her, and she seemed delighted to see him. She had aged a great deal. She looked older than she was. She had grown larger and her face had become thin, it was white and heavily lined, and there were black shadows under her eyes. She looked ill and coughed a good deal. But she was just as charming. They talked over old times and she told them all the Paris news. She asked after all her Roman friends. She was going to see a few people, but she had no wish to meet any one. She said she felt tired, and incapable of talking. The next day Madame D'Alberg asked them both to dinner, and they sat up late talking. Madame Turçin said she did not like Paris and was overjoyed at being back in Rome.

The next evening Madame Turçin asked Christopher to dinner at the hotel, and there he found Madame D'Alberg and

Pavlov. And the night after, Madame Turçin's last night, they both dined with Madame D'Alberg. There was no one else there.

Christopher asked Madame Turçin whether she still possessed the book about the Fourth Crusade that Alishan had given her.

"Yes," she said, "and I have left it to you in my will."

"To me!"

"Yes, to you, in memory of what you did for the Armenians. If you never do anything else all your life, your life will have been worth living just because of that."

They again sat up late discussing everything under the sun.

When Christopher said good-night, Madame Turçin said to him, "We may meet again if I stop on my way back, but that," she smiled sadly, "is doubtful; but if we don't meet again I want to thank you."

"Why shouldn't we meet again?"

"Because life is so uncertain," she said.

When Christopher said good-night to Madame D'Alberg she said: "Now that we know each other so well, do you feel capable of coming here by yourself just any evening without my having to write or ring you up?"

"One never knows," said Christopher, "it might be just the evening when you didn't want me."

"I am either at home, or I am not," said Madame D'Alberg, "and you can always find out by telephoning. And when I *am* at home, I shall always be delighted to see you."

"Very well, I will do that, but I am no use with people."

"To save us both trouble, if you would like to look in on Monday night, after dinner, there will be no one. You can come Sunday too, if you like, only on Sunday there will be a few people; there always are on Sundays."

"I will come on Monday," said Christopher.

"He is very *sauvage*," said Madame Turçin, "but you, dearest Antoinette, will cure him of that."

"I am trying to," said Madame D'Alberg, "I want him to get used to my old men. They are so harmless."

Madame Turçin left Rome on Saturday evening.

During that week and in company with Madame Turçin and partly through Madame Turçin, Christopher had got to know Madame D'Alberg more quickly than he would otherwise have done for months; more quickly than if he had seen her alone from time to time. The presence of a third person whom they both knew and with whom they were both comfortable drew him out. He was already at his ease with Madame D'Alberg; he became still more so; and this sense of ease increased in the presence of Madame Turçin.

Christopher went to the station to see Madame Turçin off. He thought she looked ill. She was pleased to see him.

"I want you to make friends with Antoinette D'Alberg," she said to him as they walked on the platform.

"I think I have," said Christopher, laughing. "I have seen a great deal of her this last week."

"But I mean real friends. Don't be shy of going. She likes it, and don't mind the old men. They really don't count any more than the furniture; one gets used to them and there are not nearly as many here as there used to be in Paris. You see, her life is so lonely."

"After Paris?"

"It isn't Paris – she never cared a straw for Paris. It is after what she has gone through."

"Her husband's death?"

"Yes, of course." Madame Turçin paused. "She misses him dreadfully. He was a great scholar – and her life is empty; and before she had so many friends."

"She told me that *he* did everything; that people came to see *him*."

"It's not true, although she may like to think so. Indeed, they may have thought so. They used to go at first to see him. And they went on going, thinking they were going to see him, but really to see her. Some of them realised this. She is a wonderful woman, and many people found this out. She likes you, so don't throw away the opportunity."

"As I have thrown away everything else? Can she really stand me?"

"She told me she could talk to you as if she had known you all her life. She said she felt this the very first time she had a real talk with you."

"It was at the Museo Nazionale; we met by chance."

"Yes, she told me. So please be good, and don't throw away this opportunity. Please be kind, and be reasonable; if you knew what her life had been you would do this."

"I will. I promise. I think she is charming, and nobody can have been kinder than she has been."

"You see, her life is empty; none of the people here exist for her."

There was a shout of "*Partenza!*" "There, it is time to go. Thank you so much for coming, I am very much touched. Good-bye."

"*Au revoir!*"

"Yes, *au revoir*, perhaps." She got into the train.

Christopher found himself waiting for Monday evening with impatience. He nearly went on Sunday evening to Madame D'Alberg's, but he said to himself, "It would really be too silly, and there will be a lot of people. I shall only make a fool of myself." But Saturday and Sunday seemed to him interminable.

At last Monday evening came. When he got to Madame D'Alberg's apartment, he found to his dismay and disappointment that Professor Wildenspruch was there. Wildenspruch was an oldish German professor from Munich, an archaeologist who talked guttural French. He had a stubbly grey beard and kind grey eyes, and he was kind except when it was a question of other people's archaeology. Madame D'Alberg met Christopher in the library and said to him, "Don't mind

Wildenspruch. He won't stay long." They sat down in the small sitting room. Wildenspruch bowed stiffly to Christopher and said to him: "Madame D'Alberg tells me you are also the friend of the late Professor Sackbut. I have read his books and they are good. He was a very learned man. It was a pity he was politically so narrow-minded."

Christopher made some acknowledgment.

"And you are also interested in Eastern studies?"

"I have done a little work of that kind."

"All that is outside my province, but all roads, as they say, lead to Rome also. *Ach!* Dear Madame, my cold is so troublesome tonight, that I will also leave you and go to bed."

He got up and kissed Madame D'Alberg's hand, bowed stiffly to Christopher, and left.

When he had gone, she said, "I have known him for years. He used to come to Paris sometimes. My husband liked him. He was the only German he did like. '*Il est bon et il est bête*,' he used to say, '*ce qui est aussi une qualité, malgré son bagage de science.*' And it is true, he is good although he is crotchety, and needs a lot of attention and is jealous. He has gone now, not at all on account of his cold but because he is jealous of you…jealous of your being here. He hates newcomers in my house, especially the young, but he has to put up with it, and then in a short time when he is used to them he is nice to them and likes them to come."

"I'm sorry I've spoilt his evening," said Christopher.

"You haven't spoilt it, he enjoys the demonstration. He will scold me tomorrow, and then he will soon be asking why you are not here."

"How long does it take for him to get used to a new person?"

"About a fortnight. He comes to see me almost every day, and so does Altamura, who has written a history. They detest each other, but they can't do without each other's company. They come after luncheon or at tea time and sometimes in the evening, but Altamura won't come tonight, he is away."

"Is he jealous too?"

"Altamura? Oh, yes, fearfully, but in an Italian way. He teases Wildenspruch dreadfully. He has a genius for teasing."

"And do they get on with Pavlov?"

"They don't mind him. He doesn't come so often. He likes sitting at home. He pays me a visit about once a week."

"Did you know Altamura in Paris?"

"Yes, he used to come to Paris quite often. He had many friends there."

"And does he go there now?"

"Oh, yes, every year."

"But I suppose you see many other people too?"

"Oh, yes, there are others, of course, but they don't come often, and I go out very little. I have done with all that. When I was in Paris my husband was at home every day of his life from six till dinner time, so you see I had my share of entertaining."

"You had a *salon*?"

"My husband had a *salon*. They came to see him. I was just a piece of furniture."

Christopher wondered whether anyone had ever thought Madame D'Alberg was just a piece of furniture.

"When my husband died," she said, "I tried to keep it up for a time, but I found I couldn't. It was intolerable. *Hamlet* without the Prince of Denmark with a vengeance. So I came here to bury myself and end my life quietly."

"End?"

"Yes – and even if I live to be eighty, I feel that everything is over."

"Do you feel that? I feel the same thing!"

"You! What nonsense! Why, you are a baby!"

"I am thirty-three."

"Everything that side of forty is young and I expect everything the other side is old – for a woman, that is to say. I shall soon know. Men go on much longer. Go on living, I mean. Goethe had love affairs when he was eighty!"

"And Ninon de Lenclos?"

"She went on being charming all her life. You see, when you are young, you live for yourself; I mean, you have your own life, even while you are living for others. But there comes a time when you live only for others."

Christopher wondered whether she lived only for Wildenspruch and Altamura. It seemed difficult to believe.

"Do you think," he said, "that when you say to yourself, you will never feel anything again, you are right?"

"Not at your age. And for a man, as I said, I think it is never too late to feel. Do you think you will never feel anything again?"

"I am sure of it."

"Tell me the facts and I will judge."

Christopher found himself telling Madame D'Alberg the story of his childhood, of Mabel's death, of his engagement to Alex, his years at Cambridge, about the Claydons and his engagement to Esther. He had never spoken of these things before to anyone, except briefly to Alex. But now he felt no difficulty in doing so. When he had finished his story, she said to him:

"I think you behaved foolishly. You threw away your chance. She evidently loved you."

"Oh, no. I'm sure she loved the other man."

"Perhaps afterwards, but not then. You hurt her, and she turned to the nearest first-aid."

"Then she couldn't have loved me."

"To my mind it proves that she did. The Russian lady thought so too?"

Christopher told her how the incident of the Coat without Seam had turned up at various epochs in his life.

"I know that church at Vernay," said Madame D'Alberg. "Did you tell Madame Turçin about that?" she asked.

"No, I didn't."

"What a pity."

"You see, I didn't know her well, and then I left. I will tell her when she comes back."

"Yes, if she comes back."

"But she is bound to pass through Rome, isn't she?"

"She is ill. I don't think she will live long. I think she is dying, and she knows it. However, I envy rather than pity her, she has not been happy."

"Yes, I see. I see – that is what she meant."

"She would have appreciated the story and probably seen a meaning in it. She is spiritually-minded and understands things that we don't understand."

"You think there is a meaning in it."

"Probably; my husband used to say that every man, the most insignificant as well as the vilest, has his task allotted to him by Providence, but does he ever know what it is? We can't see the pattern of our lives, but I suppose it is plain to the Designer of the tapestry; all that happens in our lives is like stitches of *petit-point*, and we ourselves are small squares of canvas on a huge stretch of tapestry.

"I expect this incident of the Coat without Seam is a significative bright stitch. It is odd I knew that church at Vernay. Do you know, I think our lives, although they seem patchy, untidy and purposeless, are very likely, every one of them, Coats without a Seam, and have a perfect unity, so that they could not be cut up or divided without being spoilt."

"But they appear to be cut up already."

"Yes, that is just it – but supposing that is because we can't see them properly – supposing we are looking from the wrong angle and in the wrong perspective?"

"I wonder."

"At any rate I like the story having happened in your life, even if it means nothing: even if it is just an ornament, as when painters suddenly put a bird in the corner of their pictures, just for fun. It would have delighted my father and my husband."

"I thought perhaps it would have irritated him."

"My husband? Oh, no, on the contrary."

"But he wasn't a Catholic."

"Yes, he was. I suppose you thought he was a Buddhist or a Mahommedan. French people, however great orientalists they may be, are rarely oriental in mind. All that is too vague for them, and they cannot think from right to left. That is why they are generally either Catholics or nothing. My husband was brought up as a Catholic, and then for a time had no Faith at all, or Faith in too many gods, and then went back to it at the time of the Dreyfus case. He was not pious but he endorsed it – violently. You see, with the French, directly the religious nerve is touched, they go mad. He used to say that the religions of the Jews and of the other Eastern races were like the hints of dawn and the clouds of daybreak before the sunrise of the Mass... And you, what do you think of those things?"

"I have no religious faith."

"None at all in anything?"

"None."

"But you were brought up... "

"As a Catholic. Yes, and it is perhaps owing to that that all forms of revealed religion mean nothing to me at all. I mean, in all those variations I see only one formula."

"The Catholic religion?"

"Yes, all other forms of Christianity, Eastern or Western, seem to me reflections or refractions or distortions or caricatures of the Catholic Creed and doctrine."

"But then, what is the difficulty?"

"Well, to accept that Creed you must have Faith. Faith based on reason and on Will, but Faith is *Faith* – a gift. I think any priest would tell me that I had lost it by neglecting the practice of my religion: but I can't say I have lost it. I've never really had it. The grain of mustard seed has never been given to me."

"But can't you believe in something?"

"Well, what? The oriental religions? About those I think I

agree with your husband, that they too are only different versions, well, prophecies or hints or shadows or warnings of the same thing. I think the same thing is true of Plato and Virgil and all the spiritual Pagans. Mahommedanism is to me like Calvinism and all forms of Puritanism and Protestantism: a distortion of the central idea. All that has come about from concentrating on one item, to the exclusion or overshadowing of the others. But about the East I am again like your husband, I admire it, but I can't think from right to left. I used to think I could, but I can't."

"But surely you could just believe in God."

"That is what people call 'third philosophies'; what some people call *real* religion: *natural* religion: perhaps you do – Pantheism, Positivism, the religion of duty…but duty to what, to whom? And why? Renan's agnostic optimism, which is exactly the same as Tennyson's, when one comes to look into it. Schopenhauer's pessimism which is only a variation of Buddha, and only in the last resort a distortion, of a part of Catholic dogma. Confucius, Lao-tse. All that the poets have said, all those so-called undogmatic hopes and dreams – most of them distorted dogma – they do not satisfy me. Then what is left? The certainty of suffering, the hope of annihilation? My only prayer is FitzGerald's. It isn't in Omar; the thought would have been inconceivable to him:

Oh, Thou, who man of baser Earth didst make,
And even with Paradise devise the snake,
For all the Sin wherewith the Face of Man
Is blacken'd – Man's forgiveness give – and take!

That is my philosophy and my creed. And my sure and certain hope is in perpetual sleep."

Madame D'Alberg looked at him with great pity.

"Sure and certain, is it? Nobody can say that. 'Ay, there's the rub!' Well, all that is, I think, very sad, and all the sadder because I see it is all true. People often say things like that for fun, or think they think them when they don't really; but you do. I can see that, and I can be of no help. Because I do not believe in anything *definite*, and I have a feeling that unless one does believe in something definite it's not much use believing at all. That may be my husband's influence. It certainly was his opinion. Vague religions used to annoy him, and he was always quoting Renan's '*Malheur au vague! mieux vaut le faux.*' He used to say all that was muddle-headedness, but I am a woman, and I am muddle-headed, and I don't believe anything definite, but I do believe there is something to believe in; there is for me just a glimmer of light; not enough, but just a glimmer, and I always hope some day that it may grow into something brighter. I always hope that some day some tiny little thing may bring about for one the moment that came to Faust when he was dying: the moment when he suddenly felt all was worth while, just by looking at some people working to save the sea from encroaching on the cultivated land. It was in that moment, and not when he was in love with Gretchen, or saw Helen of Troy, and tasted power, that he understood life was worth living."

"Yes, but isn't that what's called conversion?"

"I don't know what it's called. Call it what you like. I only know I have never had it. On the other hand, I am certain it happens to people. That it is to be had. In other words, I believe that there is such a thing as Faith."

"And you think it isn't an illusion – that people aren't pretending to themselves?"

"Yes, I think if people like my husband thought it wasn't an illusion, I can think so too. But I haven't got it."

"But you would like to have it?"

"Oh, yes! Wouldn't you? It seems to me that if one had that, nothing else in the world would matter, and life would seem simple. I think that is what Goethe meant by the death of Faust. Life suddenly seemed to him simple, as it does when one comes to from laughing gas, and thinks one has solved the riddle of the universe. It seems to happen to different people in different ways. I have seen it happen myself."

"But don't you think it is because people *want* to believe?"

"The wish father to the thought?"

"Yes."

"No, not at all. I know, and surely you have known, people who would give worlds for Faith in anything, but it's no use their wishing."

"Yes, that is true."

"Would you like to have Faith?" she asked.

"It's no use my *liking*. I haven't got it."

"But do you want it? You said just now that Faith was founded on reason and on will. Have you the will?"

"I usen't to have it; but now – well now I'm not sure. At any rate, I could never be a practising Catholic again."

"Why not?"

"Because I could never feel *contrition*."

"Don't you regret anything you have ever done?"

"Yes; but not *everything*. Not everything that the church condemns. There are certain things which the church condemns as mortal sin which I have done, and which I don't regret. So far from regretting them, I would do them again with joy. However – " He looked at his watch.

"It's late," he said, "I must go."

It was half-past twelve.

251

CHAPTER XXVII

Madame D'Alberg had told Christopher to come and see her whenever he liked, and he had said that he would do so. He would have liked to go the next evening, but he thought it was hardly decent. Then there came a press of work. The first evening he was free, he rang up Madame D'Alberg and asked whether he could come.

"Of course," she said, "only I'm afraid you will be bored. Dolly Tolovoi will be there and some others."

Christopher realised that she was the Russian lady who was getting up the bazaar.

"I will come another night," he said. He was disappointed. Two days later Madame D'Alberg rang him up and asked him to come. He found Wildenspruch, Scalchi and Altamura, who was just back from Paris. Altamura was dark and good-looking, grey at the temples; his eyes seemed to see everything, and everything about him – especially his hands – gave one the impression of centuries and hidden stores of pent-up civilisation.

He talked of Paris. He had been to London for a few days. He had seen plays and pictures and people. He talked mostly of people. Wildenspruch made interjections every now and then, and sometimes hazarded a contradiction, but most of the conversation was carried on by Altamura and Scalchi who both of them seemed to know the same people all over Europe.

Madame D'Alberg was busy at a patience, and every now and then she said something to Christopher and to the others. Christopher no longer felt ill at ease, and he stayed late.

He soon made a habit of going to Madame D'Alberg's house in the evening. There was an understanding that she should telephone to him when *not* to come. She did this every now and then. When Christopher did go he frequently found Wildenspruch, and sometimes Altamura as well. Now and then she asked him to luncheon, but he hardly ever saw her alone in her house for more than a few moments. He resented this; at the same time he saw no way out of it. Sometimes he would suggest meeting at a Museum, or at the Villa Borghese, but she always had something else to do.

In spite of this he enjoyed being an inmate of her house. He no longer had any feeling of awkwardness when he was there. The others, too, accepted him. Scalchi was amiability itself. Wildenspruch made jokes for his benefit, and disputed the things he said in his despatches. Altamura was civil; but he did not meet Altamura so often. He did not feel so sure about Altamura. He was not sure whether Altamura did accept him so wholeheartedly. He was aware when he saw him, of a searching questioning look, which seemed to say "What are you like really? And what are you *about*?" The time went by pleasantly and swiftly until Easter. Christopher's life progressed in a pleasant groove. He saw the people at his *pension*, some of his fellow correspondents, Madame D'Alberg, and the inmates of her house, but no one else.

At Easter, Yakovlev came out to Rome. He stayed at an hotel for a day. He was on his way to Naples to see Madame Turçin. Christopher only saw him for a moment. But on his way back, he intended to stay a week. He came back to Rome, and two days later he took Christopher with him to Tivoli. He wanted to have a long talk with him. They drove there in the morning, in a motor-car. Christopher asked after Madame Turçin.

"She is no better," said Yakovlev, "her husband is coming out next week. They do not think she can live long."

"Is there no hope?"

"No real hope. It may drag on. They talked of Egypt, but she won't go. It is too far away. She likes Naples, and she knows she is dying. We talked of you a great deal. I talked of you, too, with Sergei Dimitrevitch" (that was Pavlov). "I had dinner with him last night. He tells me you will not go near him."

"I don't go out."

"I should not have thought you would find too much society in his house."

"There are always people there. Not my sort."

"Well, I should have thought they would have been. He tells me the only place where he meets you is at the *Casa* D'Alberg."

"Yes, I have seen him there sometimes."

"A charming woman."

"Do you know her?"

"I knew her husband a little, and I met her in Paris. I went to their house once or twice. That was a long time ago."

"What was he like?"

"D'Alberg? Remarkable in some ways. He knew everything, like Sackbut, only he was less…less difficult. He had a more human nature, but he was less refined. In other words he was a Frenchman, and Gallic."

"I suppose she was devoted to him?"

"Yes, she was very young when she married. She was a good wife."

"He had a regular *salon*, hadn't he?"

"She had. People came from other countries to see her, and sometimes they stayed."

"Oh, who for instance?"

"Wildenspruch."

"Oh! Wildenspruch."

"Madame Turçin was her greatest friend. She told me she

hoped you would make friends with Madame D'Alberg and not be wild."

"I have. I go there often; but it is impossible ever to see her properly. The house is always full of the same people."

"I saw Anna Feodorovna in London not long ago."

"How are they?"

"Very well. They sent you messages."

"She writes to me sometimes."

"He thinks it a pity you left Russia."

"I suppose D'Alberg adored his wife?"

"He admired her and appreciated her intelligence, but she was not really…not really *ce qu'il lui fallait.* He had a long and permanent *liaison* with a Madame Morgan."

"Who was she?"

"She was a Greek married to a French journalist who died. She used to write articles too, and once wrote a play, I think. She was vivacious, very clever, and rather common."

"Did Madame D'Alberg mind?"

"She never showed it."

"And were there lots of people in love with Madame D'Alberg?"

"There were some moths."

"And she?"

"I don't know. Does one ever know?"

"Was there anyone in particular?"

"I don't know. I didn't know them well."

"Are you going to see her?"

"Yes. Sergei Dimitrevitch is taking me there tomorrow evening."

" I will come too."

The next evening they met at Madame D'Alberg's. There was no one there but Pavlov and two Russian ladies called Olenev, who were friends of Yakovlev. Christopher enjoyed the evening. It was rest to be there without either Wildenspruch or Altamura. Madame D'Alberg said she was going to Naples. Yakovlev stayed a week at Rome, and then went back to Cambridge for the beginning of the term. Shortly after he had gone, Wilding wrote to him and said:

"You have just got to come and lunch tomorrow. There are two old friends of yours lunching with me. Mr and Mrs Norton, who are crazy to meet you."

Christopher went, and found the Nortons, whom he had not seen since the death of their daughter, and of Spence, and a young Englishman called Guy Cunninghame who was an honorary Attaché at the British Embassy, a friend of the Nortons. Cunninghame was young, elegant and affable. The Nortons were pleased to see Christopher. Both their faces bore the stamp of sorrow, and Mrs Norton looked twenty years older. Cunninghame seemed to know numbers of people in Rome and England and America. Madame Turçin was mentioned.

"Poor woman," said Mrs Norton, "I hear she is so ill. Is she out there at Naples all by her lonesome self?"

"Turçin is coming out at once," said Cunninghame.

"They don't expect her to live long."

"I'm glad he's coming," said Mrs Norton, "otherwise I suppose she would have no friends."

"Not at Naples," said Cunninghame, "of course she had lots of friends here. Her greatest friend is Madame D'Alberg. She has gone to Naples to be with her."

"Is she a Frenchwoman?" asked Mrs Norton.

"No," said Cunninghame, "she is the widow of Auguste D'Alberg, the writer, who wrote long books about the East which I haven't read. She was English, the daughter of de Luce, the painter, and she lived in Paris all her life. She is attractive: beautiful eyes, and I believe, charming, but one never sees her now."

"Not since her husband's death, I suppose," said Mrs

Norton.

"Yes, and anyway she lives entirely in a tiny circle of friends, all rather intellectual, except Altamura of course; and even he, although not an 'intellectual,' is highly cultivated and has written books."

"That's that dark Cicero one sees at the club," said Wilding, "doing Mark Antony stuff."

"Yes," said Cunninghame, "he was wildly in love with Madame D'Alberg for years, and is still... I think he would marry her, only he can't because although he's separated from his wife, they can't of course be divorced."

"His wife is alive?" asked Christopher.

"Very much alive, and she still leads poor old Philip Buontresori a fearful life, although he is sick to death of her."

"And how do you like Rome, Mr Trevenen?" said Mrs Norton.

"Mr Trevenen," said Mrs Wilding, "lives like a perfect bear. It's as difficult to get hold of him as it is to flog a Wilding from a high-ball. If it hadn't been that you were coming, we should never have had him here with us today."

"I expect he's too busy," said Cunninghame. "He writes the best articles that have been written from here for ages. The Ambassador thinks they are first rate. He was saying only yesterday what a pity it was one couldn't get hold of him."

Christopher said nothing, and Mrs Norton came to his aid.

"You know," she said, "I think he's right; when people who have got work to do – real work – start chasing round, they end by doing just nothing at all."

"It's terribly easy to waste time in Rome," said Mr Norton, "at least I've always found it so."

"Yes," said Cunninghame, "I agree, but if one is writing despatches to England one ought to see a lot of people."

"I guess our friend sees quite a few," said Norton.

"Sure," said Wilding, "everyone except his old friends."

"Don't you listen to him, Mr Trevenen," said Mrs Norton. "I

understand you."

After luncheon, Mrs Norton said a few words to Christopher about Spence.

"I can't say much," she said, "but I know that you understand what I feel, and I understand what you feel."

There were tears in her eyes. Two days later Cunninghame asked Christopher to dinner, but he wrote to say that he was engaged. He did not see Madame D'Alberg for some time. She had gone to Naples, and stayed there a fortnight. It was in the middle of May that he heard she was back. He took no steps. At last she wrote to him and asked what had become of him. "Do come tomorrow evening," she wrote, "there will be no one to matter."

Christopher went, and found nobody except Scalchi.

"Well," said Madame D'Alberg, "what has happened to you? We wondered whether you were alive."

"Yes," said Scalchi laughing, "we wondered whether we had done something awful, something that you couldn't forgive."

Scalchi spoke English as easily as an Englishman, without affectation. Christopher envied him.

"He is at home everywhere," he said to himself, "and in every language. That is really the kind of person Madame D'Alberg prefers, although she would not admit it."

"I have been busy," he said. "I had to get up a lot of tiresome facts and figures for an article which nobody will read."

They talked on for a time, and presently Scalchi got up to leave. He was going to a party.

"I am going to the Torelli; are you coming?" he said.

"No," said Christopher, "I'm not dressed."

Scalchi left them.

"Why haven't you been near me?" asked Madame D'Alberg.

"You never asked me."

"I thought it was agreed that I would only tell you when *not* to come."

"I thought I would save you the trouble by guessing those

occasions."

"You have guessed them often."

"Perhaps not too often."

"Yes, too often. Listen to me, Mr Trevenen, I am going to be quite frank with you. You are complicated, and I am not. When I say I want to see someone, I mean it; and when I say I will tell you when I would rather you did not come, I mean it. So to imagine extra things is, with me, a waste of time. You must take me as I am, and believe me, or else have nothing to do with me."

"I do believe you, but I don't want to be a nuisance."

"I have told you you are not a nuisance."

"Yes, but you have many other friends."

"Yes, but you don't interfere with them."

"Perhaps they interfere with me."

"You mean you don't like my friends?"

"No, I didn't mean that. I meant that perhaps they make me feel in the way. I daresay it is my fault."

"They do not feel you are in the way. They all like you."

"All? I wonder."

"Yes, all of them. Wildenspruch was only asking yesterday what had become of you."

"But you haven't been back long, have you?"

"I have been back a week."

"How is Madame Turçin?"

"When I left she was very bad; she recognised me, but she could hardly speak. Her husband is there. I told her you had sent your love, and she smiled and nodded. I am expecting to hear that she is dead any minute. I am glad I went. He was pitiable. I never saw a man more miserable."

"He was fond of her?"

"Oh very."

"And was she fond of him?"

"Yes, she was fond of him. She was a good wife."

"Does that always happen?"

"What?"

"Well, I mean for a wife to be what is called 'a good wife'; and that means she endures her husband and loves someone else."

"I don't think she did love anyone else."

"You wouldn't say so, if you did."

"No, of course I shouldn't." She laughed.

"Then what's the use of discussing such things?"

"It was you who discussed them, not I."

"But tell me, was she fond of someone else? I really want to know."

"I don't know anything about her early life. I don't think she was fond of anyone else, while she was at Paris. And here I don't know. But at Constantinople I think she was nearly fond of someone and would have been if that person had not gone away."

"Who was it?"

"Well, if you don't know, I can't tell you."

"How should I know?"

"Don't you really know?"

"Of course I don't."

"I don't believe you do: the stupidity of men comes to one with a fresh shock at every hour of the day. One never gets used to it."

"Well you see, I only knew her a little. I was just beginning to get to know her when I went away."

"Yes; that is just it."

"So you see I had no opportunity of seeing her, and I used not to go out there any more than I do here."

"Well, I won't tell you, because I don't think it is fair on her. If you had guessed I would have told you. But you haven't guessed."

"No, I haven't the slightest idea, but I'm sorry they weren't happy."

"They were happy in a way. He was devoted to her and she

was fond of him. They had two children, a girl who is at a convent, and a boy who is at school: but they were too different. He was a conscientious official and she loathed diplomacy, and liked the country. She was fond of reading, and of all sorts of queer things. He liked going to parties, and doing his social duty. He isn't stupid; on the contrary, but he is what Germans call a *formalist*, and he has a heart of gold. If you could have seen him the other day. Mind you, I think it is a good thing for husband and wife to be unlike; to have different tastes. But they can be too unlike; and Mina and Turçin were too unlike. She married too young. That is a common mistake. It is a good thing you did not fall into it."

"Do you think it is better not to marry at all?"

"Why shouldn't you marry? You are just the right age now."

"I shall never marry, because I could only marry a particular person."

"That is what everybody thinks they are going to do when they are engaged to be married."

"Do you believe in happy marriages?"

"Wasn't your father and mother's marriage a happy one?"

"I believe it was."

"Marriage has pains, as Dr Johnson said – what was it he said?"

"I don't know."

"Well, marriage, like everything in life, is a compromise, a give and take." She paused. "You mustn't stay away like that again. I have missed you."

"What have you been doing? Who has been here?"

"The usual people."

"Wildenspruch?"

"Yes."

"And Scalchi and Altamura?"

"Altamura is away. He has gone to Aix-les-Bains for a cure. I had a letter from him this morning."

"And are you going to stay on?"

261

"No, at the end of the month I am going to stay with my sister-in-law. She has got a house in Touraine. And then I may go to Switzerland for a time. And you?"

"I am going to stay on right through the summer. I could go to England for a fortnight, or three weeks, if I wanted to, but I have nowhere to go to."

"Why don't you go and stay with those nice Claydons Yakovlev told me about?"

"Oh no!"

"But why not?"

"Because I never want to see him again; he ruined my life."

"I think that is absurd."

"Possibly, but I feel like that."

"Yakovlev told me it was absurd. He knew the whole story, and Lady Claydon told him it was absurd."

"Oh I know she thinks so, but she doesn't understand him."

"Understand whom?"

"Her husband."

"My dear child!"

Madame D'Alberg laughed. Christopher enjoyed her laugh. It was a low laugh with a soft pedal on it, but none the less infectious, and when she laughed her eyes lit up.

"You think I am talking nonsense."

"I do indeed; I am sure Lady Claydon understands her husband."

"But you see she is a Russian."

"Have you ever known a Russian not understand anything?"

"Well, I doubt if they can understand a particular form of English snobbishness; it is so foreign to their nature."

"Believe me, if it was there, she would understand it. She says, so Yakovlev told me, that they are both fond of you, very fond of you, and both hurt that you take no notice of them."

"One rebuff is enough."

"Well, it's no good my arguing."

Wildenspruch walked into the room.

The next morning, Madame D'Alberg telephoned to Christopher to tell him that she had had a telegram from Turçin at Naples, saying that Madame Turçin was dead, and a week later, Turçin sent him by hand the illuminated book about the Fourth Crusade which contained the story of the Coat without Seam.

CHAPTER XXVIII

At the end of May, Madame D'Alberg left Rome. Christopher saw her once more before she left, but not by herself. He stayed on till the end of July. All the inmates of the *pension* had left except the Italians; and at the end of July, Miss O'Connor and the signora went to Castellamare for three weeks. Christopher and Ansoni went with them. At the end of August, they returned to Rome. At the end of September, new and some of the old inmates arrived. Christopher only heard from Madame D'Alberg once. She sent him a postcard. She expected to come back to Rome at the end of October. She did not come back till the end of November, as she was obliged to go to England to look after a cousin who was in difficulties. Madame D'Alberg telephoned to him the day after she came back, and he asked if he might go round that evening, but she said, no. There were some tiresome people, friends of her husband, whom she had to see as they were only in Rome for two days. She would let him know when to come. Two days later, she asked him to come in the evening, and he found her with Scalchi and Wildenspruch. She seemed glad to see him. Wildenspruch had spent the whole summer in Germany, and Scalchi had been to England and Scotland.

Christopher asked after Altamura. Madame D'Alberg said, "He has gone for his yearly holiday to Paris. He started this morning."

During the next month, Christopher saw Madame D'Alberg constantly. He even consented to meet her at Pavlov's house, where he now found that he enjoyed himself. Countess Mühlendorff had left Rome and had migrated to Cannes. Altamura came back before Christmas. Christopher did not see him often, but when he did he met nothing but civility from him, and he began to think that he had been mistaken in thinking that Altamura disliked him. Sometimes Madame D'Alberg would ask him to luncheon, but there would always be someone else there. But he managed to see her from time to time alone in the evenings either before the other guests arrived, or after they were gone. These occasions, though rare, gradually became more frequent.

Just after Christmas, Brierley, the editor of the *Messenger*, came out to Rome for a week's holiday. He asked Christopher to dinner, and in the course of dinner, made him an offer: to go to Paris as correspondent; he would have a handsome salary, and an assistant. Christopher asked Brierley to let him think it over.

"Well, I am going back to London next week," said Brierley, "and I should like you to make up your mind before that."

The next day Christopher rang up Madame D'Alberg and told her he wanted to see her if possible alone on an important matter. She asked him to dinner. Wildenspruch was there, but he went away directly afterwards. He was going to a large reception at the German Embassy. Christopher told Madame D'Alberg about Brierley's offer. She listened to his story and all the details in silence.

"I suppose you ought to go," she said. "Do you want to?"

"No, I don't," he said, "I don't want to go away at all. I am happy here, happier than I have ever been. Of course it is a fine offer and the terms are excellent, and the work would be interesting, far more interesting than it is here, or anywhere else."

"How is your Persian book getting on?" she said.

"Well, I have begun it, but I haven't got far. The fact is, I can't really work at it except in the summer. It is impossible to settle down to anything when one is doing newspaper work."

"And in Paris you would of course have less time?"

"Yes, I suppose so."

"I think it would be a pity to give up the other thing altogether. If you stayed here you would be able to go on with it?"

"Oh, yes, in the summer, certainly. I did work in July. But it is stupendously difficult. More difficult than if I were doing something entirely on my own."

"Going to Paris would mean staying there?"

"Yes, as long as they would keep me there."

"Then it would mean practically giving up Sackbut's book?"

"I suppose so."

"I suppose it is an opportunity that won't happen again."

"I shouldn't think so. The man they've got at Paris is going, and if once they get someone else they won't want to change."

"After all, it wouldn't prevent your going somewhere else later, if you wanted to, would it?"

"No, but I am happy here."

"They are pleased with your work here."

"I think they must be."

"Yes, of course, but I think you ought to do the book at all costs. I think that is more important than being a successful correspondent. And you are right in saying that the work in Paris would take all your time. We used to know some of the correspondents, and they worked like slaves, that is to say, they went about such a lot, and saw people from morning till night, and all night. The actual work wasn't so much, but they had to be everywhere. Every day – every night, all day – all night."

"A terrible life. I think I should hate it. I like comfortable places, like St Petersburg and Rome."

"Of course, Paris is always interesting."

"I don't think I should like it."

"I am not sure you would. But one never knows. You would make friends with interesting people."

"I doubt it."

"But whether you would like it is another matter."

"Do you honestly think I would?"

"No. I honestly think…well, I'm not sure I may not be wrong. I don't like to say anything. I don't want to influence you."

"But you know Paris so well."

"I think there are many things about it you would like."

"What?"

"Well, the French are so intelligent and have so much life. Rome after Paris is like being in a backwater, a castle of the Sleeping Beauty. That is why I like it."

"Well, I will settle not to go."

"Don't settle anything in a hurry. It's a pity Yakovlev isn't here. He would have given you good advice. I am a bad person to advise you."

"Who could possibly give me better advice? You lived in Paris for years. You knew all worlds there."

"Intimacy is almost impossible in Paris."

"I won't go."

"Think it over for a day or two. When do you have to give your answer?"

"In a few days, and I think Brierley would wait longer if I asked him."

"Well, you must think it over carefully."

"And then I should miss coming here so dreadfully."

"Oh, you mustn't think of that. You see, I can do so little for you here. You know how full my little life is; how tied I am; tied by all my husband's friends and by the past. Next summer I shall probably be away still longer. I may have to go to England again. You know, one of my aunts is alive, and there is a daughter who is dreadfully difficult to deal with, and my aunt is hopeless. She is my mother's sister. Of course, I should miss you dreadfully."

"You would miss me?"

"Yes, of course I should."

"What – as much as Wildenspruch and the others?"

"My old men!"

"They aren't old at all to me. Scalchi is quite young."

"They are all old to me. And honestly, I think that if you go to Paris you won't much care for it, and it will be the end of all hope of your writing a book or going on with your private work. I shouldn't like that to happen. I am ambitious for you, I want you to make a name in the world of learning. I think you could do something magnificent, something epoch-making, with what Sackbut has left."

"He would have done something magnificent."

"And so can you. I have no doubt of it. I believe in you."

"Nobody else does."

"What does that matter? On the other hand, it would be a pity to refuse and then to regret it. Why shouldn't you go for a time, and then come back if you don't like it?"

"I couldn't do that, because in the meantime they would send someone else here. If I leave Rome it would mean leaving for good. And I don't feel capable of leaving Rome just now."

"Above all things I don't want you to refuse to go and then regret it afterwards. Nothing is so bad as that."

"But you don't think I would like Paris?"

"Honestly not."

"And you don't think I would have time for any other work?"

"Honestly not."

"And you would miss me if I went?"

"Yes, I would miss you."

"Then I won't go."

"You must not make up your mind until it is necessary."

The telephone bell rang in the next room. Madame D'Alberg went to answer, and had some conversation.

"It's Angelica Ubaldi," she said, "she wants to see me about her society for animals. She is coming round. One never has any peace."

"Well, then, I will go."

"Then think it over carefully."

"I will."

Christopher went home. The next morning he got a long letter from Madame D'Alberg.

"*On thinking things over,*" (she wrote), "*I have come to the conclusion that you had better go. I think such an opportunity may never happen again. I think it would be a pity to throw it away; if you find you don't like it, I am sure you could arrange to come back here, and it wouldn't matter giving up the book just for the present. You could have a holiday in the summer and work at it then. I am going to France this summer with my sister-in-law, Berthe Mortier, and you could come and stay with us. I feel it will be best for you to go. I think it is best to follow one's career, whatever it is. It is a pity to give things up. So do think over seriously whether it wouldn't be best. Come and see me before you send your answer. Not tomorrow night, because Angelica and the Olenevs will be here, but the evening after. We shall be alone.*"

Christopher went to see Brierley and told him that he did not think he could accept the offer. Brierley was a man of dash and energy, and he was persuasive and eloquent. When Christopher told him this, his black eyes flashed behind his spectacles, and he set to work to lay siege to Christopher. He swept away his objections.

"I have got a piece of work of my own to do," said Christopher, "to edit Sackbut's remains, a book he left unfinished, almost unbegun."

"Paris is the best place to do that," said Brierley. "You will have plenty of time to yourself and you will be able to consult the best authorities. You won't have to do the drudgery. I am willing to pay an assistant £400 to do that. All you will have to do is to write despatches and wire the important news. You can have a holiday in the summer. Work? What work do you do here, except for the paper? Whoever heard of anyone working at Rome?"

"I feel that once I left Rome I should never come back, and I can do that work here. At least I could do it in the summer."

"There's nothing to prevent your coming back here if you don't like Paris. But I know you would like Paris. We must have a good man for Paris, and you are the man we want. We must have a man who knows French and who can talk to the French people."

He argued with him for an hour, and when Christopher left him he refused to take 'no' for an answer.

"I am going away tomorrow morning," he said, "come round and see me before I start."

Christopher went for a walk on the Pincio to think things over. It was a brilliant and transparent winter day; hot in the sunlight. There he met Cunninghame, who greeted him in a friendly way. They walked together and discussed the political news. Altamura passed them. He was driving in a carriage. Cunninghame waved at him.

"There's Altamura," said Cunninghame. "I expect he's just off to see Madame D'Alberg."

"I suppose he sees her often," said Christopher.

"Every day of his life," said Cunninghame. "That's why it's no good going there at tea time. That's his hour. Sacred to him. She receives in the evening. She's at home to everyone after dinner. But you, I expect you know her. She always knows the interesting people."

"Yes, I do know her," said Christopher, "I go there sometimes in the evening."

Christopher left Cunninghame and said he had to go home. He was mad with jealousy of Altamura and angry with Madame D'Alberg. "She has been playing with me," he said. Nevertheless, he went there after dinner and found her alone.

"Well, have you settled?" she said.

"Yes," he said, "I have settled to go."

Madame D'Alberg's face changed; a wave of pain passed over it. She was lighting a cigarette, and she dropped the matchbox.

"I expect you are right," she said.

There was a long pause.

"I went for a walk in the Pincio, and I met a man called Cunninghame – do you know him?"

"I have met him."

"And we saw Altamura."

"He must have been on his way here. He came to tea. He has tea here every day. In the evenings he is so busy. He is so *mondain*. That is why we see him so seldom. But he's faithful to me at tea time, and it's good of him, because it must bore him. This afternoon he met two dreadfully dreary old ladies, both wives of friends of my husband."

"Are you at home to tea, then?"

"Yes, of course, except when I'm out. But I advise you not to come then, as you would find the people who would bore you: mostly old ladies."

"I thought you shut your door at tea time?"

"I may have done so sometimes, just as I do in the evening, sometimes, but one must have some time to oneself; I find it on the whole simpler to be always at home than to have a day. Let us talk about your future. So you are going. Well, I expect you are right." She said this cheerfully.

"Brierley persuaded me. He said that I should have an assistant; that I should have time for myself, that I should have a holiday in the summer, and that if I wanted to come hack here I could."

"Yes, yes. I understand. I am sure you are right. I will give you letters to some people in Paris. I do hope you will he happy there, and not hate it. When will you go?"

"He wants me, if I go, to go at once."

"Oh!"

There was a long silence.

At last Madame D'Alberg said: "Well, of course, I shall miss you – we shall all miss you. But I daresay you are right, only I shouldn't build hopes on having any time to spare."

There was something poignantly sad in the way she said this. Christopher had often seen her look sad, but never quite so sad as when she said this.

"But after all it's life. Directly one makes friends, something happens."

And then she suddenly began to laugh.

"Why are you laughing?" said Christopher.

"I am laughing to think how relieved my old men will be at your going."

"Because they hate me? They look down on me?"

"On the contrary, they like you very much. But they are jealous. They are jealous of anyone, and especially of anyone younger than themselves."

"Jealous of me?"

"Yes. They are all jealous, especially Altamura and Scalchi. Wildenspruch is jealous because he dislikes a stranger in his nest, and Altamura is jealous because he is an Italian. That is why I ask you not to come sometimes. It is so as not to annoy him. He has accepted your being in my life, but at the same time I don't want to exasperate or to hurt him. That is why he likes coming here at tea time, because he seldom meets any men at that time. I have told you about my tea hour. It's mostly old ladies who come. Sometimes some French people. Altamura comes then, because he feels that he has no rival, and it has become a habit. Of course he comes at other times too, as you know, but he likes that less."

Christopher believed her. He was certain she was speaking the truth.

"Well, I won't go," he said.

"Don't be so silly, you must go!" But her face couldn't help lighting up.

"I thought," he said, "that I was perhaps becoming a nuisance to you. That was the only reason why I was going."

"Is that true?"

"Perfectly true. Otherwise I should simply hate it, as you know. You know I should hate Paris, and you know it will mean the end of work – of *my* work. It will be the end of me as a human being, whatever I become as a correspondent."

"Well, I shall miss you, but I think you had perhaps better go."

"No. I've settled now, I'm not going. It's no good discussing it any more."

"But… "

"There isn't any but. It's settled, once and for all."

And so it was settled.

The next day Christopher went to see Brierley before he left. He told him he had settled not to go to Paris, and that his decision was irrevocable.

"In spite of what you say now," Brierley said, "I won't take this as a final answer, and you can still wire to me when I get back. It won't be too late. I promise you, you are throwing away the chance of your life time. I beg you to reconsider it."

But Christopher sent no such telegram. The *Messenger* was obliged to get another correspondent. When he told Madame D'Alberg the news, which he did that same day, she said to him:

"I'm afraid you may perhaps be wrong, and I rather wish you had thought it over longer; but I can't help telling you that it is a *great* joy to me to think you are not going, and I don't think it's entirely selfishness, because I do want you to do something big, and I feel that if you had gone to Paris it would have meant an end of all that. You would have frittered away your life. And now you must finish Sackbut's book."

"Yes," said Christopher, "I must finish Sackbut's book."

CHAPTER XXIX

A few days later, Christopher rang up Madame D'Alberg to know whether he might come in the evening, and he was told that the Signora had gone to England. They had no idea for how long. This came as a great blow to Christopher. The worst thing about it was the difficulty of hearing any news of her. At last he got a postcard from London saying she was staying with her aunt. She had had to leave at a moment's notice; she had no time to write at present but would write soon. But time went on and he heard nothing. Then he met Scalchi in the street and he asked him for news.

"It is most tiresome," said Scalchi. "It is her aunt, or rather her cousin. Her aunt is a Mrs someone, her mother's sister. She is younger than Madame D'Alberg's mother. A Bohemian without talent. She married an actor who left her, and she has a daughter who is now grown up and she has done the same thing. She went on the stage and married an actor last year and the girl's mother was against it, and she tried her best to prevent it, and Madame D'Alberg went over to England to smooth matters. It was impossible to prevent this marriage, and now history threatens to repeat itself the other way round. The girl wants to leave her husband, who is devoted to her, for some worthless person with no money, and the mother is helpless and distraught."

"Is there anything to be done?" asked Christopher.

"I don't know. It appears that the girl is clever and self-willed and doing well on the stage, and the mother is hopeless; and I believe it was the mother's fault."

"How long will she stay?"

"I have no idea, but I don't think long."

This surmise proved incorrect, for no sooner had Madame D'Alberg arrived in England than she developed typhoid fever and she was laid up at her aunt's house and was dangerously ill for weeks.

Christopher only heard of this by chance some time later. In the meanwhile he lived without news in a state of aching, gnawing grievance. He regretted not having accepted the Paris offer and of course blamed Madame D'Alberg. He thought it was too bad of her not to write to him and he was too proud even to ring up and ask for news on the telephone. It was Wildenspruch who told him the news of her illness. He met him in the Vatican library and then his gnawing grievance changed to an aching, excruciating anxiety.

He rang up for news at the flat now constantly, but they knew little.

It was only some weeks later that he got a telegram from Madame D'Alberg herself, saying: "Much better, staying Brighton. Hope come back soon."

She did not come back to Rome until after Easter, at the beginning of May.

She let Christopher know at once.

The first time he saw her, her house was full, not only of her old friends, but of many other Italians. Christopher thought she looked better since her illness. She was like Eurydice back from the shades. Her complexion was fresher, and she seemed as if she had been through the shadow of death to acquire a fresh lease of life.

A few evenings later he saw her alone and she told him all that had happened to her. She had had time to settle her cousin's difficulties before she fell ill. She had restored harmony in the distracted household. She told Christopher that she and her sister-in-law had been lent a house at Sorrento for the summer and that he could come and stay there whenever he liked.

"Wildenspruch is coming for a little while before he goes to Germany and Alfredo Scalchi may look in, otherwise there will be no one."

"Will Altamura be there?"

"He may come for a day or two, but he is going for a long yachting cruise to Constantinople with some Americans."

Madame D'Alberg seemed delighted to see Christopher again, and he was overjoyed at seeing her. He settled once more into the old rut of intimacy. Early in June she left Rome for Sorrento. She asked Christopher to go there in July. She would let him know when. Rome was hot and deserted. He began to work again at Sackbut's book. He had left the *pension* as the signora and Miss O'Connor were going away to spend the summer in Switzerland and he had taken an apartment in the modern part of the town. He soon became immersed in his work. He was beginning to think Madame D'Alberg had forgotten him when he got a telegram from her early in July telling him to come when he liked. He started the next day. The house at Sorrento was a villa facing the sea. He found Wildenspruch and Madame D'Alberg's sister-in-law, Madame Mortier. She was an elderly lady, a widow. She had once had a husband, but nobody seemed to have seen him. She was small, grey-haired and so short-sighted as to be almost blind, but few things escaped those blind eyes. She had beautiful hands, and a fund of devastating common sense. She spent her whole day doing needlework and she never appeared to open a book, but she had read everything.

The weather at Sorrento was miraculous. Christopher bathed. They went out in a boat sometimes, and they sat in the evenings on the terrace looking out on to the phosphorescent sea and watched Vesuvius changing from a veil of pink transparent haze to a purple shadow, with its immortal glow-worm on its crest. Life there seemed to Christopher like a dream. He had brought some work with him, but his work there was more a pretence than a reality.

One day it was settled that they were to go to Capri, but at the last moment Madame D'Alberg said that she had a headache and Christopher said that he would stay behind too. He had a piece of work he wished to finish. Madame D'Alberg stayed in her room all the morning, but at luncheon time she sent word to say that she felt better and was coming down.

They had luncheon together. Madame D'Alberg seemed restored to health. They talked and laughed without stopping; after luncheon they sat in the shady sitting room. The outside blinds were down. It was too hot to sit out of doors.

After they had had their coffee, Madame D'Alberg went upstairs to rest. She said she would come down later. Christopher was working at a Persian book, but he could not fix his attention on it. The world was still, but every now and then echoes of singing voices came to him. Christopher looked out on the verandah. "It is a beautiful world," he said, "too beautiful to be true."

He was standing by the window which opened on to the verandah and which he had thrown open, letting in the hot haze and looking upon the bay, absorbed in the beauty of the spectacle, when Madame D'Alberg came in without his noticing her. He suddenly became aware of a presence and turned round and looked at her. She was dressed in something light and mauve-coloured, and in the dark, cool shadow of the room, her dark eyes shone like stars.

"She is very beautiful," thought Christopher, "with a beauty different from that of anyone else in the world." They stood looking at each other in silence. There was something overwhelmingly sad in her expression, but not the old sadness he was accustomed to. It was something new; something tragic and calm and final.

"I want to ask you something," she said. "Don't think me mad."

"What is it?" his voice shook a little.

"I want you to go away. I want you to go away at once."

"But why?" asked Christopher, and his words sounded strange to himself, as if they were not the words he meant to say, but substitutes. "I have only just come."

"I want you to go away because I am too fond of you."

They looked at each other.

"And I am fond of you," he whispered.

"Oh no!" she said, with a look of frightened wonder in her eyes. She was as white as a ghost, and her eyes blazed.

He went up to her on tip-toe and kissed her, and they said nothing more.

Madame Mortier and Wildenspruch did not come back till late and Madame D'Alberg did not come down to dinner.

After that day everything was different. The sense of dream became permanent to Christopher; but now it was not only a dream of beauty, it was a dream of unbelievable happiness: of ecstasy. Time seemed to have been annihilated. He felt as if he and Antoinette were floating down a broad river: the days and nights were no longer measured by the clock nor apportioned by the sun and moon. It was one long stretch, neither day nor night; an unearthly twilight. A silvery twilight lined with melancholy, and steeped in a sadness of which they never had enough. They never were tired of one another for a moment. They could not notice the passage of time. Every time they looked at each other it was a fresh joy. They were like people who had drunk of a magic potion. One day Christopher said to Antoinette: "I think we have been bewitched."

"Yes," she said, "I believe Marianne" (that was her sister-in-law) "has left a Love-philtre lying about, or given it to me on purpose as Isolda's maid did. What was her name? Brangäne? I understand that story now. I used to think that was not the way

279

things happened."

"It doesn't matter how it has happened," said Christopher, "it has happened, and is happening."

It was impossible for them to think of the future, and time seemed to them at the same moment to have been lengthened into eternity, and yet to be slipping by like a puff of smoke.

The first event that brought them back to reality was Wildenspruch's departure at the end of the month. Then soon after he had gone, Christopher received a telegram recalling him to Rome. Something had happened which his newspaper was anxious to know about, and he was wanted. He had to go.

The last evening and the last night were tragic to them. They could not disguise it. Madame Mortier had divined what had happened at once.

"*Ma chère Antoinette,*" she said to Madame D'Alberg, "*prends garde; tu es en train de te préparer un Purgatoire sur terre.*"

She understood that she was speaking to deaf ears.

Madame Mortier left them together that last evening. They wandered out into the orchard on the hill, and remained a long time hand in hand, speechless and spellbound, in the darkness: and sometimes they whispered to each other. When they came back, they sat up late in the sitting room, and they talked a little of the future.

"I am afraid it will be all over, it won't be the same when we are back in Rome," she said.

"Why shouldn't it be the same?"

"I shall never see you. My life is tied up by a thousand fine almost invisible threads, each one of them as slight as gossamer, but impossible to break. I don't know what we shall do, and then there are all the others. Altamura has got the eyes of a lynx and the sixth sense of an animal. I told you he was jealous, but the real reason was that he was not only jealous, as only an Italian knows how to be jealous, but he has the profound instinct of the *male*, as well as of the Italian, which let him guess instantly not only that I liked you better than I liked him, but that I *loved* you. He saw that, at once, long before you did."

"I never thought such a thing possible till I came here."

"He saw it at once, and told me so, and I laughed him out of it in a way, but he never really believed me. He always suspected. When he comes back, he will see what has happened, whatever I do."

"Does it matter?"

"Not really, not to us – not to what I feel for you – but the past is the past, one can't help that. He has loved me for years, and he loves me still."

"And you?"

"I loved him a long time ago…for a very short moment, and then it all passed away; and for years he might just as well have been dead as far as I was concerned. You see I married when I was very young. Eighteen. I had no idea what marriage meant, and it was a terrible shock to me. My husband was good, but he did not understand. He was French, and I was English. Directly we were married, I realised that I didn't love him at all. In some ways, the most important of all ways for married people, he was to me repulsive. The result was, of course, that I drove him elsewhere, and he had a *liaison* for years with a Madame Morgan. She was clever and he loved her at first, but afterwards, I think, he was tired of her. However it went on till he died. I think I made him a good wife in other ways – I tried to. But no words can express to you the loneliness in which I lived during all those early years in Paris. Then Altamura came. He was in love with me, and for a time, for a very short time, I was in love with him. I was carried away. He was so good-looking and so understanding. He behaved wonderfully. He filled my life, and I can't tell you all the things he did, the sacrifices he made. He ruined his life for me. So I am under the deepest obligation to him – I owe him what I can never repay – and I must never do anything to make him suffer. He gave up everything: his wife, because it was owing to me she left him, and nothing else, although the world never knew that: the world thought it was because she was in love with Buontresori. She took Buontresori because he happened to be there. She would have taken anyone. It was only a pretext. A way out.

"She never cared a pin for him and they have led a most miserable existence ever since.

"And then I ruined his career. He was a diplomatist; they say he had a brilliant future, because he is a man of the world, and a man of brains and culture at the same time. He gave up his career, and he gave it up for me. He practically lived in Paris, which he loathed, that is to say in *a* Paris he loathed, my *husband's* Paris – he likes *ordinary* Paris – and he never uttered a word of reproach, and I gave him so little – almost nothing in return."

"I think he has nothing to complain of," said Christopher, "and I am sure he feels the same thing."

"Well, however that may be, that is the situation. One can't unmake the past, and Altamura is a factor in my life. I have my duties towards him which are more binding and more inexorable than the written law. The unwritten law. But I am only wondering."

"Wondering what?"

"What will happen to us. I see no solution. It is impossible to see anyone in Rome. You know that as well as anybody."

"But you saw Altamura."

"Yes, I did. It is easy to see anybody in the way I see him, but to see someone *really*."

Christopher sighed.

"I shall go and stay with my sister-in-law in France. You can come there, if you would like to, for a bit, but I shall have to come back, and then it will be awful."

"As long as I am in the same place as you are, I shan't mind," said Christopher.

"I shall mind," she said. "It will be a daily torture. Just as it has been. You have no idea how much I have suffered already."

"Did you want to see me before?"

"Of course I did, from the very first moment, and I felt like an animal in a trap with no means of escape, with no power of even being able to give a squeak."

"Things are never so bad as one expects; something is sure to happen."

"I think it is the other way round. I think things are always worse than one expects. Something does happen, but it is the wrong thing. At any rate I shall look forward to France. Marianne knows everything. She guessed at once. She disapproves because she thinks we shall both be unhappy, but she will help and not hinder. But don't let's think of the future any more for the present."

They went out once more for one last look at the orchard and the sea and Vesuvius: to look on the spot where they had tasted of perfect happiness and to say farewell to it.

Christopher left the next day. He went back to Rome, and found that the underling who had been replacing him was ill. There was something to do, not anything important, but nevertheless something that had to be done. He wrote to Antoinette every day and she wrote to him. At the end of August she passed through Rome on her way to her sister-in-law's house in France. They spent two happy days together. Then she went to Madame Mortier's. Christopher could not get away, but he went to France at the end of September, and stayed a week with Madame Mortier.

Madame D'Alberg came back to Rome at the end of October. She had been longing to come, so she told Christopher, and at the same time she was dreading it. All her friends were there Wildenspruch, Scalchi, Altamura: the army of acquaintances and the host of non-acquaintances, who, in Rome, had the eyes of an eagle for anything that was happening in private. She could hardly see Christopher, and with skill she contrived to behave as if nothing had changed: to see him no more and no less, and yet to be able to see him.

To Christopher, the situation was intolerable; to feel her so near and so infinitely removed from him. Madame D'Alberg told him she was more frightened of Scalchi than of anyone. "We mustn't let him notice," she said, "that there is a hairbreadth's difference in our relations. You must come just as often as you used to, not more often and not more seldom, and you must behave exactly in the same way. Otherwise he is so sharp that he will guess everything." Altamura came back, but went as he usually did to Paris in November, for a short time. Wildenspruch was there as before, but he saw nothing.

Christopher pretended to be busier than he had ever been, but he made a point of going to see Madame D'Alberg when he knew the others were there and of behaving as if he were what he had been before, one of the minor fixtures of the house. And so the time went on. Christopher gave up all idea of Sackbut's book, for the present. He had only one thought in his head and that was Antoinette. At least he could telephone to her every day of his life, and they met at odd moments, and in stray places as if by accident. But it was not satisfactory or satisfying. Nobody paid attention to him. Then, in the spring of the next year, there was a crisis at Constantinople, and Brierley telegraphed to Christopher and asked him to go there as correspondent. Again he refused; this time without hesitation and without even consulting Madame D'Alberg. It was impossible for him to leave the place where she was. Easter came and passed. Madame D'Alberg was not going to Naples because, had she done so, she could not have avoided inviting Altamura, who was at a loose end. One day just as she was preparing to start for France she telephoned to Christopher, and begged him to come to meet her the next morning, early, at nine o'clock, at St Peter's.

Christopher was punctual at the appointed hour.

"Christopher," she said when she met him, "an appalling thing has happened. Altamura's wife is dead and he wants me to marry him."

"But you won't do that?"

"I may have to."

"For his sake?"

"Yes, and for yours."

CHAPTER XXX

Nobody at Rome was surprised when at the end of the following October it was known that Madame D'Alberg had married her old friend Carlo Altamura.

Christopher made several final appeals to Madame D'Alberg both by letter and by word of mouth to reconsider her decision and to marry *him*. But she only repeated what she had told him before about the inevitability and binding force of the prior claim. She gave him other reasons as well; but no one will know, until the Day of Judgment, exactly why Antoinette D'Alberg did not marry Christopher and married Altamura instead.

They were married in Paris and they spent the winter in Egypt going up the Nile. When they came back to Italy they went to Florence, where Altamura had a villa, but he had lived there rarely, while Madame D'Alberg was at Rome. At Rome he had only had a flat.

Christopher began to feel that recent events had been a dream, that had happened to someone else. He imagined that his life would now become different and that he would begin work in earnest, but when he came to try, he found he had no desire and no power to do anything but journalistic work. It was as if a spring inside him had been broken. He had not done much before; but he had felt that he could if he would. Rome was an empty place to him now, and yet he had no wish to go anywhere else. He had imagined that he would not be able to live there now that everything would be different, with the cornerstone of his life removed. But he found this was not so. He felt rather as someone who has undergone an operation and feels better for having had it done and yet is lacking in something essential.

Madame D'Alberg was at Florence and not at Rome, and this made things easier. If she had lived at Rome as before, life to him would not have been tolerable. But after a year had slipped by, and he had done nothing but his regular work for his newspaper, he became alarmed. The ghost of Sackbut seemed to haunt him saying, "What have you done with my work?" It was living at Rome, he thought, which prevented him from working. Rome was too full of ghosts. He wrote to Brierley, asking him whether he could be sent to the Near East or the Far East.

As the Balkans were in a permanent state of unrest, Brierley was willing that he should go to Constantinople, and he left Rome in the spring. He took a room at the "Little Club," and settled down to the life he knew so well. There were still a certain number of his old acquaintances there.

In sending Christopher to Constantinople Brierley had warned him that the sympathies of the newspaper were with the Young Turks, and that he was not going to tolerate anything reactionary, and remembering Christopher's previous record in Turkey, he thought he would be safe.

"I perhaps need not say that, now, because you know better," he wrote.

Christopher detested the Young Turks, but he kept his dislike in check for a time.

"Now that I am in Turkey," he thought to himself, "I shall really be able to get on with Sackbut's book." He made the acquaintance of a well-known Persian scholar to whom he showed Sackbut's notes and what he himself had done. Of his own work there was not much to show, but what there was to show was excellent, so the scholar said. The scholar was enthusiastic, and encouraged Christopher to go on.

But as time went on, Christopher found he could do even less than at Rome. He became convinced that the source of his inspiration had been Antoinette. The Wildings were transferred to Constantinople soon after he arrived, and through them he made a certain number of friends. He was no longer shy of society. He did not care whom he met nor where he went, and the life at Constantinople suited him. It was easy, and everyone seemed to accept everyone else, and to take them as they were. All went on well so far in his journalistic career, until war broke out between Bulgaria and Turkey, and Christopher at once took a Turkish line. After the first successes of the Bulgars and the Serbs, he refused to believe in a swift end to the campaign, and he prophesied that the Turks would not be defeated. In one way he was right, but this was more than Brierley and the owner of the *Messenger* could stand, and they recalled him.

He came home at the beginning of 1913, and they offered him no further post abroad, but they gave him work to do in the office. It meant working late every night, and it was not remunerative, but it kept him alive.

Among other things that he did for the *Messenger* was to write criticisms about foreign plays. One night just as he was coming out of the theatre in a hurry to reach the office so as to begin his article, he met Lady Claydon and Sir Joseph. They begged him to come and see them.

The next day Lady Claydon wrote to him and asked him to dinner, and he dined alone with them. The hatchet was finally buried: although he never really entirely absolved Sir Joseph from his complicity in bringing about Esther's marriage, nor did he ever forgive him: but of this Sir Joseph was unconscious, and Lady Claydon smoothed things over by her tact and intelligence.

Christopher never saw Esther again, but he heard that she

and her husband lived at Windsor, and that Lawless was doing well.

Christopher saw Yakovlev several times, and each time Yakovlev asked him how the book was getting on.

"I have given it up," said Christopher, "I have no time and I have forgotten all I knew about it."

"Then what will you do with it?"

"I have sent the translations which he left to a literary agent asking him to place them with a publisher, if possible, and I have written a preface. The work I did trying to continue what Sackbut had done besides the actual translations, I have thrown away. I have kept Sackbut's notes, and I will offer them to William Farren."

"He's more of an archaeologist than an orientalist."

"Yes; but he knew Sackbut and understood him."

"You have not done what he asked you."

"No, and I am not capable of doing it; it would be too late now, even if I were."

"Why too late?"

"Because I still have to earn my living, and the only way I can earn it is by working in such a way as makes that kind of work an impossibility."

"It is a pity and a waste," said Yakovlev.

"If you mean I have made a mess of my life, I agree. I am myself to blame, no one else. I have had not only one opportunity but many, and I threw them away one after the other."

Yakovlev sighed.

"You ought to have stayed in Russia," he said, "that is what suited you best."

"But there I did less work than anywhere."

"It would have come in time. There was too much going on just then, but you see, now, everything is quiet again, for the moment."

During that year a small event happened which turned out to

have a future importance for Christopher. He stayed at Westleigh in the autumn, and there he met a friend of Sir Joseph's, a certain Harold Fresham, an eminent doctor. He was a man who had travelled in the East and had written books on tropical diseases; he was interested in what Christopher had to say. They made friends. Christopher reflected that this oldish man was the first new friend he had made for years.

He also met Anne and her husband. He was now a well-known Member of Parliament and a parliamentary Under-Secretary. She had become an accomplished woman of the world, but she had lost none of her simplicity. They did not mention Esther.

One night, in the summer, the dramatic critic of the *Messenger* asked Christopher to write a notice of a new play. It was a comedy. Christopher went and found an average first night audience, not of the most brilliant order, because the new play, although produced at a good theatre, under a well-known management, did not promise anything exciting or original. An actor-manager was playing the leading part, and the play, which was an adaptation from the American, had been successful in the United States. Although this was before the great invasion of crook plays, the play dealt with an underworld of criminals, and a special kind of conflict between it and the police that had no counterpart in England, and as the setting of the play had been transposed into English terms it produced a sense of unreality.

Christopher was at once arrested by the appearance of the heroine. She was young and graceful and had large dark eyes, but there was something in her voice, and especially in her laugh, that reminded him of Antoinette. This fleeting reminder cast a glamour over the play to him. This actress whom he had never seen and never heard of, although she was fairly well-known, transported him into a region of melancholy fairy land. He went to the bar after the first act and heard critics and others discussing the play, but he could not heed what they were saying.

"It won't be a success, not here," one critic said to him, "it's thoroughly American; and if they want an American play they ought to have kept it American, and had an American cast."

"Yes," said Christopher absent-mindedly, "but I think she is good."

"Who?"

"Jane Farringdon."

"Oh yes, she's clever: but she's no experience."

Christopher pondered over the subjective nature of criticism and wondered what the value, the intrinsic value of Jane Farringdon's talent might be. To him she illuminated the play and lifted it from the commonplace. Her eyes shone to him like stars, and she seemed to be different from any other actors he had seen. Whatever the public thought of the play, they were pleased with her performance and she was applauded. During the second interval Christopher sat in the stalls. In front of him were a lady in blue, wearing a rope of pearls, and a middle-aged man. He knew neither of them by name; he had seen both of them, but he could not for the moment place them.

They discussed the play, which they said was "awful."

"I like Jane Farringdon," said the lady.

"Yes," said the man, "she is promising, but she's sure to be spoilt. I saw her in an Ibsen play at a matinée and she was remarkable. She is already getting spoilt and mannered. That's what happens to all of them."

"I like her voice," said the lady.

They then talked of the audience. The man pointed out Miss Ella Dasent, the actress, in one of the boxes; Mr Peebles, the politician; Hodgkinson, the critic; Lady Harriet Clive; Fresham (Christopher's doctor friend); General Lyle, who was at the War Office.

"Who is that sitting in the stage box?" asked the lady, "with lovely hands?"

The man put up his eye glass.

"I can't see."

"I think she is a foreigner. She is beautiful. She reminds me of a spray of lilac."

The man looked again.

"The lady in black?"

"Yes."

He looked again.

"Now I've seen her," he said. "She is a Contessa Altamura, but she's not an Italian, although she looks like one. Don't you remember seeing her at Rome one afternoon at the Torellis'? She was a Madame D'Alberg then."

"Oh that woman! Well, I shouldn't have recognised her. She looks much younger and more beautiful than she used to."

"When we saw her, her first husband was only just dead and she had given up things. Now she has blossomed out again."

"With her second marriage?"

"I suppose so. It's love that makes people look young…or old."

"Was she always in love with that Italian?"

"Oh, always; her first husband was awful. A fat professor with a loud voice."

"Well, she certainly looks happy now. It's an odd thing that Englishwomen who marry Italians and who live in Italy, end by looking more Italian than Italians."

"Yes. I think Italy suits Englishwomen when they are good-looking."

After the next act, Christopher walked past the stage box to go out, and Antoinette who was leaning out of the box recognised him, caught his eye and beckoned to him. He went in to see her. In the box were Altamura, Scalchi and an oldish English lady whom he did not know. He was introduced to her. She was called Mrs Jarvis. Altamura was friendly and civil, but Christopher thought there was something subtly sinister in his welcome.

"We are here because Jane Farringdon is my first cousin,"

said Antoinette. "'Jane Farringdon' is her stage name, and this is the first important part she has had at a big theatre. Doesn't she act well?"

"I admire her enormously," said Christopher.

There was a pause, and Christopher asked if they were staying long.

"No, we have been here a fortnight. We are leaving in three days for St Moritz. We came over for this really, to be here on my cousin Helen's first night, but it was put off for a week so we had to stay. We are staying at the Carlton, so come and see us."

"Yes, do," said Altamura, "we are always in at tea time and you will probably meet some Roman friends. London is full of Italians just now."

Scalchi asked him how he liked Constantinople, and they talked of one thing and another till the last act began.

Christopher was so upset by this meeting that he could not follow the last act at all, the more so because Jane Farringdon continued to remind him more and more of Antoinette. He left the theatre with his head in a whirl, and as he left he met Nigel Hemans, the critic of the *Falcon*. Christopher offered him a lift, and they drove together to the Strand.

"By the way, tell me the story of the last act in a word," said Christopher.

"But surely you were there," said Hemans, who was an amiable small man with shaggy hair and a good-humoured face.

"Yes, but I wasn't listening."

"Well, she gets the best of it. She is had up in the police station, all very improbable, because it's an American police station," and he outlined the rest of the play. Christopher got to his office, and somehow or other he wrote an account of the performance. His account of the plot was incomplete, and presupposed some knowledge on the part of the reader. But he ended up by writing:

"Miss Jane Farringdon who already made such a remarkable impression in her performance of the 'Rat Wife' in Ibsen's 'Little Eyolf'" (Hemans had told him this) *"more than fulfilled the expectations she had raised. Her performance can only be described as rare. She lifted the play out of the region of the commonplace, and her acting had at moments that careless artlessness which can be achieved by only the most consummate art."* There was more of it.

After the newspaper had gone to press, Brierley sent for Christopher and said, "Who is this genius you have discovered?"

"Oh," said Christopher, "she is not my discovery. Nigel Hemans discovered her last month."

Brierley was satisfied.

Christopher went back to his rooms in Gower Street full of dreams, and spent a night of memories and sighs.

The next morning Jane Farringdon had many good notices, but none so enthusiastic as Christopher's.

The next day he went to tea with Antoinette at the Carlton. There he found a small slice of Rome. Antoinette was sitting at a tea-table, and round it were sitting two Italian ladies, Scalchi and a Russian, and they were all smoking and talking. He stayed about twenty minutes, but he did not have the chance of exchanging more than commonplaces with Antoinette. Her last words to him, were: "Mind you come and see us if you come to Florence; we live at the Villa Malten, on the Fiesole side."

"I shall never see her again," he thought. But he was wrong, for the next morning when he was walking across St James's Park, he met Antoinette by herself.

"Oh!" she said, "this is providential! I did want to see you so much and I did not know how to do it. I couldn't ask you to anything because Carlo...well, he's the same as when you knew him, only worse. Even now I haven't got long. I promised to meet him at Queen Anne's Gate in a quarter of an hour. But I came here because this is my favourite spot in London, although for a long time I only knew it by hearsay. This is where my father proposed to my mother. I believe there used to be a cow somewhere here. He told us about it. Now tell me everything that has happened to you."

"Nothing has happened to me," said Christopher. "I have just existed. I stayed in Constantinople till the war with the Bulgars began, and then I wrote things they didn't like, so they wouldn't have me as a correspondent any more, and now I write things in the newspaper here. I wrote an article about your cousin."

"I read it, and I knew you had written it. Helen was delighted. And what about the book? Sackbut's book?"

"I have given it up. William Farren is going to do it."

"The man who used to be at Rome?"

"Yes, I believe so. He is at Oxford now. I have written a short preface about Sackbut, which will be published with his translations, but Farren is going to do the book."

"What a pity! However, it was my fault."

"Your fault?"

"I prevented you writing. I made you fritter away your life."

"You? On the contrary. It was when I left Rome that I found I couldn't write any more. Directly you went out of my life all power of writing anything except journalese left me at once, and for ever. But tell me about yourself."

"My life is just as it used to be at Rome; if I had gone on living at Rome I could not have borne it. At Florence I don't mind. There is a group of people who come every day: new ones mostly, but some of the old ones. Wildenspruch comes to stay with us, and he stays with other people too, and he spends most of the winter at Florence now. Scalchi is there often, but then, Alfredo Scalchi is everywhere. We see some English people and the people who are passing through. Carlo seldom goes to Rome; he has given up his flat, and I, never. Marianne comes to stay with us sometimes. Angelica Ubaldi, Kitty Tolovoi and others whom you know. I have made no new friends. I read a good deal – more than I used to. I do patiences and tapestry. I am trying to work in tapestry that picture which was in the little book Mina Turçin left you in her will."

" 'The Coat without Seam?' "

"Yes. Have you still got the book?"

"Oh yes."

"I thought it such a remarkable story."

"I have often thought about what you once said to me... "

"What?"

"That perhaps everybody's life is really a Coat without Seam. But mine seems like a patchwork full of holes, and seamed and darned and ragged and tattered and dirty."

"Perhaps we only see the wrong side of the needlework."

"Yes, that is what you used to say."

"I still think it."

"Do you?"

"I do."

"Then you have got Faith?"

"Not more than before; not much more; but the gleam, just the gleam. And you?"

"Not more than before. There's no gleam yet."

"Well, one can't force these things. One must just wait and hope. I can't pray much. I mean I don't think my prayers are real prayers, but whenever I say them, and I don't quite know who I am saying them to, I always mention your name. Yours, no one else's."

"Then you haven't forgotten me?"

"No, dearest, dearest Christopher, I haven't forgotten you, and I never shall forget you. I want you to know this. I must go in a minute because I am late already, but I do want you to know this, and I was so frightened that I might die without ever seeing you, to tell you that to me all is exactly the same as it was. I haven't changed. I never shall change. I feel just the same about you as I did at Sorrento, and I shall, as long as my life lasts, and if there is anything after life I shall feel the same then. Nothing can ever change it. That is what I wanted you to know."

Her face was pale and her eyes as sad and as bright as they used to be, and there was the same accent of quiet truth in her words.

"And I haven't changed either," he said, "only I am dead. Dead to all feeling that is to say, and all the past is like a dream to me, because I was dead before you knew me. You brought me to life for a time, and now I have gone back to my dead state. I am just like a dead dog."

"Don't say that."

"It's true, and you know it's true."

"You don't hate me?"

"Hate you? I have felt bitter about everything else in my life, almost everything else and almost everyone else. I have felt bitter about almost all my friends, but never about you."

"Stop being bitter. It's no use. The only thing that matters in life is *not* to be bitter: not to be sour."

"I know that, but I can't help it; however, I will try. I know that I have been unfair and unreasonable and unjust, and that I have blamed others for what was really my fault. At least I suppose so, but I can't help blaming those who consciously or not made such a havoc of my life."

"All except me?"

"Yes, all except you."

The clock struck and Antoinette said:

"I must go. Good-bye, Christopher. Good-bye my dear, dear."

She pressed his hand and then hurried away.

CHAPTER XXXI

When the war broke out, Christopher, thanks to Sir Joseph and Dr Fresham, managed to get out with the RAMC. He wore khaki and a brassard, and acted as a stretcher-bearer with an ambulance. He did not come into contact with actual war until September 1st, and on that morning, about eleven o'clock, he found himself at the corner of a road near a wood with his motor ambulance. The German attack had begun, and after a morning of shining peace, there was suddenly a tremendous fire; leaves and branches were falling in the wood. Christopher was with a trained RAMC man called Simpson, and a driver called Tuke, who in peace-time had been a clerk in a Government office.

Towards one o'clock they saw an officer galloping up the road across which bullets were snapping. He disappeared into the wood. Christopher and Tuke followed him and when they got there they saw him dismount and give his horse to someone, and lie down on the ground. He beckoned to them. He was wounded. Simpson dressed the wound. The firing was hot. Christopher looked at the man and saw that it was Bruce Lawless. Lawless recognised him. Just behind them a horse was shot, and Lawless said:

"You fellows had better go, as you can do me no good, and you will only be killed or get taken yourselves."

They put Lawless on a stretcher and gave him morphia. He gave them his revolver, and at that moment Christopher tripped up over the stump of a tree and shouted to the others: "All right, go on, I'm coming."

A moment later, he was hit himself and must have lost consciousness for a while; the next thing he remembered was finding himself lying next to Lawless on the ground.

Lawless said to him: "You know, these aren't dumdum bullets, they are allowed by the book, but one can't carry a book about with one to prove one is playing the game." He took some bullets out of his pocket, and threw them into the grass. They could hear German voices. Lawless said to Christopher:

"I say, I'm for it, and I want to tell you something. I'm sorry about what I did to you. I mean taking Esther from you. They say all's fair in love and war, and I was madly in love with her, but it's been on my mind all my life that I didn't quite play the game. Because I took advantage of your making a fool of yourself, just at that moment. I didn't think you loved her – enough. She loved you...*then*. Of course it's been all right in a way, and I hope I made her fairly happy. But she gave up her music for me. That was all my fault. I don't believe she would have given it up if she had married you. I wonder if you would mind saying that I can die easy."

Christopher looked at him, and his life-long bitterness surged up in him, and his heart hardened like a stone.

He said nothing.

"You can't?" said Lawless. "Very well. I suppose I deserve it. I daresay I should do the same."

At that moment there was a shout of "*Schnell, Kinder*" and swarms of Germans came up and passed them. Lawless had closed his eyes and seemed to be unconscious. Some of the Germans spoke to Christopher. One of them, seeing the red brassard on his arm said "Red Cross!" One of them gave him a coat for a pillow, some water and cigarettes. Another said, "Why didn't you stay in England? We fought together at Belle-

Alliance." Another said something about the Boers; and another said: "*Verdammter Englander.*"

Christopher saw the Germans passing as if he were in a dream. He did not know whether he had been given morphia or not. He seemed to lie there for hours. Lawless neither spoke nor moved. Christopher supposed he was dead and felt neither regret nor remorse. After a time some German stretcher-bearers came and carried Christopher to a collecting place for the wounded. They left Lawless where he was, saying he was dead. It grew dark, and in the darkness you could hear the wounded crying like children. Christopher was put in an ambulance and taken to a village. Towards midnight he was carried into the hospital and his wound was dressed. Then he was taken to a shed which was full of English and German wounded. He lay upon the straw, which was covered with blood. Men were moaning and groaning all round him, and one man was raving. The next morning he was taken in an ambulance to another village. The enemy had occupied the village and had only just left it. It was stripped bare, as if a swarm of locusts had devoured its substance. There Christopher found Simpson and Tuke and an RAMC Colonel. Christopher and the other wounded were put in the church. It was, Christopher thought, a beautiful church, with stained glass windows. It reminded him of the church at Vernay. A soldier who was lying next to him was telling his beads.

Christopher was half delirious. He had no idea how long he lay in that church; whether it was hours or days. The Curé visited the wounded and did what he could for them. There was a great shortage of bandages. The Curé was an old man. Christopher thought he was the Curé at Vernay, and called him by his name, although he knew he was not the Curé at Vernay, just as in a dream one casts a figure of a person for a particular part and one knows at the same time that the actor is someone else. The Curé asked him whether he was a Catholic. He shook his head and said: "*Autrefois.*" "Did he not want to make his confession?" "No," said Christopher, "no, no, no." He relapsed into unconsciousness. When he returned to life, he was told that the Germans had been defeated; they had all gone, and the French had come and gone. Many of the wounded had gone, too. He was still lying in the church. He had no idea how much time had passed, and when the recent events were explained to him, incoherently by the men next to him, he could not understand. The men were English.

It was a fine September morning. The English soldiers were complaining of the heat and said the church was stuffy, and that they ought to break the stained glass.

"We asked the Padre to do it," one of them said, "but he said it was too valuable."

Early in the morning the Curé said Mass in the Sanctuary. Many of the wounded followed it. Some of them had rosaries, and told their beads. Christopher watched the Mass from afar, like one in a dream. When the bell rang for the Elevation, he saw the church at Vernay, the old Curé whom he remembered was different, or seemed to be different from this Curé. Why were there two Curés? It was all wrong. And where was his *mirliton*? Surely a *mirliton* was necessary at Mass? And where was Mabel? She ought to be there with him. Perhaps she was late, as usual. She was always late. Mademoiselle would scold her, and Mamma would be so cross. Mamma had got on her Sunday gown, the mauve one, and his father had got on his Sunday coat. It was shiny, and his tie was above his collar, and crooked.

He wondered whether the Curé would give him a pear after Mass, a pear, and perhaps a *Baba*. Mabel didn't like *Babas* and always gave him hers. Mabel was going to be the Queen of the Gypsies some day and a great singer: Queen Mab. They would take the horses from her carriage and drag her in triumph through the streets of Warsaw.

And he was going to be an explorer. He was going to be like Ponce de Leon, and discover Eldorado and the fountain of

301

perpetual youth; where was Eldorado? Somewhere near the Fortunate Islands, the Hesperides? Or would he find a forgotten temple and read the inscriptions of a dead language: Etruria, or perhaps it would be in Africa, the caves of Kor; or perhaps he would go to the Holy Land and find a lost relic: the Holy Grail, or the Coat without Seam.

How quickly Mass went by, and yet what a long time it seemed to take. After the Elevation it seemed to last for hours. Christopher wondered what Feast it was. Of course, it was, it must be Sunday. A Sunday after Pentecost. Where was the Chapel with the Holy Coat? It was there, but it was not in its right place. There was the Holy Coat. He could see it distinctly. Reddish brown. Hanging high up, on a pillar. That was the real one. He knew that. That was the *Agnus Dei*. It was not a *Requiem* today. He heard the words, and then the bell again.

"*Domine non sum dignus*"

The words were distinct, and went straight into his mind, if not into his heart.

There was a long silence.

The Server said the Confession, and Christopher repeated it mechanically. A little girl and a boy and some old women received Communion. Now it was the Blessing. Christopher mechanically made the Sign of the Cross. And then came the last Gospel, and the prayers after Mass. Christopher said them, too, mechanically. He remembered his early instruction and murmured the words *ex opere operato*. "*But whereas the Sacraments of the New Law though they take effect* ex opere operato, *nevertheless produce a greater effect in proportion as the dispositions of the recipient are better, therefore care is to be taken, etc.*" Perhaps, then, even his mechanical prayers were efficacious, but his dispositions had never been good. And ought he to confess that he had killed Mabel? Murder was mortal sin, but it was the intention that counted. Had he meant to kill Mabel? No, but he had meant to bathe, and he knew that bathing might kill her, so he had killed Mabel. It was just the same. Yes, he had killed Mabel. He was a murderer. He would tell M. le Curé, and he would never give him a pear again. He was sure of that. And what would his mother say? She loved Mabel: she did not love him. She had never loved him. Nobody had ever loved him. Esther had never loved him, in spite of what Lawless said. She had loved Lawless. Nobody had ever loved him except Annette: or was her name – Antoinette? And she was dead. Who had killed her? He tried to remember her face, and failed. It was mixed up with Madame Turçin's face, and the face of an actress he had only once seen: Jane Farringdon. Was she dead or had she not married a Hungarian noble? How hot it was! Would not Mass be over by now?

It was over. It had been over for hours. One of the RAMC men came and spoke to him. It was neither Simpson nor Tuke. It was someone he had never seen. There was a stale smell of blood, iodoform, incense and khaki in the church. Couldn't he be taken out of doors? He asked the RAMC man. He was an orderly, and he called him Tuke, although he knew it was not his name. Couldn't he be taken out of doors? He was himself in the RAMC – his tunic and brassard had gone and he bore no signs of it. The man asked another man, a doctor. They talked to each other, and then presently he was carried out on a stretcher into the courtyard of a small house.

It was a beautiful day. Very still. Cocks were crowing in the distance, the sun shone on the yard. The yard was a square, one side of which was a small house with green shutters and steps leading up to a door; two of the other wings of the yard were stables; the stable doors were open. There were no horses in the stalls, and the remaining wing was a wall with a door that led to the street. The sun shone on the dry white walls. The yard was full of wounded soldiers. There were two Germans lying there on stretchers. They were bandaged and there were veils of thin pink gauze over their faces to keep away the flies.

One of them had a purple lump on his forehead as if he had been stung by a wasp. Their faces were like wax. Christopher wondered whether they were dead, but presently one of them said to the other that it was cold.

He heard the doctor say to the orderly that they had telephoned to the...what? A string of letters, and *they* had promised to send a lorry and an ambulance to get these men away who were left. The men from the church had been evacuated. There were no bandages left. Not a scrap of linen or lint. They asked Christopher whether he was all right. He nodded. Did he want any water? No, the last time he had drunk some it had made him sick. Would he like to go indoors? No.

The doctor and the orderly went indoors.

Christopher was left with the soldiers, none of whom were badly wounded, and with the two Germans. They were all asleep. He slept too, for a short time or a long time. He did not know which. He was awakened by the sound of a motor horn, and two officers walked into the yard. One of them was an RAMC doctor. The doctor in charge came out and spoke to them.

Christopher was not only wide awake now, but he had lost all numbness of mind and of body. His wound was hurting him fiercely, and his mind had that merciless lucidity which goes with physical pain. Possibly he had been given drugs and their effect had worn off. Christopher listened to the conversation. He heard the newcomers exchange greetings. The two RAMC men knew each other well. One of the newcomers said:

"Two cars and an ambulance. A Daimler and a Crossley."

"Splendid," the doctor in charge said. "We had better get busy at once and evacuate these cases. None of them are bad. Only three stretcher cases." He pointed to Christopher and the two Germans.

The newcomers and the local orderly moved towards the Germans. The soldiers began to give vent to complaints. "It was a shame to take the Germans first." They then prepared to move Christopher.

"I belong here," he said. "I'm in the RAMC, a volunteer stretcher-bearer. At any rate those men must go first." The new doctor shrugged his shoulders. "Very well," he said, "it's no distance, the cars can come back for the Boches, and for him – " (he pointed to Christopher) "then there will be nothing for anyone to grouse about."

They evacuated the men and packed them into the cars, and the men went away whistling and singing. The doctor in charge said to the newcomers: "Come into the house and have a drink."

Christopher was left alone with the Germans. They felt cold. One of the officers who had brought the cars came out of the house, and the Germans complained to him of the cold. He fetched some blankets and gave them tea out of a china pot with a spout, and wrapped the blankets round them. During the last few days the heat had been scorching, so Christopher thought, but the Germans complained of the cold. They had marched, they said, for days and nights in the cold.

The officer and an Orderly carried them into the stable. "They will be warmer there, you see," the officer said.

Christopher shut his eyes and slept once more, but not for long. When he opened his eyes again he saw the Curé talking to one of the officers who had brought the ambulance.

"They rang us up," said the officer, "at our HQ, and said there were a lot of wounded men here, and asked us to lend some cars. We were able to bring a small ambulance and two cars. We have got all the soldiers away now except these two Germans who are in the stable, and that fellow" (pointing to Christopher). "They are coming back for them presently." The officer went into the house. Presently there was a noise of shouting and a crowd of villagers, men, women and children, came into the yard shouting, talking and gesticulating; headed by a farmer who was dragging a man in rags.

The Curé asked what it all meant.

"They caught this man," said the farmer, pointing to the man he was dragging, "red-handed, signalling to the enemy with this." The man was holding a tattered red rag and the farmer pointed to it. All the people shouted, "Spy! Spy!"

The man was wounded and bruised and battered and streaming with blood. His clothes had been torn to shreds.

"It is a lie," he shouted. "I am innocent, I swear it. They lie. Save me, *M. le Curé*. They have half-killed me already. I am dying."

Then the farmer's wife stepped forward. "He lies, *M. le Curé*," she said. "He has been signalling to the enemy. They caught him in the act, and with our *Holy Relic*. He used our Holy Relic to signal with. The Holy Coat: the Coat without Seam that hangs in the church. He stole it, *M. le Curé*, and used it for his spying. From the steeple, they caught him in the act."

"They lie," groaned the wounded man.

"But the man is bleeding to death," said the Curé.

"Save me," gasped the wounded man. "I am innocent. They lie. I am dying."

The doctors came from the house. The doctor who was in charge and the doctor who had brought the cars. They asked what was the matter.

"There is a wounded man here," said the Curé, "and I wanted to know if you had any bandages."

"We haven't any bandages," said the doctor. "Not one. We've used up all the bandages and every scrap of lint. The Germans took away everything. We have sent for some more, but nothing has come. But we will see what we can do for him."

The crowd became violent and said they would not let the man be treated by the doctors. He was a spy and he must suffer his deserts.

The Curé turned to the doctor and said:

"Leave them to me, *M. le Major*, I will deal with them. Please go back to the house. If you can find some *charpie*, send it."

"Do you think you can deal with these people?" said the

doctor, pointing to the threatening crowd. "They look to me ugly."

"Leave them to me, *M. le Major,*" said the Curé. "Let me be alone with them. I know my people."

The doctor went back to the house.

The farmer advanced to the Curé and took off his cap.

"With all due respect to you, *M. le Curé,* we know that man is a spy. He was caught in the act and we will see that justice is done at once."

The wounded man groaned and protested. The Curé spoke with authority.

"My children," he said. "You shall leave him to me. He is a dying man. *C'est mon affaire.*"

The farmer protested again, and the crowd snarled. They were like wolves.

"If you take him," said the Curé. "It will be across my dead body. Now, *mes enfants,* go home. *All* of you, at once." There was a silence.

They all went away and left the Curé alone with the wounded man.

Christopher was awake and acutely conscious of what was happening. He took in every detail of the scene as if he were watching a stage-play.

He was lying in the shade. The peace of the afternoon was over everything. The Curé and the wounded man were in the centre of the yard. The man was sitting on the ground and the Curé bending over him.

"Now my child," said the Curé.

"*M. le Curé,* I am bleeding to death," gasped the man. "Bind my wounds. They would have murdered me but for you. I never spied. I swear it. They said it because they hate me. François hates me because he cheated me. His wife hates me. I was already wounded and they have half-killed me. I am dying, *M. le Curé.* I swear all this is true. Stop this bleeding. Oh! how I suffer!"

307

"My child," said the Curé, "I have nothing to bandage your wounds with; no *charpie*, not a rag. There is nothing left in the houses. The Prussians took everything away. Every scrap of *charpie* has been used for the soldiers, and I have nothing on me."

The wounded man held up the crumbling piece of faded red fabric he had been accused of signalling with, and said:

"This will do, *M. le Curé.*"

"Is that the Coat without Seam which belongs to the church?"

The man nodded.

And in that moment Christopher saw a series of pictures flash past him as distinctly as the slides of a magic lantern: the Roman soldier and his wife, Miriam, and the dying child; the Hungarians on the eve of Mohacs; Sofia about to take the veil; the sale room in London: the actress in powder and lace, Sir Horace Beaufort, her lover, with his coat of velvet embroidered with gold and his waistcoat of cloth of silver: the *Abbé.*

"How did you find it?" asked the Curé.

"They say I stole it. It is not true. I swear, *M. le Curé.*"

"Do not swear. I believe you already. Where did you find it?"

"I found some children playing with it on the road outside the church. I swear – . Quick, quick, *M. le Curé,* or I shall die."

The Curé saw that it was true. The stream of blood seemed to be beyond control. It was a question of seconds. He made the Sign of the Cross and tore the relic into shreds. It was like *charpie,* as thin as a cobweb, and it tore easily. The man was now lying stretched out on the ground as on a Cross.

The Curé rolled up a piece of the fabric into a pad, stopped the bleeding, and began to bandage him with other shreds. But as soon as the stuff touched the man, he cried out: "Stop, *M. le Curé.*"

"What is it, my child?" asked the Curé.

"Wait, I have something to say to you before you bandage

me."

"Let it wait till I have finished. There will be time."

"No now, now before. Wait a moment, *M. le Curé*! You must hear. What I said just now was not true. Not a word of it. I stole the Coat from the church after they had moved the soldiers. It is true I wanted to spy. I spied before. I signalled to the enemy with the Coat. They gave me money – but it was not for money. It was revenge. I… "

"Patience," said the Curé, "my child, till I have bandaged you. Keep still. There, quite still."

The Curé finished bandaging the man's wounds – there were many on the head, face and arm – with the shreds of the Coat, and when he had finished, he said, "Now my child, I will hear your confession."

The man began to whisper, and Christopher felt a sharp twinge of pain and lost consciousness for what seemed an eternity, but in reality for a short space of time.

When he regained consciousness, the Curé was bending over him. "And you, *mon enfant*?" he asked.

"How is he?" asked Christopher.

"He is dead," said the Curé.

"I am dying too," said Christopher, "and I want you to hear my confession."

The Curé heard his confession, and when it was over Christopher said to him:

"I found the Coat without Seam, after all, *M. le Curé*. The real one, you told me about at Vernay, when you gave me the *mirliton*, but I needn't have searched, *because it was there all the time*. It was my life that was a Coat without Seam. But I tore it into shreds and now you have mended it. There is no seam in it now."

"*Oui, oui, mon enfant*," said the Curé, thinking that Christopher was delirious.

Later, when the ambulance came back, and the doctor and the

orderly came to look after Christopher, they saw it was not necessary to send him to the base, for he was dead, but they took back the two Germans.

MAURICE BARING

C

Baring's homage to a decadent and carefree Edwardian age depicts a society as yet untainted by the traumas and complexities of twentieth-century living. With wit and subtlety, a happy picture is drawn of family life, house parties in the country and a leisured existence clouded only by the rumblings of the Boer War. Against this spectacle Caryl Bramsley (the *C* of the title) is presented – a young man of terrific promise but scant achievement, whose tragicomic tale offsets the privileged milieu.

CAT'S CRADLE

This sophisticated and intricate novel, based on true events, takes place in the late nineteenth century and begins with Henry Clifford, a man of taste and worldly philosophy, whose simple determination to do as he likes and live as he wishes is threatened when his daughter falls in love with an unsuitable man. With subtle twists and turns in a fascinating portrait of society, Maurice Baring conveys the moral that love is too strong to be overcome by mere mortals.

Maurice Baring

Daphne Adeane

Barrister Basil Wake and his arresting wife Hyacinth lead a well-appointed existence in the social whirl of London's early 1900s. For eight years Hyacinth has conducted a most discreet affair with Parliamentarian Michael Choyce, who seems to fit into the Wakes' lives so conveniently. But an invitation to attend a Private View and a startling portrait of the mysterious and beautiful Daphne Adeane signifies a change in this comfortable set-up.

In My End Is My Beginning

This historical novel tells the tragic story of Mary Queen of Scots, from her childhood until the beginning of her end, whose unwise marital and political actions provoked rebellion among Scottish nobles and forced her to flee to England, where she was beheaded as a Roman Catholic threat to the throne. The clash of opinion over whether Mary was a martyr or a murderess is perfectly represented by four eye-witnesses (The Four Maries – her ladies-in-waiting) who narrate this captivating story with distinctive conclusions.

Maurice Baring

The Puppet Show of Memory

It was into the famous and powerful Baring family of merchant bankers that Maurice Baring was born in 1874, the seventh of eight children. A man of immense subtlety and style, Baring absorbed every drop of culture that his fortunate background showered upon him; in combination with his many natural talents and prolific writing this assured him a place in literary history.

In this classic autobiography, spanning a remarkable period of history, Maurice Baring shares the details of an inspirational childhood in nineteenth-century England and a varied adulthood all over the world, collecting new friends and remarkable experiences. It has been said that Baring's greatest talent was for discovering the best in people, that he had a genius for friendship, and in this superb book his erudition and perception are abundantly clear.

'A classic autobiography'– *Dictionary of National Biography*

Tinker's Leave

Reserved and unworldly, young Miles Consterdine and his epiphanic trip to Paris is Maurice Baring's first bead on this thread of a story based on impressions received by the author in Russia and Manchuria during wartime. From here Baring allows us to peek through windows opening onto tragic and comic episodes in the lives of noteworthy people in remarkable circumstances.

Made in the USA
Middletown, DE
05 February 2024

49105785R00179